ICED OUT

ICED OUT

ELENA GRAF

PURPLE HAND PRESS

Purple Hand Press
www.elenagraf.com
© 2026 by Elena Graf

Trade Paperback Edition
ISBN-13 978-1-953195-29-6
ePub Edition
ISBN-13 978-1-953195-28-9

Cover photo © Wirestock - Freepik.com, used by license.

05.15.2026

To the memory of Dr. Joseph D. Connors,
a true friend

Notes

For a character guide to the inhabitants of Hobbs, Maine, please visit: https://www.elenagraf.com/hobbs-characters/

Chapter 1

The scuffs of high-heeled shoes on the tile floor got Lucy's attention. Across the table, Maggie looked up from the print edition of the *New York Times* and stared. "Liz, are you wearing *heels*?" she asked incredulously. Because Liz towered over other people, she usually wore flats. "And a *skirt*?" In cool weather, Liz's usual office outfit was a blazer, button-down shirt, and dress slacks.

"Ah-yuh," Liz replied. Her attempts at imitating a Maine accent never quite succeeded because there was always the faint trace of New York in her intonations. After casually filling a coffee pod, she emphatically jabbed the button of the coffee maker. "Maggie, don't look like you've never seen me dressed like this before," Liz said with barely disguised annoyance.

Maggie carefully folded over the newspaper. "But only when absolutely *necessary*."

"I'm giving a talk at the school board this morning," Liz said in an even voice, but Lucy could hear her impatience. Liz never liked to explain herself, especially not to Maggie.

"You didn't get dressed up for school board meetings before." Maggie sat back and perched her reading glasses on her head.

"I'm doing a Q&A about the new vaccine recommendations from the CDC," Liz grudgingly explained. "Since Covid, no one trusts government agencies. Now that we have an antivaxxer running Health and Human Services, it's even more confusing. Bobbie Brainworms swore he wouldn't take a position against vaccines. They all lie during confirmation hearings."

"So you dressed up to look as credible as possible," Maggie concluded. "You're channeling your old persona as a world-renowned surgeon and breast cancer guru."

"Bingo," said Liz, stirring cream into her coffee.

Maggie gave Liz a head-to-toe inspection. "Gotta hand it to you, honey. You still know how to rock a power suit."

"Thanks...I guess." Liz grinned at Lucy. "But I have an ulterior motive. Since Lucy decided she's a leg woman, I like to give her something to look at." Liz hiked up her skirt to mid-thigh. With a reedy whistle, Lucy admired Liz's shapely legs.

Maggie turned in Lucy's direction. "I used to beg her to dress up, even just a little. Now, you've got her wearing skirts because you like her legs. Lucy, what's your secret?"

Lucy raised her shoulders. "Nothing special. Maybe I don't reinforce other people's expectations. That gives Liz the freedom to express herself in any way that feels right to her."

"Spoken like a true shrink," Liz said cynically as she brought her coffee to the island. "Sometimes, I enjoy getting a rise out of people, and I know when I dress like this, people pay attention. Look at the two of you staring at me, like I'm an alien from another planet. When I was at Yale New Haven, I used to dress like this every day."

"You look great, Liz, and thank you for the view." Lucy blew Liz a kiss, which she pretended to catch. "I totally get it. When I wear my collar, people look at me differently. Do you mind if I come to your talk? I don't have any meetings until two. I might get questions from my therapy clients or members of the congregation."

Liz didn't look up but arched her brow. "Luce, you know you shouldn't be giving medical advice. What are you supposed to say?"

Lucy mimicked the dry tone of a TV drug commercial: "If you have concerns or questions, ask your doctor."

"Exactly. Those influencers with their unfounded ideas about medicine are dangerous. You're better off *not* offering advice because it's not worth any more than Bobby Brainworms' or Maggie's."

Obviously indignant, Maggie puffed herself up, ready to launch a vigorous defense. Lucy sighed. It was too early in the morning for a quarrel. "At least, I try to stay informed," declared Maggie. "Why can't I say I believe in science? Or say that vaccines eradicated many of the dangerous childhood diseases you and I had as children? I spent the entire time I had measles in a dark room because people believed it could keep kids from going blind. Liz, was there anything to that idea?"

Liz stopped scrolling her phone and looked thoughtful. "Measles causes light sensitivity. Being in a dark room could make a patient more comfortable, but it wouldn't prevent blindness. Measles retinopathy can be a serious complication, but it's uncommon in healthy children, who get enough Vitamin A."

"Maybe I'll come to your talk too," Maggie said. "I always learn something when you talk about medicine. I'm off today."

Liz looked from Maggie to Lucy and back again. Lucy guessed she sensed a conspiracy. She often accused her two wives of "ganging up on her." Liz frowned, then shrugged. "You know where the school board meets."

"In the administration building," said Maggie.

"Not anymore. Since the right wing began focusing on local politics, we need more space. We're in the middle school auditorium now. The school board meetings used to be boring as hell. I'd plan my next woodworking projects while pretending to pay attention. Now, *everything's* an issue: the books in the library, trans girls in sports, and of course, vaccinations."

"Maybe it's a good thing people are taking an interest in their kids' education," said Maggie. "I just wish it weren't so politicized." When Liz pulled out one of the stools from the island and sat down, Maggie pointedly said, "Liz, you could join us."

"Thanks, but you and Lucy look comfy, and I need to leave soon." She went back to scrolling her phone. "Anything interesting going on this morning?"

"They're organizing a nationwide protest of Musk's DOGE cuts," said Maggie, looking across the table to get Lucy's attention. "We're going right?"

"You bet, and this time, I'm wearing my collar. Cutting medical care for the poor is an issue that should concern every Christian."

"The Medicaid expansion was the best thing that happened for the working poor since food stamps," said Liz. "If they intend to cut healthcare, I'll even carry a sign."

Lucy and Maggie turned in Liz's direction. Her statement counted as an even bigger change in her behavior than wearing a skirt or spike heels. During the heated fall campaign, she'd refused to attend any rallies for their candidates, insisting that it would reflect badly on Hobbs Family Practice to see the senior doctor standing on the street waving a political sign.

"That doesn't sound like you, Liz," said Maggie, folding up the newspaper to signal she was done with it, now that the conversation had become more interesting.

"Well, even I have my limits," said Liz. "We're long past the old norms. Firing those scientists and vaccine experts will put people's lives in danger. I can't just sit back and watch."

"I'm glad you realize things have changed." Maggie cut a generous piece of apple bread, slathered butter on it, and brought it to the island. "Here, you should eat something before you go."

Liz murmured her thanks and took a bite. "When the markets plummeted after he imposed his stupid tariffs, I'd hoped that the business community would influence his behavior, but the indexes floated back up like nothing ever happened." Of course, Liz would use the stock market as a barometer of political sentiment. Although she'd reluctantly turned over management of their portfolios to Olivia Enright, a former hedge fund manager, she watched their positions like a hawk. "When all the billionaires began bending the knee, and the legacy media settled those absurd lawsuits, it was obvious he owns them. The conservative Supreme Court justices are in his pocket. No one is coming to save us, but *us*."

"Fortunately, there are more of us than there are of them," Maggie said.

"But they have more guns," Liz said gravely.

"Don't let that be an excuse for you to buy more," Maggie warned. "You already have an arsenal."

"They're for training," Liz replied and took a big bite of apple bread.

Maggie looked across the table for support, but Lucy knew better than to get involved in this conversation. After the school shooting, Tom Simmons had shocked her into action by alerting her to Liz's suicidal ideation. Liz had her guns back now, and Lucy had to trust her to make good decisions.

"Don't worry," Liz replied with a shrug. "If I got more, I'd need another gun safe, which would be expensive, and we don't have the room."

Maggie glared at her and shook her head with a sigh.

The calm that had existed before Liz's pervasive energy had disturbed it returned. Lucy went back to reading her email. Maggie picked up the newspaper and continued to browse.

"Holy fucking shit!" Liz's sudden outburst made Lucy jump.

"What is it now?" she asked as calmly as her shaken nerves would allow. With this administration, it could be anything—more government workers fired, more agencies shut down, more hacks into people's sensitive information.

Liz's eyes were glued to the screen. "Brenda, are you insane! *What* the *fuck* were you thinking?"

"Stop screaming profanity and tell us what's going on," Maggie prodded anxiously.

"Listen to this from the Portland paper: 'Police Chief Brenda Harrison said the department has signed a 287g agreement with the Department of Homeland Security. She explained that it would expand the toolkit of Hobbs officers. She said that the training would help keep the town safer because they wouldn't have to wait for ICE agents to come up from Boston.'"

"That sounds reasonable," Maggie said.

"It is reasonable," Liz agreed, "but it goes on to be critical of the decision and suggests the Hobbs PD wants to align itself with ICE."

"Is that supposed to be a news story or an opinion piece?" asked

Maggie. Long ago, she'd been the editor of their college newspaper and often lamented the demise of objective journalism.

"Nowadays, who can tell?" Liz said. "Forget the spin, and look at the optics. We all think ICE is over the top. Now, our police chief has allied herself with them. Not a good look for her or the Hobbs PD."

"Liz is right," Lucy said. "It doesn't look good, but before we jump to conclusions, you should talk to Brenda." The vibration of the phone in Lucy's hands startled her. The photo of an attractive, dark-complected woman appeared on the screen along with the name Cherie Harrison. "That didn't take long," said Lucy, swiping open the call. "Good morning, Cherie."

"It's in the paper already," Cherie said, clearly agitated. "Brenda says she has no idea how the press got hold of the story, but she tried to answer their questions as best she could."

"Cherie, mind if I put you on speaker?" asked Lucy. "Liz is here, and I'm sure she'd like to listen in."

There was a moment of hesitation. "Sure, put Liz on. I'd like to hear her take."

Liz sat down in the breakfast nook beside Lucy. "Cherie, tell Brenda not to make *any* more statements to the press."

"I think she figured that out," Cherie said with a sigh. "She kept trying to explain herself. She thought the facts would speak for themselves. But you know how those reporters are."

"She might have a perfectly fine explanation for getting involved with ICE," Liz continued, "but reporters won't see it that way. They just want a story. Trust me, I have experience after that actress didn't follow my medical advice and then sued *me* for malpractice."

"Brenda's pretty upset," Cherie said, adjusting the pitch of her voice to a calmer level. "Liz, please talk to her. She really needs advice, and she won't listen to me."

"I'll swing by the station after my talk at the school board," offered Liz.

"Is there anything I can do to help?" Lucy asked Cherie. "I wasn't going to come in until my afternoon meeting, but I can if you need me."

"Thanks, Lucy. I'd love your advice, but I think the only one Brenda will listen to is Liz."

"Why don't you and Brenda come over for dinner tonight?" Maggie suddenly suggested, which drew a sharp look from Lucy. No one was supposed to know that Maggie was not just living next to them; she was living *with* them.

"You're over there early, Maggie," said the voice on the phone with more than a hint of suspicious curiosity.

Maggie gracefully shifted into actress mode. "I came over to make breakfast because Liz has that early meeting. I figured she needed fortification," she said, fabricating a relatively plausible explanation. "We all know how much Lucy hates to cook."

"I do not!" Lucy protested. "I'm just not very good at it." At the kitchen island, Liz snickered.

Maggie waved to Lucy to indicate she should play along. "Cherie, I'm making a big pot of stew, so there's plenty. After dinner, the kids can watch a movie in Liz's media room. You know how much they love watching their Disney favorites on that big screen. That will give the adults the privacy to strategize how to deal with this situation."

"Liz, is this okay with you?" Cherie asked tentatively.

"Absolutely fine," Liz replied. "We don't see you enough outside of work. Right, Lucy?"

Lucy was staring at Maggie in a futile attempt to make her understand how her presence at that early hour would raise questions. Maggie conspicuously ignored her. Frustrated, Lucy finally gave up. "Yes, fine," she replied in a flat tone.

"Are you sure it's not too much with the kids, Lucy?" Cherie asked. "I can ask Aunt Simone to watch them tonight. Those kids love time with their auntie."

"It's up to you, Cherie," said Liz, "but we'd be happy to have the kids, too."

There was a long moment of hesitation before Cherie said, "Honestly, I'm really stressed, and *I* wouldn't mind a break. We need to speak honestly. Keith, especially, gets so anxious when there's any conflict."

"I'm going to the school board meeting to hear what Liz has to say about vaccinations," Lucy said. "Then I'll come to the office. We can talk more."

"Thanks, Lucy. Meanwhile, I'll let Brenda know we're invited for dinner. What can we bring?"

"Nothing," said Maggie. "We have everything we need. Come at six."

After Cherie ended the call, Liz got up. "Sorry, ladies, but I need to go. If you decide to come to the meeting, I'll see you later."

"I'll be there," Maggie promised.

"Me too," Lucy called to Liz's back. The garage door opened, but Lucy waited until she heard it close to address the issue. She focused on Maggie's hazel eyes, moody now because she knew she was guilty.

"Lucy, I know what you're going to say," she said, showing her palms. "I'm sorry, but I forget that I'm not supposed to be here."

"Maggie, you *are* supposed to be here," said Lucy with a sigh of impatience. "We just need to be careful who knows about our life together."

"Brenda is Liz's best friend, now that Sam is gone," protested Maggie petulantly. "How can she keep this from her?"

"Brenda is a sweetheart, but she's very conventional, and so is Cherie. Finding out about us could wreck our relationship with them. Besides, every new person who learns the truth could be the one who blows our cover."

"I still think it's no one's business what we do in bed. Besides, I live right next door, practically in the same house. Why shouldn't I be here? I was here all the time, making dinner or breakfast, before we all got involved. No one knew about it, and no one cared. We're just being paranoid, which makes us look guilty and causes more suspicion."

"I'm sure they already suspect," Lucy reluctantly admitted. "But we don't need to confirm anything. And you're right. It's no one's business what we do in bed."

Maggie shook her head and occupied herself with clearing the breakfast dishes. Lucy realized she felt hurt by the criticism. After all, she'd meant no harm. She wanted to help, and extending an invitation to Cherie was generous. "Maggie, I'm sorry," Lucy murmured.

"No, you're right, Lucy...as always. I need to be more careful, or you'll lose your job." Lucy smiled because Maggie was taking responsibility instead of becoming defensive. She might be seventy-one, but she was still making progress.

"Thanks for understanding."

Maggie nodded and began rinsing the dishes. Lucy glanced at the clock over the sink. If she intended to show up at the school board meeting, she needed to get dressed, and she should probably wear her collar.

✳✳✳

When Lucy gave her admin one of those furtive therapist's assessments, a palpable ache formed in her chest. Jodi looked completely exhausted, understandable because the young woman had two preschoolers at home. Fortunately, her mother looked after them during the workday. Both Jodi and her husband needed to work to pay the mortgage, but day care was so expensive. And people wondered why young people didn't have more kids. How could they afford them?

Simone Ballou, Cherie's aunt, had suggested adding another day to the after-school program that Denise Chantal, their transgender music director, had started before returning to her singing career.

Working mothers loved it, especially Jodi, who could use the extra hours of pay and the convenience. Her mother dropped off the kids after school, and Jodi could just walk downstairs after work to bring them home.

Jodi finally turned and noticed Lucy standing there. "Good morning, Lucy. I didn't hear you come in."

"These ballet flats are nearly soundless. Taking lessons from Mother Susan on how to approach with stealth." Lucy raised an auburn brow.

"Mother Susan has perfected that trick." Jodi emphatically pointed to the door of Lucy's office. "By the way, she's waiting for you." The message that Susan wanted to see her had pinged into Lucy's phone just as she was leaving the house. The idea of starting the day with Susan brought on a long sigh, but meeting with clergy was part of her duties as a rector.

Lucy had no good reason to avoid Susan. Although her tenure as an assistant priest at St. Margaret's had gotten off to a rough start, Susan had turned herself around. Bobbie, the always smiling nurse practitioner in Liz's family practice, had a steadying influence on her. To Lucy's knowledge, Susan had been faithfully attending her AA meetings, and now she led the one at St. Margaret's. There was a time when Susan was too ashamed to even show her face there, which was partly Lucy's fault. She'd been so unwelcoming when her former lover had first returned to Hobbs.

Lucy took a deep breath and summoned her trademark smile before entering her office. "Good morning, Susan!" she said warmly. Susan's eyes lit up, but fortunately, the cloying lovesick expression was absent. Maybe her relationship with Bobbie had finally cured her of her obsession with Lucy.

Susan always rose when her "superior" came into the room, one of those annoying convent customs she'd probably never lose. Lucy hung her coat on the vintage coat stand near the door. "Susan, how nice to see you on a school day," said Lucy, a forgivable lie. "To what do I owe the pleasure of your company this morning?"

"Something significant happened over the weekend. I thought you'd want to know as soon as possible...as my rector...and my *friend*."

As a therapist, Lucy's eyes never missed a detail. They settled on the large, glittering stone on Susan's hand. "You're engaged?" Lucy struggled for the appropriate emotion. She wanted to show that she was happy for Susan, but no matter how much she tried to force the feeling, she just couldn't. But why wasn't she overjoyed? This meant the end of Susan's crazy infatuation after years of trying to gently ease her away.

Susan held up her hand. "Last night. Bobbie asked me out to La Scala for a date night. Over an obscenely rich 'death by chocolate,' which we were virtuously sharing, she produced this."

Lucy managed to remember that all women wanted their engagement rings admired by their friends. "Let me see," she said, reaching out.

Blushing, Susan approached. "It's nothing compared to that huge diamond Liz gave you."

"It's an antique. After Liz's grandfather became rich, he bought it for her grandmother in the 1950s. Liz said they don't find natural diamonds like it anymore." Lucy took Susan's hand and inspected the ring. "It's beautiful. I love the little diamonds around the big stone. I bet it cost Bobbie a fortune."

Susan shrugged and withdrew her hand. "She inherited all that money from Joyce. She might as well spend it." Lucy heard an echo of what Bobbie had probably said when being questioned about the cost. Susan had grown up poor. The vow of chastity she'd taken in the convent had only reinforced her frugal inclinations. "Most of the young women I work with think giving a diamond engagement ring is a silly idea," Susan said. "They talk about blood diamonds and colonial exploitation."

"Well, they're right. In some countries, diamond miners are exploited, but you can buy what they call 'ethical diamonds.'"

"I'm sure that's what Bobbie did," Susan said with obvious pride in her voice. "She cares about such things more than you know."

Lucy brushed off the implied criticism and gestured to the visitor's chair. "Thanks for letting me know. You should also tell Tom and Reshma."

"Tom knows. He's my spiritual advisor, so I told him first."

"Good. What did he say?"

"He said he's so happy for me. He told me how much his life has changed for the better since he'd married Jeff."

"And you're sure about this marriage?" asked Lucy, frowning a little. She hated to sound skeptical, but it was easier to revert to her role as a couples' counselor than to sort out her real feelings about this development.

"Yes, I think so," Susan said, finally sitting down. "I've known Bobbie since I returned to Hobbs. We were friends for more than a year before we got involved. And at our age, we can't waste any time. Who knows what tomorrow may bring?" Lucy could bet that was another direct quote from Bobbie. "I feel like I should give Bobbie something, but on a teacher's salary, I can't afford anything expensive. Did you give Liz something when she proposed?"

Lucy smiled at the memory of Liz in the restaurant after the concert in the park. She'd waited until dinner was over before popping the question. Blushing and speechless, she pushed the velvet covered box across the table. In the end, Lucy had to do the asking. "No, and I think she would have been uncomfortable. Usually the person who proposes gives the ring. Don't worry. You'll have your chance to give her a ring...at the wedding."

Susan exhaled a long sigh and finally sat back in her chair. "That's what I thought. Bobbie looked so relieved when I said yes."

"You're not easy to figure out, Susan. You could have just as easily said no."

Susan made a sad face. "That would have crushed her."

"That's not why you agreed to marry her? Because you didn't want to disappoint her?" Lucy said in her neutral counseling voice.

"No, no! I want our relationship to be honorable. Getting married means we can finally live together openly."

"So that's your reason?"

"No, Lucy, it's *not*. I love Bobbie."

"Good. That's what I wanted to hear. So, obviously, you'll be moving out of the rectory."

"Yes, maybe Reshma could move into the rector's quarters. That curate's studio is so cramped. She loves to cook and you can barely put down a spoon on that little countertop."

"I'll think about it," said Lucy vaguely. "I've also been thinking about your request to come on as a full-time priest. Are you sure you want to quit your teaching job?"

"Bobbie says I won't need to work anymore, but she intends to keep working, so I think I should too. Of course, I want to follow my vocation as a priest." She lowered her eyes, another maddening convent custom. "But if you don't want me...."

Lucy fought the temptation to roll her eyes at the obvious passive aggression. "It's not that I don't want you, Susan. It's just that St. Margaret's doesn't need four full-time priests, especially when some churches have none. Have you considered applying for openings in other parishes?"

"But you and Tom are always off traveling, and Reshma is too young and inexperienced to handle it on her own."

"You're right about that, and she appreciates your mentoring. But I also know you really like teaching. It was your first vocation."

"If I teach another three years, I'll get a nice, little pension."

"That's something to consider. As you said, who knows what tomorrow may bring?"

Susan eyed Lucy suspiciously. "You don't want me as a full-time priest."

Lucy stifled a sigh of exasperation. "That's not what I said,

Susan, but it will be hard to get approval from the vestry for the additional salary. We need the money for the work on the church. It's an old building and eats up our budget. It's not personal. You're an excellent priest. We just can't afford it."

Susan didn't look convinced, but she murmured, "I understand."

"I hope you do." Lucy glanced at her phone. "Now, I'm sorry but I have to go. Liz is giving a talk about vaccination policy at the school board meeting."

"And I must leave too. I asked for personal leave this morning to talk to you. I wanted to tell you in person, of course. I owe you that."

Lucy gave Susan a firm look. "You don't owe me anything, Susan. We've both paid our debts to one another. But I appreciate you coming to tell me in person." As an afterthought, Lucy added, "Congratulations."

Susan got up, but she didn't leave. Lucy realized she expected more—some gesture of affection. Lucy went around the desk and gave her a quick hug. "Please pass along my congratulations to Bobbie too."

"I will," said Susan, finally looking satisfied.

After she left, Lucy put on her coat. She needed to hurry, or she'd be late for Liz's talk. On the way out of her office, she ran smack into Cherie Harrison. No one was hurt in the collision, and they fell into one another's arms, laughing. "I was just coming to see you," said Cherie, "but it looks like you're on the way out the door."

"I'm heading to the school board building for the meeting," Lucy explained. "I want to hear what Liz has to say...in case I get vaccination questions."

"You shouldn't be giving medical advice," Cherie said, echoing Liz's earlier warning.

"I know. I should tell people to ask their doctor."

Cherie laughed. "I see Liz has you well trained."

"That she does. She would take over everything if I let her." Liz had suggested folding Hobbs Family Counseling under the LLC she'd formed for her medical practice, but Lucy had resisted the idea. It was enough to have merged most of her other assets with those of her wives. Lucy wasn't sure why, but she wanted to keep this small part of her world independent. Maybe it was because Liz had such little respect for psychotherapy and could be so bossy. Lucy also didn't want to hear her advice on how to run her practice, even though it would likely be practical and sound.

It suddenly occurred to Lucy that she should encourage Cherie, who had two school-age children, to attend the school board meeting. "You should be going to the school board meeting, not me."

Cherie smiled. "Oh, I already heard Liz's speech. She used me as her practice audience because I have kids."

A little flash of jealousy surprised Lucy. Before Maggie had moved in with them, Liz would test all her presentations on Lucy. As her sermons came together, Lucy read the drafts to Liz. With Maggie there, they seldom exchanged their half-baked concepts, probably because it felt like holding a third-party hostage. Now, Lucy realized how much she missed being able to speak her thoughts aloud without deliberation, asking for permission, or wondering if it would annoy someone.

Lucy became aware of Cherie's striking blue-green eyes studying her curiously. Yes, it was obvious Lucy had become lost in her own thoughts. She smiled an apology. Cherie gracefully said, "It was so nice of Maggie to invite us for dinner tonight. Does she make breakfast for you often?"

Every muscle in Lucy's body tensed. Did Cherie suspect what was *really* going on at their house? Cherie peered deeply into Lucy's eyes, but there was no suspicion, merely curiosity.

"That kitchen in the garage apartment is so tiny," Lucy said quickly. "It must be terribly confining for a trained chef to even fry an egg on that little stove. Plus, our kitchen used to be Maggie's. She's comfortable there."

"I'm just glad to hear you're all getting along so well. There was a time Liz and Maggie couldn't even be in the same room together, never mind cook in the same kitchen."

"I remember it well," Lucy admitted with a sigh. "But I don't mind having someone make breakfast for me or bake tasty treats. You know I'm helpless when it comes to cooking."

Cherie studied her coolly. "You're not helpless, Lucy. You can cook when you want to."

"But why bother stressing? Liz likes to cook, and Maggie is professionally trained. It seems to make them happy, so why not?"

"Lucy, you've got everyone wrapped around your little finger, don't you?" Cherie clucked her tongue and made a low chuckle of disapproval that had a decidedly Southern drawl to it. Unlike her racial identity, Cherie's place of origin was never in doubt. Her Louisiana accent was unmistakable. "All you need to do is smile that big, beautiful smile, and everyone wants to take care of you."

Lucy mimed horror. "Is it that obvious?"

"No, of course not. You're just applying your knowledge of people's personalities to manage their behavior. Half the time people probably don't even realize you're doing it, and, as far as I know, you don't do any harm. Using feminine wiles on your partner is something I've been known to do myself!"

"Never try to trick another therapist," Lucy said with an exaggerated sigh.

"Nope, we can spot a manipulation a mile away." Cherie glanced at her watch. "Lucy, you'd better get going if you don't want to be late. You know your spouse is a stickler for punctuality."

"Even though she's late all the time!"

"She's a doctor. She has an excuse."

"I have one too. I'm a priest."

Cherie's eyes were merry. "Yes, you are, and you have an answer for everything."

Lucy winked. "That's my job." But she could see the wall clock over Cherie's shoulder and knew she needed to get moving or she'd miss Liz's talk.

Driving to the school, Lucy reflected on the dreariness of early spring in Maine. The ground was thawing. The water, trapped all winter, bubbled up in the roadways, spitting through the asphalt like millions of tiny goblins. The plow piles along the road were dirty and rounded from melting in the growing sunshine. Maine was the most beautiful place Lucy had ever lived, but there was nothing endearing about mud season.

Despite the date on the calendar, it was brisk that morning. Lucy wished she'd remembered her gloves. The parking lot was packed, requiring her to walk some distance to the school entrance.

Liz and Maggie were sitting near the front. Being late looked bad for the rector of Hobbs' Episcopal Church, so Lucy summoned the confidence to stride down the center aisle like she owned the place. From her opera career, she'd learned that, when things went wrong, acting like everything was perfectly normal was the best strategy.

Liz picked up her coat, placed on the neighboring chair to save Lucy a seat. After Lucy sat down, a long-fingered hand surreptitiously reached over to take hers—Liz's way of making amends for the dirty look she'd given her wife when she'd arrived. Liz's warm hands were always welcome, but especially when they walked on the beach on chilly mornings, and she took one of Lucy's hands into the pocket of her sweatshirt with hers. On cold winter nights Liz was like Lucy's private furnace. Maybe Cherie was right and Lucy did use people. She was a compulsive hugger. Often, she gave hugs just to get them back.

Stop, she told herself. There's nothing wrong with needing human affection. That's why God gave us arms!

The booming voice of the school board chairman interrupted Lucy's examination of conscience. "And now, we're going to hear from Dr. Stolz, who, as you all know, is the senior doctor at Hobbs Family Practice and the medical advisor to the school board."

Liz took her place at the podium on the stage. "Good morning. The board asked me to talk about vaccines. I know many people are confused. You hear opinions from your friends or read things on-line. What should you believe?" Lucy had heard Liz speak at medical conferences in a very different tone. Then, she was all business, efficiently citing facts and figures, to prove her points. With this audience, she'd adopted a relaxed, almost folksy tone. One would never know that she was once chief of surgery at Yale New Haven and one of the world's leading authorities on breast cancer. To the townspeople of Hobbs, she was just "Dr. Liz."

We all manipulate our listeners to encourage them to listen, Lucy thought, which she knew from her training for the ministry and psychotherapy. *I'm still defending myself against Cherie's observations,* she finally admitted.

She listened to Liz gave a quick summary of her opinions about vaccination. They're safe. They have centuries of experience behind them. (She told a little anecdote of how George Washington gained military advantage by vaccinating his troops against smallpox.) Lucy watched the guys in the audience suddenly lean forward and pay more attention. Men loved history, especially military history. Liz now had them hooked.

She didn't short-sell the risks of vaccines, but she spoke in a way that seemed to put people at ease. Then she asked for questions. Dozens of hands shot up. Lucy glanced at Maggie's face and saw she was as proud as she was.

***

"Hard day?" Maggie said, turning away from the stove to give Lucy a kiss.

Lucy heaved out a sigh. "You don't know the half of it!"

"It must have been bad. You're still wearing your collar."

Lucy's hand flew to her throat. The inflexible band of white linen was still pinned to her blouse. Usually, Lucy took it off as soon as she got into her car to drive home. Today, she'd been too distracted by the jumble of memories from a day when nothing seemed to go right.

With everyone being so jumpy since the president had been inaugurated, the emergency counseling sessions were understandable, but even her staff was needy. Her young curate, Reshma, had been brought as a refugee from Sudan as a child. She was a naturalized citizen, but she worried for her friends, Teresa and her daughter, Grace. They had arrived more recently, victims of yet another Sudanese civil war. Teresa and Grace were terrified that they'd be swept up in an ICE raid, even though they had all their papers and were "legal."

In the last election, Reshma had campaigned for the Democratic candidates, but now she was afraid to join any political event. "It's bad enough that I stick out in lily-white Maine, I don't want to endanger myself or the church by standing on the street with a sign." Lucy's heart ached watching her protégée wrestle between her impulse to fight back against what she perceived as injustice and her instincts for self-preservation.

Shaking her head, Lucy finally reached up to unpin her collar.

"I'd help you," said Maggie, watching her struggle with the pin in the back, "but I'm afraid I'd get grease on it. Liz works so hard to press your linen collars just right." She sighed. "When I lived here, she always let Ellie do all the ironing. I never saw her iron anything since we were in college."

"I'm almost sorry I told her how well Erika used to iron my collars for me. Liz took it on to prove she could do it just as well," Lucy said, but it was strangely affecting to watch an ex-surgeon take on this humble duty.

Maggie nodded sadly. "I heard her promise Erika she'd take care of you if anything happened to her. You know how Liz is. She'd rather die than break her word." Maggie's tone rang with the certainty that came from knowing someone for half a century.

Lucy was too raw from the stressful day to talk about Erika. It was true what she said in grief counseling. The pain never goes away completely. It simply becomes less intense. "Where *is* Liz? Don't tell me she's late at the office again."

"She's outside bringing in firewood." Maggie turned and landed a quick peck on Lucy's cheek. "Go on, honey. Get out of your work clothes. I'll have snacks ready by the time you come down. Brenda and Cherie should be here soon."

Gazing into the living room before ascending the stairs, Lucy reflected on how much she appreciated the quiet domesticity of their lives together. The scent of a wood fire smelled like home. Its mellow, penetrating warmth soothed her. When she lived in the old building that served as rectory and parish house, it was always cold. In that drafty place, the cast iron radiators could never crank out enough heat. They clanged loudly when the steam came up, but she loved warming her nightgown on the hoops before going to bed.

Her nostalgic memories of the rectory also brought back the loneliness she'd felt before Liz and Maggie had 'adopted' her. Coming home to delicious smells from the kitchen was a blessing. When Lucy was a brand-new rector and lived alone, she was too busy to cook for herself. Her meals were usually salads topped with a protein like chickpeas or a hardboiled egg. The minimalist fare had helped her maintain her trim figure. Once she'd moved in with Erika, who was an excellent cook, she'd had to watch her weight for the first time. Now, with Liz and Maggie, both gourmet cooks, it was even more of a struggle. Fortunately, as rector of a large church, Lucy was always running around so much, she burned off calories just doing her job.

She quickly changed into a cozy sweater and lounge pants. Feeling the need for an extra dose of comfort, she put on her sherpa-lined clogs. Dinner with Brenda and Cherie would be informal. She could bet that Liz would be in her jeans and a hoodie, her usual cool-weather, off-duty outfit. Maggie was always dressed—hair perfect, a full complement of makeup, even on her days off from teaching.

They'd been best friends for over a year before Lucy had seen Maggie without makeup. She'd finally figured out that the polished glamor was an inextricable part of Maggie's persona as an actress, and she was always "on." Although Lucy had also spent a good part of her life on the opera stage and in the public eye as a priest, she firmly believed in "downtime" when she could show her naked face and be herself.

Someone came up the stairs. Lucy instantly knew it was Liz. Her step and movements were distinctive. Air molecules made way for her. "Hey, Luce. Glad you're home. Brenda and Cherie just arrived." Liz caught her in a sturdy hug that almost lifted her off the ground. Lucy gratefully molded herself to Liz's warm body. The heat in the bedroom was turned down as usual. "How was your day?" asked Liz, nuzzling her ear.

"Busy as hell."

Lucy could feel the low chuckle rise in Liz's throat. "That's no way for a priest to talk!"

"Too bad. As you well know, this priest throws the F-bomb too."

"Come downstairs, and I'll pour you a glass of wine. I'm sure you deserve one." Liz bent to offer a sweet kiss, lingering just long enough to be provocative, then let her go. "Later, you sexy thing. I promise." After Liz released her, Lucy immediately felt chilled and wanted her back. She heard Liz's rapid footsteps on the stairs but resisted the urgency because she'd been rushing all day.

Chivalrously, Brenda rose when Lucy came into the room. Like Liz, she'd absorbed the "gentlemanly manners" their parents had tried to teach their brothers. "How's my favorite priest?" Brenda asked, kissing her on each cheek and giving her a tight squeeze. Cherie, who knew Lucy could never get enough hugs, opened her arms and embraced her warmly.

"Just some snacks to start us off," said Maggie, trying to herd them all back to their seats. "The stew can sit for a while."

"Thanks for inviting us on such short notice," said Cherie, giving Maggie a half hug.

Liz poured herself a glass of Irish whiskey. "I can't have my friend making a PR nightmare for herself without offering some unsolicited advice."

"I'm glad for any advice. I was totally shocked at how fast this thing blew up. I don't even know how the press found out I signed the 287g agreement. We didn't tell anyone, not even the town manager or the select board. We sign up for lots of trainings no one ever knows about."

Liz took a long, reflective sip of whiskey. "Unfortunately, the press has a way of discovering anything that will get eyeballs. Reporters can search public records for a good lead. And you conveniently supplied it."

"Liz, I swear to you, when my administrative chief brought this training opportunity to me, I thought it was a great idea. Right now, if we apprehend someone here illegally, and they have a criminal record, we need to wait for ICE to come up from Boston. That can take two hours. More, if they're busy. Meanwhile, I've got a patrol officer waiting on the side of the road with a potentially dangerous perp. The officer is out of commission until ICE shows up. It's a real public safety issue."

"So what will this ICE training do for you?" Maggie asked, offering a tray of beautifully presented canapés. Lucy, who hadn't eaten much for lunch, hungrily collected a few.

"Once my officers are trained," Brenda explained, "they can deliver the suspect to a federally approved facility, where they will be held until ICE can pick them up."

Munching on a piece of cheese, Liz looked thoughtful. "Sounds perfectly reasonable to me."

"I thought so too, and still think so," said Brenda, accepting some olive tapenade bruschetta from Maggie. "That's why we signed up. The Feds take our problem off our hands so we can get back to keeping Hobbs safe."

Lucy turned to Brenda's wife. "Cherie, what do you think?"

"I'll always support Brenda because I love her. I didn't even know about it until all the ruckus started."

Brenda turned to Cherie. "Honey, I never thought of telling you because I never thought it would cause all this commotion."

Liz idly inspected her fingers like a man would, fingers curled into her palm. "Brenda, what planet do you live on?"

"Liz!" Maggie hissed. "Brenda is your *friend.*"

"I know. As her friend, I need to be honest with her. This is by far the dumbest thing I've ever seen her do." Liz peered at Brenda. That imperious stare, once used to intimidate junior doctors, made everyone in the room sit up and pay attention. Brenda, occupying the leather club chair by the wood stove, squirmed. "Brenda," said Liz slowly, "do you watch the news?"

"Cherie and I stopped watching it since the former guy got in again."

"We all have," Liz said, finally releasing Brenda's gaze. "We hope by not watching TV, we can pretend all these awful things aren't happening, but they are. ICE is acting lawlessly and with impunity. Stephen Miller has set a goal of deporting three thousand undocumented people *a day*. They say they're only after violent criminals, but they're picking up grandmothers who have lived here for decades. Don't you see that associating with them makes you look *bad*?"

Brenda blinked. "As chief of police, I'm obligated to cooperate with other law enforcement agencies. Doesn't matter if it's other states or the Feds."

"I understand. But that assumes the agencies are acting within the law. Come on, Brenda. You see how bad this looks."

Brenda sat back in her chair as if pushed back by Liz's steady gaze. "I know what people are saying, but this is good training."

Lucy nudged Liz's thigh, hoping she'd get the message and back off. It was clear that Brenda thought she hadn't done anything wrong. "Brenda, I know you always try to do the right thing," Lucy said gently. "This isn't as clear to other people as it seems to you."

"I'm getting that now," Brenda said, her blond brows dipping towards the base of her nose. She turned to Cherie, who reached for her hand. "So what should I do?"

"For one thing, stop talking to the press," Liz said emphatically.

"But I want them to understand!"

"They won't understand. Your reasons don't matter to them. All they know is people hate ICE, and this story will get lots of clicks."

Brenda looked reflective as the information penetrated her mind. Lucy realized Brenda had never even considered how this would look to the public.

Maggie leaned forward. "I put a lot of effort into this dinner, and I want everyone to enjoy it. Can we pause this conversation until after we eat?"

Cherie looked like a huge burden had been lifted from her shoulders. "Thanks, Maggie. That's a good idea. What can I do to help?"

***

When Lucy came to bed, she found Liz with her hands clasped behind her head, staring at the ceiling. Lucy slipped into bed beside her. "What are you thinking, gorgeous?"

"That Brenda is between a rock and hard place." Liz raised her arm so Lucy could nestle against her breast.

After the hard day and the evening's tough conversation, Lucy would rather cuddle than analyze a dicey political situation, but she'd asked what Liz had on her mind. "How so?"

When Liz sighed, her breath smelled sweet and minty from toothpaste. "In a leadership position in a male dominated profession like law enforcement, you can't switch positions just because someone objects. If you roll over that easily, you risk looking weak or admitting that you made a bad decision. Sometimes, you find yourself backed into a corner with no escape."

"You think that's how Brenda feels?" Lucy asked, genuinely curious.

"I can't say how Brenda feels, but that's how I felt many times when I was chief of surgery. A situation changes and you're stuck with the decision you made under other circumstances. Even worse, one of your staff has done something stupid, and you're trapped between supporting them or courting a lawsuit. It's easy to say, 'just do the right thing,' but what's right isn't always obvious or something you can do."

Lucy thought back to some of the hard decisions she'd had to make as rector of St. Margaret's, like when she more or less forced the vestry to hire a trans woman. Denise Chantal was clearly the most qualified candidate, so it was the right thing to do. The old guard's pearl clutching was expected but almost comical. The decision to continue the mask requirements during the waning days of the pandemic was certainly unpopular with the conservative members of the congregation.

While she'd asked for input from others, Lucy had made those tough calls. Yet if she had realized she'd made a wrong decision, she wouldn't think twice about changing her mind. *Did I appear weak?* she wondered. "I've had to make some hard calls. Liz, you helped me decide some of them, but what good is digging in and refusing to admit you've changed your mind?"

"That's what a woman would do because it's common sense. Guys think differently. Brenda, like me, works in a male culture, or at least, I did when I was a surgeon. I'd meet with the chiefs of obstetrics or pediatrics, which were more female-friendly departments. They handled things differently. Discussion and collaborative decision-making was the norm. Like the military, the surgical service was a hierarchy with a top-down, command-control-coerce leadership style. In those days, being a surgeon meant being decisive and confident and always *right*, even when you were wrong. Things are changing now, but not fast enough. In old boys' professions, like policing, the pace is even slower."

While Lucy considered what Liz had said, she reached up and teased her nipple. Liz grunted. "Lucy, what are you up to?"

Lucy grinned against her breast. "What do you think?" She slid her hand under Liz's shirt and began rubbing her belly. "I'm surprised Maggie didn't join us tonight."

Liz yawned. "I told you she'd lose interest in sex. By the third year of our marriage, she'd push me away unless it was one of our designated nights."

"You had designated nights?" Lucy leaned up on her elbow and peered into Liz's blue eyes. "That must have been hard on you. You LOVE sex."

"I do, especially with you." Liz rolled Lucy over on her back and began kissing her. She was gentle, which was perfect for Lucy's mood tonight. She was tired and wasn't even sure she could stay awake for sex. Once Liz raised her nightgown and began kissing her breasts, Lucy was completely awake. Feeling Liz's mouth on her nipples stirred sensations in other places that Lucy hoped Liz would kiss. She didn't have to wait long. Liz worked her way down Lucy's body, kissing and licking the most erogenous zones, before parting her legs with her shoulders.

The feel of her tongue on her sex was warm, curious, gentle, then probing. This wonderfully ordinary lovemaking was exactly what Lucy needed tonight. She opened her legs wider to get more of the sensuous teasing. Not only did Liz have perfect pitch, which could be annoying when Lucy rehearsed, she had a musician's sense of rhythm. She advanced, withdrew, increased pressure, then lightened it in perfect sync with Lucy's needs. Then, Liz frustrated her with a course change without warning, but she always came back just in time. On cue, Lucy's body vibrated with a shimmering orgasm. She threaded her fingers through Liz's hair and pulled tight.

When it ended, Liz returned to Lucy's arms. "See? Better watch what you start, because you know I'll always finish it."

"I love it when you make love to me like that."

"The old-fashioned way, without toys or acrobatics? Like an old married couple?"

"We're married and old, so I guess so," replied Lucy with a lazy smile.

"Not dead yet," said Liz, frowning.

Lucy's finger flew to Liz's lip. "Don't even say such a thing." Liz looked sad, obviously reminded of Erika, her best friend, her wingman, and Lucy's first wife.

"Don't catch Maggie's Irish superstition, please," Liz warned gently.

Lucy changed the subject by digging into Liz's lounge pants. "Don't worry. It's not contagious." She smiled against Liz's cheek when she found her lover wet and open. "Oh, my heroic and strong wife needs attention. Here's proof." She found her way inside.

"Your wife is putty in your hands, Lovely Lucy. Put me out of my misery...please."

Lucy had barely gotten started, when Liz came in her arms. As always, when Liz was excited, it took barely a touch to produce an orgasm. Lucy had yet to come up with a strategy to slow the process other than making Liz come first. It didn't matter tonight. They were both warm, satisfied, and blissfully alone.

Liz gave Lucy one last appreciative caress before pulling down her nightgown. "Thanks. That was nice and unexpected. I could see how tired you are."

"Never too tired for you, lover," Lucy said in a sultry voice.

"Keep on like that, and I'll have no choice but to make you come again."

"Not tonight." Lucy snuggled more deeply into Liz's body. "Did I tell you how much I liked your talk at the school board today? I loved how well you deflected that woman defending that debunked autism study. Just the right amount of kind but firm rebuttal. She thought you were on her side until you convinced her to see it your way."

"I'm learning that a quiet voice speaks louder than shouting or cutting someone off at the knees."

"I can see a definite improvement in your approach. You've finally figured out you don't have to crush your opponent to get your point across."

"Only took seventy years," Liz said, stifling a yawn.

"Stop talking about your age. People will think you're obsessed with it."

"I'm not, but seventy is a big birthday."

"It is, but you have months before then." Lucy decided that Liz needed a deep tongue kiss to reassure her that she wasn't "dead yet."

Chapter 2

Cherie loved the feel of Megan's hair as she plaited it, like strands of pale-yellow silk between her fingers. Although Megan's adoptive mother was a blonde too, her hair had a coarser texture from her African American heritage. Cherie's coloring made her ethnicity hard to place. Many Scandinavians were olive-complected and had blond hair and sea-blue eyes. Cherie was light-skinned enough to pass, but she made sure everyone knew she was *black* and proud.

Cherie remembered her own mother's dark fingers winding her hair into braids, all the while telling her daughter how beautiful her hair was, what a pretty girl she was—compliments that still caused her heart to swell all these years after her mother's death. She wished all mothers could instill a positive body image into their daughters, especially when they began adolescence and felt gawky and ugly.

Obviously, Brenda's mother hadn't. Her wife was always self-conscious about her looks. Why, Cherie had no idea, because Brenda was a damn good-looking woman. Her face had good bones. Her fine features were elegant, especially her perfectly shaped and proportioned nose. Brenda had stopped dyeing her hair blond and cut it short because her new duties as a parent meant she had less time. Also, she'd grown tired of the monthly ritual of mixing smelly chemicals and waiting patiently for them to work. Closing in on sixty, Brenda wasn't fooling anyone.

"Oww!" Megan howled when Cherie twisted the braid tight. At least she wasn't squirming this morning like she usually did. She was eight now and should be past fidgeting when her mother did her hair.

Despite her annoyance and under pressure from the clock, Cherie spoke gently. "If you'd hold still, honey, Mama C wouldn't have to pull so hard to gather your hair. Just sit quietly, and I'll be done in no time!"

Megan huffed but relaxed her body. As promised, the braids came together quickly. Cherie tied the bows at the end of Megan's braids, an old-fashioned look, but a little extra touch that showed how much she cared. She kissed the top of Megan's head, pleased that her hair still smelled floral from a recent shampoo. Her mother always said, 'you can tell a good mama by how clean her babies' clothes are and how they smell.' Cherie took pride in her children and always made sure people knew it.

Even more, she wanted to show her babies how much she loved them, knowing they needed the extra special attention after they'd been orphaned by domestic violence and forced to relive their terror when a crazy kid shot up their school. Keith had only escaped because he was in the nurse's office with a fake bellyache. Afterward, he stuck close to Brenda, whom he saw as the only one who could protect him. Although Brenda had been reluctant to become a mother, she loved and protected her children fiercely. Keith responded by following her around like an eager puppy. Megan insisted on sitting in Brenda's lap when she read the kids a story.

Cherie glanced over at Brenda, who was mechanically eating her oatmeal while scrolling her phone. "Oh, fuck! Not another one! I can't fucking believe it."

"Brenda!" Cherie shot her wife a sharp look. "Language!" Brenda, despite her tough act perfected over her years in police work, shrank back from the scolding. Cherie emphatically nodded toward Keith. Fortunately, their son was too wrapped up in his tablet to notice his mother's profanity, but Cherie knew that small ears were always listening. "Now, tell me what's going on, but spare us the F-bombs, please."

"There's a story on Channel Eight about the ICE agreement. Of course, it hammers on one point over and over." Brenda pounded the air with her fist. Keith looked up from his tablet and cautiously stared at his adoptive mother.

"What point is that?" Cherie asked as if she didn't know.

"That Hobbs is the *only* police department in Maine to voluntarily sign an agreement. That's because the other departments chickened out once they saw what happened to us. This story is so biased and skewed I could *spit!*" She dropped her phone in disgust.

"Sweetie pie, everything gets twisted. The news people don't care. They just want clicks."

"I know, but it makes me so damned...." Brenda glanced up guiltily and covered her mouth. "Sorry. It makes me so darn mad. Want me to read it to you?"

"No, thanks," said Cherie. "I don't want to upset the kids. Text me the link. I'll read it later if I can find a few minutes."

The furrow in Brenda's handsome brow grew deeper as she continued to stare at her phone. "So unfair," she murmured. "I'm just trying to keep them safe."

"I know, honey bear. Maybe you need to explain it better," Cherie said, then caught her lower lip in her teeth. She'd vowed not to discuss how she really felt about this whole stupid thing. When they'd first begun the relationship, Cherie had resolved to avoid making comments about Brenda's work unless she was specifically asked for her opinion. So far, she'd stuck to that policy. She knew she was prejudiced since a state trooper had shot her obviously black half-sister at a traffic stop, and she'd be the first to admit that she knew next to nothing about law enforcement.

One thing she did know for sure. ICE was no ordinary police force. They dressed like they were going into combat, carried assault rifles, and wore masks like militias in Third World countries, all clearly intended to intimidate people. Breaking into homes in the middle of the night was a scare tactic. And what kind of officer chases an old man out into the cold in his pajamas? Why would Brenda, *her* Brenda, want to associate with such horrible people?

When Cherie looked up she saw Brenda eyeing her curiously. "You don't approve of what I'm doing."

Cherie weighed her response carefully. "That's not entirely true.

I believe our immigration laws should be enforced. I don't know enough about this ICE agreement to approve or not. I can tell you that those ICE people are the bad guys, and I don't like you hanging out with them."

There was suddenly fire in Brenda's blue eyes. "I don't *hang out* with them. I don't even want to see them in Hobbs. But my officers don't have time to deal with undocumented immigrants with criminal records. We're busy arresting speeders and busting shoplifters or rushing to the house of someone having a heart attack."

Cherie involuntarily narrowed her eyes in skepticism. "You sure that's all this is about?"

Brenda raised her hand like a scout. "I swear."

Cherie exhaled long and slowly. "Sweetie, I believe you don't mean any harm, but I don't know if you completely understand what you've gotten yourself into."

"It's just training, Cherie. It means we can transport a suspect to a federal facility and get on with our day."

"Uh huh," said Cherie with just the right note of skepticism.

"Okay, then don't believe me," Brenda huffed.

"I do believe you, Brenda. I just don't think you're seeing the whole picture."

"I don't do politics when it comes to law enforcement. No one should ever know my party membership or which candidate I support."

"That's appropriate, but this goes beyond who you vote for. You're a smart woman. You know what I'm trying to say."

"Oh, yes, baby, I do," Brenda said. "But *everything's* political now. Everything."

"Which is why you need to watch *everything* you say and do." Cherie noticed the clock over the sink closing in on the hour. "Brenda, you need to get these kids to school."

Brenda turned around and looked at the clock. "Hell, yeah, I do." Brenda gave Keith an affectionate pat on the arm. "Come on, buddy. You need to put that tablet away and brush your teeth." She grimaced at him with big teeth for emphasis.

Keith groaned but he turned off his tablet. The house rule—no tablets allowed during school hours—was inviolable. Glowering beneath his blond brows, he handed his device to Cherie. "Thank you, sir," she replied. She reached out to Megan. She wasn't as addicted as her brother and surrendered her tablet without a fight.

When Keith returned from the bathroom, Brenda handed him his jacket and helped her daughter into hers. Now that all kids in Maine got free lunch at school, Cherie felt empty handed at the door. They got breakfast too, but she insisted on giving them fruit and yogurt in the morning before they left. Not feeding her own kids just didn't feel right.

✳✳✳

Cherie was grateful to be alone in the practice's breakroom. Solitude was such a rare state since she and Brenda had adopted the kids. She tried to savor each and every single moment. Not that she didn't love her wife and children or resented the presence of her colleagues. Sometimes, she simply needed some blessed moments alone to catch her breath and listen to her own thoughts. With all the political background noise, the influx of stimulation from other people was often overwhelming.

As a therapist, Cherie knew how important time alone was to mental health. Between parenting duties, a half-time job at Hobbs Family Practice, and her second job at Hobbs Family Counseling, so little of her time was her own. Brenda had encouraged Cherie to cut back and conserve her energy, but where?

Along with other mental health volunteers, she'd been happy to help Lucy deal with the unprecedented demand for counselors after the school shooting. Almost two years later, most people had gone back to normal life, such as it was under this new administration. One shock after another to political norms and the rule of law, often several in a single day, was increasing everyone's stress. The human nervous system simply wasn't built to adapt to so many threats in rapid succession. Even with help from their semi-retired therapist, Gloria Parrish, Lucy needed help in the counseling practice. Reshma was taking classes to earn her therapy credential, but it would be years before she qualified.

Brenda said Cherie should choose whatever gave her the most satisfaction, which was hard. She'd gone back to school to become a PA after years as a psychotherapist because she enjoyed practicing medicine. She loved working with patients, and now that Liz was cutting back her hours to accompany Lucy on her singing engagements, the family practice needed her more than ever.

Filling her jealously guarded Café du Monde mug, Cherie reflected on her impossible choices. The idea that she had to choose closed in on her like the relentlessly moving walls in old black-and-white horror movies.

She heard female voices in the hall and knew her precious solitude was about to be invaded. Bobbie, the practice's nurse practitioner, came into the break room, followed by their refugee nurse. Teresa had been a fully certified nurse in South Sudan before the last political upheaval, but she'd had to take classes to qualify for a state nursing license. Following in Bobbie's footsteps, Teresa was training to be an NP herself.

Usually, a tune or bubbling laughter accompanied Bobbie and her protégée. Today, it was conspicuously absent. In fact, their conversation sounded downright grim. Cherie's own thoughts were enough to weigh her down. She didn't need help from others to sink into a morass of negativity.

"Good morning!" she said heartily, defending in advance against the gloom. The newcomers responded with less enthusiastic greetings, but at least Bobbie managed a smile.

"Queenie, I saw your customers lined up for you out there," Cherie said, addressing Teresa by her practice nickname. After Dr. Liz had dubbed Teresa "queen of the blood draw," the affectionate moniker had stuck.

"Those early birds think they can get preferential treatment," Teresa replied with her British accent graced with lilting African notes. "They must find some patience this morning. This nurse needs a strong cup of tea."

Cherie changed the subject to a more positive topic. "We so enjoyed your Grace's performance in the school play. She's really adapted to her new school."

Teresa suddenly yelped like an injured puppy and fled the room. Meanwhile, the electric kettle she'd set to boil began to hiss and gurgle. Cherie waited a moment to see if Teresa would return before switching it off. She turned to Bobbie for an explanation. "Was it something I said?"

Bobbie heaved out a frustrated sigh. Her face was red. She carried more than a few extra pounds, and Cherie often worried about her blood pressure. "She's terrified, like everyone in Maine's African community. I don't blame them. He ran on the promise to deport millions of immigrants, and it looks like he means to make good on it." Although the practice had informally banned political talk, lately, it was impossible to avoid.

"But she has all her papers," Cherie protested. "She waited years in that awful refugee camp for her chance to come to America."

Bobbie sighed. "Yes, I know, but that doesn't seem to matter to those goons. They'll scoop up anyone with brown skin. You're lucky you don't look black." Cherie gave Bobbie a sharp look because passing for white had always seemed like a deception.

It was hard to be mad at Bobbie, who was kind to a fault. She'd taken in Teresa and her young daughter, Grace, when they were stuck in a homeless shelter. Now, she was mentoring Teresa in her quest to qualify as an NP. "They canceled all the refugee visas. Some of the friends Teresa made in the camps were all packed and ready to come to the US. They were so excited to come to Maine. Now they're stuck in a country on the edge of starvation." Maine might seem like an odd place for people from Sub-Saharan Africa, but decades ago, it had become a haven for Somali and Sudanese refugees.

"I don't blame her for being scared. I'm scared myself," said Cherie, "and like you said, I can pass."

"We're all scared. I might be white, but I'm a gay woman. Soon, they'll be coming for us too. This is worse than I imagined, and I was pessimistic!" Bobbie absently spooned two sugars into her coffee. Cherie worried about her A1C, but obviously, Bobbie didn't share her concern. After a grim moment of silence, Bobbie suddenly brightened. "How about some good news?"

"That would be nice," said Cherie cautiously, afraid to hope.

"I'm getting married," Bobbie proudly announced, strutting a little as she carried her coffee to the table.

"Oh, wow! Congratulations! When?"

"Soon. At our age, why wait?"

Through Bobbies' break room tales, Cherie had been following the ups and downs of the couple. Susan was still adjusting to sobriety. For the first couple of years, Bobbie was the caregiver to her partner with dementia. As a member of St. Margaret's clergy, Susan felt she had to hide their relationship from public view. They'd recently been talking about marriage, but Susan worried how it would look for Bobbie to be in a relationship so soon after her partner's death.

As much as Cherie admired Susan for turning her life around, she grew impatient with her excuses for not doing things. There were times when she wanted to throttle the woman and scream, "Get on with your life!" But how could anyone yell at someone who looked like a holy card saint and shrank from the gentlest criticism? The therapist in Cherie recognized classic passive-aggression, but she expected more self-confidence from a priest.

Bobbie's brows dipped toward the base of her nose. "She still doesn't trust me when I say she doesn't need to worry about money. Joyce left me everything—the beach house, all her investments, her shares in the company. I'll never be able to spend it all in this lifetime." It must be nice to have inherited so much wealth. Cherie tried to think of something neutral to say. Bobbie apparently mistook her lack of response as disapproval and hurried to add, "People think I didn't really care about Joyce, but I did. She wasn't just my sugar mama. In the beginning, I loved her. Not everyone would stick around to take care of someone with Alzheimer's, especially since we weren't even married."

Cherie soothingly stroked Bobbie's shoulder. She knew how sensitive she was to criticism of her relationship with Susan because they'd gotten involved while Joyce was still alive. Most people stayed away from people in such relationships, as if dementia were catching. Some people looked at family caregivers as masochistic martyrs. Cherie, who'd taken care of her ailing father when she'd first moved to Maine, saw them as unacknowledged saints. "You were so good to Joyce," Cherie said tenderly, "right to the very end. And you should spend her money. She wanted you to have it." She wanted to add, 'and you earned it,' but that would only reinforce Bobbie's fears about people's perceptions.

Dr. Liz came into the break room. Usually, she was hard to read because she wore that perpetual surgeon's scowl. This morning she was wearing the kind of satisfied smile that meant she'd probably had a very good night. Cherie was glad her permanently tan skin hid her blush. She shouldn't be thinking about what her boss did in bed, but it was hard not to imagine. Liz's wife simply exuded a lush femininity that made it easy to visualize her passionate response in bed. Lucy might try to mute her vibrant sexuality under an appropriate priestly demeanor, but desire constrained by a collar was exponentially more potent.

"Bobbie, do you have a few minutes for me?" Liz asked, smiling. The polite request was another effect of Lucy's influence. Before Lucy worked her wiles on her, Liz would simply command someone's presence.

"Mind if I bring my coffee?" said Bobbie, getting up. She grimaced a little and shifted her weight to one leg. She'd been complaining about that knee.

"Not a bit," Liz said amiably, lifting her own cup. She nodded in the direction of her office, and Bobbie followed her out.

Cherie tried to figure out whether she liked being alone again. Having her coworkers around her had been a welcome break from debating her hard choices. She reminded herself that she didn't have to decide anything this morning and stayed to finish her coffee.

❋❋❋

When Cherie arrived at St. Margaret's rectory, she tried to muster the energy for a busy afternoon. She'd seen her first patient at Hobbs Family Practice at eight am. It was only a quarter past noon, but she already felt like she'd put in a full day.

Lucy was trying to convince Gloria Parrish to formally join the practice as a partner after months of volunteering to help the families recover from the school shooting. The clinical psychologist claimed she was bored in retirement. Coming back to work as a volunteer, had clearly reinvigorated the septuagenarian, who was too full of life to lounge on the beach. Gloria had recently bought a condominium in Hobbs, which Lucy took as a sign that she was considering their offer. The mere thought of possible relief gave Cherie a second wind.

A delicious aroma emanating from the common kitchen instantly activated Cherie's taste buds. She'd meant to pick up a sandwich from the supermarket on the way but she was running late. Brenda had been the lucky recipient of the chili left over from last night's supper. Now that Keith was in a growth spurt, his appetite was voracious. At the same time, their grocery bills were skyrocketing thanks to the economic policies of the new administration. The price of ground beef had surpassed what rib-eye steak used to cost. Brenda and Cherie were lucky to have secure, well-paying jobs, but how did poor families feed their children?

Cherie came into the kitchen, where she found Lucy reading from her laptop while she ate. She looked up and smiled with genuine affection. "Cherie! You're just in time to help me eat some of this stew. Liz always gives me portions the size she would eat. She forgets how much smaller I am." Lucy pointed to the bowl on the counter. "If you're hungry, help yourself!"

The container held more than enough for Cherie and another person with a light appetite, but she was famished and decided to help herself to what remained. While it heated in the microwave, she leaned against the countertop. "You're lucky to have such a good cook in your house. Brenda can cook, but she's happy to let me do it."

"I'm doubly lucky because I have two talented ladies cooking meals for me. Maggie often comes over and makes dinner. I'm completely spoiled."

Cherie tried to keep her eyes from narrowing at yet another confirmation of the unconventional arrangement in that household. She'd sensed that things weren't quite what they seemed, but Liz was her boss, and since Lucy had invited her into the counseling practice, she was as well. *What they do in private is their own business*, Cherie firmly told herself.

She sat down across from Lucy and dipped her spoon into the stew. One taste told her that it was the creation of someone who really loved to cook. Cherie could identify mustard and something sweet, maybe cider. Delicious didn't even begin to describe it. "This is wonderful," said Cherie. "I want the recipe. Who made this, Liz or Maggie?"

"Liz made it, but it's Maggie's recipe, if that makes any sense. They cook each other's recipes all the time." Lucy's green eyes held Cherie's. For a long moment, it seemed she wanted to say something important. Then her gaze dropped to her bowl. She'd changed her mind. "I hate to bring up a sore subject while you're eating, but I saw the Hobbs police were on the evening news again last night."

Cherie shook her head. "Those reporters won't let it go. Maine doesn't have enough going on, so they jump on anything juicy."

"I'm sorry for you and Brenda. The press can be relentless, but

I'm glad someone is keeping track of what's going on. So many newspapers and TV channels have caved to partisan pressure."

Lucy was right. The press had a job to do, but the media often took things out of context or twisted their meaning, making it hard to tell fact from fiction.

"Cherie, you've never said what you think about Brenda's decision," said Lucy in a kind voice. Her superpower was getting right to the point while making the other person feel perfectly safe.

Cherie had a choice to make. As the wife of a police chief, she'd learned to be careful about what she said. Confiding in Lucy was so tempting. Cherie knew her priest scrupulously observed professional boundaries, although sometimes she complained about Liz keeping medical secrets that people could see with their own eyes, like the fact that elderly Mr. Gleason's cancer was in its last stages.

Lucy seemed to be in no hurry, so Cherie gave herself until she finished her meal to decide how to answer her question. "Honestly, Lucy, I don't know what to think. Clearly, people have come into the country illegally, but most of them are only trying to find a better life for their families, just like all the immigrants who came before them. But those ICE guys wear masks so no one will know who they are, just like the Klan. They won't show their badges. I don't trust them."

"I don't either," Lucy admitted. "If you're really law enforcement, show your face and your credentials. Otherwise, anyone can pretend to be ICE."

Cherie hadn't considered that possibility. There was no official uniform, so anyone could dress up as an agent and do anything they wanted. Behind the mask could be a rapist for all they knew. Lucy had been raped, so to her, the danger was real.

Cherie decided to speak frankly. "No, I don't like it that Brenda and her officers are mixed up with that bunch. Even if they are technically required to cooperate with federal law enforcement. Why volunteer to help bullies?"

"Exactly," Lucy agreed.

"But to hear Brenda tell it, she thinks the training will help keep Hobbs and our police safer. It sounds reasonable to transport someone with a criminal record to a federal facility." Cherie leaned forward to speak confidentially even though there was no one in the building apart from Jodi, the admin, and she was down the hall. "I asked Brenda if she really thought this agreement would keep us safer. She said she hopes by taking the initiative and getting the training, they won't ever have to call ICE."

Lucy frowned. "That makes some kind of sense, but it assumes that she can maintain control of the situation. So far, ICE isn't playing by the rules."

Cherie inhaled sharply and sat back in her chair. "You won't tell anyone what I said," Cherie said anxiously. "...not even Liz."

Lucy looked at her as if to say, "You have to ask?" Finally, she said, "No, of course not. But we need to figure out how to support Brenda without making it look like we condone what ICE is doing. That's tricky."

"Tell me about it," said Cherie with a long sigh.

Lucy glanced at the smartwatch on her wrist. "I need to get my dishes cleared away before my client shows up. Anything left in that container Liz sent?"

Cherie smiled. "Not a bit."

❊❊❊

Brenda came into the kitchen after tucking the kids into bed. Although Keith was at an age when boys started to push their mothers away, he loved to hear Brenda read to him. He had a different bond with her because she was the one who'd rescued him and his sister after their parents had died in a murder-suicide. Huddled in their closet, defended by an army of stuffed toys, Keith had held his sister close. Their mother had told them to hide there until someone came for them. The one who came was Brenda.

Cherie watched her wife pour herself a beer. Her shoulders drooped as if they bore the entire weight of the world.

Brenda had been a popular police chief. Kids drew pictures of her, which she proudly displayed in her office. The girl scouts baked cookies for her. Along with Liz, Brenda was one of the heroes of the horrible shooting at Hobbs Elementary. She was revered by the townspeople. And now this stupid business over the ICE agreement. What a horrible way to end a long, distinguished career.

When Brenda was growing up in Brooklyn, she never wanted to be anything but a New York City cop like her dad and brothers. She started in the homicide division before the department discovered she had a special knack for community policing. They assigned her to create a training series to help ease interracial tensions in some of New York's toughest neighborhoods. By the time she'd retired from the force, she'd worked her way up to lieutenant.

When she'd moved to Hobbs with her first wife, Marcia, Brenda joined the Hobbs PD with no ambition other than earning enough to supplement her pension until their mortgage was paid off. Marcia's untimely death in a car accident changed the calculus. Without her income, Brenda needed to accept the promotions to make ends meet. No one was more surprised than she when they appointed her chief. Now, she was approaching actual retirement, and this cloud of suspicion and anger hung over her like an incoming Nor'easter.

It just wasn't right. No one worked harder than Brenda. She would never knowingly do anything wrong. She might have a blind spot where it came to this 287g agreement, but she'd gone into it for the right reasons. Of that, Cherie was sure.

"Sweetie pie, I don't want to encourage you to guzzle your beer, but I'd like to go upstairs and cuddle. You look like you need it."

Brenda's slightly defective smile took effort. "Oh, believe me. I do!" She watched Cherie close her laptop and anxiously asked, "You're not still working, are you?"

"No, no. I was messaging with Maggie Fitzgerald to get a recipe for a chicken stew that Lucy shared at lunch. I need to come up with more meals that use ingredients we can afford."

Brenda shook her head in despair. "Every week our grocery bill goes up. At this point, I'll be working until I drop dead...if I make it that long. Fortunately, the select board and the town manager are staying out of it...for now."

"You know Olivia supports you, Brenda. She wouldn't let you quit when you had long Covid, and she got you that job at Fox News."

"It was good money. Unfortunately, it didn't last long," said Brenda in a woeful tone, slumping in her chair. "The right has gotten so radical they won't listen to reason."

"Right. Left. The extremes are the same. Neither side will listen."

"Unfortunately, that's the goddamned truth!" Brenda turned to Cherie. "Did you ever think it would come to this?"

"No, never. It's worse than I ever imagined, and God knows, I thought it would be bad. What pisses me off is they're making you the bad guy. After all you've done for this town!"

"I know. I can't believe it! My own friends are turning on me."

"Like who? As far as I can see, Liz and Olivia are standing behind you, and Mother Lucy and Father Tom. Chief Duvaney has your back and so does the rest of the fire department. Your guys are all in your corner. The town clerk, the select board..."

"They don't want to take sides, but there's a faction in town, old hippies who still think the police are 'pigs.'"

"Oh, you mean those assholes protesting outside your office? Ignore them. They're pathetic."

"I try, but can you imagine going to work and seeing pickets every day?"

"They'll get tired of it."

Brenda sighed. "Oh, God, I hope so!"

Cherie got up to plug in her laptop to charge. When she turned around again, she saw the pure despair in Brenda's face. "Oh, baby. Finish that beer and let's go up to bed."

Brenda emptied the bottle in a few gulps. She carefully washed it out and put it in the bin with the other deposit cans and bottles. The deliberation of her movements meant she was desperately trying to control her anger and frustration.

"Come on, baby girl," cooed Cherie. "Let mama take care of you."

Brenda's grin was full of mischief. "Is that a promise?"

"You bet it is," Cherie replied enthusiastically. She pulled Brenda's arm around her shoulders like she was carrying a wounded soldier, which she was. Brenda's heart was broken by all the criticism. She tried to pretend it didn't matter, but it did.

They ascended the stairs and Cherie locked the door behind them. The kids no longer invaded their bedroom like when they first arrived, but Cherie didn't want them to see Brenda like this.

While her wife brushed her teeth, Cherie slipped into one of her sexy nightgowns that she reserved for special occasions like birthdays and anniversaries.

When Brenda emerged from the bathroom, she smiled and whistled. "Wow, the sight of you makes me want to leave the lights on."

"You can if you want," Cherie replied in a sultry voice. "Whatever pleases you tonight. I am completely yours."

"No, I can enjoy you just as well in the dark," Brenda switched off the light and slid into bed beside Cherie. Usually, Brenda liked to make the first move, but she just collapsed on her pillow with a sigh. "I know you're just trying to make me feel better," she said bitterly.

"No, baby. I want you. I really do. Let me make love to you, and we'll both feel better." Cherie began to kiss her with soft, open lips. Instead of responding, Brenda let out a big, soul-shaking sob. "Oh, no, sweetie pie! It's all right," said Cherie, gripping her shoulders. "Everything will be all right."

"No, it won't. Things won't ever be the same again. They hate me now."

"No, they don't. Some people just want to use you to make a

point. They don't know you like I do. They don't know how good and kind you are, how you would literally give someone the shirt off your back." Cherie stroked Brenda's hair and clung to her while the sobs shook her whole body. Cherie opened the buttons of her nightgown so she could cradle Brenda's face against her bare breasts.

"You know my secret, don't you?" Brenda asked in a tear-soaked voice. "That I'm really just an old softie."

"Yes, baby, I do, and it's all right to be sad and upset. You don't have to be big, strong Chief Harrison here. I love you. Your secret is safe with me."

Chapter 3

Lucy heard Liz come in through the back door. She banged her boots against the door sill to shake off the sawdust before sitting down to take them off. Now that Maggie was back, she had Liz well trained. In her socks, Liz headed to the kitchen sink to wash her hands. Maggie would have preferred she use the bathroom, but she tolerated this practice rather than listening to Liz's complaints. After Liz dried her hands on the towel designated for the purpose, Maggie handed her a plastic tube. "If you plan on touching me with those hands, Dr. Stolz, put on some hand cream." The order elicited a minor grumble and an eye roll, but Liz complied.

Lucy found the behavior of her "roommates" fascinating, like she was living in a bush station, where she could watch the grooming rituals of bonobos. Maggie was always fussing over Liz, how she dressed, her hair, her makeup, or lack of it. Maggie preened for Liz's attention, dressing to perfection to empower her Alpha female mate by looking attractive. Maggie loved to play with Lucy's hair, her touch reinforcing their bond.

"Lucy, put away your laptop," said Maggie, sounding like an indulgent mother. "We're going to eat now."

Lucy stowed her computer but kept her phone handy. Reshma was on call this weekend. Lucy was her backup, and for some reason she still hadn't figured out, weekends were a busy time for pastoral calls. She wondered if busy church members finally had time to pay attention to their families. Maybe grandma was sicker than they thought, or the need to have an intervention in their son's alcohol abuse became more obvious after a Friday night bender or near-fatal accident.

"What are you building out there?" Maggie asked, ladling bean soup into Liz's bowl.

"One of the medical assistants is having a baby, so I'm building a cradle."

"Wow, that's a pretty nice gift," said Maggie. "I wouldn't mind a handcrafted cradle built by my boss. Isn't that a little extravagant?" Everyone knew how generous Liz could be, especially when it wasn't expected.

Liz shrugged. "Not a big deal. I have lots of scrap cherry in my shop. When I worked out the design, I made router templates. I just rough out the parts on the bandsaw, trim them, drill the holes for the spindles, and done! If I wanted to, I could go into business making these cradles."

"Maybe you should," Lucy said. "They're beautiful. People would certainly buy them."

"Nah, woodworking is no fun when you do it for money. But with all the political drama, my shop has been sitting idle. It needed some love." Lucy knew that it wasn't the idle shop that bothered Liz. Her surgeon's hands needed to be busy, even more so now that she'd retired from the OR. Her ability to fix things was nothing short of phenomenal. She could just look at something, figure out how to take it apart and put it back together. Her fabricated parts made things better than new. "The cradle is a quick project. I'll have it glued up by this afternoon."

"You could make things for us," Maggie suggested.

Liz helped herself to a homemade dinner roll and generously slathered on butter. "We have everything we need. That's why I only build furniture as gifts."

"I could use a couple of bookcases in my apartment," said Maggie, helping herself to homemade bread.

"I'll put it on my list, but don't hold your breath. Now that you two have gotten me involved in your political activities, I don't have as much time."

"It's for a good cause," Maggie said, sitting down.

"I wonder about that..." replied Liz skeptically. "Both sides are being incredibly stupid. Look what they're doing to Brenda."

As usual, Liz finished her meal before the others. She was

fidgety, but after Maggie had recently dressed her down for bolting from the table, she patiently waited for her slower companions to finish their meal.

Out of the corner of her eye, Lucy saw a green bubble pop up on her phone. She waited until she finished eating before tilting the screen so she could read it. Her breath hitched when she saw the identity of the sender. "Excuse me. This is important," she said, inputting the code to unlock her phone. The message was brief and simple: *Can we talk?*

"Don't tell me you need to go," Liz said in a disparaging tone. "I thought Reshma was on call this weekend."

"She is. This is personal." Lucy engaged Liz's inquisitive gaze. "It's Rebecca Morgenstern."

Liz made a face. "I wonder what she wants. She hasn't spoken to you in almost a year."

"I know. Not that I haven't tried." Lucy got up. "Would you two excuse me while I respond to this message?"

"No problem," said Liz, not even trying to disguise her anger, "but she'd better have a good explanation for cutting you off." To calm her, Lucy placed a quick kiss on her forehead before she left.

Lucy went upstairs to the former guest room that had been turned into her private space. Here, she kept the most important things from the beach house: her theological library, Erika's desk, and the queen-sized bed made of solid cherry that Liz had built for her wedding to Erika. Sometimes, Lucy slept there when Liz was too restless to sleep.

As usual, the heat was down in the parts of the house they weren't occupying, so Lucy burrowed under the duvet. Before she responded to Rebecca's message, she tried to formulate a position or at least an attitude about the sudden contact after almost a year of silence. Their friendship went back to when Lucy was in seminary. Despite coming from different faith traditions, they saw 'eye to eye' on all the important things. They'd bonded over their work in an organization supporting homeless LGBT youth and had been friends ever since.

Rebecca had gotten Lucy through some of her worst spiritual crises. She'd held Lucy's hand through her dark night of the soul when she doubted her faith. She'd talked Lucy through deciding to marry Liz so soon after Erika's death. She was the one who'd finally persuaded Lucy to give her singing career a second try. Half-joking, Lucy called Rebecca her "rabbi."

Over the years, they'd had their disagreements, but never a rift in their friendship. Then, after one ill-considered remark, Rebecca had stopped talking to Lucy. Her texts and emails went unanswered. Finally, Lucy realized things weren't the same between them and might never be again.

She stared at Rebecca's text for a long time before she typed a response. *May I call you?* The request sounded so deferential and formal. Lucy held her breath until the little gray bubble on the screen began to move.

Of course you can. That's why I messaged you! Lucy could almost hear the smart-mouthed, sarcastic tone behind the words. With a smile she found Rebecca's number in her contact list. After such a long period without hearing from her, she'd moved it out of her favorites because seeing it refreshed her pain.

"Well?" asked Rebecca when she answered. "How are you?"

"I'm okay. Pretty good, actually. How are you?"

"The same." Then they blurted out at once: "I'm sorry."

"No, Becca, *I'm* sorry," insisted Lucy. "What I said was insensitive."

"But you were right, Lucy," Rebecca replied. "I just couldn't hear the truth."

"Oh, Becca! It must be so hard to accept."

"Sometimes, the truth is hard to bear. I'm just glad to have Judith home. Her parents have moved to a safer location, which is a big relief, but her brother is in the IDF. We're still worried about him."

"Oh, Rebecca, I've missed you so much," said Lucy. "When can I see you?"

"What are you doing this afternoon?"

The spontaneous invitation startled Lucy. It was especially surprising because Saturdays were a rabbi's busiest day. "Don't you want some time to decompress after your service?"

"I have the rest of the weekend. Judith took the girls to see colleges. They may only be twins by virtue of sharing a birthday, but they want to go to the same school. Joined at the hip."

Lucy visualized Rebecca's daughters. They'd been conceived using the same sperm donor and delivered on the same day by Caesarean section. Although they didn't share the same mother because Rebecca and Judith had become pregnant with the other's fertilized egg, they'd been raised like twins, even dressed the same. Wanting to attend the same college proved they liked being considered such, despite the technicalities.

"If you'd like to come up here and talk, I have a pot of chicken on the stove. I know it's a cliché, but even Jewish mothers need nurturing."

"I'm glad you're practicing self-care, Rebecca. Too often clergy forget they need to take care of themselves."

"You're lucky. You have your personal doctor living with you."

"Well, for ethical reasons, she's no longer my doctor, but she does take good care of me. She makes me soothing soups when I'm sick, just like you're doing for yourself. But Becca, you haven't talked to me for almost a year, why now?"

There was a long silence before Rebecca admitted softly, "You know how you always say I'm your rabbi? Well, it works both ways. I need my pastor."

"I'll drive up as soon as I can make myself decent. I can be there in an hour. Will you save a bowl of soup for me?"

"You bet, Lucy. I knew that would get you up here."

Lucy was tempted to say something sassy, but the emotional

climate between them was still uncertain. Teasing would have to wait until they could trust again. "Let me get dressed," said Lucy. "I'll be there soon."

Lucy put on a pair of corduroys and a coordinating sweater. She plaited her hair into a French braid and applied some makeup. Liz wasn't the only one Maggie encouraged to dress up. Lucy wasn't in the mood to listen to criticism.

"I've been invited to South Portland for chicken soup," she explained, coming into the kitchen.

Looking skeptical, Liz folded her arms on her chest. "What made her suddenly decide to start talking to you?"

"I don't know," said Lucy, giving her a kiss on the cheek, "but I'm about to find out."

She could feel Liz tense. "She'd better apologize. Cutting you off like that was really shitty."

Across the table, Maggie gave Lucy a sympathetic look. "Liz tried to explain what happened between you and your friend. I could have told you that mentioning genocide in the same breath as Gaza would have gotten you in trouble. I've become very careful about what I say to my Jewish friends."

Lucy appreciated Liz's attempt to explain, but her biased opinions could give Maggie the wrong idea. "It was early in the war in Gaza. I was reading the history of how the Palestinians had been mistreated. I didn't realize the Jewish settlers drove them out of their towns and poisoned their wells so they wouldn't return. Rebecca and I had discussed the abuses of Israel's right-wing government. I thought we were on the same page. Then I made the mistake of using the loaded word, 'genocide' and..."

"...and Rebecca was triggered and stopped talking to you," said Maggie, completing Lucy's sentence. "Nowadays, people's emotions are in overdrive. You need to watch every word you say, even when you mean no harm. Some people act like they're just waiting to catch you."

"But I should have been more sensitive," said Lucy, more willing than her wives to give Rebecca some grace.

"You talked to her about everything," said Liz, shaking her head. You thought you could be honest with her. She could have given you the benefit of the doubt."

Lucy nodded. "Yes, or at least given me the opportunity to explain and apologize. Instead, she ghosted me."

Maggie sighed and assumed a look of sympathy that was no act, although on the stage, she could have produced a totally convincing facsimile. "You didn't deserve that."

"No, but she wants to talk about it now, and as her friend, I'm willing to listen."

"You're a better woman than I am," said Liz, frowning.

"Liz, don't give me that," said Maggie. "You forgive your friends all the time, even Sam when she got involved with me."

Maggie got up and put her arms around Lucy. "Good luck, honey. We'll be rooting for you." She gave Lucy a tight squeeze.

"Thanks, Maggie. I need all the help I can get. This reunion isn't going to be easy. If it's appropriate, I'm going to tell her about us. Are you okay with that?"

"Fine with me," said Liz. Maggie nodded.

✳✳✳

The drive to South Portland gave Lucy too much time to worry. She tried prayer, but God wasn't saying much today. To make it all worse, the March landscape was dreary and cold. Dirty snowbanks along the Thruway were evidence of the long winter. More than other years, Lucy longed for spring and its warmth. Easter would be late, and Lent with its sad purple pall dragged on. Reshma, in charge of the Lenten liturgies, was distracted by the administration's hostile actions towards refugees. The political divisions in the church had deepened as people took sides. The unrelenting shocks from the administration wore on everyone's nerves. On top of that, the skies were constantly gray.

Maybe singing about spring will help it come faster, thought Lucy and streamed the accompaniment to the first of Strauss' Four Last Songs, *"Frühling."* Filling her lungs with air and freeing her vocal cords to embrace the notes made Lucy feel suddenly lighter. She remembered the performance with the New York Philharmonic under Morales, her first solo concert after her comeback. She'd told herself she'd forgiven Alex for blacklisting her and destroying her career. Not only had he left her pregnant and broken, he'd deprived her of something that gave her great joy. She loved connecting with an audience when she sang. It felt warm and intimate, not merely a performance.

"Congratulations, Lucy. Now, you're in a worse mood," she said aloud to herself. How could anyone get to their sixties and not have regrets? Life was so full of wrong turns and misfires, like this extended hiatus in her relationship with Rebecca. Lucy had tried so hard to model Christian forgiveness, but this hurt was so deep and personal. "If I hadn't been such an insensitive asshole, we wouldn't be here," Lucy said aloud, then glanced in the rearview mirror as if the driver behind her could hear her.

Oh, Lucy! Don't be so hard on yourself, said a mellow contralto that sounded British by way of Berlin. Lucy's imagination could play tricks on her. When she prayed, she often found herself in dialog with an inner voice she liked to think was God, but that was absurd, wasn't it?

Why? According to your theology, God can do anything. Why wouldn't She talk to you? I'm certainly not the deity, but you're hearing me.

"You're dead, Erika."

That's what they say, but don't your kind believe in an afterlife?

Lucy glanced around anxiously to assure herself she was the only one in the car. Liz had talked about having conversations with Erika. Was this what it was like?

Yes, Liz and I chat from time to time. I try to keep an eye on her. I am her wingman, after all.

If Lucy weren't driving seventy miles per hour, she would have stopped in the middle of the Turnpike. "Erika! What are you *doing* here?"

You summoned me with your beautiful rendition of Frühling. No one sang it better than you. Well, maybe Lucia Popp...in the day. Betty Blackhead's version was rather good.

Lucy wasn't about to debate the relative merits of her performance versus that of other singers, especially because she was a fan of Lucia Popp. The irreverence toward Elizabeth Schwartzkopf was pure Erika.

Lucy, since I'm here. Would you mind terribly if I offered you some advice?

"Go ahead. You will anyway."

Let your rabbi friend fall on her sword. She was clearly in the wrong. Israel has no business killing innocent civilians. But you don't need to rub her nose in it. Tread lightly.

"Good advice. Thank you."

You're welcome, Lovely Lucy. I wish I could kiss you goodbye, but I can't. This is the best I can do. Lucy felt a light brush on her check. Then she was as startled to feel the absence of Erika as strongly as her sudden presence. She raised one hand off the steering wheel to assure herself of her own reality.

She discovered she was shaking.

***

The soothing aroma of homemade chicken soup greeted Lucy when Rebecca opened the door. Lucy's plan to hang back a little and listen before jumping into a tearful reunion was blown to bits in their first seconds together. Rebecca's hair smelled of sauteed onions when she tenderly, then fiercely hugged Lucy.

"Oh honey, I've missed you soo much! All my fault," Rebecca admitted, nearly crushing Lucy's ribs. Her friend's powerful embrace was full of raw emotion that Lucy couldn't resist. Even after the hug ended, Rebecca didn't completely let her go. She clung to Lucy's arm as she closed the front door and led her into the house. They came into the kitchen, where evidence of two women parenting a pair of adolescents was everywhere. Flyers papered over one side of the refrigerator. Two lacrosse sticks leaned against the bench on which sat a stylish computer bag. Judith and the girls might be physically absent, but their presence lingered, not unlike Lucy's strange encounter with Erika in the car.

"How long will Judith be away?" asked Lucy, slipping out of her coat. Rebecca took it and hung it on a peg by the door to the backyard.

"They're coming home tomorrow night, probably late. That's why I made the soup. I used a whole chicken, so there will be plenty left over for sandwiches."

"Oh, and I thought you made the chicken soup for *me*," teased Lucy with a brilliant smile.

"I did make it for you...and for me, and for anyone who finds their way to my kitchen."

Lucy had always found Rebecca's idea of "kitchen ministry" compelling. She'd come up with the idea from watching her grandmother, the wife of a rabbi, become the confidant and teacher of the women in her husband's congregation through cooking with them and chatting about their lives. "The women were often overlooked while the men handled the important business and discussed the Torah," Rebecca had explained. "I won't have half my congregation getting half my attention, so like Bubbe, I open my kitchen. That's one way having women in ministry makes a difference."

"People complain that women are taking over the Anglican communion. Supposedly, that's why our priests are joining the Catholic Church."

"That's bullshit," Rebecca stated flatly. "Men will do anything to preserve their privilege. Catholic priests love playing dress-up with their long gowns and lace. They forget that faith was meant to be a way of life, not the handshake of a secret society."

The adamance of Rebecca's response surprised Lucy, but her friend had never tempered her opinions of religious hypocrisy. "Oh, I like the ritual too," admitted Lucy. "Don't you?"

"I adore it, but how we dress for worship isn't the point, is it?"

Lucy shook her head.

Rebecca looked her over from head to toe. "You look good, Lucy. You've even put on a few pounds. Guess you didn't miss me too much."

"I did miss you. You have no idea. But you know how Liz is. She feeds people. And we now have a trained chef living in the garage apartment."

"Really? Lucky you."

Lucy wanted to bite her tongue. She hadn't meant to lead by telling Rebecca that Maggie had moved in with them. Fortunately, Rebecca didn't question the identity of their tenant.

Studying Rebecca's back as she ladled soup into two bowls, Lucy wondered what to say about Maggie's role in their marriage. The thought of hiding something so important from Rebecca would have been unthinkable before now. Rebecca never had expressed any unconventional opinions about marriage except to affirm the right of same-sex unions. Lucy couldn't predict how she'd react to the idea of polyamory because they'd never discussed it. Lucy made an instant decision. Until their relationship was on solid ground again, she would avoid a debate about sexual morality by keeping her domestic situation to herself.

Rebecca set a steaming bowl of soup in front of her. "What's the matter, Lucy? You look stressed."

Lucy instantly smiled to deflect Rebecca's suspicions. "Oh, just wondering how to talk to you about some things. It's been so long." It was a vague explanation but close enough to the truth. Rebecca nodded knowingly.

"If you're still worried about the G-word, don't be. I think we all need to have an honest conversation about what Israel is doing in Gaza."

"We had a special collection at St. Margaret's to support the Episcopal bishop of Jerusalem. The bombing of the Al-Ahli Arab Hospital was a horror."

"Maybe Hamas has tunnels under schools and medical buildings, but bombing a hospital sheltering women and children is never right."

Lucy exhaled a sigh of relief. "Liz says that Zionism is so embedded in the identity of American Jews, it's hard to separate criticism of Israel from antisemitism."

"She's right, of course," said Rebecca, sitting down across from her. "Liz carries a lot of guilt because her father was in the German military in World War II, so she bends over backward to support us, but she thinks critically. Israel's actions in Gaza go way beyond self-defense or even retribution for the Hamas attack. It's heinous."

Lucy looked at her friend sympathetically, realizing how difficult this must be for her to say. "But there have been attacks on Jews in retaliation."

"That's because people will use any excuse to hate us."

With a sigh, Lucy picked up her spoon. She wasn't hungry because she'd eaten lunch before coming, but when she tasted the delicious soup, her appreciation was spontaneous. "Oh, Rebecca, no one makes chicken soup like you do."

"Oh, you should taste my mother's."

"Actually, I have. Once, Melissa gave me a container along with the rent check."

"I always forget you know my sister. Another one of your tenants. You're quite the slum lord, Lucy," said Rebecca with a wicked grin.

Talking about renters skated too close to Maggie's new role in her marriage, so Lucy quickly changed the subject. "How do you talk to your congregation about what's going on in Gaza? I'm sure they have questions."

"Some do, mostly the younger people. The older ones have been groomed since the cradle to support Israel, right or wrong. It was part of the campaign to reinforce Jewish identity when so many Jews were intermarrying with people of other faiths. For most of them, Zionism means what it is to be a Jew. We deserved Israel because of the Holocaust."

Lucy read between the lines. "Are you speaking for yourself, Rebecca?

"No, well, yes. I was raised with that kind of thinking, but give me some credit, Lucy."

"Oh, I do, and that's why I was so shocked by your reaction to my comment about the G-word."

Rebecca put down her spoon. "Okay, let's stop this right now and say the bad word out loud. *Genocide.* Netanyahu's right-wing supporters want to wipe out the Palestinians or force them to move. They want their land, and they will bomb everything into oblivion to get it. What else should we call it?"

Lucy studied her friend and saw how admitting this pained her. Rebecca stared into her soup as if it contained divinatory entrails. "It's so sad," said Lucy. "I'm disappointed too. I always thought Israel had good intentions, that they were a beacon of liberal democracy in the Middle East."

"It's all those orthodox Jews that moved there. Back in the day, they didn't support Zionism. Now, they're all in, building new settlements in the West Bank, even though they're technically illegal."

"Invoking the vengeful God of the old testament," said Lucy.

Rebecca gave her a hard look. "I'm not a fan of all that smiting of enemies. There are days when I think Jesus was right. Maybe he is the Messiah. I'm too culturally Jewish to change at this point, but I think about it."

"Is that why you needed your pastor?" asked Lucy softly.

"No, no. I needed to talk to you because of..." Rebecca's voice dropped and she looked away. Lucy realized she was holding back tears.

Lucy reached for her hand. "Rebecca, tell me… I'm here for you."

"Judith has been different since she returned from Israel. She doesn't talk to me the way she used to. Now, I think she's keeping things from me because she knows I don't approve of what Israel is doing."

"Oh, Becca, I'm sorry. She was born in Israel. She was there during the October attack. Her allegiance to Israel is different."

"But Lucy, even when we disagreed about politics, we talked about everything. We were so in line with one another, we even got our periods together." Lucy hadn't thought about menstruating for years, but she knew that females living together often bled on the same schedule, and it was no sign of intimacy.

"Her distance might be temporary," Lucy suggested. "The viciousness of the Hamas attack shocked everyone. I can't imagine being there while it happened. Maybe Judith needs some trauma counseling."

"Are you volunteering?" asked Rebecca with a hopeful note in her voice.

"No, of course not. Given our close relationship, that would be unethical. But I can help you find someone, if you want a recommendation."

"I may take you up on that. I need to do something. She won't talk to *me*."

Lucy squeezed Rebecca's hand. "I know how that feels. After killing Peter Langdon, Liz completely shut down. I begged her to talk to me, but she just wouldn't. She'd sit on the enclosed porch and drink whiskey."

"Oh, my word. That's the worst. Judith doesn't have any self-harming behaviors. At least, not that I know of. She's still engaged with the girls. She's performing as she should at her school. But she just won't talk to me."

"Be patient. She may come around on her own once she gets used to being home again."

Rebecca sighed. "I hope so." She forced a smile. "At least, she gave me an excuse to reach out to you."

Lucy wanted to ask why Rebecca had waited so long, but she didn't. She simply basked in the warm smile of the woman across the table.

***

Huddled under the colorful Afghan crocheted by Liz's grandmother, Lucy and Maggie sat side by side on the leather couch in the living room. Liz was making one of her famous sheet pans—shrimp and assorted vegetables seasoned by a spice mix known only to her. Lucy was putting the finishing touches on tomorrow morning's sermon. Maggie was grading papers on her tablet.

"I still can't believe they submit all their papers online," Lucy said, watching Maggie's finger flick across the screen, highlighting passages for comment.

"We have to run everything they write through anti-plagiarizing software," Maggie explained. "That's the real reason they submit their papers through a portal. Didn't Union accept papers electronically when you were in graduate school?"

"Sort of. I attached a Word file to an email and sent it to my professors."

"I guess they're more trusting in a seminary," Maggie speculated.

"It seems like an eternity, but it was only a few years ago," said Lucy, remembering the endless train rides into New York City, Liz helping her study for her comps and brutally editing her thesis. All that for the right to call herself 'Dr. Bartlett,' which she seldom did.

"We've been all in with this digital dance since I came back to teaching. Everyone's worried the kids are using AI to write their papers."

"How can you stop them?"

"Supposedly, the AI in the portal software catches AI-written passages, but I don't believe it. My view is, why bother to pay for an education if you don't want to learn from it? If you want to screw yourself, go right ahead." Maggie closed the cover of her tablet. "Lucy, why are we working on a Saturday night? I don't know why you write down those sermons. You end up ad libbing anyway."

Lucy put aside her tablet and reached for her glass of wine. "In fact, I memorize my sermons, so they seem spontaneous. You know, like you learn your lines for a play or the lyrics of a song."

"They teach you that at Juilliard?"

"Actually, my mom trained me early to memorize music and librettos."

Liz came in and flopped down beside them on the couch. "Dinner is in the oven. I came out to see what you two are up to."

"Just comparing notes on preparing for a performance," Maggie volunteered.

"I want to hear how the conversation with Rebecca went. Did she admit that what Israel is doing in Gaza is *criminal*?"

"Well, any being with an intelligence bigger than an amoeba's can see that," said Maggie.

"Yes, she used the G-word, even said it out loud. But she's in a tough spot. Even Jews disagree about this stupid war. Rebecca is married to an Israeli. Obviously, Judith would see it differently."

"I don't know about that," said Liz, shaking her head. "You see the demonstrations in Israel. Liberal Israelis aren't buying it. They want the hostages returned more than anything. I bet most are horrified by the destruction in Gaza and the needless killing of civilians."

"It's a horror," Maggie agreed. "But at least you and your friend are talking again. That's the important thing."

Lucy could feel Liz's blue eyes boring into the side of her face. "Did you tell her about us?" Of course, Liz would ask so directly.

"No, I was focused on getting our friendship back on track," said Lucy, returning Liz's steady gaze. There was a long moment of silence. Lucy guessed Maggie was trying to figure out whether to get involved. Finally, she sat back, evidently deciding this was dangerous territory. Maggie certainly knew how to read an audience.

Liz's expression softened. "That was probably a smart move, but it's got to be hard not to be completely honest with your rabbi."

"Your rabbi?" Maggie repeated. "What does that mean?"

"It's an old New York expression," Liz explained. "In business, your rabbi is the person you go to for advice. Leave it to Lucy to have an actual *rabbi*."

"Rebecca and I go back to my seminary days," Lucy explained. "She's gotten me through some tough times. One thing I thought I could always count on her for is absolute honesty, and she got the same from me. I never held back."

"But this is the first time you can't tell her everything," Maggie guessed.

"Right. And after being ghosted over saying the G-word, I'm obviously going to be more careful what I tell her."

"Well, that's just a shame," said Maggie and began rubbing Lucy's back sympathetically. "I'm sorry, honey. That must hurt so much."

Maggie's kindness finally broke Lucy. After holding herself together since her visit with Rebecca, she burst into tears. "Oh baby," said Liz, gathering her in her arms. "I'm sorry. Not being able to trust her again must hurt worse than when she stopped talking to you." Naturally, Liz had no idea that spelling it out made it hurt even more.

"It does," admitted Lucy through the tears. "And I know she might not approve, so I'm afraid. I've told her all kinds of things I've done or said, but I always trusted she would love me even if she didn't agree. Now, I'm not sure."

"You would be crushed if she rejected you again," Liz concluded. Lucy wanted to punch her for being so blunt. Instead, she began to sob, deep heaving shudders. Maggie stroking her arm to soothe her and Liz holding her tight were making it all worse. Lucy melted into a puddle of sadness and grief. No matter that she and Rebecca had made peace. Their relationship would never be the same again. Something had broken and couldn't be fixed.

Annoyingly, the timer on the stove went off. "I'll get it," said Maggie and headed to the kitchen.

Lucy burrowed into Liz's shoulder, wetting the soft fabric of her sweatshirt with her tears. Liz's familiar scent comforted her. "I'm sorry, sweetheart. Losing someone you thought you could tell anything is so hard." By now, Lucy was drowning. She tried to wipe her nose on her hand. Liz encouraged her to sit up straight and handed her the box of tissues from the side table. "Here. You're a mess."

"Gee. Thanks," said Lucy, mopping her face.

Maggie returned. "Dinner's ready and it smells outrageously good." She kissed the top of Lucy's head. "Eat something, Lucy. You'll feel better."

The attention Liz and Maggie were showing her made Lucy feel selfish for melting down so completely. But when she looked into Maggie's sympathetic hazel eyes and Liz's calm blue eyes, she saw such perfect love that she wanted to start crying all over again.

"Come on, Luce. Maggie's right. You'll feel better after you eat." Liz reached into her armpit and hauled her to her feet. "Even if you can't tell Rebecca everything, you can tell us, and we'll always listen."

Lucy stood up, feeling a little uncertain about her balance, but there was Liz, holding her up on one side, and Maggie on the other.

Chapter 4

Liz pulled the door closed against a gust that threatened to rip it off the hinges. After the storm that had come through during the night, the wind was fierce. It was still roaring in Liz's ears, leaving her with slight vertigo. Although her feet knew every dip and rise in the patched linoleum floor of the Hobbs Diner, she steadied herself with a hand on the counter until she got her sea legs.

"Mornin', Doc," called Paula, the counter waitress. "Your date's already here." When Liz had first come to Maine, Paula's hair had been an unnatural shade of red only seen on Saturday morning cartoons. Around sixty, she'd figured out the men no longer paid attention, so she'd finally stopped dyeing it. "I'll put in your order," Paula offered. She opened the kitchen door and shouted, "Doc's here!"

When Liz arrived at "her" table in the back, Brenda looked up from scrolling her phone. "'Bout time you got here, Stolz."

"Sorry. Had to make a quick stop at the office." Liz tossed her parka on the bench seat of the booth. She gave Brenda one of those instant physician assessments. "You look awful."

Brenda scowled. "What do you expect? My life sucks right now."

"I bet it does," Liz said. "It's not fair what they're doing to you."

"I'm done talking to the press. They twist everything I say into something bad. And those assholes who keep showing up at the select board meeting to make a public comment, even when it's not on the agenda. The board chair tells them their time is up, but they keep talking."

"Rude as well as stupid. Some people don't think the rules apply to them."

"I know those people, and I thought they respected me. They were always pleasant. Now, they can't say enough bad things about me." Brenda stared over Liz's shoulder with a scowl. "Someone's staring at us right now. Better watch out, Liz, or my bad rep will rub off on you."

"Not a bit worried. I've been the town doctor here for years. Most people in Hobbs have been my patient at one time or another. You've been here longer than I have. We have squatters' rights, or something like that."

"She's really staring at you," Brenda reported, studying the woman over Liz's shoulder.

"Well, then fuck her," said Liz, turning around, ready to give whoever it was a filthy look. When she saw it was an influential member of St. Margaret's vestry, she changed her mind. Instead, she gave her one of those piercing stares guaranteed to put junior doctors in their place. It wasn't obviously disapproving, but it certainly showed she meant business. The woman broke eye contact and turned to her companion.

"Hey, that's a good trick, Liz. You'll have to teach me how to do it."

Liz grunted. "Your cop stare is plenty intimidating. You don't need lessons from me."

"Cherie yells at me when I use it on the kids. Keith runs and hides behind her."

"Yeah, your kids have been through a lot. I probably wouldn't scare them more than necessary."

"I do my best." Brenda sat back so their waitress could serve her breakfast. "Thanks, Lois." The elderly woman gave Brenda a beaming smile for the simple acknowledgement of calling her by name. She served Liz, who also thanked her. After she left, Brenda said, "At least, there's one person in town who doesn't hate me."

"Oh, Brenda. Don't think like that. There are lots of people in town who don't hate you. I don't. Lucy doesn't. Neither does Maggie...or the people at the school, the staff at the church. To most of this town, the people who really know you, you're a hero."

"I appreciate everyone who comes to the select board meetings to speak up for me, especially you and Lucy. You're important people in this town, so your presence means a lot."

Liz dipped the corner of her toast into the golden egg yolk. "Maggie would come too, but she teaches on Tuesday nights." Brenda gave her a funny look that Liz couldn't quite identify, but fortunately, she didn't ask any questions.

"I know my old friends support me because they're my friends, but what about other people in town?"

"Believe me. Even if people don't agree with your decision, they don't approve of shaming you for doing what you think is good for your department."

"It *is* good for the department. It keeps my officers on patrol like they're supposed to be instead of babysitting federal perps. It's good training. I took it myself, great refresher on things we don't usually encounter in a small town like Hobbs, and it's free. I'm always looking for ways to make the force better, especially if it doesn't break the budget. Olivia watches the town's money like it's her own."

Liz laughed out loud. "Olivia takes her fiduciary responsibilities *very* seriously. Hobbs should be glad to have someone of her caliber...and yours."

"Include yourself in that, Dr. Stolz. Don't ever retire."

Liz shrugged. "I'd find it hard to give up medicine and put my feet up, especially with Lucy working not one, but two jobs—three, if you count her singing engagements. I can't have my wife working harder than I do."

"Does she have any gigs coming up?" asked Brenda, mopping up her egg with a piece of toast.

"She's singing the *Verdi Requiem* in Boston next month and at the cathedral during Holy Week. Her buddy, Yannick, is coming up to conduct the Boston performance."

Brenda chuckled. "That guy is really a character with his painted fingernails and two-tone hair. I guess in the arts you can get away with that stuff."

"I don't know, but Lucy is very careful. Too many people know she's a priest. Before a concert of religious music, we always have this silly conversation about whether her gown is too low-cut. My view is, she should flaunt her assets. She has the most gorgeous boobs I've ever seen, and I've seen a lot of boobs!"

Brenda laughed and slapped her thigh. "I bet you have." Her expression suddenly turned serious. She gestured toward her own bosom. "How's Maggie doing with the...you know?"

"Oh, her tests are all in the range I like to see. She's still self-conscious about the reconstruction, but I think it came out great. I would have been happier with less lymph resection, but it wasn't my call." Liz looked up and saw Brenda had no idea what she was talking about and realized she'd been talking to her like she was another doctor. "To answer your question, Brenda, Maggie is just fine, and I'm very happy about it."

Brenda wiped imaginary sweat off her brow. "Gotta hand it to that woman, she's been through a lot, but she keeps coming back."

"Like all of us," said Liz, pushing back her plate. She always left some home fries and a piece of toast so she could feel virtuous about her carb consumption.

"What's it like having your ex living right next door to you?" Brenda asked, her blue eyes bright with innocent curiosity.

Liz made a conscious effort to relax her shoulders so she wouldn't look anxious about the question. "It's fine. Maggie likes her privacy and gives us ours too. I tell you I don't mind coming home to her meals, and she makes a wicked tarte tatin. Part of the reason I married her was for her cooking." Brenda loved Maggie's cooking, so that sounded like a good excuse.

But Brenda frowned. "You married Maggie for lots of reasons, Liz. She's beautiful, kept you on your toes, and she loved you. Do you regret the breakup?"

Now, Brenda's questions were probing uncomfortably close to the truth. "Of course, I regret it. I loved Maggie, and when I give my word, I believe in keeping it."

Brenda grinned. "Yeah, but you like to look at the ladies. I do too, but I'm not as obvious about it."

Liz grinned. "Yes, you'd think by my age, I'd have learned to be more discreet, but old habits are hard to break." Liz so desperately wanted to tell Brenda the truth, but she'd promised her partners they'd discuss it first. "It's always sad when a relationship ends," Liz continued philosophically. She gazed out the window. The wind was rattling the letters of the specials sign. "Maggie and I are in a good place now. We're like one big happy family." There, she'd revealed the facts, if somewhat euphemistically.

Brenda looked skeptical. "If you say so. I think Cherie would kill me if I kept my ex right next door."

Liz wanted to say, 'I don't think you have to worry about that,' but it would have sounded cruel, since Brenda's first wife had passed. "Well, Lucy and Maggie were best friends before things got out of hand. They go do their girly things together and leave me alone. I'm not big on small talk. They're chatterboxes who can talk each other's ear off for hours on end. It works."

"That was kind of you to give Maggie a place to live when her daughter threw her out."

"The place was empty. No one was using it, so why not? We offered her the beach apartment, but she chose to live with us."

"Crazy. I would have lived at the beach. Great view. Just a short walk to the ocean. You and Sam turned that apartment into a cozy, little place."

"Sometimes, I think I should go into the real estate business and give up medicine," said Liz. "I'm always finding places for people to live. I should get a commission."

"Except you let them live rent-free, so you'd never make any money. You're just an old softie, like me," said Brenda glumly.

"Yup, I guess I am. But I'll keep your secret if you keep mine." Liz winked rakishly.

"Deal," said Brenda like the New Yorker she was.

"Deal," Liz agreed, not to be outdone. She tried to say it with the Brooklyn accent she never really had.

***

Liz hung up her parka in the staff locker room. When she turned around, she looked down into Bobbie's smiling face. How had she crept up on her like that? Liz pulled at her ear lobe, wondering if something had gone wrong with her hearing.

"Good morning, Bobbie. I didn't hear you come in."

"Oh, it's these nurse's shoes," she said, sticking out one leg. "They're practically silent. Drives Susan crazy. She thought she was the only one who could sneak up on people. Learned that trick in the convent, she says."

Liz frowned. Susan wasn't her favorite person after trying to break up her relationship with Lucy. "Next time, say 'good morning' or something, even *boo*!" Like a Halloween goblin, Liz had suddenly raised her voice on the last word, making Bobbie jump. "There. Got you back."

"Dr. Liz, you are such a kid."

"Guilty as charged," Liz agreed, grinning. "Now, what can I do for you?"

"Can you spare a few minutes to talk...privately?"

Liz glanced at her watch. She had a good fifteen minutes before her first appointment. "Sure, Bobbie. Let me get a cup of coffee. Meet me in my office in two minutes, and we'll chat."

As she prepared her coffee, she wondered what Bobbie wanted to discuss. Liz had mostly handed over her senior partner's duties, including personnel matters, to her second-in-command, Amy Hsu. Even so, many people still came to her with administrative questions. Bobbie had been covering for Liz, since Cherie cut her hours to help Lucy in her practice, so it could also be a patient issue.

"Well, you'll find out soon enough," said Liz aloud to herself. One of the medical assistants, who'd come in to put her lunch into the refrigerator, looked at her curiously. "Yes, I talk to myself," Liz volunteered. "Not a sign of dementia...yet." The medical assistant responded with a nervous smile and hurried out of the room. "Still scaring the shit out of junior staff. Good job, Stolz," Liz said, splashing half and half into her coffee. In fact, she was proud that Lucy's efforts to help her unlearn almost fifty years of negative medical training hadn't been completely successful. She liked the idea that she could still strike terror in people's hearts with a mere look.

Bobbie was seated in the visitor's chair when Liz came into her office. She was a little flushed. Liz was about to remind her to check her blood pressure, then told herself Bobbie, a longtime nurse practitioner, should know to do it herself. That was another indication of Lucy's intervention. Liz had mostly stopped trying to control everything.

Liz tasted her coffee. It wasn't as good as in the diner, but on a blustery morning like today, its warmth was welcome. "What's on your mind, Bobbie?"

Bobbie took a deep breath and said, "I have two terrified immigrants living in my house. I need to know what this ICE agreement Chief Harrison signed means for them. I keep telling them they're safe. They came in through legal channels. Teresa has a valid green card. She goes to all her court hearings and check-ins. But now ICE is snatching people outside the court room. I don't blame them for being scared. What do I say to them?"

Liz studied Bobbie's face for a long time while she tried to figure out how to answer her question. Everyone assumed that because she and Brenda were friends, she had an inside line on what was going on with the police. She did, but only because she asked probing questions. "I can't speak for Chief Harrison, Bobbie. I thought the chief explained it well at the last select board meeting. My understanding is that it's training so the Hobbs police can transport undocumented immigrants with an outstanding judicial warrant to a federal facility."

Bobbie shook her head. "I really wanted to get to that meeting, but Susan had something going on at her school. I promised to go with her."

Liz grimaced. "Ugh. I remember having to go to the school plays when Maggie was drama coach at Hobbs High."

"I can't complain. This was pleasant. The State Police presented awards to the teachers and staff who exhibited special courage during the shooting. Courtney Barnes, the principal, got one. The school nurse, and the principal's secretary." Bobbie puffed up with pride. "And of course, Susan."

Liz involuntarily shuddered, remembering the hostage situation in the principal's office. In her mind, she could smell the pot smoke and see Peter Langdon's glassy eyes. She had a flashback to him holding a gun to Susan's temple, the pool of blood growing under his body after Liz was forced to shoot him in the throat.

Bobbie's voice roused her out of the grim memories. "I thought they should all get recognition, and they did. Every staff member got a certificate acknowledging their bravery that day."

"Everyone should have been recognized. The school and the town performed courageously that day."

Bobbie gave Liz a hard look. "Never mind you. The real hero."

"They offered. I declined."

"You deserve it more than anyone. If not for you, Susan wouldn't be here. You *are* a hero."

Liz didn't feel like a hero. She would never forgive herself for killing that boy, but she forced herself to follow Lucy's advice about what to say when people said she was. "Thanks."

"But back to my question," Bobbie pressed. "Will this agreement mean that the Hobbs police will be going after immigrants?"

"You mean, actively pursuing them?" Fortunately, Brenda had answered this question in the select board meeting. "No, they're not enforcing immigration law. It's not a felony to be in this country illegally. It's a violation of civil law, which isn't the business of the local police."

"So, if someone calls the dispatcher at the police station and says, 'Hey, I think Bobbie Lantry has undocumented immigrants living in her house,' the Hobbs police won't be knocking on my door?"

"Absolutely not," said Liz emphatically.

"How can you be so sure? ICE is doing strange things. And why do they wear masks and not show their badge?"

"Supposedly, they're protecting their identities and their families."

"But if they're not doing anything wrong, why do they need to hide? I've never heard of police who won't show their badges. I mean, anyone could pretend to be ICE." Liz frowned because Bobbie was right. "Plus, they're so aggressive. That's not how any police I know behave. There's no need for dressing up like they're heading into combat, or the violence. It almost seems like cruelty is the point."

"It does indeed," said Liz with a sigh. "But Teresa and Grace have nothing to fear from Brenda's officers. They're not coming after them. From what I understand, if someone tries to report them to the Hobbs police, they will be told it's not their job to enforce immigration policy."

"That should piss off the hateful busybodies. We all know Hobbs is full of them."

"Unfortunately, I do," Liz replied with a sour look. "That "Hobbs Speak Your Mind" Facebook group is full of nasty posts."

"I can't even stand to look at it. Just makes me so angry!"

"Would you like me to talk to Teresa about it?" Liz asked.

Bobbie thought for a moment. "Actually, that's a good idea. She thinks you walk on water, so it would mean more coming from you. She knows you and the chief are tight."

"Okay, as soon as the opportunity arises, I'll talk to her. Feel better now?"

"Much."

"Good," said Liz and opened her laptop, but Bobbie didn't leave. "Something else?" Liz finally asked.

"Yes, actually."

Liz closed her laptop again. "Go ahead."

"I'm getting married," Bobbie said with a sly smile.

"Well, congratulations!" Liz held out her hand.

Bobbie's eyes grew large with surprise. "You mean you didn't know? Lucy didn't tell you?"

"Lucy believes in strict professional confidence. You'd be surprised at the stuff we don't tell each other."

The look on Bobbie's face indicated she probably didn't follow that practice with Susan. "It must be hard keeping all those secrets."

"But we do." Liz narrowed her eyes. "You're sure about this, Bobbie? Susan has a lot going on. Don't get me wrong. I admire her for sticking to her recovery, but you've barely had a life, taking care of Joyce during her decline." There she was, giving unsolicited advice again, but it was hard not to intervene with people she liked and respected.

"It's not like it's sudden. Susan and I have been friends pretty much since she came back to Hobbs. The only reason she wouldn't consider getting married was that Joyce was still alive."

"It's so strange how people thought about that situation," Liz said, reflecting. "You weren't married to Joyce."

"I know. It's almost like I was being punished for my loyalty."

Liz hadn't thought about it that way, but Bobbie was right. Joyce had resisted marriage because her conservative politics conflicted with the idea, yet she'd set up her estate and legal arrangements as if they were. It made no sense, but then, Liz's relationship with Lucy and Maggie probably only made sense to them. And why was it anyone's business anyway? Everyone was always judging other people for doing things that had no impact on them whatsoever.

"When is your wedding? I suppose you'll want time off for a nice, long honeymoon." Liz grinned to show that she approved, despite the implied grievance as Bobbie's employer.

"Well, I will want to take Susan to some nice places, like Joyce took me. That's one thing Susan and I have in common. We didn't have much growing up. I was lucky when Joyce took me along while she enjoyed life. Now, I want to do the same for Susan. And we're not wasting any time. We're looking for a date this summer."

"You could be married at St. Mary's by the Sea. The summer chapel is a perfect venue for a wedding."

"Yes, I love that place, but we want a big wedding, and the summer chapel would be too small. Do you think Lucy would agree to marry us?"

"I don't know. You'll have to ask her. I wouldn't dare speak for my wife." It was an exaggeration, but where Susan was concerned, Liz never knew what Lucy would do.

"Well, you can't speak for her, but I hope you can speak for yourself."

"What do you mean?" asked Liz, shifting uncomfortably when she realized what Bobbie was about to say.

"I want you to be my best woman."

"Me?" Liz wondered why Bobbie had chosen her over one of her colleagues. She knew that Bobbie and Cherie were close. She would be perfect.

"Yes, you," said Bobbie. "You've done so much for both of us. You gave me this job when you knew all about my situation with Joyce and how it could complicate my schedule. You were always there for Joyce and me when I needed you. And you not so subtly encouraged me to keep after Susan when things got so crazy. Susan always says you were the one who saved her life by pulling strings to get her into rehab."

"But, Bobbie, I was just doing my job as a doctor and the manager of this practice."

"Liz, you never just do your job. You always go above and beyond."

"Not everyone likes that," Liz said, noting again Bobbie's

reddened face. "And I'm going to piss you off right now by insisting I take your blood pressure."

Bobbie sat back, obviously surprised. "Yes, I've been running high. Kathy upped my dose."

Liz opened a drawer and took out a blood pressure cuff. "Take your arm out of your lab coat." She whipped on the cuff and inflated it. As she suspected, Bobbie's pressure was high. "One-seventy-three over one-hundred-five," she said, as the cuff deflated. "Not good."

Bobbie sighed. "I guess I'll ask Kathy to check later and tell me what to do."

"You'd better if you want to live to go on your fancy cruise or whatever you're planning for your honeymoon."

"Good guess, a cruise of the Greek Islands followed by a romantic weekend in Paris."

"Nice," Liz said, smiling as she remembered the island cruise she'd taken with Maggie shortly after they got married.

"So? Will you stand up for me at my wedding?"

"Sure," said Liz, although she was still reluctant. "I'd be honored."

✳✳✳

Liz's last patient canceled, so she had the rest of the afternoon free. She looked out the window of her office, enjoying the afternoon light. Despite the unrelenting wind off the ocean, she loved the longer days of early spring because they meant summer was coming. In self-defense, she presented to the world as a grumpy skeptic because she was so hopeful. When she was a surgeon, she dove into the direst cases, not to be a hero or for the challenge, but because she had faith she could achieve the best outcome.

Faith. What a strange word. In her role as a priest, Lucy talked about it often, but Liz had her own opinions. Unlike hope, which always carried a whiff of desperation, faith conveyed the arrogance of certainty, like Liz's trust in her own skill. She studied her hands.

Once, her fingertips could tie the tiniest knot, or route a catheter though the thinnest vein. Now, there were days she could barely separate two pieces of paper or open one of those infernal plastic bags in the vegetable aisle.

Stop feeling sorry for yourself. Summer is coming, and if you get your ass out of here, you can enjoy the rest of the day. She got up, unlocked the safe where she kept her gun purse and headed to the locker room to pick up her coat. When she got into her truck, she turned on the NPR classical music station. It was playing her favorite duet from *Don Carlo*. Singing along at the top of her lungs, she could almost hear Maggie admonishing her, "Liz, you're an alto, not a tenor," and Lucy responding, "Let her have her fun."

How different the two women in her life were. Maggie was always trying to reform her. Lucy just let her be. Why had Liz chosen to invite Maggie, with her criticism, pointed remarks, and supposedly unfulfilled expectations back in her life? Liz brushed the thought out of her mind because it was spoiling her hope for a fun afternoon.

When she opened the door to her garage, she saw the overflowing trash can and remembered she'd meant to go to the dump on Saturday, but got busy in the shop. With a sigh, she flung the bags into the back of the truck and broke down the cardboard boxes with a razor knife. The noise got Maggie's attention, and she opened the door to her apartment.

"Liz! What the hell are you doing down there?"

"Getting ready to go to the dump, and I have to hurry because it closes in twenty minutes."

"Can't it wait until tomorrow?"

"I don't have time tomorrow."

"Well, come up when you get back and I'll give you a piece of the apple pie I baked. I'll leave the door unlocked." Before closing the door, Maggie added. "Don't dilly dally at the dump yakking with your friends."

Although her back was turned and Maggie couldn't see, Liz rolled her eyes. She heaved the last bag of recyclables into the back of the truck and headed out. She watched in the rearview mirror for cops as she deliberately exceeded the speed limit. Nowadays, the race to get to the transfer station before the gate closed was the one way she spiked her adrenaline. *Pathetic,* she thought.

She was relieved when she arrived to see that the attendant was locking up the gatehouse, but she still had a clear path. Like the others desperately trying to unload their trash, Liz hurried. No one was stopping to talk because time was short, but people shouted their hellos across the cardboard compactor. "Hey, Dr. Liz!" called one of the select board members. Even the town big shots were guilty of last-minute trash disposal. Liz wondered if he got the same thrill from rushing to beat the gate at closing time.

When she got home, she wondered if she felt up to a visit with Maggie. But her "wife" had been keeping to herself lately, so Liz decided she owed her a visit. She still cooked dinner most nights, but after the evening news, she usually retreated to her own apartment instead of joining them in bed. The exception was chilly nights when she came solely to cuddle.

Liz recognized the pattern. Falling out of the "habit" of being physical killed the sex lives of so many lesbians. After long dry spells, approaching a partner felt so alien. Where do you even start? Fortunately, Lucy would never allow it, at least not where Liz was concerned. Lucy kept encouraging Maggie to join them, but she seldom agreed.

Maggie opened the door as Liz ascended the stairs. Apparently, she'd been listening for her return. "Come on, old girl. You can make it."

"Don't remind me," Liz growled.

"Oh, we're like that today," said Maggie, reaching up to give her a sweet kiss on the mouth. That was the most puzzling thing about this hiatus in her sexual interest. She loved affection—kisses, cuddling on the couch while they watched a movie together, being embraced, especially by Lucy, who gave full body hugs that melded her to the receiver like a warm cushion. Needing to stay away from people during the pandemic had driven Lucy crazy. Many clergy were wary about offering affection, but not Lucy. She was a hugger through and through.

Maggie gestured to the little table for two, where the pie and a teapot had been set out. "I heard your truck come in," Maggie explained, pouring the tea.

"I love your apple pie almost as much as your tarte tatin," Liz admitted.

"I know you do," said Maggie, affectionately rubbing the small of her back. "That's why I make it. Plus, it's so quiet now that I've cut back on classes so I can travel with you and Lucy. Baking gives me something to do."

"You could bake for St. Margaret's coffee hour," Liz suggested.

"Oh, I do. Their freezer is full of my quick breads and muffins."

"This is what we're reduced to," Liz mused sadly as she sat down, "rushing to the dump for a thrill and baking to fill the church freezer. We've outlived our usefulness."

Maggie gave her a hard look. "Liz, that doesn't sound like you. You're always so busy, looking for the next thing to do. Are you depressed?" She spooned some honey into Liz's cup and added a splash of milk.

"You don't have to fix my tea," said Liz. "I can do it."

"I know, but I like to do it, and after all these years, it's a habit. Just say, thank you, Liz."

"Thank you."

"So what's going on with you? Why are you moping? Think it's because the winter just won't quit? That makes me sad too."

"Playing shrink now, Maggie? That's Lucy's job."

Maggie looked mildly offended. "What? I can't care when I see you looking down?"

"No, of course you can. But look at the state of the world right now. They're firing all those federal workers. Those are real people losing their income. They have families. That DOGE team is nothing but a pack of over-educated brats running rampant through our personal data. Kids that age don't even have fully developed brains, never mind a sense of ethics. They killed USAID. Hundreds of thousands of people will die. Israel is blocking food going into Gaza. Every day there's some new cruelty, and there's nothing we can do to stop it. I feel helpless, and I hate it! Isn't that enough reason to be depressed?"

Maggie sighed. "I know you feel frustrated. You live to fix things, whether it's sick people, stuck plumbing, or the state of the world."

Liz shook her head. "But I can't fix this."

"No, not all by yourself. But you're going to the 'Hands Off' protest, so that's something. We absolutely must stand up to them. We knew it was going to be bad."

"Not this bad. Even I couldn't imagine it, and you know what a pessimist I am."

"Don't try that on me. You're a realist, not a pessimist. You're a fighter. Now, eat your pie. It will make you feel better."

Liz looked up and smiled. "You know me so well."

"I should. I've only known you for fifty plus years."

"When you say it like that, it sounds so long, but it feels like yesterday when you seduced me in our dorm room."

"Hey, wait a minute. Let's get the story straight. *You* seduced me." Maggie gazed out the window reflectively. "I guess we seduced each other, didn't we? Neither of us knew what we were doing. I only knew a little more from Barry groping me in the car after football games."

"You knew enough to get me going. And I'll never forget when you were taking that twentieth century French literature class and handed me Anaïs Nin's memoirs so I could read the description of cunnilingus."

"I never liked that word," Maggie said.

"I know. It even sounds like a dirty word."

"I wanted you so much then I thought I would die without you," Maggie looked suddenly sad, then distraught. "When I lay in that other twin bed, I burned for you."

"I didn't know that. After you left, I told myself I was just your experiment."

"You know that's not true. I loved you then, and I love you now."

The intimate confession encouraged Liz to ask the question that had been bothering her. "Then why don't you join us in bed? You seduced Lucy with that erotic movie. You seemed to enjoy it in the beginning. That's why we brought you into our marriage."

"I love being in a relationship with you and Lucy."

"But not the sex."

"Sometimes, I do. But I'm not you, Liz. I don't need multiple orgasms every night. And if I need to come, I know how to take care of myself. Sometimes, it's more convenient and less complicated."

Liz blinked in surprise. This was the first time Maggie had ever admitted that she masturbated. "Why do it when you have the opportunity? You're welcome in our bed."

Maggie released a long sigh as if preparing to say something difficult. "Honey, at this point in my life, I sleep better alone. Just like you, I'm exhausted by the antics of this administration. It's hard enough to sleep. Sometimes, you snore, and you don't like anyone to touch you when you sleep."

"But Lucy loves to cuddle."

"I can get cuddles from Lucy anytime. It doesn't have to be in bed."

"So, it doesn't bother you that we don't all sleep together?"

"No, Liz, it doesn't. You and Lucy are like two horny teenagers. I love watching you go at it, but I feel like a voyeur. Some things are best left to the imagination." Maggie frowned and compressed her lips. "That's not fair. You two are passionately in love with each other. If you didn't express it physically, you'd probably explode. You need sex with Lucy like you need air."

"And that doesn't bother you?"

"It used to. That's because we're trained to think having sex means being loved. Sex is only one form of love. Listening to you talk when you're feeling down is one way. Making you apple pie and fixing your tea is another."

"So, you're fine with how things are?"

Maggie stared into her tea cup while she considered the question. "Not always. I don't like having to watch every word I say, hiding the truth from our friends. I don't like when you and Lucy appear as a couple, and I'm just the third wheel, the pathetic ex hanging around for crumbs."

Liz frowned. "I can see why you'd feel like that. I hate that part too."

"But unless Lucy wants to give up her job, there's nothing either of us can do about it."

"Maybe there is. We could trust more people with the truth. I was tempted to tell Brenda today."

Maggie shook her head. "Hmm. I don't know about Brenda. She may be gay, but she's very conventional. She wants a mirror of a heterosexual marriage. She's the big strong one taking care of everyone. Cherie's her pretty little wifey. Two kids, home on a cul-de-sac, perfectly manicured lawn. She might as well be a guy."

"Maybe, but that doesn't mean she'd reject us."

"Liz, I'd think about that long and hard before I told her. Plus, Brenda's going through a tough time right now. You don't want to add to her stress by forcing information on her that will upset her even more."

Liz knew Maggie was right about Brenda. Despite being annoyingly critical sometimes, Maggie was an astute observer of human nature. Her instincts were usually spot on, and Liz counted on them in social situations. "You're right. I don't want to add to her stress."

"I know Brenda's your buddy since Sam ran off to build sky-scrapers, but we need to be careful to protect Lucy." Maggie leaned forward to underscore her message. "Listen to me, Liz. Don't do anything rash."

***

Lucy was home by the time Liz had left Maggie's apartment. In the garage, Liz put her hand on the hood of Lucy's car and felt it was cold. She'd been home for a while. Liz filled the brass bucket with kindling before going into the house. Instantly, the smell of the comforting braise Maggie had started earlier, greeted her.

At the sound of the door opening, Lucy came into the hallway to see who'd come in. She was wearing one of Liz's old hoodies that used to be black but was now an off shade of gray. Liz just couldn't understand why her wives always wore her old shirts. From the alumni shops of their shared alma maters, Columbia for Lucy, and Yale for Maggie, Liz had bought them brand-new hoodies in the correct sizes. Maggie swam in Liz's shirts, but not as much as Lucy. Given the choice, they both preferred Liz's shirts, whether or not they were freshly laundered. Liz finally gave up complaining and bought herself new ones.

Lucy was also wearing her fuzzy slippers, which meant it had been an especially rough day, and she needed to be cozy. She threaded her arms through Liz's and hugged her with all her might. "Bad day?" asked Liz, gathering her close and stroking her silky hair, bending to inhale its floral scent, chamomile and lemongrass, according to the shampoo bottle. Whenever Liz smelled Lucy's red hair, she imagined bright sunshine on a field of daisies.

Lucy didn't answer her question. She just tightened her embrace. "Very bad day," Liz surmised. "Let's go into the living room. After I get the fire started, I'll give you a foot rub." Lucy finally let her go, indicating her delight at the prospect of a foot massage with a big smile.

"I'll get us some wine," she volunteered and headed back to the kitchen.

Liz opened the glass door of the wood stove and pulled close the bench she'd built when her knee became cranky. By the time Lucy returned with the wine, Liz had the beginnings of a blazing fire.

Lucy set down the glasses, kicked off her slippers and struck an eager 'I'm ready for my foot massage' pose. Liz took her feet into her lap, remembering how she'd used this trick to seduce Lucy, supposedly shocking her by rapidly rubbing a finger between her big toe and its neighbor. But Lucy's toes were covered today by black tights. Liz found a small hole in the heel and wiggled her finger into it. "Did you know about this?"

"Yes, but it wasn't big enough to throw them out yet."

"Like you're a pauper."

"I'm glad I have anything left after that agent cheated me. Plus, I have Erika's money, but that doesn't mean I should waste it."

"Spoken like a true New Englander."

"Well, I am a 'Bay Stater.' At least, I come by it honestly. Not like you, Ms. Brooklyn."

Liz settled into the rhythm of the massage, starting with the ball of Lucy's foot. Her wife showed her appreciation with a sigh. "So what made your day so awful?" Liz asked, moving her attention to the arch.

"This ICE thing has taken over everything. First, we had that new vestry member insist that we write a letter to Brenda complaining about the agreement. She even wanted to censure her as a member of the congregation. Brenda only joined the church because of Cherie and the kids. I don't want to make her feel unwelcome."

"Is it that Darla woman who insisted the Hobbs schools change the name of their sports teams because it was offensive to Native Americans?"

"How did you guess?" asked Lucy with a sigh. "She is a full-blooded Wabanaki, so I kind of understand."

Liz compressed her lips to avoid saying exactly what she thought. "Does that woman have a day job?"

"She works for some progressive group. Maine Action…something or another."

"Professional activist. Figures," said Liz, frowning.

"Liz, advocacy is important. At least, she's on the right side."

Liz often wondered if there was a "right side," but she didn't argue. She switched to Lucy's other foot. "So, how did the vestry vote?"

"Olivia reminded us that we should avoid taking political positions because of our tax-exempt status. The conservatives in the group looked relieved."

Liz grunted skeptically. "Like the Evangelicals honor that rule."

"Just because they break the rules, doesn't mean we can." Lucy winced when Liz hit a sore spot in her instep.

"Sorry, I'll be gentler."

"You're fine," sighed Lucy. "I'm just so tense." She picked up her glass of wine and began to guzzle it down.

"Take it easy, Lucy. It can't be that bad."

Lucy put down the glass with more force than needed, and Liz worried about the integrity of the stem. "Okay, it is that bad. What happened?"

"After all the craziness in the vestry meeting, Reshma cornered me." Lucy's young curate, one of the few black women in Hobbs, had been a refugee from Sudan, brought as child by her mother, the last surviving member of her family. They'd waited for years in a camp to be admitted to the U.S. Reshma became a priest partly to thank the Maine Episcopal Churches who'd supported her education. "Reshma is one of the organizers of the 'Hands Off' protest. Now, she's afraid to even show up."

"But Reshma's a citizen," Liz protested.

"He's threatened to reverse naturalizations and deport people. Reshma's taking him seriously." Liz ended the massage. Lucy swung her feet around and put them on the floor. "Liz, what can I say to her?" Liz thought of her earlier conversation with Bobbie.

Meanwhile, Lucy's green eyes glistened with tears. Then a sob erupted. Liz put her arm around Lucy and held her close.

"You tell her that we won't let anything happen to her," Liz whispered near Lucy's ear.

"But how can we stop it?" she asked between sobs.

"We can. And we will," Liz said bravely to give herself courage.

"Liz, I'm afraid."

"I know, sweetie." Liz gathered Lucy closer. "Me too."

Chapter 5

Brenda drew a sigh of relief when she saw Courtney Barnes. The elementary school principal often stood outside to greet the students when the buses arrived. Courtney's presence guaranteed that Brenda would see at least one smile this morning.

Fortunately, Megan had outgrown the need for a booster seat, so unloading her passengers was easier than it used to be. She checked to make sure the kids had their hats and mittens. Thank God winter would soon be over. Technically, it was, but April temperatures in Maine could still be frosty. Today was one of those chilly days. Cherie had made sure the children were bundled up before they walked out the door.

Once Brenda rounded up all their paraphernalia, she put on her campaign hat. She liked to look sharp when she appeared in a public place like the school, even more so now that she was apparently the most hated woman in town. Other mothers glared as they drove out of the parking lot. One flipped her the bird. Brenda smiled in return and touched her fingertips to her hat brim. *Gotta keep up a good front*, she thought.

Fortunately, Courtney's smile was completely genuine. The young blonde's golden-brown eyes, the color of good bourbon, literally glowed with warmth. The two of them went through their usual morning formalities like a re-enactment from an earlier time.

"Ms. Barnes," said Brenda, raising her hand to her hat. "How are you on this brisk morning?"

"I am well, Chief Harrison. I'm hoping that spring will finally come," she said, glancing at the bare trees lining the walkway. "I bet you are too." Courtney gave each of the Harrison kids a gentle pat on the shoulder as they passed.

"I hear it's supposed to get warmer next week. It was pretty chilly for that protest on Saturday."

"Melissa and I dressed in layers, and we were walking up and down to make sure people stayed on the sidewalks, like you said."

"With Melissa involved, I always expect things to be well organized, but you exceeded my expectations. There were no incidents except that woman who tripped on the curb, but she might have fallen with nothing going on."

"I'm sorry we had any incidents at all. We were hoping for a perfect record. And we had Dr. Stolz and your wife standing by if anyone got hurt."

"I can't complain about anything you did. There was no trash left behind. The sidewalks were spotless. No one would even know there were so many people on that street just a few hours before. Do you know how many showed up?"

"It's hard to count a crowd because people keep moving, but we think we had close to a thousand."

Brenda allowed herself to show surprise. "Wow, that's amazing, considering there are only ten thousand people living in Hobbs."

"I know. We were shocked." Courtney widened her eyes to show just how much. "Even after we filled the parking lot, more kept coming. Glad we planned overflow parking. The library was still open, and they were crabby about people parking there, despite the signs we put up. The library staff is sensitive after the other side accused the new librarian of using the space for 'woke' activities." Brenda raised a brow, not understanding right away. "We had a poster making event before the protest. The fact is that any organization can reserve that space, even the Hobbs Republicans, who meet there every month."

"Oh, some people will use any excuse to complain and point fingers."

"We left lots of room for the library patrons to enter and exit, but one guy just sat there until someone walked over and moved the barrier. Then he shouted something like, 'you're all nuts. How much are they paying you?'"

Brenda laughed heartily. "Bet you'd love to get a check for all that planning and hard work."

"Not coming anytime soon," said Courtney, shaking her head. She waved to one of the parents dropping off their kids.

 "How about my officers? Did they do a good job?"

"Well, we could have used some help directing traffic. Your guy just stood outside his squad car while everyone was trying to leave the parking lot. Finally, he got the idea and stepped in."

"I told them to leave you alone unless they were needed," said Brenda.

"This guy didn't look happy about having to help us."

Brenda leaned closer to speak confidentially. "I keep telling them they can't be showing their political stripes in the line of duty. Some of the younger guys need to learn how to put on their game face."

Courtney's soft laughter was musical. "It's something we all learn over time. I've only been principal for two years, and I'm still learning not to show everything I'm thinking on my face." She waved to the students as they passed and answered their greetings with a smile and a good morning.

Brenda lowered her voice. "You're doing a great job, Courtney, especially after all you've been through."

"We've all been through a lot. First, the pandemic, then the shooting, now this craziness."

"I know, but keep up the good work. We appreciate it. And tell your girlfriend her organization of that event was amazing. She's welcome to protest in my town any time."

"Well, thank you. I'll pass along your compliment to Melissa. She'll be happy to know you thought she did well. We're all new at this. Before he got into office, I never got involved in politics. Like you, I need to pretend I don't have any politics."

"Hard, isn't it?"

"Almost impossible, but like your patrol officer, I need to put on my game face."

"I think your regular face is just fine," said Brenda with a frankly admiring look. *Jeeze! I don't want her to think I'm flirting with her,* thought Brenda and wiped the grin off her face. *She's taken. I'm married. Cherie would frigging kill me.*

Most of the students had arrived, and the parade into the school had thinned to a trickle. "I need to get to work, Chief Harrison. I hope you have a great day." The friendly warmth in Courtney's voice reassured Brenda that she hadn't taken offense at the admiring look. With a sigh of relief, Brenda headed to her car.

❋❋❋

Brenda knocked on her administrative captain's open door. "You ready to meet the enemy?" she asked.

Sean Gaulin, a graying, handsome man with a young face, looked up with a smile. "You're not afraid of a bunch of young women with good intentions, are you, Chief?"

"I'm not afraid of anyone but my wife in a temper," Brenda said with a laugh.

"I get it." Sean frowned, then looked sad. She knew he felt responsible because he'd brought the announcement of the ICE training to Brenda's attention. Since the press coverage had created an uproar, Sean had confessed how bad he felt about causing trouble for his boss.

"Let's just stay calm and answer their questions," said Brenda. "Hopefully, it will go as well as the meeting with the officers of the Hobbs Democrats."

"They seemed to agree our decision made sense."

"That doesn't mean they approve. They probably don't, but we'll go to their meeting and answer their questions. That's the best we can do."

"You're not going to back down?" Sean asked anxiously.

Brenda shook her head. "Nope. That would make us look like we don't know what we're doing. Like we make bad decisions, which we don't."

Sean grinned. "Not even sometimes?"

Brenda gave him a hard look and frowned before she realized he was only teasing. "Well, of course, sometimes, but not often. Sean, you don't know how hard it is to be a woman in law enforcement. People are always questioning everything you do. If you waver, even a little bit, they think you're not a strong cop. You need to be tough as nails every single minute."

"That must be hard for you, Chief. You're tough, but kind. Remember during the pandemic, when you asked for volunteers to read online to the kids? I doubt a man would have thought of that."

Brenda shrugged. "It was good publicity for the department," she said gruffly. "I had an ulterior motive."

The grin on Sean's face mellowed into a warm smile. "But not a bad one. My kids loved it. It was fun watching Gilbert with his huge hands and linebacker shoulders hunched over a kid's story about saving dandelions. Who picked the books?"

"My wife's aunt. She knows what kids like. She's a retired elementary school principal. "

"Did she pick that one for Gilbert?"

"Nope. He did. He said it's his daughter's favorite."

An amused light shone in Sean's blue eyes. "I forgot he has a little girl."

"You can always tell girl dads. They might be the gruffest guy in the pack, but they'll put on a tutu and paint their fingernails for their daughter." Brenda smiled at the memory of Megan putting purple nail polish on her toenails while Cherie howled with laughter. That was last summer, before the fateful election, when life was still fun. Back then, Brenda felt like the town appreciated her and accepted her as a lesbian mom, raising two adopted kids with her biracial wife. Now, wherever she went, she got scowls and angry stares.

Brenda patted Sean on the shoulder. "Come on, let's get this meeting over with. I have other things to do today."

As she headed down the hall to the conference room, Brenda

steeled herself. She'd already met separately with some of the members of Activate Hobbs. Their leader, Darla Combs, was particularly obnoxious. She stood too close when she talked, practically spitting in Brenda's face. Her questions were really statements of her disapproval and disgust, and she asked them questions repeatedly. What did they think, that Brenda would crack and admit an ulterior motive, like a wish to terrorize the immigrants in town, or a secret desire to dress up in combat gear?

Sean opened the door to the conference room, where half a dozen women sat. The oldest had long gray hair and vaguely reminded Brenda of Maggie Fitzgerald, but this woman wasn't nearly as attractive. The youngest, a blonde, was the proprietor of the local pâtisserie. She was the only one who smiled when Brenda and Sean came in. Beside Tiffany Taylor sat St. Margaret's curate, Reshma John, herself a refugee from South Sudan. She was wearing her game face and her collar.

Usually, the clergy of St. Margaret's tried to avoid showing their religious affiliation at obviously political events, but as Lucy had explained, all that had changed. The Christian Left, whose influence had waned since its heyday during the civil rights movement and the Vietnam War, was finding its voice again. Despite Reshma's stern look, Brenda could see the warmth in her eyes. Apart from Reshma and Tiffany, everyone else glared.

Brenda tried to muster a cheerful attitude from her experience with hostile groups. In the NYPD, she'd often had to tamp down tensions in minority neighborhoods. As she'd developed her training program for community relations, she was shocked to discover how many white cops were secret racists. They saw people of color as a creeping invasion, encroaching on their neighborhood and taking their jobs. They believed the propaganda that affirmative action meant less qualified people were in line before them. In fact, Brenda, along with many in the NYPD, had come into the force through nepotism. When she'd tried to explain that the old boys' network that fed the police academy was unfair, many of the white cops couldn't hear it. Looking at the stern faces gathered around the table, Brenda realized this audience was just as impervious to reason, but she'd keep trying.

Brenda offered a broad smile and said, "Good morning! Thanks for taking the time to come meet with us. For those who don't know our administrative captain, this is Sean Gaulin." She gestured in his direction as he sat down. "You asked for this meeting. What can we do for you?"

A glowering, dark-haired woman unfurled a piece of paper. "I collected the questions," Darla explained, "but there might be others."

"Shoot," said Sean, and Brenda shot him a disapproving look. With this crowd, gun metaphors probably weren't a good idea. "I meant, let's hear your questions," Sean said, trying to clean up after himself.

Darla frowned ominously at him. "We want to know if this agreement was reviewed by the town lawyer before you signed it."

Sean looked to Brenda to field this question. "No, it wasn't. Prior to this, we've never submitted an agreement with any government law enforcement agency to the town attorney. We read it carefully and understand our obligations."

"Did you know it can obligate you to participate in ICE actions in our town?" asked the woman with the long gray hair.

"I'm sorry, I didn't catch your name," said Brenda, smiling to disarm her.

"Allison," the woman said with a bitter look. "I'm a lawyer."

"Well, Allison, then you'll know that federal law takes precedence over state and local laws. Federal agencies can ask us to join a law enforcement action with or without this agreement."

"Unless the legislature passes the law they're considering, banning local law enforcement from being involved in immigration enforcement."

Brenda looked thoughtful, although she had researched this question thoroughly and consulted Harriet, her personal lawyer. "In that case, there would be grounds to refuse to participate, but such laws haven't been tested in the courts."

The lawyer looked surprised that Brenda knew what she was talking about. She studied her with narrowed eyes. "Your agreement could leave the town open to liability in the case of an unjust detention or civil rights infringement."

"I suppose it could," said Brenda after a moment of thought, "but as you know, law enforcement enjoys broad immunity, so it would have to be an obvious civil rights violation. In Hobbs, we try to be sensitive to everyone's rights, including those of our immigrant neighbors. We depend on them to keep our businesses going."

"So, you realize they might be intimidated by the agreement you signed. They might even be afraid to report actual crimes. That means if someone experiences domestic violence, they won't call you."

Brenda tried to keep her face neutral. "I suppose that's possible, but I think the local population knows they can trust us to come when called for any crime."

"But what if the assailant or the victim is undocumented? Will you turn them over to ICE?" asked Darla.

Brenda nodded to Sean to take this one. "If a person we detain has a previous judicial warrant against him, we will turn him over to the agency seeking his arrest, whether state or federal. That's standard procedure."

"But what if the scan shows an administrative warrant?" Brenda assumed that Darla was trying to prove to her friends that she knew what she was talking about. In private meetings with her, Brenda had repeatedly answered this question. Brenda took a deep breath to summon patience.

"We don't act on administrative warrants."

"What if someone calls and says, 'I think the people next door are here illegally.'"

"We will tell them we don't enforce immigration law," Sean said with a shrug. "Not our job."

"Do you tell them to call ICE?"

"No, we tell them exactly what I said. If they want to report someone, I'm sure they can figure out who to call."

Brenda studied each face around the table. None of them looked satisfied by their explanations, which was to be expected. They hadn't come looking for answers. They'd come to push their positions. Only Reshma, who kept her expression neutral, and her girlfriend, Tiffany, sitting beside her, didn't look overtly contemptuous.

The leader folded up the paper with the questions. "Let's go," she said, and they all got up in unison. She left without any thanks for taking up their time. Everyone followed her except Tiffany and Reshma, who watched their friends walk down the hall until they were out of sight.

Tiffany took a large white box out of a canvas bag emblazoned with the logo of her store, Forbidden Pleasures. It was tied with old-fashioned, red-and-white bakery string. "This is for you and the other officers," she said with a warm smile. "I haven't forgotten how kind you were when my ex was stalking me. We don't like you getting involved with ICE, but we don't all hate you."

Brenda didn't know what to say. Fortunately, Sean reached out to take the box. "Thanks," he said. "That's very kind."

"What would your friends say if they knew you'd brought us treats?" asked Brenda.

"I don't care what they think. I know you're a good person," Tiffany proclaimed defiantly.

"Then why do you hang out with them?"

"Because this administration is dangerous and needs to be resisted in every way."

"Even if it means turning against your friends?" Brenda asked. She'd been dying to ask a friendly person on the other side this question.

"They don't see you, Chief Harrison," Reshma explained. "They see ICE. Everyone hates them. It's not personal."

"Reshma, I know, and I guess I should be grateful they're respectful enough to come and ask questions, although it feels like an attack instead of an honest attempt to get information."

The woman's dark eyes searched Brenda's face. "Ideology always tends to dehumanize the other. But look at it from my point of view. I'm a refugee. I came to Maine after years of waiting in a refugee camp."

"But you did it legally. You waited your turn."

"I did, and now, I'm a naturalized citizen. But that doesn't seem to matter if you're from a 'shit hole' country like South Sudan. It doesn't matter that all my family except my mother was killed, and women and girls are still being raped by the thousands. We were just trying to escape, but my suffering doesn't matter because my skin is brown."

Reshma's dispassionate but completely factual description of her situation made Brenda's eyes fill. She opened her arms. Reshma searched Brenda's eyes, cautiously weighing the invitation. Finally, she stepped forward. Fighting back tears, Brenda held her in a firm but gentle embrace.

❋❋❋

While Brenda's lunch heated in the microwave, the eyes of everyone in the breakroom stared enviously. Brenda smiled back, proud of her wife's good cooking. Gingerly, she carried the hot container back to her office. Just as she was about to plunge her spoon into Cherie's savory gumbo, the dispatcher's line lit up on her phone. Brenda sighed and pressed down the lit button. "Yes, Nicole?"

"You have a visitor, Chief."

Brenda adjusted her attitude so that she wouldn't sound as frazzled as she felt. "Who is it?"

"Rev. Bartlett."

Brenda blinked. Lucy almost never came to the station, so a visit from her was something of an honor. Either that, or there was a serious problem that couldn't wait. "Thanks Nicole, can you ask Cynthia to walk her up?"

"Sure thing, Chief."

Brenda quickly rearranged the papers on her desk, so her office didn't reflect the chaos she felt inside. Lucy never missed a trick. As Brenda stacked things into reasonably neat piles, she wondered what had brought Lucy. As the rector of a large congregation, she was a busy woman, and now that she'd gone back to singing, even more so. Liz sometimes dismissed her wife as "silly," but that wasn't Brenda's impression at all. Lucy was savvy to everything going on around her and a shrewd judge of character. She might not be a brainiac like Liz, but she was whip smart. If she'd come to the station today, she was likely on a mission.

Brenda had managed to find the surface of her desk barely a moment before Cynthia came to the door. She knocked on the frame. "Chief, Rev. Bartlett is here to see you."

The red-headed priest waved from the door. She was wearing a richly colored sweater over her clerical shirt and pants that matched. Brenda's wife had wondered aloud if Maggie moving in next door was the reason Lucy was looking more stylish. Clearly, Cherie approved of the upgrade because she talked about it often.

After the admin left, Lucy came in and looked around. Her eyes spotted the bowl on Brenda's desk. "I'm interrupting your lunch. I'm so sorry."

"I'm used to it. In my line of work, there's always something going on."

"Mine too, I'm afraid. But don't let me keep you from eating."

"It's chicken gumbo. Like some? I can get another bowl from the breakroom."

"Oh, I guessed it was Cherie's gumbo from the delicious smell. But I've eaten lunch, thank you."

Feeling strange about eating in front of Lucy, especially when she was wearing her collar, Brenda, picked up her spoon, Once she tasted the gumbo and realized how hungry she was, she didn't care who was there. "What brings you over here, Lucy? You can just call me, and I'll come to the rectory."

Lucy beamed one of her brilliant smiles. "You're busy too. And I think it's good to change things up. Don't you?"

"That's right. Keep 'em guessing."

Lucy gave her a sly look. "You make me sound like a schemer."

Brenda smiled. "Oh, you are, but not in a bad way. You always have people's best interests at heart."

Lucy blushed a little. Her redhead's complexion made any embarrassment impossible to hide. "Reshma told me about your conversation this morning."

Brenda instantly scanned her conscience to see if she'd done anything inappropriate. Maybe she shouldn't have hugged the young priest. Everyone was so prickly now about physical contact. "Do I need to apologize to her?" asked Brenda, setting down her spoon.

Lucy looked surprised. "Apologize? Why?"

Brenda affected a contrite expression. "I initiated the hug, Lucy, but she accepted it."

Lucy's green eyes studying her curiously gave Brenda chills because it felt like the priest was looking right into her soul. "You did nothing wrong, Brenda," she said gently. "Reshma was moved by the gesture. She's frightened. You proved you care about her and will protect her. Immigrants are terrified, even naturalized citizens, like Reshma, and legal refugees, like Teresa."

"I don't blame them for being afraid. Who knows what this guy will do? You didn't hear me say that. No one is supposed to know our political affiliation. I drum that into all my cops. We can't do our job if people think we're acting politically."

"Come on, Brenda. You're talking to me, Lucy. You were at our election watch party...even if you fell asleep."

Now, it was Brenda's turn to blush. "Unfortunately, I didn't miss anything. She lost anyway."

"Yes, she did. But I'm saying you don't have to hide from me. I'm not here in an official capacity, and even if I were, you can always be honest with me."

"Well, that's a relief. I spent the whole morning meeting with people grilling me about the ICE contract."

Lucy's features settled into a sympathetic look. "I'm sure it's awful being constantly questioned and second guessed."

"Let's just say I'm not used to it. I thought people in this town trusted me."

"They do. It's ICE they don't trust," said Lucy. "And do you blame them? Some agents are behaving like thugs." Brenda saw a flash of Lucy's righteous anger, but then her eyes became gentle and kind. "When Reshma came back from your meeting, she cried in my office. She said that when you held her it was the first time she felt safe since those deportation quotas were announced. You think people don't trust you, but Reshma does...completely. She really needed that hug, so no, you did nothing wrong. You did everything right. I'm proud of you."

Cherie's very good gumbo stuck in Brenda's throat. She struggled to swallow. Finally, she managed a smile. "Thank you, Lucy. I was pretty moved myself. When Tiffany gave us the pastries, I realized not everyone hates me."

"They don't hate you, Brenda. They hate the lawlessness of this administration and its cruelty. There have been deportations in other administrations. Everyone agrees that immigration law needs to be enforced, but not like this. ICE agents are behaving like bullies."

"I hate bullies."

"So do I." They exchanged a smile. "When Reshma told me

about your meeting, I realized that you might need a hug as much as she did. That's why I came over...to see how you're doing."

That did it. Brenda's eyes filled. She swallowed several times before she could speak. "Thanks," she said.

"I'm sorry," said Lucy. "Now you won't be able to finish Cherie's gumbo."

"Oh, I couldn't finish it anyway. Cherie always gives me too much. I'll save it for tomorrow."

"You sure? I can leave so you can finish eating in privacy."

"No, don't go. It's not often I have you all to myself. Those times are special." Brenda forced a grin so that Lucy could see she was all right.

"You know I'm always here for you."

"I know. It's your job. You're a priest," said Brenda, glancing at the collar.

Lucy looked a little hurt. "I am a priest, but I'm here for you as your friend."

✳✳✳

Cherie's eyebrows and lower lip instantly rose in sympathy when Brenda came through the door. Before she had a chance to lock up her service weapon in the hallway safe, her wife's arms were around her, hugging her fiercely.

"Oh, baby, you look like hell," Cherie said, not mincing words.

Brenda managed a weak chuckle. "Thanks. I feel like hell."

Cherie let her go and gave her a careful inspection. "Okay, I forgive you for not coming home to make dinner like you said you would. Good thing Aunt Simone could pick up the kids and get dinner going."

"Thank God for Aunt Simone." Brenda looked around. "Is she here?"

"No, she left for choir practice. I should be there too, but someone had to stay with the kids."

"If you want to go, I can watch the kids."

"Nope, I can miss practice. My Brenda needs some loving. Get rid of your damn gun, change out of your uniform, and I'll get your dinner."

Brenda sniffed the air like an attentive yellow lab. "Smells good. What are we having?"

"A chicken casserole Aunt Simone threw together from last night's leftovers. The kids ate already. I did too, but I'll sit with you. Now, skedaddle and change into your civvies. Your dinner will be waiting for you by the time you get down."

In the bedroom, Brenda took off her uniform shirt and hung it on the back of the door to air out. No sense making extra laundry. In the cool weather, she hardly perspired. She slipped off her uniform pants and carefully hung them along the crease. She'd needed to pee for over an hour, but she'd been holding it because she just wanted to get home. She sat down on the toilet and released a steady stream with a contented sigh. As it ended, her phone pinged. She always felt weird looking at her phone on the john, so she pulled up her underwear.

The text message was from Lucy. *How are you doing?*

Brenda shook her head but smiled. *Has anyone told you you're a pest?*

LOL! My wife tells me all the time. How are you doing?

I'm home. Going to eat dinner. Cherie's taking good care of me. She's going to miss choir practice tonight. Vouch for her with Maggie.

Maggie will understand. YOU take care of yourself. Enjoy your dinner. The message ended with a yellow heart and a rainbow.

"Damn you, Lucy Bartlett, you are a pest, but you're a good priest...and friend." Brenda blew a kiss toward the dark screen.

By the time she got downstairs, her dinner was waiting, just as Cherie had promised, but there was more. The kitchen was illuminated by warm, golden candlelight. It wasn't an occasion for a romantic evening, so Brenda was confused. "Why are the lights off?"

"I'm sure you had enough stimulation today, so I'm trying to reduce the sensory overload by dimming the lights. Sit down," Cherie ordered. She flipped open a bottle of Brenda's favorite red ale and poured it into a glass. Before Cherie had come into her life, Brenda would have drunk the beer straight from the bottle. Not only did Cherie take care of her, she'd added refinements and beauty to her life.

"Thanks," murmured Brenda, taking a seat. She admired Cherie's shapely ass as she put a plate with a generous portion of casserole into the microwave to heat.

"Don't get too used to the service," Cherie warned, "...or coming home late." Her words were stern, but her eyes were smiling. She meant it because she had a busy life too, but she'd already forgiven Brenda.

"I won't do it again. We're in this together all the way. I just never expected it to be this hard."

"You mean, being married to me, the kids?"

"No, I mean his second administration. Most of all, I never expected to be second-guessed when I make decisions for my own department."

Cherie put the heated plate in front of Brenda and sat down with a glass of wine. "What happened today?" When she reached for Brenda's hand, she had that intent look that meant she was listening with her therapist's ears.

"I had four meetings with groups demanding answers. I'm so busy explaining myself to these angry people, I don't have time to do my real job."

Cherie nodded sympathetically. "I saw Reshma after she came back. I was just ready to go into a session when she came through the door."

"I heard our meeting was as tough for her as it was for me."

"Oh, that's not what I heard," said Cherie, letting go of Brenda's hand and lifting her fork. "Eat, baby. I'm sure you're starving."

Brenda took the fork and dug into Simone's casserole. Like everything Cherie's aunt cooked, it was delicious. Cherie smiled as Brenda ate hungrily. "You made a big impression on Reshma. I mean, she already admired you for how you handled the case of Tiffany's stalker, but now, you walk on water."

Brenda covered her mouth when she talked. "I think only her boss can do that. I mean Jesus, not Lucy. She showed up to check on me, which was nice of her."

"That sounds like Lucy. We're all worried about you, baby. We know that despite keeping up a good front, you're worn down."

Brenda paused her eating. "You've never told me what you think of what I'm doing."

Cherie emitted a long sigh. "Well, I support YOU completely and absolutely. That doesn't mean I always agree with what you do."

"Why didn't you tell me?"

Cherie visibly hesitated, considering what to say. "You don't tell me how to deal with my patients. I don't tell you how to run the police department."

"But you do have an opinion, don't you?"

"Yes, I do," Cherie said slowly. "But I'm not sure you want to hear it."

"Please, tell me," said Brenda, putting down her fork.

"No, you eat first, then we'll talk about it. Lucy said she interrupted your lunch, and after you talked, you couldn't finish."

"Shame on her for telling on me," Brenda said with a snicker.

"She cares about you. You need nourishment, Brenda!"

Brenda picked up her fork and began to eat. "I feel like I'm in a fishbowl with everyone watching me—you, Lucy, Liz, the press, everyone in town!"

"I can understand why you might feel that way."

"Cherie, don't give me that counseling bullshit," warned Brenda in an angrier tone than she'd intended.

Cherie's blue-green eyes widened. "I'm sorry, I only meant I can understand. I wouldn't want to be in your position."

While Brenda wolfed down the food on her plate, she could feel Cherie's eyes on her. Finally, she reached for some beer to wash down the last bite. "I'm finished eating. Say what you have to say."

Cherie was silent for a long moment. "I'm not the enemy, Brenda. I love you. Take it easy."

"How can I take it easy when everyone is on my case, even you!"

"I'm not on your case. I haven't said anything because it's your decision to make."

"But you disapprove."

Cherie inhaled a deep breath. "I don't know enough to judge what you're doing. I know you are an excellent police chief and try to make the best decisions for your department. I've heard your reasons for making this one, and they seem sound."

"But..." said Brenda.

"But ICE has been behaving badly, and everyone who cares about other people disapproves of them. It's not about you, Brenda. It's about them, guilt by association. It looks bad to voluntarily cooperate with them."

"A sheriff in another town cancelled their agreement before it was even signed. He caved to pressure."

"Well, isn't that an option?" asked Cherie, placing her hand on Brenda's arm.

"No, that would make me look like I think I made a bad decision. At least, the select board and the town manager aren't getting involved, although if they ordered me to end the agreement, I'd be off the hook."

"They aren't getting involved out of respect for you," Cherie said softly.

Brenda smiled weakly. "That's something, I guess."

"It's a lot. You built that respect through years of loyal service to this town and proven leadership. You deserve it."

"I should tell Jim and Olivia how much I appreciate their staying out of it."

"You haven't?" asked Cherie, her eyebrows shooting up.

"No," Brenda admitted sheepishly. "I haven't had time."

"Tell them. They need to hear you appreciate their support." Cherie nodded to Brenda's plate. "You done eating, or do you want more?"

"No, it was delicious. Just right."

Cherie picked up Brenda's plate. "Take your beer into the living room and turn on one of our shows."

"I'll help you with the dishes."

"No, you won't. It's just your dish. I'll join you after I tuck in the kids."

"I should go up and kiss them good night."

"Go on. Tell them I'll be up soon."

Brenda got up and stood behind Cherie at the sink. "Have I told you lately how much I love you?" she asked, encircling Cherie's waist with her arms. She nuzzled her neck under her ear and gave her a playful nip.

"Yum," cooed Cherie. "You need sex, baby?"

Brenda sighed. "I do, but I'm too damn tired."

"Then go say good night to the kids and get the TV going. Pick something good. Not the news! I can't stand to see that orange man."

"Neither can I," said Brenda, giving Cherie's soft breasts an appreciative squeeze.

"Maybe you're not too tired," Cherie murmured seductively.

"Maybe not."

Cherie shooed Brenda away with her hip. "Then get going. I'll be there soon."

"Can't wait," said Brenda, giving Cherie's shapely ass a strategic caress.

Chapter 6

At the knock on her door frame, Brenda turned to see Sean Gaulin, timidly awaiting permission to enter. The explosion over the ICE agreement had left her once confident, even cocky, administrative captain deferential and confused. Brenda had been so busy dealing with her own emotional reactions, she'd barely noticed how this insane episode had crushed Sean.

Before the craziness, he'd been on a smooth course to succeed her once she finally retired. He was a good cop, who'd paid his dues, and would make a great chief. Now, it was becoming doubtful he'd even remain on the force. He had enough experience to get a high-paying job in a security agency, even government, but losing him would be such a shame.

People who'd grown up in town and committed to Hobbs, were invaluable. Being "from away," Brenda counted on them to interpret the relative importance of local customs or supply the backstory on individuals and issues. Although Sean had focused on the practical benefits and missed the potential fallout from signing the 287g agreement, he was astute. Brenda hoped he would hang in there, as she intended to do. She wasn't going to let a little bad publicity drive her from her job.

"I brought you a copy of my notes," he said, handing her a stack of paper.

Brenda flipped through the rumpled pages, squinting to read his cramped, angular handwriting. Sean was the last generation to learn cursive, but like most men, he had awful penmanship. "Jesus, Sean. I can barely read this. Why didn't you type your answers?"

With a sheepish look, he admitted, "Because I wrote them in the middle of the night when I couldn't sleep. I didn't want to fire up my laptop and disturb my wife."

So, he couldn't sleep either. Brenda's restlessness had driven

Cherie to the twin bed in Megan's room. With her wife asleep in another room, Brenda had no guilt about turning on the light while she read the negative publicity and antagonistic social media posts. Cherie kept telling her to stop reading the posts, but Brenda couldn't tear her eyes away because she still couldn't believe what they were saying about her. The latest was calling the Hobbs Police, and by inference, Brenda, "the stain on Maine." Some reporter had probably thought the phrase was catchy and made her sound smart, but to Brenda it felt like being stabbed.

Cherie was worried enough to suggest calling Liz for meds to help her sleep, but Brenda wouldn't hear of it. The lifelong police officer in her resisted the idea of taking any drugs that could impair her judgment. Instead, she sat awake, staring at her tablet, which left her bleary-eyed in the morning. Fortunately, there were eye drops that got the red out before she showed up for work. Unfortunately, they didn't help the exhaustion that left her dragging all day.

Brenda was able to make out enough of Sean's scribbles to see that the reasoning behind his answers was sound. The Hobbs Democrats had requested their members submit their questions in advance. Their secretary would combine redundant requests for clarification to save time.

When Brenda and Sean had met with the organization's officers, they clearly wanted to hold her feet to the fire, but they listened respectfully. They stated that although they didn't approve, they were satisfied that there was no malicious intent on Brenda's part and that signing up for the training made some sense. They decided to give Brenda and Sean an opportunity to appear in their monthly meeting to explain their rationale. It all sounded reasonable and well-organized. Unlike some other meetings, Brenda wasn't worried about this one.

"Sean, I want you to take the lead. This has been your project since the beginning. I know you've given it even more thought since it blew up. Plus, it will be a good experience, and the town will see you in a leadership role. Work for you?"

"You're not setting me up to take the fall, chief?" Brenda chuckled although it wasn't funny and with someone else, not outside the realm of possibility. "Just kidding," Sean added quickly, "I know you'd never do that to me."

"Damn right, I wouldn't. That's not how I operate."

"I know. And you're right, it was my idea to do this, so I should take the lead on dealing with the fallout."

"But I listened to your reasons for this training. I thought it was a good idea. It's my signature on that agreement. I promise I'm not throwing you under the bus."

Sean suddenly looked much younger than his forty-plus years, more like the young recruit Brenda had once been assigned to mentor rather than the seasoned officer he was. His blue eyes were suddenly full of unabashed admiration and devotion. Brenda only hoped she could be worthy of such loyalty. There were some things she couldn't control, but if she could help it, she would shield this young man from the fallout.

"You ready to go?" she asked.

"Yes, ma'am," he replied with a smart salute.

Brenda returned the salute and rose to get her hat.

✱✱✱

They took Sean's squad car to the public library, where the Hobbs Democrats held their meetings. As she headed to the door, Brenda found herself reminiscing about the public library down the street from her childhood home in Brooklyn. When she was growing up, the library was a revered institution. It was the place she went to research her school papers, where the helpful librarians guided her to books that answered her questions about everything from the weather to how to deal with boys. As a budding lesbian, she was more interested in how to get rid of them than attract them, but the insights in those books helped her deal with her father and brothers, and later her colleagues in the NYPD.

Now, libraries had come under fire as a tool of the "radical left."

Librarians were too "woke" because they put books on their shelves about diverse communities and sexuality. Merely by offering material covering multiple political opinions, they were implementing a liberal agenda.

"Come on," Brenda said, waving on Sean to divert him toward the main entrance. She had suddenly decided to stop in to see the new head librarian. Barely a week after the woman arrived, the righties began whipping up outrage because she'd allowed a poster-making session before a protest. They conveniently ignored the fact that any legitimate town organization could reserve the community room for a meeting, including the opposite party.

The librarian at the front desk looked surprised to see two officers fully outfitted with police vests and service pistols. Brenda leaned forward and asked quietly, "Is Brittany Stevens still here? I know it's late, but just in case." She smiled charmingly. That seemed to reassure the young woman. Despite a quick glance at Brenda's service pistol, she returned the smile.

"I'll ring her office," she offered.

Sean looked at his watch. "Don't worry," said Brenda. "We have plenty of time. There's another speaker ahead of us. We can sneak in the back way." She leaned on the counter while the front desk librarian tried to contact her boss. Finally, she hung up and nodded.

"Do you know the way?" she asked.

"Thank you, I do."

Sean, following Brenda, looked around. "I don't spend as much time in here as I should. I've only been in this new building a dozen times."

"Libraries are wonderful. You should spend time here. Bring your kids." Brenda leaned into the head librarian's doorway. "Thanks for seeing us at this late hour."

"Always glad to see you, Chief Harrison. Is there something I can do for you?"

"No, just stopped by to say hello and see how you're doing. They haven't made your first weeks in your new job easy."

The librarian's eye roll said it all, but she added, "It's never dull in Hobbs."

"Sure isn't," Brenda agreed. "We're here to answer questions in the Hobbs Dems' meeting."

"Good luck. All this controversy has made you extremely popular."

"In the worst possible way," Brenda said without irony. Over her shoulder, Brenda could hear Sean snicker. "Ms. Stevens, meet my administrative captain, Sean Gaulin. He's going to bring his kids here. I know my kids love coming to this library. I'm sure his will too."

Ms. Stevens got up to shake Sean's hand. "When you bring your kids, ask for me. I'll be happy to show you around."

Sean looked touched. "Thank you, Ms. Stevens. I will."

Brenda glanced at her watch. "I guess it's time. Have a good evening."

"Good luck with your meeting, Chief," the head librarian called after her.

Brenda led Sean to the back entrance to the meeting room. "Sean, that's why we call it community policing. I had no reason to talk to her. I just wanted her to know we are here and why. Plus, a little courtesy smooths the way when things need to get done."

"I saw that, chief. Good idea. And I will bring my kids...and stop in to see her when I do."

"Good," said Brenda, satisfied that her lesson by example had been learned. She scanned the meeting room through the glass door. As she'd expected from the full parking lot, it was packed to capacity. They'd run out of chairs. People standing in the rear were jammed together tightly, so there was no room to pass. "Maybe we should go in the other way," Sean suggested.

"They'll let us through. You'll see."

While the speaker addressed the audience on Zoom, Brenda studied the woman standing at the lectern. Although she didn't know her well, her opinion of the chair of the Hobbs Democratic Town Committee had risen when she'd brought her officers to the police station to get clarification on the 287g agreement. Instead of rushing to judgment, she'd led her group in asking calm, well-considered questions.

She'd been a model of rationality and calm, but tonight, the woman at the podium kept scanning the audience while the first speaker went on and on about prison reform in Maine. The chair's fidgeting was amplifying the tension. She caught Brenda's eye and nodded.

When the speaker took a breath, the chair quickly said, "Thank you, Christine. And now we have time for one or two questions." The audience looked relieved to skip to the "good part". Only one person asked a question. The speaker had barely finished her answer when her Zoom feed was cut.

"And now, let's welcome our Hobbs police chief, Brenda Harrison and Captain Sean Gaulin." The chair clapped to encourage the audience, but this time, the applause was hesitant and thin.

Brenda took a long deep breath before she stepped into the room. She could feel the eyes on her, some curious, some supportive, and others openly hostile. When she arrived at the front, she turned to the crowd with a tense smile plastered on her face. Then she saw Cherie, sitting between Maggie Fitzgerald and Lucy Bartlett. The three were beaming warm smiles in her direction.

Brenda looked around for Liz, finally spotting her in the back. She must have come in late. She had a flinty, no-nonsense expression on her face. Her blue eyes were cold, and the set of her jaw was hard. Her arms were crossed on her chest like a bouncer in a cheap New York bar. Her stance showed a clear message: I've got your back.

Encouraged by the presence of her supporters, Brenda cleared her throat and began. "Thank you for inviting us to answer your questions about our 287g agreement with the Department of

Homeland Security. You've probably heard about it on TV and don't know what to think. When we're done here tonight, I hope you'll understand why we signed up for this training and why it will help us keep you safer. My administrative captain, Sean Gaulin, has been taking the lead on this project, so he'll be answering most of your questions this evening."

A tall, older woman with gray hair rose. She was the same woman who had stopped by the station that afternoon to review how the group planned to manage the Q&A. As the secretary of the Hobbs Democrats, she had compiled the questions submitted in advance by the membership. There were a few late comers, so she'd brought those to the station in person. She was all business, a little stern, but pleasant. "I sent the late questions by email too, to both you and Captain Gaulin." The secretary explained that she would read questions distilled from similar ones to prevent personal attacks against the officers and grandstanding.

"Thank you for coming tonight, Chief Harrison and Captain Gaulin," the secretary began. "The first question is, can you briefly explain how the Hobbs police became involved with ICE? Let's start with how you found out about the agreement."

Brenda glanced at Sean. He looked confident answering this simple question. "As the administrative captain, I'm in charge of relationships with other jurisdictions, including the federal government. I also oversee our training program. When we got the email from DHS, uh, that's the Department of Homeland Security, I went to the chief. It looked like a good opportunity for us to get an important certification."

"Please explain."

"The training would allow us to transport undocumented people with a judicial warrant to a federal holding facility. Right now, if we detain someone with a judicial warrant and they're undocumented, we have to wait until ICE comes up from Boston."

"How many times have you called ICE?" the secretary asked.

Sean glanced at Brenda nervously, but he answered the question truthfully. "We've never had to call ICE."

The secretary nodded, having drawn the obvious conclusion. They were preparing for a threat they had never encountered. Brenda jumped in to explain. "We're always looking for opportunities to improve our ability to keep Hobbs safer. Thankfully, we have had few incidents requiring officers to draw their guns, but we practice on the range once a month to maintain our skills. We saw this agreement as a way to get training to do our work better."

"So, you didn't seek it out to solve a particular problem with undocumented people?"

"No," said Brenda. "We often get notices of training opportunities from Federal agencies such as the FBI, ATF, and DHS. These trainings are usually online and there's no charge for them. We try to take advantage of as many as we can."

"Well, that answers my next question, who paid for this training?"

"Not the town," Brenda said.

"Was the town involved in your decision to sign this agreement? Did you run it by the select board, the town manager, or the town attorney?"

"We did not. We have never asked for a review of any of our agreements with federal agencies, and we have never had any question about our decision to sign up for anything until now."

Brenda was waiting for the secretary to ask if, in retrospect, she should have consulted the town administration, but she didn't.

The eyes of one of the select board members, sitting in the front row, locked on hers. Obviously, he didn't think she'd made a good decision, but she had to give them all credit for not getting involved. At first, she'd interpreted that meant they trusted her to make a good decision. It could also mean they would let her sink or swim on her own.

A cold feeling of unease fluttered inside Brenda, so she glanced at Cherie, sitting with their friends. Her blue green eyes were full of warmth and encouragement. At least one person still believed in her.

"Let's turn to the agreement and what it obligates the Hobbs Police to do. Will the Hobbs Police be acting on behalf of ICE to pursue undocumented people?"

"Absolutely, not," said Sean, suddenly finding his tongue. "It's not the role of a town police department to enforce immigration law. And I see one of the questions on this list is, 'what would you do if someone called to report they think someone is undocumented?' The answer is, we would tell them we don't enforce immigration law, just like I'm telling you. The next question is, 'don't you think the agreement will have a chilling effect on immigrants, documented or not. They might be afraid to report crimes, like domestic violence. How will you reassure them that if they come to you, you won't arrest them?"

Brenda realized that Sean was going through the submitted questions, one by one, not the consolidated questions that the secretary had provided. The tall woman sat down, realizing the group's careful plan was rapidly unraveling. Sean had taken over the meeting.

There was no way that Brenda could gracefully remind him of what had been decided without making him look bad. Instead, she chimed in when appropriate. He was clearly on a roll, and it was hard to insert a word into Sean's rapid-fire stream of questions and answers.

The secretary crossed her arms on her chest and exchanged a look with the chairwoman. They knew they had lost control of the meeting. Finally, Brenda put her hand on Sean's arm. When he turned to her, his eyes were wild, but he instantly fell silent. Although the secretary had tried to distill similar questions, she had included the originals, minus the identity of who had asked them. Brenda hadn't realized it before, but Sean had found some of them personally offensive. That explained why his paper was completely covered with extensive notes. Maybe she should have read them more carefully.

The chair used the opportunity to say, "We have time for about two or three clarifying questions. You may ask the chief and the captain to elaborate on what they said, not ask new questions."

A tall, thin woman in the back raised her hand. Brenda's eyes instantly narrowed. This was the same woman who parked herself in her office yesterday, interrogating Brenda for over an hour. What more could she possibly need to know?

"Could this agreement possibly keep ICE out of Hobbs?" Brenda's brows shot up. What was this woman's game?

"Well, if we don't have to call them to pick up someone, there's less chance they'll be here," said Brenda. "So, yes, it could keep them away from Hobbs."

Another hand shot up. "Can this agreement be terminated?" asked a dark haired, portly woman.

Sean answered, "Yes, it can be terminated at any time by either party."

"Then why don't you just terminate it?" asked the woman in an aggressive tone. "You admitted that you've never had to deal with an undocumented person with a criminal record. You just want to help ICE lock up innocent people!"

Brenda responded in the most measured tone she could muster. "As I explained, we always want to be prepared for any situation. This training provides us with another tool to help keep Hobbs safe."

"That's bullshit and you know it!" the woman shouted back.

"All right, enough questions," the chairwoman said in a raised voice. Its pitch and a slight tremor undermined her ability to speak with authority. She gulped air before she spoke again. "We will adjourn now, because we've already run over time, we need to be out of the library by eight o'clock."

People started getting up and folding the chairs. The low rumble of confused conversation was broken by a man shouting from his seat. "You're not shutting me up. I have a First Amendment right to speak!" Brenda focused on the man. He looked close to eighty and had a crazed look in his eyes. As he continued to ramble about 'First Amendment rights,' he looked like he could be choking. Brenda braced herself for a medical emergency. She glanced at Liz, who also looked ready to spring into action.

Then the secretary got up, cupped her hands around her mouth, and called across the crowd, "Greg! That's enough! It's time to stop."

Furious, the man got up and allowed himself to be led away by some people. When he stood, Brenda could see that, despite the wild look in his eyes and his age, he was fit and agile. This was no dementia outburst. It was the raving of an extremist.

She was distracted by a small crowd that had gathered around her.

"I'm so sorry for the disrespect," the secretary was saying. "This is what we were hoping to avoid."

A woman said, "We're not all against you, chief. Some of us support you and the Hobbs police. We know you're only trying to do the right thing."

The man standing beside her seconded the opinion, but he said, "If you really don't need this, why not terminate the agreement? It only makes you and the town look bad." Although the comment rankled, Brenda managed to remember the man meant well and what he said was only common sense.

The crowd around her hemmed her in and prevented her from escaping the room. Helplessly, Sean stood by. Although he'd unwittingly created this controversy, Brenda was clearly the focus of any blame. While she was a captive, she answered a few more questions, and accepted declarations of support. Finally, she said, "Thanks, folks, but Captain Gaulin and I need to get back to work." She smiled a big smile. That always worked for Lucy Bartlett, so Brenda had been practicing how to use it to defuse stressful situations. Finally, the people gathered around her opened a path. Waving Sean on, Brenda quickly took the escape route.

Before she got to the door, she saw the chairwoman trying to talk to the man called Greg. Brenda heard her trying to explain that First Amendment rights didn't apply to a local political committee. "Greg, you were out of order. It's the job of the officers to run an orderly meeting." She was trying to sound reasonable, but the frustration was evident in her tone.

The tall, skinny woman, who asked if the agreement could keep ICE out of Hobbs, interrupted. "An officer just yelled at Greg!"

The chairman turned and peered at her with a deadly look. "Pat, you just put my head through a buzz saw. As far as I'm concerned, you have nothing more to say!"

Brenda leaned between them and said, "Thanks for inviting us to speak, but we have to go!"

Never in her life had she been so glad to leave a meeting.

***

Brenda was glad they'd parked in the lot behind the library that most people didn't know about, instead of in front, where people leaving the meeting could see them. Commiserating with Sean about the spectacle they'd just witnessed, Brenda hoped her wife would guess her strategy. A moment later, Cherie drove into the parking area and pulled into the spot beside the squad car. When Sean rolled down the driver's side window, she said, "Don't mind me interrupting, but I came to take my wife home."

Sean smiled weakly. "Can you take me home too?" He pouted like a six-year-old.

"Your wife will take care of you, Sean," said Cherie. "Go home and get a hug."

As Brenda was getting into Cherie's SUV, Sean called out to her, "I'll pick you up in the morning, chief, so you can get your car at the station."

"Thanks, Sean. It was a tough meeting, but you handled yourself the best you could."

"I'm sorry I couldn't keep my personal feelings out of it. I really tried."

"You did your best." Brenda hoped her disappointment didn't show in her voice. She didn't need to underscore that his best hadn't been good enough.

As Cherie drove away, Brenda watched Sean in the rearview mirror. With his limbs hanging off him like the arms and legs of an idle marionette, he looked totally defeated. Finally, he shook his head and got into his car. "Poor guy," murmured Brenda, "he knows he lost it in that meeting. Those people tried so hard to organize the meeting so it wouldn't blow up, and he wrecked their plan."

"Once he lost control," Cherie observed, "it was clear that things would go downhill fast. People picked up on his frustration and anger. The sharks smelled blood in the water and swam in for the kill."

"You mean that Greg guy?"

"He and the others. I was sitting in front of him. When he was shouting at the end, I thought he was having a stroke."

"Hmm. I saw Liz getting worried too. Jeeze, could you imagine even more drama?"

"Unfortunately, I could. I'm just glad they shut him up when they did."

Brenda's cell phone rang in the pocket of her police vest. "Oh, hell. Now, who's this?" She looked at the screen. "Hey, Liz."

"You all right?"

"Mostly, Cherie rescued me from the back parking lot. She's driving me home."

"Good. Want me to come over for moral support or do you just want to crash?"

"Thanks, Liz. I just need some quiet. It's been quite a day."

Brenda heard a soft chuckle. "Believe me. I get it. Besides, I have my gang with me, and you'd have to put up with them too."

"Well, Lucy always knows what to say in tough situations, but I have my personal shrink sitting beside me."

Cherie shot her a filthy look.

"I wouldn't call her that, Brenda. Lucy hates it." Brenda could almost hear Liz grinning. "But, dammit, I call her a shrink anyway." Now, Liz was laughing outright. Brenda couldn't help but smile too. "I'll call you tomorrow. Maybe we can set up a fishing date. We all need a break from this craziness."

Brenda imagined sitting on the deck of The Wet Lady, fishing pole in one hand and a cold beer in the other. "Oh, my God, that sounds just wonderful."

"I agree. Night, Brenda."

"Good night, Liz."

Chapter 7

While Liz was waiting for her coffee to brew, Lucy came into the kitchen and hugged her from behind, pressing her breasts suggestively into her back. After the chaotic spectacle they'd witnessed in the usually staid, boring meeting of the local Democrats, they'd felt the need for pure animal comfort. Even Maggie had crawled into their bed, looking for safety and warmth. After they had made love slowly and deliberately, they'd clung to one another. Although she hated to be touched when she slept, Liz didn't shoo them away. After that civic nightmare, she needed them close.

Lucy reached down to massage Liz's crotch through her pants. "You were amazing last night," she whispered.

Liz closed her eyes to focus on the pleasurable stroking. "You were pretty damn amazing yourself. I'm sure poor Maggie didn't know what hit her."

Lucy abruptly let her go and declared indignantly, "You know I don't approve of violence during sex!"

Liz eyed Lucy from her full height. "You know I meant it metaphorically."

Lucy nudged Liz with her hip. "Your coffee is done. My turn."

Liz stepped aside to give Lucy access to the coffee maker. She splashed cream into her coffee and took a sip. The jolt of caffeine was welcome. The wild night in bed had been fun, but the lack of sleep hadn't done her any favors. "I'm sorry we didn't get to our beach walk this morning. Want me to pick you up at lunchtime? We could walk along the ocean road."

"Good idea," said Lucy, wagging her hip in approval. After good sex, Lucy was always so coquettish.

"We could ask Maggie to meet us and grab a lobster roll," Liz suggested.

"She'll be up in Biddeford when you take your lunch break. She has a department meeting today," said Lucy, who kept up with the household calendar that Liz usually ignored.

Liz took another welcome sip of coffee, finally beginning to feel like she was waking up. She was grateful that they'd left Maggie in a stupor while they'd quietly gotten up to shower and dress. Lucy's sunny energy was enough to deal with this morning.

Liz's phone vibrated in her pocket. The screen showed the photo of an attractive, perfectly coiffed woman in her mid-sixties. The message preview read: *Can you join me for lunch today?*

Liz could guess the reason for Olivia's invitation. Although the town manager avoided political events for fear of appearing partisan, Olivia had by now heard about the near riot at the Hobbs Democrats' meeting.

In answer to Lucy's unspoken question, Liz held up her phone showing Olivia's photo. "I think our lunch walk just got preempted."

Lucy sighed. "We can take a walk on the local roads when you get home this evening. That's one benefit of the longer spring days. We need the light. It's been such a long, hard winter."

Liz lightly pinched Lucy's shapely rear, which made her jump. "Hey, no pessimism, Mother Lucy. You need to be cheerful and hopeful for your flock. Besides, being an old grouch is my job."

Lucy laughed. "Everyone knows it's an act, Liz. You're wasting your time."

Liz harrumphed at the suggestion, then smiled. Lucy reached up for a kiss, which started out merely friendly but devolved into something more passionate. Caught up in the fervor, Liz's hand strayed under Lucy's sweater to caress her breast. An appreciative moan encouraged Liz to keep on going into her slacks, but before her hand reached her goal, Lucy gently pushed away. "If we go on like this, we'll land back in bed. You need to get to work, and so do I."

"Maybe it's time for us to retire," Liz suggested.

Lucy reached up to caress Liz's nipple through the perfectly pressed, button-down shirt. "On mornings like this, retirement sounds very appealing, but it's not happening today." She gave Liz a perfunctory kiss. "Now, drink your coffee and let's get going." Liz pouted until Lucy pinched her arm. "I'm sorry to be the one to spoil our fun, but I mean it. Wait for me. I need to fix my lipstick."

❋❋❋

On her way to the offices of Hobbs Family Practice, Liz smiled at the memory of their bedroom adventures. Particularly amusing was Maggie "remembering how to have sex." Maggie had never been as expressive as Lucy, but when thoroughly aroused she became a molten volcano of passion. Liz remembered her legs clamped around her while they used one of Lucy's favorite double-ended toys. This morning Liz felt a little sensitive below after all the enthusiastic activity. Her hips were a bit cranky. Although the attention of both women flattered her ego and made her feel like a stud, sometimes making love with the two of them wore her out. *Stolz, you need to stop thinking about sex*, she thought, then found herself picturing Lucy's face when she came.

Without even remembering how she got there, Liz pulled into her reserved space in the practice parking lot. She squinted against the bright sun in the Eastern sky. Yes, it was wonderful to have its warm light, now that the season was finally turning.

She accepted the sleepy greetings of the patients in the waiting room as she passed and headed to the staff office to review her morning schedule with the practice manager.

"Cherie is in your office waiting for you," Ginny said in a grave tone. Liz had never known her to be especially interested in politics, but as the admin for the town's only family practice, Ginny heard everything. By now, the news of the drama at last night's meeting must have reached her ears.

"Please ask Bobbie if she can meet with my first patient if my meeting with Cherie runs long."

"You got it, Dr. Liz." Ginny handed her a printout of her morning schedule.

Usually, Cherie beamed a smile when she saw Liz, but this morning she looked positively grim. She raised her compelling blue-green eyes as Liz closed the door. Clearly, she'd been crying.

"What's going on, Cherie?" asked Liz, dropping into her desk chair.

"Brenda doesn't deserve this."

"She certainly doesn't."

"She's awake all hours of the night, staring at her tablet, rehearsing responses she wished she could say to those damned reporters. Because she can't sleep, I can't sleep. I need to take some time off to deal with her and the kids, and my own stress. Lucy needs me more than you do, but I'm going to ask her for some time off too."

"That's fine, Cherie, I completely understand. But why are you coming to me? Dr. Hsu is the managing partner now."

Cherie rolled her eyes and waved dismissively. "Everyone knows you're still the boss." Then, she shook her head. "I'm sorry, Liz. I'm cranky because I haven't been getting much sleep."

"That's not good. Do you need a script for a sedative?"

"Hell, no! I want this whole nightmare to go away!" Cherie said in a voice louder than usual, then looked shocked at her own outburst. "God, Liz, I'm sorry. I'm just so stressed. We all got through Covid together. We started rebuilding our lives, and then this asshole gets in and creates all this division!"

"It's worse than any of us imagined," Liz commiserated. "This division is making us hate one another. The Hobbs PD isn't the enemy. It's the same community force it was before the ICE surge. They're the same good, decent people who run marathons for breast cancer and let kids dunk them at Harbor Fest. It's not fair!"

Cherie covered her face with her hands. Liz realized she was weeping. She got up and gently rubbed Cherie's shoulder. "If you want a hug, I've got one for you," she said quietly. Cherie began to sob. Liz soothingly rubbed her back until Cherie stood up and buried her face in her shoulder.

When Cherie finally let her go, Liz snatched some tissues from the box on her desk and handed them to her. "This might sound wrong, but I'm more worried about Brenda than I am about you. You express your emotions and know how to process them. Brenda is an old-style butch like me. We were trained to emulate male grit. Not good for men...or women in times like this."

"Oh, Brenda cries. She might act tough, but like you, she's an old softie."

"Well, thanks," said Liz with an off-center grin. "I see you too."

Cherie sputtered out soft laughter. Then she became completely serious and looked Liz straight in the eye. "Thank God for you and Brenda. We need your strength and courage. She was telling the truth when she answered that question. She *was* trying to keep ICE out of Hobbs."

"I got that, but I don't think that was her plan."

"We don't all plan consciously."

"Sounds like something Lucy would say."

"Well, listen to your wife, Liz. She's smarter than you are about some things. You may be a brilliant doctor, but Lucy knows how people work."

Liz nodded, perceiving the truth of Cherie's statement. "Well, here's the bottom line, Cherie. I am here for you and Brenda in any way you need me to be. Yes, you can take off as much time as you need. We'll manage. And I don't expect you to tell on your wife, but please tell me how I can help Brenda. We both know she'll play stoic instead of admitting she needs help."

"Oh, believe me, Liz, I will make Brenda ask for help if I have to put dynamite under her ass!"

Liz drew back a little at Cherie's fierce words. "I know how much you love her."

"I do, and I will not let this stupid thing destroy her!"

"Neither will I, if there's anything I can do about it."

When their eyes met, Liz felt like she was swearing an operatic blood oath.

❄❄❄

Liz's meeting with Cherie had been brief, so she was able to meet with her first patient, stay on schedule, and even leave for her lunch date with Olivia a few minutes early. Liz lived for those days, when everything went right. She smiled at the green arrow at the light where she needed to turn on the road leading to Dockside, the restaurant where Liz and Olivia had been meeting for lunch and cocktails since they were officers of the Hobbs Chamber of Commerce.

Before Olivia had become the town manager and began keeping regular hours, she'd often whipped up one of her gourmet lunches at her enormous oceanside home. The Pseudo-Victorian building was the largest house on Gull Island, and all of Hobbs, for that matter. Maggie liked to emphasize how ridiculous it was by describing it as "obscenely large."

Today, Liz didn't mind eating at their familiar haunt because they always had her favorite version of "lazy lobster" on the menu. She was wearing a brand-new jacket today and didn't relish the messy job of cracking lobster claws. The memory of spurting lobster juice all over Tom Simmons' glasses suddenly brought a grin to her face.

When Liz arrived, Olivia was seated at their usual window table overlooking the harbor. Turned to gaze at the light dancing on the water, she was unaware of Liz admiring her elegant profile. With her fine features, perfect makeup, and hairdo, Olivia looked every inch an old-money patrician. In fact, she'd come from humble circumstances. Her enormous wealth came from her own hard work. She'd earned her scholarships to Ivy League schools but had deliberately chosen Michael Enright as her husband to get a seat on the stock exchange. Her persona of effortless elegance had been carefully crafted. Everything about Olivia Enright was a fabrication, except the cunning and business acumen that had allowed her to create one of the most successful hedge funds on Wall Street. Liz loved her chutzpah and brilliance, but most of all her determination to make it in a man's world, no matter what it took.

Olivia glanced at her gold watch when Liz sat down. "You're on time for a change, Dr. Stud."

"Stop it, Olivia," Liz hissed as she sat down. "Someone will hear you."

"Who?" Olivia swept her hand dramatically around her. "There's no one here except us."

It was true. At that time of year, the only patrons were a couple of men at the bar, watching hockey reruns while they ate their lunch.

Olivia looked Liz over from head to toe. "You're looking quite natty, Dr. Stud. New Jacket? It suits you. Love that plaid. Très chic!"

"I'm glad blazers are in again. Throwing on a jacket makes it easy to look professional."

The waitress, another woman past retirement age but still working, approached. "Hi, Dr. Stolz, we have a new IPA. Would you like to try it?"

"Thanks, Kathy, I'm going to pass on the alcohol today. I'll have tonic water with a lime twist."

Olivia stared at Liz with exaggerated horror. "A virgin tonic? Liz, you're kidding."

"Nope. I have patients to see this afternoon."

Olivia shrugged and took a sip from her martini, obviously to rub it in that she could imbibe while Liz couldn't. The waitress chuckled and went away with Liz's drink order.

"I bet I know why you wanted to have lunch with me," Liz said after the waitress was out of earshot.

Olivia's piercing blue eyes engaged hers. "You do, do you? Tell me." She leaned forward showing her intention to listen.

Liz wanted to laugh at the idea that Olivia thought she could play that game with her, but she didn't even crack a smile. "You heard about the near riot at the Hobbs Dems last night."

"Who hasn't? That was quite a scene. The town police chief

and her captain scurrying away to escape an angry mob. 'Off with her head!'" Olivia quoted from the old movies. One of Olivia's best qualities was her penchant for dramatic sarcasm.

"It was impressive," Liz agreed. "A few minutes more and there could have been a fist fight. I could have punched a few people myself." Liz barked out a chuckle. "I'm exaggerating, of course, but I'd never seen a pack of septuagenarians come so close to blows. It was like watching a food fight in a nursing home." Liz shook her head, thinking, *what am I saying? I'll be seventy soon myself.* "I shouldn't make fun of old people, being one myself."

"You are not *old*, Liz. You will never be old. You think and live *young.*"

"Oh, I'm sure younger people would beg to differ. It's a matter of perspective." Liz looked up to see Olivia's curious stare. "But you didn't invite me to talk about my age. What are your thoughts about what happened last night?"

"Well, as you can guess, I'm not happy."

Liz nodded. "Things are getting out of hand. But Olivia, you're the town manager. You could do something about it."

Olivia appeared momentarily pensive. "First of all, I have enormous respect for Brenda Harrison. She is an excellent police chief with far more knowledge and experience than this little town deserves. Second, this whole controversy is ridiculous. The Hobbs police aren't cosplaying ICE. Third, I'm trying not to use my usual tactics. I've turned over a new leaf."

Liz doubted the truth of that statement. From the cut-throat world of finance Olivia had to learn to control her subordinates with a steel grip, exactly the same way Liz used to keep her junior staff in line. Unlearning such harsh conditioning at this point in life was virtually impossible. Yes, Olivia had somewhat modified her imperious style, but the need to oversee every single detail persisted. Rather than dispute Olivia's claim, Liz allowed her to enjoy her delusions.

The waitress arrived. Liz ordered the "lazy lobster" over pasta. She sat drumming her fingers on her thigh while Olivia made the waitress repeat the specials four times and then ordered her favorite off the regular menu. As much as Liz admired Olivia, people who abused their privilege annoyed her. Not that Liz was innocent. She flagrantly disregarded the local speed limits because of her friendship with the police chief.

As soon as the waitress left, Olivia returned to their earlier conversation. "I've wondered why the select board hasn't gotten involved. They listen to those idiots go on and on about this ICE business at every meeting, even when it isn't on the agenda. And those people just won't shut up!"

"I think the select board members respect Brenda and the work she does," Liz opined. "They should. She's done a great job for Hobbs."

"Let's be real, Liz. They're afraid of her."

"What? Afraid of Brenda?"

"They don't know her like we do. I can see why they'd be taken in by her tough New York City cop act. She plays it as well as your take-no-prisoners surgeon's game." Liz made a face, but she was flattered by the idea that people were still afraid of her.

Liz gave her a canny look. "Of course, you've talked to the board. What's their *official* opinion?"

"Dear God, Liz. In a small town like this, there are no "official" opinions. One guy runs a property management business. One owns the hardware store that his great grandfather founded. There's a lobsterman, and the headwaiter at La Scala. The rest of them are retired from inconsequential jobs. Half of them sleep through the meetings, even though it's on closed circuit TV and everyone can see them nodding off. What do you expect?"

Liz could see Olivia's point. "It would be better if the town had a point of view and professional media advice. My lawyer advised me to hire a publicist when my malpractice suit from that actress hit. Good thing too. I would have told the press to go fuck themselves."

"Of that, I have no doubt," said Olivia with a knowing look. "Yes, a professional spokesperson would certainly help. The Hobbs Police Department is so small they share admins with the other safety services. They come up with these cutesy public relations campaigns like letting the kids shoot them with paint balls and drown them at Harbor Fest, but none of them has a clue what to do with negative publicity, Brenda included."

"See, that surprises me," said Liz. "She had a high-profile community relations job in the NYPD before she came up here."

"Yes, but that doesn't apply because this is the media we're talking about. And she has a blind spot because what she did wasn't *wrong*. It just looks wrong because of the politics."

When the waitress arrived with their meals, they instantly changed the subject to expectations for the summer season. "And that's another thing. This silly controversy is getting national attention," said Olivia, stabbing her fork into her pasta like she loathed it. "That certainly won't help the tourist business!"

Liz put on her chamber of commerce hat and looked at the problem from the business perspective. As it was, tourism was down since the pandemic ended. People had flocked to the great outdoors as a respite from the misery of confinement, but once the rebound was over, the number of summer visitors had declined. Posting on news stories, commenters swore they would never return to Hobbs again or would skip it on their next trip to Maine. While the catchy alliterative moniker, "The stain on Maine" pertained to the police department, it had given the entire town a black eye.

Liz picked out the chunks of lobster before digging into the overabundance of angel hair pasta on her plate. "So, what are you going to do about it?" she asked and popped a big piece of claw meat into her mouth.

Olivia took a long sip of her martini. "Right now? Nothing."

"You could throw her a lifeline."

"Of course, I could. But it's always been my policy to let my subordinates fix their own messes. Hopefully, they learn something from the experience."

"At this point in her career, Brenda isn't going to benefit from the lesson."

"No, but if I or the select board involve ourselves, then we'll go down with her." Olivia focused her piercing blue eyes on Liz. "And why don't you do something? You're her friend."

Liz exhaled a long sigh. "I've tried to explain why it looks so bad, but she just doesn't get it, or if she does, she's resisting my advice. She thinks backing down would make her look like she's incompetent."

"Oh, for God's sake!" exclaimed Olivia rolling her eyes. "After all these years, we all know she's competent. Refusing to budge just makes her look stubborn and contrary. Her blindness is going to sink her career."

"I hope not. She needs this job, even more since they adopted those kids."

"Well, then she should think long and hard about what's really important to her—being right, or her family." Olivia's harsh statement sounded like a threat.

Liz's phone vibrated in her pocket. She pulled it out and glanced at the screen. "Excuse me while I take this. It's my wife."

"Which one?" asked Olivia, arching a brow.

"The legal one."

"Oh, Lucy. Yes, you must take *her* call," replied Olivia primly and went back to her meal.

Chapter 8

Lucy could hear the brittle irritation in Liz's voice. "Yes, Lucy?" she asked in a brisk professional tone that barely concealed her impatience.

"Are you eating?" Lucy asked tentatively.

The terse reply: "Yes."

"So, you can't talk now," Lucy ventured.

"No."

Lucy began to wonder if calling Liz had been a good idea. Yes, she knew that Liz was having lunch with Olivia and probably sitting right across from her, but Lucy's panic had momentarily gotten the best of her.

"Can this wait until I finish eating, or should I step away for privacy?"

"No, no. Finish your lunch," Lucy said. "I just wanted to tell you that Maggie invited the Harrisons for dinner."

"That's nice," Liz replied in that bland tone Maggie called her 'doctor voice.'

"Finish eating. Call me when you can. I love you."

"Me too," said Liz. She ended the call without saying goodbye, but that wasn't unusual for Liz. She seemed to find the awkward final amenity a bother. When Lucy asked why, Liz blamed the pace of surgical practice, when every minute counted.

Analyzing Liz's lack of social grace calmed Lucy despite her nearly paralyzing panic.

Why couldn't Maggie get it through her head that she had to keep a low profile in this marriage or whatever it was? Lucy knew that she wasn't deliberately trying to sabotage Lucy's priesthood. She was being generous and spontaneous when she'd invited Cherie. They'd all witnessed the devastating effect the previous night's meeting had on Brenda. Maggie was merely trying to help.

Lucy could understand why her wives didn't feel her urgency about keeping their domestic situation to themselves. Liz considered herself retired, although she probably worked as hard as when she was a full-time surgeon and chief of the department at Yale, maybe even harder because she had revived a dying family practice. There was such a shortage of primary care providers in Maine, that no matter how many new doctors or practitioners Liz and Amy added to their staff, they couldn't keep up. Now that Liz was approaching seventy and really wanted to retire, she couldn't justify it. Because she was the senior partner, no one was going to fire Liz for an unconventional sexual relationship.

Maggie, who was two years older than Liz, had retired three times from college teaching, but they kept begging her to come back. She was a gifted theater director, who had impeccable credentials, including a starring Broadway run in *Les Misérables*. With her dramatic long white hair and eclectic style, Maggie had become an icon of aging creativity. Everyone forgave brilliant artists their eccentric lifestyles.

If Lucy were merely an aging opera star, she might be able to get away with their unconventional arrangement. As a priest, she was supposed to set a moral example for her congregation and the community. As a woman and a lesbian, she was already doubly held to a higher standard. Although her bishop was himself an out homosexual and open-minded, polyamory was probably a bridge too far, even for him.

Hoping to ease her nerves, Lucy got up and went into the breakroom to make herself a cup of coffee. Because she drank so much coffee, caffeine paradoxically calmed her. But today, her hands were shaking as she attempted to spoon the grounds into a single-use pod.

"Lucy!" said a male voice behind her. Lucy turned around and saw the associate rector, Tom Simmons. She could now doubly relax because Tom already *knew*. He'd sensed something different when she'd returned from her retreat with Liz and Maggie after last year's disappointing election result. As her priest and spiritual director, Tom had deserved the truth, so she'd told him.

When Tom saw the look on her face, his bushy gray brows shot up. "Oh, no! Lucy, what's wrong?" She opened her mouth but couldn't speak, no matter how hard she tried to form words. When he opened his arms, she fell into them. "Oh, Lucy, whatever it is, it will be okay," he said, soothingly stroking her back. She clung to him with all her might. He strengthened his embrace but held her tenderly. "You're shaking."

"I know. I couldn't even fill my coffee pod."

Gently, Tom released her. "Let me do it for you," he said with a smile. He skillfully filled the pod and set up the coffee maker to brew a cup. He leaned against the counter while the dark liquid brewed into Lucy's special cup. Her daughter, Emily, had given it to her. It had a cartoon of a woman wearing a horned helmet with the caption: "Don't make me use my opera voice." Tom glanced around to make sure the room was empty before asking, "Now, what's going on?"

Lucy took a long deep breath. "I thought I'd be okay living with this big secret. Now, I'm not so sure."

Tom nodded knowingly. "I understand. Before I moved to Hobbs, I was in the closet for almost forty years. It's not easy living a double life."

"But you finally came out. I'm not sure I ever can."

"Oh, you could, if you weren't the rector of a significant church." He spooned a teaspoon of sugar into Lucy's cup and added exactly the right amount of half-and-half. What a good friend he was to know how she took her coffee, but Tom was also an extraordinarily observant priest. He handed her the cup, which she sipped gratefully, holding it with two hands, because they were still shaking. Tom glanced at his watch. "I came in early to deal with my email, but I have half an hour before my first appointment. Come down to my office and tell me about it."

Tom's office, like all the rooms in their rectory *cum* parish house, was furnished with vintage fumed oak furniture from the era in which the building was constructed. As a woodworker, Liz had instantly recognized its value and suggested auctioning it to pay some of the church's debts. Lucy would never agree. The Craftsman furniture was part of St. Margaret's legacy in Hobbs, and it needed to stay with the building for posterity.

The heavy leather sofas were reminiscent of a Victorian men's club. The wall-to-wall bookcases were filled with theology and exegetical texts. Tom, with his mild-mannered, scholarly demeanor, fit perfectly into this environment that exuded academic refinement.

He invited Lucy to sit down before taking his usual seat in a worn leather club chair. He got right to the point, but his voice was kind. "Okay, Lucy, tell me all about it. What precipitated this meltdown?"

Lucy took a moment to collect her thoughts which lay scattered around her like fallen leaves. "Maggie ran into Cherie Harrison in the supermarket and invited her family to dinner."

Tom steepled his fingers and tapped his lips to hide a smile. "It's always that one little, innocent thing that blows up our carefully constructed wall of protection. That's kind of Maggie to offer Cherie and her family comfort. That was quite a scene at that meeting last night. The Harrisons need all the support they can get. I hope the kids aren't being bullied at school for what their mother is doing."

Lucy couldn't help but look shocked. She hadn't even considered that possibility. "That's so unfair. Between losing their parents and that shooting at their school, they've gone through so much."

"That's how we see it, Lucy, but in this era of unbridled cruelty, no one seems to have any guardrails. At another time, Brenda's decision might not even be questioned. Now, she's 'the stain on Maine.' I know they mean the whole police department, but it's obviously directed at her personally. I don't envy her one bit."

"Neither do I, and I know she needs her friends more than ever. Liz and Brenda go back a long time. But the more people come into our family life, the greater the chance our secret will come out."

"That was always a risk, Lucy. I know you. Within the bounds of professional confidence and your counseling roles, you are the most genuinely honest person I know. You live your truth in the best possible way. The duplicity must be excruciating for you."

Tom's astute observation nearly caused Lucy to burst out crying, but she restrained herself because she didn't want him to see her out of control again. Unfortunately, she couldn't keep her eyes from filling. Tom saw the tears forming, and his expression softened. "Oh, Lucy. I'm so sorry."

"Don't be sorry, Tom. I got myself into this mess."

"But Lucy, it's not a mess, and you did it out of love. Give yourself some grace. You entered this admittedly unconventional relationship because you *love* these women."

"That doesn't mean I should have acted on my love. There are some boundaries that shouldn't be crossed."

Tom's blue eyes, usually so merry, became serious as he studied her. "That's what we are taught to say as priests, but we both know the wide variety of human behavior doesn't fit tidy rules. I'm sure you're not the first member of the clergy to be involved in such a relationship, nor will you be the last. The rules exist to keep people from hurting themselves and others. Ergo, if you're not hurting anyone, or yourself, what's the harm in what you're doing?"

"I know, Tom. I know!" said Lucy jumping up from her chair, mostly because she was now too agitated to remain seated, but also because she needed a tissue to blow her nose. "How can I keep this secret and be there for the people I love? The more people know, the more likely it is that *everyone* will know."

Tom leaned on his hand while he thought. Finally, he asked, "Lucy, what's the worst thing that could happen?"

"There's a scandal. The vestry fires me. The bishop pulls my priest's license, and I'm done. Maybe I should just confess to the bishop and get it over with."

Tom stoked his salt-and-pepper beard. "I don't think that would be a good idea. Greene may be one of us, but he's also under a microscope as a gay bishop. Plus, I've never considered him a theological powerhouse. He has a winning smile, and he's great at publicity for the Church, but he's not especially skillful at pastoral matters."

Lucy stared at Tom because he rarely criticized their bishop. She knew that Tom and his husband had decided to get married in Connecticut to preempt the bishop's offer to do the honors, but otherwise, her associate rector mostly kept his opinions of Greene to himself.

"So what do I do? Wait until it explodes?"

"I don't know," said Tom honestly, but then added, "I think you wait and see what happens. There is no immediate threat. Why not take things one day at a time?"

"As you aptly described the situation, it's excruciating."

"Only because you keep worrying about what other people think. Poor Brenda and Cherie are so wrapped up in their own troubles, they're not even thinking about who's in your bed. They're focused on their own troubles."

Lucy sat down again. Tom was right. Of course, he was right. "I'm making my own hell," she admitted.

"Yes, you are. If you truly love these women and aren't using them for your own pleasure, you aren't doing anything objectively wrong. Yes, you are violating the Christian principles in your ordination vows, but really, who completely honors them? I know I don't. Maybe that makes me a liar or a bad priest, but, like you, I am only *human*."

After a long moment, Lucy finally said, "Maybe I should leave the priesthood."

The statement made Tom sit up straight. He frowned, then settled back into his seat. "Yes, you could, but the congregation adores you. You care for your flock like a parent, gently guiding them and loving them fiercely. To them, you are truly *Mother* Lucy. They would be devastated if you left. You don't want to hurt them, do you?"

Directly confronted with the facts, Lucy realized that leaving her congregation would break her heart. She stared at her feet and shook her head.

"But if I were forced to leave because of a scandal, wouldn't that be even more hurtful?"

"Perhaps, but we're not there yet, are we? And it may never happen. Meanwhile, you will have preemptively ended your career as a priest."

"But how can I continue without being a hypocrite?"

"Aren't we all? I know how your theological studies challenged your faith. Things are no longer black and white. Lucy, you share that burden with most progressive theologians. You and I have studied Bible history and criticism. We know that scripture is a patchwork quilt of iron age stories written by human beings, not the literal word of God. We've read religious history and see the common threads with other faiths. Ours is neither unique, nor even the most inspiring. We know how European culture changed the Church for better or worse. In short, we are overeducated doubters. I know it sounds harsh, Rev. Dr. Bartlett, but welcome to the club of grown-up Christians."

The words hit Lucy's ears like sharp stones, but she knew they were completely true. The coziness of believing the dogma and Bible stories was for simpler minds and children, not professional theologians and priests. As if trying to digest this painful truth, Lucy swallowed hard. In the silent room, the sound seemed unnaturally loud.

Unfortunately, Tom wasn't finished delivering his painful message. "Living your faith means following Jesus, and you do it better than anyone I know. You listen with your entire body. You love with all your heart. You give until you have nothing left. That's what makes you a perfect priest, not how well you follow the rules. Don't give up so easily, Lucy. Many people need you, including me."

Lucy's heart was so full that the dam finally broke. Tears silently streamed down her face. Tom got up to bring her the box of tissues. He bent to speak near her ear. "Do you mind if I use your office to meet with my client?"

Ripping tissues out of the box by the fistful, Lucy shook her head.

***

By the time her first client showed up an hour later, Lucy's emotional storm had calmed but she was still unsettled. She could retreat behind her neutral therapist's face to avoid showing her internal turmoil, but she felt sad her client wasn't getting her full attention. With Tom's words ringing in her ears, she strained to concentrate on what the young woman was saying. Like many, she was finding the news a daily threat to her mental health. She was prone to panic attacks, and the constant chaos was making them worse.

"Have you tried the meditation techniques we practiced?" Lucy asked.

"I've tried everything! Deep breathing. Guided meditation. Blocking social media and the news. I'm still stressed!"

"Maybe you should ask your doctor to adjust your medication," Lucy gently suggested.

"That's my last option, but I'd rather not take more pills. That's why I'm here talking to you."

Lucy tried to keep politics out of her therapy sessions and her ministry because she considered it inappropriate, but these were extraordinary times and the threat was grave. Even the bishop of Washington had taken a stand in her inauguration day sermon at the National Cathedral. She'd begged for mercy for LGBT people and immigrants. For speaking a Christian truth, she was trashed by right wing media and politicians. Tiny Marianne Budde was one of Lucy's heroes, because she had stood up to the president before, when he'd invaded one of the churches in her diocese for a photo op. Lucy blocked the image of him holding a Bible upside down so she could come back to the conversation.

"You're not the only one losing sleep over this chaos. The human mind isn't built to be shocked every day with new threats."

"I'm glad you said that. I kept thinking it was just me."

Lucy shook her head. "It's not *you*, Amanda. It's everyone who cares. It's everyone who believes in the rule of law and our Constitution. Everyone who thinks women should have a voice, and people of color aren't less than we are. Everyone who thinks immigrants aren't all drug dealers and criminals!" Lucy managed to stop herself before continuing the rant, realizing the conversation with Tom had wound her up. The last thing her client needed was more agitation. "Sorry about the political speech," Lucy said, lowering her eyes.

"No, thank *you*. I wish more people would speak up, especially ministers and priests. No offense, but I hate religion because of what the Evangelicals have done to hurt gays and women. They're not afraid to be political. Why should you be?"

"I'm hoping liberal churches like mine take a higher profile position, but I try to avoid alienating people."

"The Christian Nationalists don't care. Why should you?" The young woman's eyes were suddenly glowing with passion. Before Lucy had mentioned politics, they had stared dully or glittered with anxiety. "I feel crazy because I'm so helpless. Just hearing you share your worries makes me feel better."

"Have you read Marianne Edgar Budde's book, *How We Learn to Be Brave*?" Lucy asked. "If not, I recommend it."

Amanda's lips curved into a sly smile. "No, but I tried to read your book on sex. Couldn't get past the first chapter. More religion than I expected."

"It was my doctoral dissertation for a theology degree," Lucy explained. "I simplified it for lay readers."

"Not this lay reader. I tried, but it was way over my head."

Lucy doubted that claim. Amanda was a middle-school teacher with a good head on her shoulders. More likely, her anxiety had made it difficult to concentrate. When Lucy's nerves were jangled, she found it difficult to read and had to do something active instead. Sex was a favorite solution to that problem, she thought with a little smile.

"If you're really interested, I can give you the Cliff Notes version, but not during our session."

"What are Cliff Notes?" Amanda asked, looking puzzled.

"Never mind. Before your time," Lucy said with a laugh. "We have a couple more minutes. Do you want me to send a note to your doctor to recommend an increase in your medication?"

"Sure. That would help."

"Who's your doctor?" Lucy asked, opening her tablet to make a note.

Amanda suddenly giggled. "My doctor? Your wife, Dr. Stolz. Couldn't you just tell her when you get home?"

Lucy felt her face warm and pursed her lips. "I'll send a note instead."

❋❋❋

When Lucy drove in, she found a volleyball game in the parking area in front of the garage. Against tall, competitive women like Liz and Brenda, the Harrison kids didn't stand a chance, but the adults passed them the ball and rescued their fouls.

Lucy parked in the woods. She tried to pass, but a red-faced, sweaty Liz landed a kiss on her cheek while still managing to spike the ball across the net.

"Hey, Lucy! Heads up!" called Brenda. In a surprise to them all, Lucy punched the ball back over the net. She waved as she carried her bags into the house.

Before she could get away, Megan, Brenda's youngest, tackled her legs. "Lu-u-u-cy," she crooned. "I want to come with you." Lucy, who didn't enjoy active sports either, sympathized, so she took the blond child by the hand and led her into the house. "Smells good," the girl said, as Lucy hung up their coats. With both Maggie and Cherie cooking, dinner would be a kid-friendly feast with a gourmet flair. Like an obedient puppy, Megan followed Lucy into the kitchen. She helped her up into one of the island stools.

Maggie pointed to her throat. Once again, Lucy had forgotten to take off her collar. "It was a long day," she explained with a sigh and reached up to unpin it. Maggie carefully wiped her hands on a towel and came around to help.

Lucy tried to ignore Cherie's curious stare. All the women gathered there tonight were comfortable with casual affection—a hand on an arm or thigh, a half hug, or a light, teasing punch. Liz and Brenda were always pawing at each other like teammates in a locker room. *Why should Maggie's helping me be any different?* Lucy thought, defending herself against imaginary criticism.

"We're having a Tex-Mex celebration tonight," Cherie announced. "Tacos, of course, because the kids like them, but we also have enchiladas and burritos, along with the fixins'. We decided to eat ourselves into feeling good again."

"Sounds like a plan," said Lucy, slipping her collar into the pocket of her cardigan. It didn't quite fit and the linen loop stuck out. "Would you mind if I changed, so I can really join in on the fun?"

"You do that, honey," Cherie said, kicking up a leg to show off her yoga pants. They clung to her elegant figure in exactly the right places. "I'll mix some more Margaritas. We have a head start on you, but you can catch up when you get back."

Lucy looked both ways to make sure no one was looking before pressing the elevator button. Tonight, climbing the three flights to the bedroom felt like an impossible feat.

She had just changed into yoga pants and a hoodie when Liz swept into the bedroom. "I've been sent to tell you that dinner is ready." Damp with perspiration, she scooped Lucy into her arms.

"Don't mind the sweat. I came up to change my shirt." She peeled it off and wiped her armpits with it before putting on another Tee. "Cherie has your Margarita waiting for you."

"I just need a moment to myself. I've been "on" all day and coming home to a whole gang and active children is a lot."

"I get it, but don't be mad at Maggie. This is exactly what Brenda and Cherie need, a relaxing night with friends."

"I'm not mad. I panicked when Maggie invited them again without warning. I guess I'm a little paranoid today."

Liz stepped back. She arched a brow as she studied Lucy. "Lucy, you're overthinking this."

"That's what Tom said."

"Well, good for Tom for talking sense to you," said Liz, sitting down on the bed. "Obviously, you're not listening to *me*."

"I do listen to you, but Tom and I can discuss it on another level. I can hear what he tells me differently."

"If Tom knows how to cut through the static and send you a clear signal, I'm glad. I know how scared you are that someone will find out about us, but if they do, they do. We can't live in constant fear. Besides, it makes us look weird, which is like a neon sign flashing that something's wrong. Nothing's wrong. We're fine. So, let's act like we are."

Lucy sighed and shook her head. "You make it sound so easy."

"It is easy. Besides, we have no choice. This is how it is now." Liz grinned that endearing off-centered grin and got up. "Now, let's go downstairs or people will think we're fucking up here."

Lucy swatted her arm. "Liz! You are so bad!"

"Which is why you love me," said Liz, stealing a kiss. "Now, come on!"

Chapter 9

"This is the fucking longest meeting they've ever had," growled Liz, glancing at Lucy for sympathy. Liz was cooking tonight because Maggie had a hastily scheduled Zoom meeting with team leaders of the Hobbs Democrats. Fortunately, the meal Liz had planned was incredibly quick to make—Haddock with beurre noisette and capers.

More than anything, Liz hated unproductive downtime. Tonight, she was especially impatient because she was famished. "What the hell can they be talking about for almost two fucking hours?" she asked, glaring at the clock over the sink like it had offended her.

"Maybe they're debriefing about that crazy meeting last month?" Lucy suggested mildly.

"It was crazy, wasn't it?" Liz refreshed Lucy's glass of pinot grigio. "Have you ever seen anything like that?"

"Church meetings can get hot sometimes, but Episcopalians tend to be understated. They hide behind their nervous smiles. That's also why they never get anything done."

Liz snickered. In a fit of generosity, she'd made the mistake of volunteering for the church property committee. Once she'd figured out the group of retired men had no intention of fixing anything, she quit in disgust. "It's always the same in volunteer organizations. Little people, who never accomplished anything in their lives, suddenly want to be big shots."

"Ego plays a big part," Lucy agreed. "But what can you do? My main role in my church committees is trying to get people to play nice together. Unfortunately, I don't always succeed."

"Remember last year when Hobbs Rod and Gun wanted to throw me out because I supported the new yellow flag law? I'm their only NRA-certified gun safety instructor. They need me because they get their insurance through the NRA." Liz still carried a grudge against the club members who'd voted her out of office and then wanted her thrown out of the club. What hurt most of all was that she used to call some of those people her friends. "We used to agree on the importance of gun safety. Now, you either support 'Constitutional carry' and want no constraints or you're a *librul*." Liz drawled the last word to imitate what the other side called anyone on the left. "Everyone who uses a gun needs to learn basic safety. This is why kids kill themselves with their parents' guns, and guys shoot themselves in the crotch. Dumb asses!"

Lucy's eyes glazed over as they usually did when Liz talked about guns. She didn't hate them with Cherie's passion or fear them like Maggie, but she'd made it clear she didn't like them. Seeing Lucy wasn't listening, Liz shut up on this subject. "I'm going to cook. Maggie can eat when she gets here."

Liz cut a generous knob of butter into the pan she would use to sauté the fish. While she waited for the butter to melt, she opened the refrigerator and took out a beer, an IPA she hadn't tried before. Despite her foul mood at dinner being delayed, she felt adventurous.

"Better put it in a glass before Maggie gets here," Lucy warned, watching her drink straight from the bottle.

"Goddamned women," Liz grumbled under her breath and opened the cabinet to get a beer glass. "Can't live with them or without them!"

"Stop complaining, Liz. You love us."

Shaking her head, Maggie came into the kitchen.

"About time you came down," said Liz to her as she passed. "What the hell were you talking about for almost two hours?"

"Guess," said Maggie and poured a glass of wine for herself. "The chair said she wanted to clarify what the roles of the team leaders should be before the next meeting. She invited us all to this meeting, but its real purpose was to call Greg on the carpet. First, we had to listen to that annoyingly deferential Maura deliver a sermon on how there would be growing pains because the team structure is new. Then Greg took over the meeting with a fifteen-minute diatribe on how frustrated he was that the meeting with Brenda was adjourned while he still had so many questions."

"He's so full of shit!" Liz said. "Brenda told me he met with her privately and grilled her for hours before the meeting. What other questions could he have? That fucker just wanted to grandstand!"

"Yup," Maggie agreed. "And I'm sure everyone in the meeting saw through his nonsense, but no one dared to stop him."

"Did he have that crazed look in his eye?" Liz asked. "People are afraid of crazy people."

"Liz..." Lucy gently warned.

Liz turned to her. "Okay, maybe he's not crazy, but I keep telling him he needs to stop getting so excited or he'll have a stroke."

"Obviously, he's not listening to your advice, Dr. Stolz." Maggie sat down beside Lucy at the kitchen island.

Liz grunted in disgust and picked up the sauté pan to distribute the melted butter. "Greg thinks a lot of himself. His fake humility annoys the hell out of me. Classic passive aggression."

"Since when did you become a psychotherapist, Liz?" Lucy asked dryly.

"Lucy, you don't need a degree in psychology to diagnose that asshole!"

Lucy sighed. "In this case, you're right. He's passive aggressive... and an asshole."

Maggie stared at Lucy with faux shock. "Lucy! You're a priest."

Lucy assumed a demure expression. "So?"

At the stove, Liz laughed heartily.

"But wait, there's more!" said Maggie, sounding like a late-night TV commercial hawking a hot new invention. "Each team went through its mission and scope. Then we got to Greg. He's been trying to start a Substack blog to influence persuadable voters. The secretary tactfully explained that opinion blogs aren't part of the mission of a town political committee. Of course, Greg lost his mind."

"Of course, because it's all about Greg, and his pet projects," said Liz, easing the fish into the pan.

"He turned purple," said Maggie.

"He turned purple?" Liz asked, frowning. "That's not good."

Maggie continued her description. "Then he said in a dramatic whisper, 'If that's so, I'll have to resign from this team.' He left the meeting. Maura pleaded with the chair. 'Please ask Greg to come back. We need him. He's brilliant! A visionary!'"

Liz opened her mouth and pointed to her throat.

"I agree," said Maggie. "It was nauseating."

"What are they? A cult?"

Maggie laughed. "It's beginning to look like it. I can't figure out what happened. I worked with Maura and Pat on the scholarship committee. They always seemed like sensible people, retired high-school math teachers. Apparently, they took that news literacy class Greg taught at the community college, and now, they're his disciples."

"Jesus Fucking Christ!" Liz exclaimed. "You don't mean that stupid class the community college canceled because no one signed up?"

"Yes, that one," Maggie confirmed.

Liz flipped the fish and spooned some capers into the frying pan. "Okay, Lucy, pour yourself a glass of wine. We're going to eat dinner."

"I see someone already set the table," said Maggie, glancing into the breakfast nook. "Is there anything I can do?"

Liz handed her the salad bowl. "Toss the salad."

"What's new in your world, Lucy?" Maggie asked, mixing the greens in the bowl.

"My agent told me I'm booked for *Four Last Songs* at Aix, and La Scala wants me to sing Marguerite in Gounod's *Faust* in May. I have a bunch of European gigs along with the Chicago Lyric and San Francisco Opera."

"But no Met?" Maggie asked gently.

"She embarrassed the fuckers by making them apologize for covering up the sexual abuse," Liz said. "Now, they're getting her back."

This time Lucy just rolled her eyes at the F-bomb. It had been one too many. "They're having a lot of financial problems. They were trying to get younger subscribers with original operas, but it's not working. They've had to dip into the endowment just to keep the lights on."

"God, that would be awful!" said Maggie. "I remember Liz taking me to see *Madama Butterfly* when we were in college. I was in awe to be in *The Met*."

"Maybe I'll get a role next season. We're negotiating," Lucy said, but she didn't sound hopeful. Suddenly, she brightened. "But Simone suggested I teach a girls' martial arts class for the youth group."

"Like you have time with all your other gigs," Maggie said, shaking her head.

"But it would be so much fun. Don't you just love the idea of empowering girls?"

"All right, gang. Dinner's ready." Liz took the vegetables warming in the stove out and brought them to the table. "Please sit down." After the others took their seats, Liz served the fish directly from the skillet.

"This is my favorite meal," said Maggie as Liz put a portion of fish on her plate.

"That's why I made it," Liz replied.

Maggie raised her face, and Liz kissed her before moving on to Lucy's plate. "It's my favorite too. Don't I get a kiss?" Lucy asked and puckered up. Liz laughed, then bent to kiss her.

***

"Your pal's already here," said Paula, nodding in the direction of their usual table. She lowered her voice to say, "She does *not* look happy."

Liz sighed. "Bet it's about that story on the evening news last night."

The local station had run an extended segment on the protests in front of the police station. Every day, a handful of elderly people stood there, holding signs that said, "No ICE in Hobbs" or "Keep Hobbs Police Local" as well as nastier versions of the same sentiment.

When the reporter interviewed their leader, Greg Blackhead, he spoke in a trembling, barely audible voice. His disconnected sentences made little sense, and he looked old and pale, squinting into the bright sunlight. Watching, Liz felt torn between concern for a patient, and contempt for the man who was making her friend's life hell. Of course, Greg's followers, Pat and Maura, were there and glad to offer their opinions.

"The news people are just terrible," Paula said, shaking her head. "Anything for a story. I remember when that actress sued you for malpractice. It was in all the papers. Maybe you can give the chief some advice."

"I'm trying, but my situation was different. That actress didn't listen to me and then got sicker. I'd done nothing wrong, except treat her in the best way I knew how."

"What ever happened to her?"

"She died of breast cancer like I said she would if she didn't get additional treatment."

"I wondered. You suddenly didn't hear about her anymore."

"She was a third-rate actress to begin with. She used the malpractice suit against me to get attention. It didn't matter whether I was right or wrong, or how it impacted me and my practice, as long as she got the publicity."

"That's awful," said Paula, shaking her head. "What a bitch! How did you feel when she died?"

Liz searched her feelings. "Sad because if she'd listened to me, she'd probably still be alive. It's always hard for a doctor to lose a patient, even the ones you don't like."

"So, you're not still mad at her?"

"No. The malpractice suit made my life hard, but it wasn't about me and my competence. It was about her. I was happy when the lawsuit was dismissed, but things were never the same after that."

"That's why you came up to Hobbs. Funny how life is," Paula mused, looking thoughtful. "Everything happens for a reason."

"Not really, but significant events or choices constrict the causal net." Paula stepped back and eyed Liz cautiously. Obviously, she wasn't prepared for a philosophy lesson this morning. "Talk to you later," said Liz, patting the countertop. "I'd better go and console my friend."

Brenda raised her eyes from her phone when Liz appeared at their table. "Stolz, are you *ever* on time?"

"You'd be disappointed if your doctor didn't keep you waiting."

"I'd probably think she wasn't busy enough."

"I'm always busy."

Brenda glared at a woman at the next table who was paying too much attention. "Jeeze. Maybe I need to save my public appearances for after dark, like a vampire."

Liz tossed her parka on the bench and sat down. "Feeling sorry for yourself?"

"No one else is feeling sorry for me, so why not? Did you watch the news last night?"

Liz nodded sympathetically.

"All the stations are streaming news and loop their top stories. So, I get to watch it over and over again."

"Don't watch it. Stop looking online. Turn off the TV."

"It won't make it go away."

"Of course not, but it might help you stay sane."

Brenda turned her sad eyes on Liz. "Are you giving me advice as my doctor?"

Liz inhaled a deep breath. "Not exactly, although it's good advice. I know, because it worked for me. Sometimes, you need to look away."

Brenda tilted her head, curious. "You don't. I've been at accidents with you where there were guts strewn all over the highway. When you rolled over the bodies of the kids shot in that gym to see if they were still alive, most of them had no faces. It was all I could do not to retch, but you coolly went on doing your job." As Brenda spoke, her eyes filled. She was exhausted, and the pressure was obviously getting to her.

"It was our duty to be there for those kids," Liz said, "for them and their families, and the staff at the school. I'm a doctor and you're the police chief."

The waitress came with their breakfast order, so they sat back. "You two look like you're havin' a barrel of fun," she said, hands on hips.

"Good morning, Lois," Liz said, smiling in an attempt to recover from the grim conversation.

Lois looked directly at Brenda. "Chief, I saw that news report on TV last night. Those ICE people are mean SOBs. You shouldn't be working with them, but you've done a lot for this town. You don't deserve this."

Liz heard Brenda swallow hard. She was holding back tears, but she needed to hear that not everyone hated her. "Thanks, Lois," Brenda managed to say after clearing her throat.

"People should be ashamed of the way they're treating you! *Ashamed!*" Lois added in a voice loud enough to be heard at the nearby tables. The woman who'd been glaring at Brenda suddenly found her breakfast fascinating. After her brave speech, Lois devolved again into a pale octogenarian. "Need more coffee?" she asked.

"Nope, I'm good," Liz said, and Brenda chimed in that she had enough too.

After Lois left, Liz peered at Brenda. "See? Not everybody hates you. What Lois said is what most people in this town think. They might not agree with what you did, but they support you and the Hobbs PD."

"Somebody put up signs along the sidewalk in front of the safety building. 'Support our police.'"

"I saw that," said Liz, smashing the egg yolks so she could sop them up with toast. "That's not necessarily a good thing. That black American flag with the blue stripe is a symbol of the right wing. They only support the police when they protect white people. People of color don't count."

"Yup. The hypocrites had no problem beating the shit out of the Capitol Police on January sixth," said Brenda.

Liz realized they would both descend into a darker mood if they persisted discussing these sad topics. "You know, I'm sorry I had to cancel our fishing trip because Cathy was sick that day. We need to do something fun to get our minds off all this misery."

"I'm off tomorrow afternoon," said Brenda, mopping up the remaining egg yolk with her home fries.

Liz whipped out her phone to look at her calendar. She saw that she had a meeting with Amy Hsu to go over the business of the practice. Finance and organizational management weren't Amy's forte, one reason they'd agreed she wasn't ready to completely take over the managing partner role. The other reason was Liz was a self-confessed control freak.

"Tomorrow, I have a meeting with Amy at lunchtime, but I can easily switch it to another day. How about I pick up a couple of lobster rolls and some beer and meet you at The Wet Lady at noon?"

"That's perfect," said Brenda. "That way I can get some things done around the house before I meet you."

Lois arrived to deliver their bill and collect the empty plates. "Now, you hold your head high, chief," she said before she departed. "People in this town better get a grip, if they know what's good for them."

"Well, there's a message," said Liz after Lois walked away with their plates. "And we thought New Yorkers were tough. We can't hold a candle to old Mainers."

Brenda picked up her bill. "Jesus Christ! When did it cost almost twenty dollars for a couple of eggs and bacon? I used to take Cherie and the kids out after church. Now, four breakfasts cost a hundred bucks!"

"Give me your check," said Liz, repeatedly flexing her fingers toward herself.

"Like hell I will," said Brenda, still furious. "I'm no charity case."

"No, you're not, but you have a mortgage to pay, and you're supporting a family."

"No way. We've always paid for these breakfasts, even steven."

"Brenda, just give it to me," Liz said in the firm voice she used to use in the OR. "If you're really my friend, you will accept my help. I give money to the food pantry, but as my mother used to say, 'charity begins at home.'"

Brenda still didn't look happy about it, but she handed the check to Liz.

When Lois returned with the little portable card reader, Liz said to her. "From now on, Lois, one bill and it comes to me. Okay?"

Lois smiled. "Glad you're showing your support for the chief. We all should."

"Damn right, we should," Liz said loud enough for the annoying woman at the next table to hear.

✳✳✳

When Liz came into the kitchen that evening, Maggie pointed to a plate on the kitchen island. "Eat," she ordered. "We have to be out of here in twenty minutes."

Liz glanced at the multilayered sandwich that Maggie had prepared. The multigrain bread alone looked delicious, but between the slices was all kinds of goodies, including bacon and tomatoes sliced as thin as paper. "Your sandwich looks like a picture in a food magazine, but what kind of greeting is that? Eat, we have to leave."

Maggie rolled her eyes. She stood on her toes to offer Liz a kiss because she refused to bend down. "There's soup too. Think you can gulp it down before we need to go?"

"I eat fast, but I think I'll pass on incinerating my esophagus. I can eat the soup when we come home tonight." Liz sat down on a stool at the island and began wolfing down her sandwich. "Where's Lucy?" she asked, covering her mouth while she chewed.

"Upstairs, changing into her civvies."

Liz swallowed before she spoke. "I thought she was into this new Christian Left look."

"For non-partisan events, like protests," Maggie explained. "This is a political organization."

"Oh, right," said Liz in a cynical tone. "We must protect the church's tax-exempt status at all costs!" Liz finished the first half of the sandwich and picked up the other.

Maggie watched her intently. "I never could figure out how you can eat that fast."

"You learn to eat fast when your meal might be interrupted at any minute. Otherwise, you would starve."

"I put a lot of effort into that sandwich, and now it's vanishing right before my eyes."

"That's because it's delicious as well as beautiful." Liz interrupted her eating to give Maggie a quick kiss. "Thanks for making it for me."

Lucy came into the room, looking relaxed in a polar-fleece zip-up and jeans. "Are we almost ready to go?" she asked, looking at Liz, who continued scarfing down her sandwich. "It's crazy that they have the meetings at five-thirty on a work night," said Lucy.

"Technically, the meeting doesn't start until six," Maggie explained, "but as a team leader, I'm supposed to be there on time."

"I'll drive," Lucy volunteered. Usually, Liz insisted on driving, but she was tired and saw an opportunity to project the kinder, gentler persona Lucy would like her to cultivate, so she didn't argue. She grabbed the last bite of sandwich off her plate and followed them out to the garage.

As they sped down the Post Road to the library, Maggie, sitting in the backseat, said, "I hope this meeting is less eventful than the last one." Liz, gazing out the window, frowned at the protest signs in front of the police station as they passed it. Obviously, the pressure on Brenda hadn't let up. "The treasurer came up with the idea of adjourning the business meeting before the speaker," Maggie continued. "That way, we don't have to ask to adjourn when people won't stop asking questions."

"Sounds reasonable," Lucy said, "but Liz is our resident expert on *Robert's Rules of Order*."

"I don't remember that particular article, but it sounds good to me."

The room was less crowded than it had been during the previous meeting. While Maggie and Lucy went to check-in and get a name badge, Liz stood at the back scanning the group for threats. Maggie headed to the officers' table to make amends for being late. A moment later, the chair rose to call the meeting to order.

"We're going to try something new tonight," she announced. "First, we'll conduct our business meeting, then we'll adjourn to give our guest speaker from Immigrants' Legal Defense more time to answer your questions. I want to remind everyone that, according to our agreement with the library, we need to be out of here by eight pm."

"That's not true!" shouted a white-haired woman, jumping up from her seat. "I called the library, and they said groups can meet until ten o'clock!"

The chair and secretary exchanged a look. "It's true that meetings can go until ten," said the chair, "but the agreement I signed specified we would end by eight pm." There was a low rumble of dissent. This meeting was not getting off to a good start. "So, can I have a motion to adjourn our business meeting before the speaker begins?"

A woman put up her hand. "Does that mean anything the speaker says won't be part of the minutes?"

The secretary stood up. "That is correct. Technically, the minutes only reflect the business meeting. Other notes are at the discretion of the secretary."

Someone shouted out of order. "We don't want to adjourn early!" Others loudly voiced their agreement.

Liz noticed the chairwoman looked stressed. She exchanged glances with the other officers. "Very well. So, let's get on to the treasurer's report." It was approved by voice affirmation. "And now, the minutes." Maggie had related how hard the secretary had tried to create objective notes from the last meeting, which had ended in chaos. "Can I have a motion to approve the minutes?" the chair asked.

Pat, the tall skinny woman, who'd been interviewed the night before on TV, stood. "I object to the following points summarizing the police chief's positions." She read them. "And I object to including the reports on immigration arrests published by the Department of Homeland Security. I want them removed."

The secretary stood. "This is the first time in my years as secretary that the minutes have been questioned. Those reports were given to me by Chief Harrison for distribution to our members. It isn't my job to choose which handouts to give people. When a speaker provides them, I attach them."

"This is nothing but government propaganda," Pat replied in a brisk tone.

The secretary looked to the chair for guidance. "Let's take a vote," the chair suggested. Her tone was amiable but her eyes darted around the room nervously. "Raise your hands if you approve of the corrections to the minutes." Nearly every hand went up. The secretary's face grew dark with anger. Her voice trembling, the chair said, "Let's move on to welcome our speaker from Immigration Defense Alliance, Attorney Michelle Griswold."

There was an enthusiastic round of applause as a heavy-set woman in her forties approached the front of the room. To Liz's ears, the lawyer's opening remarks sounded biased—all immigration enforcement was wrong, which was plainly false. Violent criminals and drug traffickers should be imprisoned and deported.

As the speaker went on, Liz realized this wasn't an informational Q&A. It was a pep rally. She suddenly wished she had brought her own car, so that she could leave in disgust. She noticed the chair and the secretary huddling in the front of the room. Finally, the speaker concluded her opening remarks and asked for questions. The chair came forward. "We'll allow questions until seven thirty and then we will adjourn."

Some of the questions were reasonable. Others genuinely sought insight on the deliberately cloudy status of immigrants under this administration. Some were just statements of opinion to which the audience offered their approval or vocal disapproval. The atmosphere was beginning to feel as tense as last time.

Suddenly, the chair interrupted. "We are going to adjourn the meeting here. We thank Attorney Griswold for coming tonight to answer our questions. But I also have an announcement to make. It seems that this committee has lost confidence in my leadership. We can't even agree when to adjourn a meeting. So rather than prolong this, I resign as chair of the Hobbs Democrats."

The secretary stood up. "And I resign as secretary of the Hobbs Democrats. I will not revise the minutes from the last meeting, and there will be no minutes from this meeting."

The two of them grabbed their coats and walked out the door. As the secretary passed, Liz reached out her arm. "Are you okay?"

"I'm fine," said the woman in a flinty voice. "Fuck them!"

Lucy and Maggie headed in Liz's direction. "Let's get out of here," Maggie said under her breath.

"Good idea," said Liz. "I need a stiff drink."

Chapter 10

Brenda couldn't find her favorite lure. She hadn't been fishing since last fall, right before Liz put The Wet Lady into dry dock for the winter. It was always funny to see all the boats in the marina shrink-wrapped in white plastic like enormous cans of cat food.

Until Liz had bought her boat, they'd mostly fished at Sam McKinnon's place on Jimson pond, but now its owner was off in Chicago, teaching architecture and designing buildings. It was good for Sam to leave for a while. Although the furor over her role in the school shooting had died down, people in a small town never forget. Sam hadn't sold the house, which made Brenda wonder if she intended to come back. Meanwhile, she'd given Liz and Brenda permission to use her boats and fish off her dock, but they never did. Liz said it didn't feel right fishing without Sam there, and Brenda agreed.

The garage door opened, and Cherie called, "You all right out there, Brenda?"

"I'd be better if I could find my favorite haddock plug. The last time we went fishing, we brought the kids, so who knows where it ended up."

"I keep telling you to clean up that tackle box. It has fish guts in it from God knows when. Better yet, buy yourself two new boxes—keep one for salt water and one for fresh. That's what my Daddy used to do." Brenda smirked, although it was a good suggestion. She knew she kept Cherie around for a reason, and it was for more than sex, mind blowing though it was. That woman could do things with her mouth and hands that Brenda had never even imagined! "Why don't you just pick up a new lure on the way?" asked Cherie, hands on hips. "Isn't there a bait shop right there in the harbor?"

"There is, but it's really expensive."

"Maybe so, but you better get a move on, girl, or you'll be late."

Brenda snapped closed the smelly tackle box and ran up the garage steps to kiss her wife. "Good luck, sweetie pie," said Cherie. "If you catch anything legal, make sure to bring it home. I love fresh fish."

Growing up in a big Irish Catholic family Brenda associated eating fish with Friday abstinence. Cherie had Maine in her blood through her French-Canadian father, whose people had come to the state hundreds of years ago. Mainers loved their haddock every which way: fried, broiled, sauteed, baked in fish pies, or floating in seafood chowder. To make her wife happy, Brenda would happily bring home her catch.

She knew that Cherie was right about her tackle box when she turned on the heat and the ripe aroma of fish guts permeated the car. Brenda lowered the rear window to vent some of the stench. Despite being a city girl, she had mostly accustomed herself to the disgusting smells that went with fishing because she enjoyed being on the water and the company of her fishing buddies.

Liz's truck was already in the harbor parking lot when Brenda arrived. Brenda could hear the boat engine puttering when she walked down the dock. "Took her out for a little test run," Liz explained when Brenda arrived. "I wanted to make sure the new plugs I installed were firing."

Brenda handed up her gear to Liz before she climbed aboard. She smelled fish guts and saw that Liz had been cutting up bait. "How long you been down here?"

"Oh, an hour or so. Ran all the engine checks, picked up our lobster rolls at Down the Hatch. I found some new beer at the brewery. I bought a red ale I think you might like." Liz plunged her hands into a bucket half full of water already pink from fish surgery. She scrubbed them with soap and a fine brush that she'd once explained surgeons used before an operation. Even here on the boat, she was compulsive about hygiene. "You ready to go?" she asked.

"Can't wait, but I can't find my best haddock plug. I think the kids might have stuck it someplace I'll never find it again."

"Don't blame the kids. Your tackle box is a sewer," Liz said dismissively. "Never mind. I have lots of lures. You can borrow whatever you need."

They went into the pilot house. When Liz revved the engine, the entire floor rumbled until the pistons fell into their rhythm.

"We couldn't have picked a better day. It's supposed to hit seventy by noon," said Brenda.

"Might be warm enough for some early stripers," Liz said. "We can start in the inlets and then head out to deeper water."

"Sounds like a plan," Brenda said.

Liz's gaze was focused intently on the buoy to make sure she navigated away from the shoals and shallow water. Once they were through the narrows, she upped the throttle. "I want us to have a relaxing day, so I wasn't going to bring up the other problem." Liz turned her blue eyes on her with a significant look, as if Brenda didn't know what the "other problem" could be. "But I heard something this morning that might be of interest to you."

Brenda gazed at Liz from under her eyebrows. "Well, after that introduction, Liz, I think you need to tell me."

Liz returned her eyes to the path ahead. "I'll tell you, but then we don't need to talk about this again today unless you really want to discuss it. Then I am happy to talk to you about it."

"Sounds like a good deal. Now, come on, Liz, spit it out."

Liz turned to her with a grin. Brenda guessed she knew exactly how annoying she was being. "Remember our state rep? I became tighter with him after I testified on reforming the yellow flag law. We stay in touch. He said the initiative to prohibit local law enforcement from engaging in immigration enforcement is sure to pass. They have the votes in both houses. Do you see what that could do for you?"

It didn't take long for Brenda to put the pieces together. "It would give me cover on the 287g agreement."

"Exactly. You could back out because it may soon be illegal in Maine to cooperate with ICE."

"But they haven't even voted yet," said Brenda, frowning.

"No, but you could make a public statement that you understand this initiative will come before the legislature, and you will 'pause' the agreement pending the outcome."

Brenda pounded on Liz's shoulder. "I always knew you were smart, but you're an absolute genius!"

"Thank you." Nearly everyone knew that Liz had skipped two grades in school because she was so smart, but she smiled at having her intelligence acknowledged. "If this works, it might get your critics off your back. At least it might hold them off for a while. Even a little break would help the department to get back to normal. Not to mention how good it would be for you and your family."

Brenda exhaled a huge stream of air. "Oh, my God! Would it ever!"

"Okay. Now, let's stop talking about this stupid ICE thing and get down to business. We are going to catch ourselves tons of fish today." Liz pointed toward to a rocky inlet ahead. "What do you think about dropping anchor there?"

Brenda grinned. "I think that cove is damn near perfect!"

***

Brenda watched Cherie mentally catalog the clear plastic bags of perfectly filleted fish. "My, my, my," her wife crooned, "Isn't this a beautiful sight to behold? Tonight we are going to have fish fry like nobody's business! And such variety!" Cherie read off the names of the fish species written in blue permanent marker in Liz's blunt print. Haddock, of course, but also halibut, winter flounder, and cod. "You and Liz could open a fish store. And such clean fillets. Not a bone in sight."

"Liz cleaned the fish. She's like a factory!"

"Well, she is a surgeon. And surgery is just butchering of another kind." Cherie gazed at her from under her brows. "Now, don't you go telling her I said so." After Brenda had spent the day on the receiving end of Liz's merciless teasing, it would serve her right. Brenda had learned to have fast mouth in the NYPD, where sarcasm was a matter of survival. For some reason, she held back with Liz, even when her good natured ribbing cut a little too close.

"Well, let's see," said Cherie, rubbing her hands together. "We could put some of these filets in the freezer for another time, or we could invite some guests to help eat them while they're fresh. Why don't we invite Liz and Lucy?"

"Liz can cook her own fish. She brought a haul like this home with her," Brenda said quickly. Now that she had a plan to get people off her back about the ICE agreement, she was feeling relaxed enough to think about bedroom activities after dinner. Lately, sex had been a way to relieve tension rather than something romantic.

"A big fish fry is more fun with other people. Let's see. I'll also invite Aunt Simone and Maggie."

"Maggie?" asked Brenda. "We don't always have to invite her when we invite Liz and Lucy. They're a couple, like us. She's just the ex."

Cherie stared at her, apparently hoping she'd change her mind. Finally, she said, "Brenda, when we were hurting, Maggie was the first to reach out. She fed us when I was too upset to cook, and you needed your friends to love you up! How can we even think of leaving her out?" Cherie's explanation made Brenda stare at her feet. Cherie, who could practically read her mind, said, "I know, baby, I find it strange too. I couldn't have my ex living right next door, never mind waltzing around my kitchen like she owns the place. But she and Liz were at war for years, and now they're at peace. If it works for them, it's okay with me."

"When we were out on the boat today, it seemed like Liz really wanted to tell me something, but then she suddenly changed the subject."

Cherie nodded knowingly. "Same with Lucy sometimes." She emitted a long sigh. "As we both know, things are not always what they seem. And if they want to tell us something, we'll just have to wait until they do. Until then, it's none of our damn business."

"You're right...as always. Good thing I have you around to translate the world for me." Brenda grinned affably.

"You do just fine on your own, and you weren't born yesterday," Cherie said. "Now, we have lots to do. First, you call Liz and invite them...*and* Maggie for dinner. I'll call Aunt Simone. Then do me a favor and bring one of those five-pound bags of potatoes up from the basement. We have a lot of peeling to do." Brenda took her phone out of her pocket, ready to make the call, but Cherie obviously sniffed around her. "Brenda, before you call anyone, please take a shower. I like the smell of fresh fish, but not on my lover. Now, skedaddle!"

Laughing, Brenda headed up to the bathroom.

***

After the amazing fish fry, complete with fresh Cole slaw, and homemade French fries, or *pommes frites*, as Cherie called them, Brenda and Liz sat in the living room for a beer. The Disney Channel had the kids glued to the screen, giving the adults relative privacy.

"I feel guilty letting the ladies clean up the kitchen after they cooked," Brenda said. "And it's a mess with all that cooking grease everywhere."

Liz shrugged. "We did our duty by providing the fish. Now, it's our time to relax."

Brenda howled. "Liz, you're more primitive than I thought!"

"Social conditioning from another era. Always makes a good excuse. Try it sometime." Liz grinned.

"Oh, believe me. I play that card regularly. Unfortunately, Cherie sees right through it and calls me on it."

Liz compressed her lips and slow nodded for emphasis. "Lucy does the same. She says, 'Liz, despite your fantasies, you are no more a man than you are a tenor. You are a woman, which I know better than most people!'

"Woohoo! Leave it to Lucy to put you in your place and come on to you at the same time."

"That's my Lovely Lucy. Always has something to say, and it's meaningful, not just chatter, which I appreciate."

"Must be boring sometimes, having a conversation in a house full of PhDs."

"I don't have a PhD," Liz replied with rare modesty. "But I am a doctor."

"A real one."

Liz sat up straight, covered her lips with a raised finger, and glanced toward the kitchen. "Sh! Don't let them hear that."

Brenda roared. Hearing her mother's laughter, Megan crawled up on the couch next to her for a cuddle. Keith looked up and snuggled in on the other side. Liz moved to one of the armchairs, so the kids would have space with their mom.

"You know, Brenda, I've been thinking," said Liz, looking reflective. "With all this bad publicity, the Hobbs PD should consider hiring someone who knows how to deal with this kind of thing."

Brenda dramatically shook her head. "Never happen. You know the town doesn't have that kind of money. Hell, we can't even get the potholes fixed in our parking lot."

Liz assumed her 'I'm serious now' look. "I know the town won't okay the cost, Brenda. Their attitude is 'you got yourself into this; you get yourself out.' But I might be able to help. The publicity manager I hired for my malpractice suit became a friend afterward. She's retired now, and I think I can talk her into giving you a very good price."

"Liz, you know how strapped I am for money. I can't afford that kind of help." Brenda had tensed, which Megan instantly sensed and tightened her grip.

"I'll help you Brenda. This is money well spent for you and for Hobbs. The bad publicity is not just hurting you. It's hurting the whole town."

"Liz, can you imagine some hot shot New York publicist speaking for me? They hate us up here. How many years did it take for you to be accepted? I bet they still look at you and say, 'she's not bad...for a New Yorker.'"

"Deborah is not like that, Brenda. I promise. That's why I chose her. As a doctor and chief of surgery at Yale, I couldn't have a brittle, hard-charging,   ask-me-the-wrong-question-and-I'll-chew-your-face-off kind of person defending me. I needed someone who spoke quietly and thoughtfully. That's what you need too. Please, Brenda. Just talk to her. I promise I'll pay any fees."

"Liz, we've had this discussion. I won't have you paying my bills. Jeeze, I let you pick up my breakfast tab, and now you want to take over my life!"

Liz pursed her lips. She knew she'd pushed too hard. "I'm just making a suggestion..."

Brenda needed a moment to calm down before she spoke. "I know you are. And I appreciate your offer of help. Your idea today was pure genius, and I wouldn't have known about that law going through the legislature without your connections. But please, just let me handle this."

Liz showed her palms in surrender. "Okay, Brenda. It's your call. Just remember I'm here to help."

✳✳✳

Brenda arrived at work early. She loved Cherie's fish fries, but at her age, fried food didn't like her. She'd awakened with indigestion around three, and despite chewing some antacid tablets, she'd had trouble going back to sleep. After hours of staring at the ceiling, she decided to get dressed and go into the office. These days, it didn't matter when she left for work. Since Cherie had taken leave from Hobbs Family Practice, she was driving the kids to school.

Opening the door to the dispatcher's office woke the sleepy crew. Once they realized it was the chief standing there, they instantly snapped to attention. "Good morning, team," said Brenda cheerfully. "Just so you know, there might be a lot of people around here today. I'm calling a news conference."

The head dispatcher sat up straight. "What's the news, Chief?"

"There's a bill moving through the Maine legislature that will likely pass soon. It forbids local law enforcement from cooperating with ICE. Since our agreement with them may soon be illegal, I'm going to pause it for now."

To Brenda's surprise, all three dispatchers started clapping.

"Smart move, chief," said the head dispatcher. "It will take a lot of heat off us."

Brenda narrowed her eyes. She knew the whole department was under pressure over this agreement, but until now no one had dared to say it out loud. "You're right, Kris. It will let us all get back to doing our jobs."

Brenda went to her office to deal with her email and paperwork. At eight o'clock, she went downstairs to the admins' room. "Cynthia, come upstairs. I want to review our press release list and figure out who we should invite to a press conference this afternoon."

Cynthia's eyes grew wide. "A press conference? This afternoon? Do we have time to get one together?"

Brenda glanced at her watch. "It's only five past eight. If we hold off until three, that should be plenty of time, don't you think?"

"But will anyone come?"

Brenda wanted to laugh out loud, but Cynthia would find that insulting. "Cynthia, we have been on the national news three times this week. We're on the local news every night. I think those reporters will get down here. Don't you?"

Cynthia blinked twice. "Yes, chief, of course they will. I'll print out two copies of the press release list and be right up to your office."

"Good," said Brenda.

Chapter 11

The long sigh was audible through the phone speaker. "I'm sorry it didn't work," said Deborah Goldberg, Liz's former publicist. Her refined voice had an accent that was impossible to place. Like Olivia, Deborah had taken elocution lessons to erase her origins. With a fellow New Yorker like Liz, she could be herself, and allow her Queens accent to come through. "Please try not to blame yourself. It was a good idea . It should have solved the problem, but it didn't."

"But, Deb, *why* didn't it work?" Liz asked, genuinely puzzled. The media had been unimpressed by Brenda's announcement and kept asking why she hadn't simply canceled the agreement.

Deborah's chuckle was low and cynical. "Liz, you're a scientist. You believe in the empirical method and logic. People's opinions don't have a logic. They listen to what their friends say, or hear a snippet on the news, and it sticks with them. Look at this mess with the author of the Harry Potter series. One day, she's the esteemed creator of beloved children's books, credited with restoring childhood literacy. She gives a thumbs up to a post objecting to trans women being housed with women in prisons, gets called out for it, pushes back, and it snowballs into a full-fledged cancel campaign."

On the other end of the call, Liz frowned in disgust. "Half of the people who hate her probably don't even know what her position is."

"Of course they don't, but because their friends told them to hate her, they do. And she makes it worse for herself by digging in and flipping them the bird."

"Ironically, she seems to have won," said Liz. "Sales of her books are strong. All the Potter franchises and video game spin-offs are booming."

"But her reputation will never be the same again," Deborah

explained. "Financial success does not equate to rehabilitation when it comes to your good name. That's why suing for libel is still a serious legal gambit."

Liz smiled. "I always enjoy talking to you, Deb. You explain things so well."

"Well, I miss you too. Now that it's getting warmer I'm thinking of getting out of town. Summer in New York is so boring because all the interesting people leave."

"Why don't you come to Maine? We'd love to have you stay with us. We have lots of room." The invitation had popped out before Liz realized the implications. With a house guest, she and her wives would have to go back to pretending that Maggie was the neighbor next door. "I should probably make sure there are no conflicts," Liz quickly added.

"And I don't have to stay with you. There are lots of summer rentals, and this early in the season, I can probably get a good deal."

"I won't have you staying in some over-priced cabin when we have room. Plus, you won't have to rent a car. I can drive the truck while you're here, and you can use my resident's pass to park at the beach."

"Now, that is a deal that I can't refuse," said Deborah. "But you probably should discuss your plans with Lucy. I promise I won't take offense if she'd rather have her privacy. After all, you're still newlyweds."

In fact, Liz and Lucy were approaching their third wedding anniversary. Their passion hadn't waned one iota, and a visitor would make no difference. Liz was more worried about Maggie's reaction. "Having my ex next door makes for a somewhat unconventional relationship."

"Oh, Liz. Why am I not surprised? You and Jenny were always having your little asides."

Deborah had become Liz's confidante during the death throes of her long-term relationship with Jenny Carson. Over the course of their twenty-year partnership, neither had been monogamous. They'd had an "understanding." Neither would ask questions about the other's affairs, and they would keep their extra-curricular activities off campus. But Liz always knew when Jenny had a new lover because their sex became supercharged. Often, Jenny came home with an exotic new technique or a clever sex toy. Compared to Jenny, Lucy's fascination with devices was tame.

"Let me talk to Lucy about having a house guest, and also Maggie, since we're living in such close quarters."

"Again, I'll find other accommodations if it doesn't work out," said Deborah, but Liz sensed she was playing hard to get.

"Deb, I know you're very enterprising, but I can't wait to see you and pick your brain about helping Brenda. What if I hired you to advise her behind the scenes? I could be the conduit. That way she'd benefit from your advice, but it would be coming from me."

"So you get the credit for my brilliant ideas? *Really*, Liz?"

"I can make it worth it for you," said Liz in a tantalizing voice.

Deborah groaned with insult. "Liz, I would never charge you! I don't need the money, and this is an interesting challenge. Your little Brenda has made herself a national nemesis. Maybe she needs to fight back more aggressively. I dug up some of her interviews on Fox News, and that address to the police chiefs of Maine during Covid. She speaks well. And she's quite photogenic, trim, attractive, and relatively feminine."

After listening to Deborah size up Brenda like she was an aspiring actress in a cattle call, Liz said, "Brenda has sworn off talking to the press after last time."

"Just because she didn't get the result she hoped for doesn't mean she shouldn't keep trying," Deborah said. "And yes, I'm happy to give you advice to pass along to her. I love strategizing with you. You're one of the few people who understands that defending your reputation is like playing chess. You must always be ten steps ahead of your opponent."

"You're the one who taught me how to look at the big picture, and how important it is not to take things personally."

"Yes, that's the key."

"It's hard for Brenda. She's been a cop her entire life. She comes from a long line of proud NYPD officers. It's not in her DNA to consider doing the wrong thing. As a consequence, she thinks her agreement with ICE is *right*."

"Because in another context, it would be. And maybe it is right, but it's how people see it that matters."

In unison, they recited Deborah's favorite maxim: "Perception is reality."

"Remember how you struggled to separate your emotions from that malpractice case?" asked Deborah. "You pride yourself in your skill as a surgeon and your medical advice. Being a world-renowned expert on breast cancer is part of your *identity*. Then some silly actress comes along and says you're incompetent. Like your friend, Brenda, you would never knowingly do the wrong thing. Being accused of incompetence and negligence was like a knife through the heart."

Deborah's quick summary instantly brought back the emotional turmoil. Liz felt the same outrage as the day she'd learned of the lawsuit. At least, the medical board saw the truth, but as Deborah had said, Liz's ego and reputation were never the same again.

"Liz, are you still there? I can feel you getting all worked up again."

"It still makes me so angry! Being unjustly accused is maddening. I know how poor Brenda feels."

"Yes, and it's an awful place to be. But I will help you...and her. Now, I must get off the phone. A certain beast is standing here with crossed legs. May I bring her along if I come?"

"Of course. We have lots of beasts here, both the two-legged and four-legged kind. But keep her on a leash. Some of our beasts eat little dogs."

Deborah did a perfect imitation of the wicked witch's famous line from *The Wizard of Oz* before ending the call.

❋❋❋

After Liz left her office, she went into the kitchen to get a beer. Maggie was there, getting dinner ready. "That was a long call," Maggie said in a neutral tone, although it was obvious she was fishing for information.

"Deb and I haven't talked in a while, so we had a lot to catch up on. I debriefed her on the fallout from Brenda's news conference. She promised to help...in the background, if necessary."

"I like Deborah. She has that earth mother, no-nonsense persona that cuts through the crap," Maggie said. "You should invite her up to visit."

"I did. It just slipped out before I thought about it."

"That's because you invite everyone to come visit...and they do."

"Now that Lucy's taken over the seashore room for her office, we have less room for guests. We'll put Deb in the downstairs guestroom. More privacy for her and us. You can still come across the second floor bridge to join us in bed." Liz took a long drink of beer before saying, "I almost told Deb."

"You didn't! Lucy would kill you."

Liz smiled smugly. "Lucy would never kill me. She likes how I fuck her too much."

Maggie gave her a playful swat. "How dare you speak about your wife in that way!" she said with mock indignation. "But you're right." She grinned conspiratorially. "And me too."

Liz turned serious. "I alluded to an 'unconventional relationship' with you living right next door."

"What did she say?"

"She reminded me that Jenny and I had an unconventional relationship too."

"I'm sure finding out that we're a throuple won't faze Deb in the least, but we swore we'd talk about it before telling anyone, so I'm glad you didn't tell her before discussing it with us." Maggie covered the Dutch oven. "Liz, this pot weighs a ton. Would you mind putting it in the oven for me?"

Liz got up from her stool and lifted the pot into the oven. "Still good for something, I guess," she muttered, which earned her another swat, this time on the backside. "You're lucky I didn't spill your stew."

"You wouldn't dare!"

"Not if I value my life."

"Glad I have you well trained." Maggie poured herself a glass of wine and sat down beside Liz at the island. "I know you really trust Deb Goldberg. She's been a good friend to you. If you invite her, I can go back to pretending to be your next-door neighbor. I am an actress, you know."

Liz leaned over and kissed her. "And a very good one, I might add." She sighed. "I wouldn't ask that of you. It's one thing when the family is here. The kids don't understand, but they're used to you being around, so they probably don't think about it."

"Has your niece told them?"

"I don't think so, but sometimes, it's not what you tell kids, but how you act around people. If you act like everything's fine, the kids usually think it's fine."

Maggie nodded. "Very true. I wish it had been that easy when we told my adult children."

"Your kids are a special case. They had childhood trauma from that awful Romanian orphanage. Alina is still on medication for anxiety and depression. Plus, adult children can be very protective of their parents, especially their mothers after a divorce."

"You've become quite the expert on family relationships, Dr. Stolz. Soon, you'll be giving Lucy real competition."

Liz shook her head. "I just observe my patients and listen to what they tell me about their lives. You can learn a lot that way."

"Humility too?" Maggie pretended to feel Liz's forehead for a fever. "What's come over you?"

Liz chuckled and shrugged. "Old age?"

"Oh, Liz, you're not going to go on again about turning seventy. I did it, and I'm no worse for wear."

Liz gave Maggie a critical inspection. "Actually, you look pretty good for someone of your advanced age."

"Oh, shut up, Liz. Here I try to be sympathetic, and you insult me!"

But Liz was still thinking about her conversation with Deborah. "I think I should tell Deb about us, don't you?"

While Maggie thought about it, she took a sip of wine. "I think if you really trust her, you should tell her. It would make her visit easier on everyone, especially me."

"That's what I think. When Lucy gets home from visiting Rebecca, we'll talk about it."

"Speaking of her return, I promised to empty the dishwasher." Maggie opened the machine. When she pulled out the top rack, she shrieked. Liz stood up to identify the problem and saw a variety of multi-colored phallic-shaped objects bobbing up and down. "Jesus Christ!" exclaimed Maggie, hand on her heart. "Why can't Lucy warn us when she's going to wash her toys in the dishwasher!" Trying to recover her dignity, Maggie took some deep breaths.

"She probably just forgot," said Liz, feeling like she ought to defend Lucy. "At least we know they're *clean*."

Liz started to laugh, then Maggie. Soon, they were doubled over, slapping their knees. They laughed until they were clutching their bellies.

❋❋❋

When Lucy returned from South Portland, she barely said hello before retreating to her room. Liz guessed from the pinched look on her face that she needed some time to think.

"Maybe you should go up and see what's going on?" Maggie suggested, nudging Liz. "She's scrunched in on herself like she really needs a hug." Being an actress and theater director, Maggie could read body language as well as any therapist.

Liz looked at the ceiling in the spot where Lucy's room was upstairs and shook her head. "If she wanted to talk to us, she would have hung around and told us how it went. She knows what she needs. Let's leave her alone for a while and see what happens. She'll come down when she's ready."

"Maybe she wants us to ask how she's doing," said Maggie, staring at the same spot on the ceiling.

"That's how *you* would behave, Maggie. You would make withdrawing a test, not Lucy. She knows we love her. When she wants our attention, she'll let us know."

Maggie frowned and once again laid the back of her hand on Liz's forehead. "Liz you're beginning to worry me. What happened to the barge-right-in-and-take-control-of-everything hero of the day?"

"I don't need to pry Lucy's hurt feelings out of her because when she's ready to share them, she tells me. Life with Lucy is simple. No games."

"That's probably why she's wrecked now. She's so truthful. It's probably killing her that she can't be honest with Rebecca about our relationship. Or maybe she told her, and they had a fight."

Liz considered this possibility for a moment. "Lucy wouldn't inflict the truth on Rebecca if she didn't think she was ready to hear it. But you're right. Lucy used to share everything with Rebecca. Now, she can't. Whatever went down in South Portland was really hard on her, or you can be damn sure she'd be sitting here telling us about it."

"Well, I'm going to set the table and get the rest of dinner prepped while we're waiting. All Rebecca ever gives Lucy is chicken soup."

Liz laughed. "Always feeding people."

"So are you. It's how you show love. You feed them."

"What can I say? Hard to break that feminine archetype. And while you do that, *I'm* going to have a glass of whiskey."

"Just one, Liz. You need to be sober when Lucy comes down. Hear me?" Maggie frowned in Liz's direction so she'd get the message.

"I hear you, Maggie. I always *hear* you."

"But you don't always *listen.*"

"Nope." Liz opened the cabinet and took down the bottle of Irish whiskey.

Twenty minutes later, Liz had kept to her promise to remain sober and had imbibed only one glass. Lucy still hadn't come downstairs. Finally, Liz's curiosity got the best of her. She took out her phone and texted Lucy: *Are you okay?*

For an extended minute, there was no response. By that point, Liz was ready to go upstairs to see if Lucy was all right. Then, a text message arrived: *Yes. Coming down now.*

"So, Ms. Patience, even you couldn't wait," said Maggie when Liz looked up from her phone.

"Well, she's been up there a long time. She's coming down now, but don't pounce on her with all kinds of sympathy. Give her some space until we find out what's going on."

"Liz," said Maggie with pleading in her eyes, "Why couldn't you be this sensitive when we were married?"

Liz thought for a moment. "Because I didn't know better. You were always playing games and criticizing me for everything I did. You were furious because I didn't blurt out everything I knew about your cancer. But I couldn't. I was trained to wait for all the data, come up with reasonable advice, and deliver it in a way a patient can understand. When you're a doctor, that's the responsible thing to do."

"But Liz, you were my *wife*," Maggie replied, looking like a very young, hurt child.

"Yes, and that's why I can't be your doctor or Lucy's. As it is, I'm too involved in your care." Liz shook her head in disgust. "Let's not make this about our old stuff. Lucy needs us, and she'll be here any minute."

Maggie used her acting skills to assume a deliberately calm, smiling face. When Lucy walked into the kitchen, Maggie opened her arms. Lucy instantly fell into them. Over Lucy's shoulder, Maggie grimaced. She remained irrationally protective of her breast implants no matter how many times Liz explained that they were built to take much more pressure than an enthusiastic embrace.

Liz patiently waited her turn for a hug. When she got it, she understood Maggie's concern about the implants. Lucy's arms gripped her with all their might. "I am so lucky to have you two," Lucy murmured into Liz's shoulder. "I hope you know *how* glad I am."

Liz gently unwound Lucy's arms from her waist. She nodded over her head to Maggie, who read her sign language, and opened the refrigerator to get Lucy a glass of her favorite pinot.

"What were you doing up there?" Liz asked.

"Well, as you can see I changed my clothes. Then I needed time to process. I prayed over it." When Liz rolled her eyes, Maggie wagged her finger behind Lucy's turned back.

"Why don't we go sit in the living room?" Liz suggested. She noticed Maggie switching off the oven. Obviously she'd sensed that this could be a long conversation.

Liz settled Lucy on the long sofa, so she and Maggie could sit beside her. Maggie brought the wine and a glass of whiskey for Liz on a tray along with cheese and crackers. After Lucy took a sip of wine, she carefully put down the glass on the coffee table.

"It's worse than I thought."

"Did you tell her about us and she rejected you?" Liz asked, cutting to the chase. Maggie sent her a warning glance over Lucy's head.

"Are you kidding?" said Lucy sarcastically. "I never even got that far. Like you, Liz, she's a New Yorker and talks so fast I couldn't get in a single word! All I could do is listen." Lucy inhaled a long sigh, which seemed to calm her. "I will have to tell her about us eventually, but now is not a good time."

"So, are you going to tell us what happened?" asked Liz impatiently.

"Do you want the blow by blow or the short version?"

"Give us the high points first," Maggie suggested, "then you can go back and fill in the details." Liz guessed that Maggie trained her students to use this trick when writing papers. Probably AI did it for them now.

"You remember when I told you that Rebecca was concerned because when Judith got back from Israel she was withdrawn? Well, today, she found out why, also why Rebecca was so desperate to see me today. I guess I should take comfort in the fact that she turned to me like in the old days. But I didn't know what to say, not as a counselor, or a priest. She was so raw and miserable, no words could ever comfort her."

"Well, after that buildup, maybe you need to give us the long version," Liz said dryly.

"I'll tell you the important part. While Judith was in Israel, she met up with an old childhood friend and they fell into bed together."

"Of course, she did," Liz said. "There she was, in a war zone, bombs falling all around her, scared out of her wits, and someone was available. You always say sex is a great comfort. That's why you mercy-fucked Erika the night her mother died."

"Liz!" hissed Maggie. "How can you bring that up while Lucy's so upset?"

Liz gave her a pained look. "I'm telling Lucy I understand. She knows what I'm saying."

Lucy chuckled weakly. "She's right. I do."

"So, what made Judith confess now?" Maggie prodded.

"When she came home from Israel, Judith said she needed to sleep in another room because of the war trauma. At first, Rebecca tried to be understanding, but Judith had been away for nearly a year, and she'd missed her. You know what they say about absence making the heart grow fonder? Well, it also makes you hornier. Rebecca had hinted that their sex life had grown cold before Judith left for Israel. Once Judith returned, Rebecca needed to make love to re-establish their bond. All that makes sense, right? But the more she approached her wife, the more she withdrew."

Over Lucy's head, Maggie's eyes met Liz's. This was a familiar tale, but, in their case, reversed. Paradoxically, the more deeply Liz fell in love with Lucy, the more sex she wanted from Maggie.

"So they were sleeping separately," Lucy continued. "The girls are seventeen and both wicked smart, so they picked up on their mothers' estrangement. This morning, Naomi asked Judith when she was going to move back in with Rebecca."

"Leave it to a child to ask the obvious question," Maggie said. "My daughters were like antennas when Barry and I were at odds, picking up all the conflict and amplifying it."

"Rebecca waited until Judith came home from dropping off the girls at soccer practice to confront her. She used all the marriage counseling tricks she'd learned as a rabbi, but it's different when it's someone you love. All the techniques they teach you in seminary mean nothing!"

"Good of you to admit it, Lucy," said Liz, which earned her a light punch on the arm.

"Be quiet, Liz. You forget you're a doctor when we have a fight and become just as irrational."

Maggie looked impatient. "Ladies, argue later. I want to hear what happened."

"Rebecca kept begging her to explain why Judith had become so distant. She pleaded with her to come back to her own bed. Finally, Judith confessed the affair. It was more than a one-night stand. They are still texting and video chatting online."

"So, it's serious?" Maggie asked.

"Apparently," said Lucy. "Rebecca told her wife to get out of the house, but Judith has nowhere to go. Except for Rebecca and the girls, all her family are back in Israel. Rebecca volunteered to leave, figuring she'd move in with her mother, but when she called Ruth, she gave her a lecture about how lesbian relationships never last. I mean, those women have been married for almost twenty years!" Lucy reached for her glass of wine before resuming. "Of course, Ruth loved the idea of having her daughter home again, so she ended the diatribe and invited her to move in with the girls. When Rebecca told Judith, she insisted on keeping her biological daughter with her. Ironically, that's the 'twin' Rebecca carried when they swapped fertilized eggs to make their motherhood 'real.'" Lucy added air quotes for emphasis. "Rebecca considers Naomi *her* child because she occupied her womb for nine months."

"Oh, my God!" Maggie explained. "Judith insisted on separating the girls, who think and act like twins? And she wants the one Rebecca carried because it was *her* egg?"

"See?" said Liz and downed her glass of whiskey in a gulp. "This is where all that romantic shit and modern medicine get lesbians into trouble. Never mind that they raised those girls as twins, and now they want to pull them apart. They're at a delicate point in their adolescence. Separating them is *not* a good idea."

"Of course not," agreed Lucy. "But neither of their mothers will listen to reason. They just want to hurt each other as much as they can because they're both in so much pain."

"No wonder you looked like you'd been hit by a tsunami when you came home," Maggie said in a sympathetic voice. "What can we do to help?"

Lucy shrugged dramatically, raising her shoulders nearly to her ears. "I have no idea. This isn't our drama. We can only watch."

Chapter 12

Brunching with the Morgensterns after Saturday temple, Lucy felt right at home. While she'd lived in New York while attending Juilliard and later, when it was home base for her first opera career, she'd had many Jewish friends. She loved everything about New York Jews—their support of culture and performing artists like her, the love she felt within their tight-knit families, and their delicious food.

Ruth Morgenstern was a phenomenal cook and made traditional dishes like no other Jewish mother Lucy had ever met. Ruth used special meals to show off her wealth, even more so now that she was married to a rich, retired plastic surgeon. The brunch spread that afternoon was lavish. It included everything from New York bagels and a wide variety of smoked fish shipped overnight from Zabar's to homemade chicken liver pâté and real *Schmaltz*, the rendered chicken fat that was richer than the finest butter.

While Lucy was helping herself to the buffet, a familiar voice said near her ear, "That's not enough to fill a cavity. Eat, eat, or my mother will be insulted." Lucy put down her plate and turned into Melissa's arms. The taller woman scooped her into a sturdy hug, then held her at arms' length. "Where have you been? Now, you even send Liz to collect the rent checks!"

"Well, I wouldn't have to send anyone if you'd just put them in the mail."

"I don't trust the post office any more. And I wouldn't have to do that either if a certain technophobe would agree to an automated EFT deposit."

"Liz says I need to set up an LLC for that kind of thing, and she hasn't gotten around to it."

Melissa's striking blue eyes were merry. "This is why amateurs should let their attorneys do certain things. We get it done."

"You know Liz. She's hands-on with everything. She says she likes to see how things work behind the scenes, so she knows what's going on."

Melissa rolled her eyes and handed Lucy's plate back to her. "I interrupted you. Carry on."

Lucy scanned the room for Rebecca. "Where's your sister?"

Melissa picked up a bagel and sliced it. "She's having a slow start this morning," she said in a confidential tone. "Since she got that retired rabbi to fill in for her, she doesn't have to get up at a certain time. She's not sleeping well."

"I bet," said Lucy in a low voice. "Is she okay?"

Melissa raised her shoulders. "I haven't a clue. She doesn't talk to me. She lectures me about making Courtney 'an honest woman' since we started dating. Now, she's ashamed that her marriage is a mess. She won't talk to anyone." Melissa turned to Lucy. "Why are you asking me? I thought she was talking to *you*."

Lucy shook her head. "No, I've called a few times, but she always says she's too busy."

"Doing what?" Melissa coughed up a skeptical grunt. "She just hangs around all day holed up in her room. Mom's worried. That's why she invited you this morning. She thinks you have some magic power over Rebecca, which, of course, you do."

"Right," said Lucy sarcastically.

"Well, get some food on your plate and sit down and be sociable," said Melissa. "You know how Jack loves to talk to you."

Lucy helped herself to a dollop of pâté, added some smoked fish and fruit to her dish, and headed to where the family was gathered at the table. Ruth's recently acquired husband, Jack, gallantly stood when she pulled out the empty chair. "Oh, really, Jack, you don't have to get up for me."

"Most certainly, I do, Madam Bartlett," he replied. "When a great diva joins our table, she deserves every honor." Jack Dreyfus had been Liz's former colleague at Southern Med, when she was still practicing surgery. She'd introduced him to Melissa's mother in a classic case of matchmaking. Jack, like Liz, was also a rabid opera fan. He bowed deeply after Lucy sat down before finally reclaiming his seat. "I can't believe after all that fuss, you're not singing at the Met this year." He opened wide to bite into a bagel heaped with smoked white fish.

"They're not staging any operas in my *Fach*."

"Too busy staging new operas nobody wants to hear," said Jack with disgust. "I hear they're going to reappoint Gelb to another term. Don't they see the handwriting on the wall?"

Lucy studied Jack, wondering how much to say. The general manager of the Metropolitan Opera had been goaded into apologizing to her for the previous administration's cover up of her sexual abuse. Estefan Morales, the Brazilian conductor, had shamed him into it. Occasionally, powerful men did the right thing.

"I think we need to stage new works to keep opera from becoming a reenactment or a quaint remnant of the past," said Lucy.

"And your friend, Yannick Nézet-Séguin, is all for it."

"I like Yannick. He's so full of energy and curiosity about everything. I completely understand why he wants to produce new operas."

Ruth gave Lucy a critical look. "You might want to tell your friend that people like me will stop contributing if the Met doesn't get its act together. Jack has already suspended his membership."

Lucy glanced at Jack. "Really, I'm sorry. I know the Met is struggling, but donors fleeing will only make things worse."

"If that's what it takes for them to get the message..."

Lucy looked up to see a sleepy Rebecca, still in her pajamas, stumble into the room. Her curly hair was flattened on one side by the pillow. There were dark circles under her eyes. She looked like something that had crawled out of a crypt. Lucy said a quick prayer asking forgiveness for such an uncharitable thought.

Ruth jumped up. "Sit down, honey. I'll get you some coffee."

"Thanks, Mom," Rebecca murmured and took the chair next to her sister. She looked across the table at Lucy. "Sorry I overslept. Thanks for coming."

"You're welcome," Lucy gave her friend a quick inspection.

"Yes, I know. I look like hell." Rebecca yawned and glanced around. "No Liz?"

"It's her week for Saturday office hours. She might come later if there are no emergencies." Lucy thought of Maggie, who wasn't invited. Fortunately, she had Saturday classes to teach, so it never became an issue.

"Dr. Stolz is a busy woman," said Ruth, glaring at her husband. "At least, she found something to do with her life instead of golfing and playing with her boat!"

Jack looked aggrieved. "Liz always had an extra dose of that responsibility gene. Good for her. Maine needs doctors."

"Maybe you could help her," Ruth suggested with a huff.

"I could, but then who would take you on your cruises, or down to the old neighborhood to visit your friends?"

"Liz has cut back on her practice to accompany Lucy on her singing engagements," said Melissa, reaching for the coffee carafe. "Maybe there's a middle ground?"

"You know, there might be. I could help out in the ER at Southern Med. They're always looking for surgeons."

"Good idea," said Ruth. "I don't want you to get fat and lazy now that you're retired." Ruth gently poked Jack's developing paunch.

Through all this good-natured teasing, Rebecca shaded her eyes against the light from the chandelier over the table and stared into her coffee cup. Lucy recognized this level of grief. She'd experienced it when Erika died. Some people thought grief only applied to deaths, but the loss of a relationship or a job could hit even harder. As if realizing what Lucy had been thinking, Rebecca raised her dark eyes.

"I'm okay. I just look bad," she whispered loud enough for Lucy to hear while the others carried on with their banter.

Lucy nodded in the direction of the living room. "Will you excuse me, please?" she said, taking her coffee and getting up. Everyone immediately fell silent. Lucy could feel their eyes following her as she left the room. Fortunately, she'd already eaten most of what she'd piled on her plate. She hated to waste food, especially now that it had become so expensive.

She sat down and sipped her coffee, wondering if Rebecca would join her. Then she heard a shuffling sound. She saw Rebecca's fuzzy slippers before she looked up to see their owner's face. Rebecca plopped down on the sofa beside Lucy. "Thanks for coming," she murmured. "Mom is trying to help. She knew that if you came over, I'd have to get out of bed."

"Thanks for the honor," said Lucy, "but I wish you'd do it for yourself."

Rebecca emitted a long sigh. "You know how it is, Lucy. You suddenly became a widow. That's how I feel."

"Except Judith is still very much alive, and you could fight to get her back, if you wanted to."

"Why should I? She *cheated* on me. Meanwhile, I was the one keeping the home fires burning while she was flirting with the IDF and her old school friend."

"Rebecca, we're *all* under such stress," said Lucy, reaching for her friend's hand, but she snatched it away.

"That's no excuse!" snarled Rebecca.

"No, it's not, but it's a way to understand why it happened. Judith hurt you, but I bet she still loves you."

"Yeah? Then why does she want to take my own children away from me? *Our* children. We were pregnant together. We shared every moment of the feelings, the changes in our bodies, each little twinge and twitch. Naomi quickened first. Judith would lay her cheek against my belly for hours to feel every small movement because that was her baby too." Rebecca covered her face with her hands and began to cry.

Lucy waited for the storm to pass before saying, "Rebecca, we know each other too well, so I'm not giving you my pastoral care spiel. I'm just going to sit here and hold space for you. I'm *here* for you."

Rebecca turned her tear-stained face toward Lucy. "Why? I was an idiot. I treated you like shit. My loyalty to my Israeli wife was more important than my own truth. I knew that you meant no harm that day. You were just asking a question. But I didn't speak to you for almost a year. Why are you here?"

"Because you're my friend, and you need me."

Rebecca's face twisted with pain. She flung her arms around Lucy. "Thank you for still being my friend. I *do* need you, now more than ever!"

The declaration made Lucy want to squirm a little, knowing there was something important she was holding back, but she closed her eyes and hugged Rebecca fiercely until the intense emotion burned itself out.

When they finally released one another, Lucy reached for Rebecca's hand. "I'm not sure being here with your mother is the best thing."

"I know. She lets me mope around like a teenager. She talks so much I can't think."

"More than anything you need time to think." Lucy squeezed Rebecca's hand. "The beach apartment is empty."

Rebecca's dark eyes glowed with interest, then went cold. "But is there room for the girls to visit?"

"Plenty of room. The sofas in the living room are really futons that open into comfortable beds. There's a wicker hamper there with the linens and blankets."

"Clever."

"It's compact but cozy, and the view of the ocean is very

conducive to meditation. You'll have everything you need. Liz even keeps a stash of alcohol there...for medicinal purposes...of course. As a bonus, you'll have your sister right next door if you need her."

"Did you plan this with Melissa?"

"I mentioned to her I would offer you the apartment...in case she had any objection."

Rebecca grinned. "We're sisters. We fight all the time, but we love each other to death."

"I know. You're so lucky. I wish I had a sister."

"I'm your sister, Lucy," Rebecca suddenly said, which made Lucy's heart twist. She consoled herself with the idea that even between real sisters there were secrets that couldn't be shared.

"So, are you interested in the beach apartment?"

Rebecca searched her face, her brows slightly raised as if she were afraid to hope. "Lucy, are you sure about this?"

"Absolutely sure."

"Don't you want to ask Liz first?"

"Why? It's my house." Lucy nudged Rebecca. "Go tell your mom. We'll finish eating, then I'll help you get your things. I think you should come with me today."

"Thanks for giving me an out, Lucy. I owe you."

"No, you don't. Friends don't keep score."

Rebecca held Lucy's cheeks, squeezing them gently. "You are a gift. Thank you for being here for me."

"You're welcome. Now, let's eat. We can talk later when we have more privacy."

✽✽✽

Lucy turned the key in the lock and stepped into the beach house apartment. Bright sunlight streamed through the picture window overlooking the ocean, but it was frigid inside. The heat had been off since September. The last time Liz and Lucy had used the place was for a quick change of venue for some passionate sex. That was before the horrible election and the lost weekend on Moosehead lake, where the couple had become a throuple.

As she watched Rebecca look around the place, she had a pang of anxiety over keeping this basic fact of her life from her "rabbi." Maybe when Rebecca wasn't such a mental wreck she could tell her, but not today.

Rebecca turned to Lucy with a big smile. Obviously, she liked what she saw, and she was looking so much better after a good meal, a shower, and some makeup. Apart from the dark circles under her eyes, which no concealer could completely hide, she almost looked like her old self.

"This is a wonderful place," she said. "Why aren't you and Liz using it all the time?"

Lucy sighed. "We're both so busy. With all the political shocks, I'm overwhelmed with counseling appointments."

Rebecca patted Lucy's arm sympathetically. "I get it. You're a busy lady. I'm grateful you can spare time for me."

"Of course, I'd spare time for you, Becca. You've always been there for me."

"I'm so sorry I cut you off," said Rebecca, looking like she might start crying again. "I was an idiot!"

"No, you were reacting to an insensitive comment I made."

Rebecca frowned and shook her head. "What terrible times we live in when we can't allow a friend to make an honest mistake!"

Lucy sadly nodded. "So many rifts look ridiculous in retrospect, don't they?"

Rebecca gazed at the ocean through the window. "But some rifts can never be healed." No further elaboration was needed to know Rebecca was thinking about Judith.

"It depends on whether the parties are open to healing or dig themselves in deeper."

Rebecca turned and stared at Lucy. "You're not suggesting I should forgive her after what she did."

Lucy needed a moment to consider her response. "Let me turn on the heat to get the stale air out of here. Then we can talk about it." She felt Rebecca's eyes on her back while she headed to the closet where the service panels were located. "There, it should be warmer in here soon." She gave Rebecca a radiant smile. "So, you'll take the place?" she asked like an earnest real estate agent.

"It's very generous, and yes, I will, but I'd like to pay you rent."

"*Fuhgeddaboudit!*" said Lucy in her best New York accent. "No one's using the place. It's just sitting here, empty. You'll have the privacy to think about your life and what you want to do next. The path to the beach is right across the street. I'm sure you'll find being near the ocean therapeutic. When Erika and I lived here, we often took long walks after dinner."

Rebecca nodded, understanding. "That's why you decided to move in with Liz when you married. Too many memories here."

"They were good memories, but Liz and I couldn't live in two houses, so I had to choose. I didn't want to sell the beach house because Erika had remodeled it especially for me and Emily." Just remembering Erika's kindness and unfailing sense of duty made Lucy's eyes fill. Then she heard a little whisper in her ear, a British accent tinged with German. *Thank you. I'm glad you noticed.*

Lucy's eyes flew open and she glanced around, expecting to see Erika lurking in a corner. She felt a light brush on her cheek and knew it was a kiss. The presence, whatever it was, disappeared as suddenly as it had arrived.

They went upstairs to look at the bedroom, positioned so that the rising sun streamed into the large window and gently woke the sleepers in the king-sized bed. "Bed looks comfy," Rebecca remarked.

"Liz built it."

"Of course, she did." Rebecca opened the closet door. "Plenty of space."

"Are you going to move all your stuff down here?" Lucy asked, merely curious.

"Not yet," said Rebecca, which Lucy took as a hopeful sign. Maybe Rebecca secretly hoped for a reconciliation.

"Come downstairs, and let's have a glass of wine. Liz always leaves some of the good stuff around here."

Rebecca glanced at her watch. "You sure? It's your day off. Don't you have things to do?"

"I always have things to do, *and* I always have time for you." Lucy descended the spiral staircase to the lower level. "I was glad Liz suggested adding the upstairs toilet when we built this level. These stairs are tricky to navigate in the middle of the night. Be careful."

"I think I can manage, Lucy. Remember, I'm younger than you are."

Lucy turned to make a face. "Don't rub it in."

"Don't worry. Even I know not to bite the hand that feeds me."

While Lucy got the wine, Rebecca continued to poke around in the built-in cabinets and closets. She pulled open one of the futon couches. "This should be more than fine when the girls come to visit. Like a sleep over."

"I know how hard it was for you to leave them with Judith," said Lucy, struggling to pull the cork. Rebecca stepped in to help her. It finally emerged with a high-pitched pop.

"I just couldn't bear to separate them. We'd already had so much weeping and gnashing of teeth."

Lucy rummaged in the kitchen cabinets and found an unopened bag of corn chips and a jar of salsa. "Not exactly a feast, but it's what we have."

"After pigging out at my mother's this morning, I don't really need more food."

"But I can tell you've lost weight," said Lucy, ripping open the bag of chips. "You should eat something." She found a bowl and dumped the contents of the bag into it.

"Salt," said Rebecca, reaching for a handful. "I love salt."

"You and Liz both. At least, these chips are the upscale variety. Less salt." Lucy put glasses and the bowl of chips on a tray and nodded to the coffee table in the sitting room. Getting the idea, Rebecca carried it to its intended destination. Lucy brought the wine bottle. "I'm glad to hear you're not moving all your stuff," she said lightly as she poured the wine.

Rebecca shrugged. "Why should I move everything before I know where I'm going to land?"

"So, it's not because you think a reconciliation is possible."

Rebecca's face colored. "Seriously? You think we can get over this? She's still texting that bitch and making plans. Sounds like she's moved on already."

"You're sure about that? Have you asked whether she might consider couple counseling?"

Rebecca peered directly into Lucy's eyes. "Are you offering?"

"Of course not. That would be unethical, but my new partner, Gloria Parrish might take you on as clients. She specializes in lesbian couples counseling."

"Really? I thought she was a trauma therapist."

"That too," said Lucy, reaching for a handful of chips. "Which could help if Judith's sudden infidelity is related to the war."

Rebecca started eating the chips by the fistful as she thought about what Lucy had said. "Putting aside my anger, which I can assure you is enormous, I find it hard to imagine forgiving Judith. Do you really think an intimate relationship can be healed after infidelity?"

Lucy took a sip of wine. "Yes, I do. There will be many bumps in the road, setbacks, screaming fights and tears, before it can happen. If you're both willing to see each other as flawed human beings instead of the enemy, you can try. That is, if it's what you both want."

"Right now, I'm not getting that message," Rebecca said, reflectively staring out the window.

"Have you asked?"

"No," Rebecca admitted. "We're not really speaking to one another, except where the girls are concerned."

"Well, maybe someone needs to make the first move."

"Meaning me."

Lucy stared at Rebecca as if to say, *do I really need to underscore the obvious?*

"Why me? I didn't go out and fuck another woman while my wife was waiting for me at home, desperately wondering if I was even alive!"

"No, you didn't. You are clearly the injured party, but that is also why you can be magnanimous and offer the olive branch. Plus, you're a rabbi and used to counseling warring couples. If you can put your anger aside for five minutes, you can look at it more objectively. Judith is the one who hurt you, so she's probably consumed with guilt."

Rebecca allowed a low chuckle to roll out of her throat. "It's not just the Catholics who do guilt. Jewish mothers invented it."

"Exactly. Ruth taught you to be an expert."

Rebecca laughed aloud. "Lucy, why are your insights always spot on?"

Lucy shrugged. "Just observant, I guess. I listen well."

"Yes, you do. But what makes you think this can work?"

"Because I've seen it before."

"You mean in your practice?"

"No, closer to home. Maggie has finally forgiven Liz for falling in love with me. Believe me, Rebecca, Liz never broke her marriage vows with me...at least not physically. We sublimated a lot, but we never had sex before the divorce, and I'm not splitting hairs like Bill Clinton."

Rebecca studied Lucy's face. "I believe you, and I've always believed you. But what makes you think Maggie has really forgiven Liz?"

"She moved into the apartment over the garage."

"What? You didn't tell me that!"

"We haven't talked in a while," Lucy reminded her. "Maggie moved back in with her daughter after her relationship with Sam McKinnon fell apart. Unfortunately, all the political stress made Alina less careful about consuming alcohol with her psychotropic drugs. One night she had a fight with her fiancé and completely lost her mind. She threw Maggie out of the house, just packed her mother's bags and carried them out to the driveway. Maggie called a cab to take her to a motel. The next day, she showed up on our doorstep. Of course, we took her in."

"Of course, you did. You always say that Liz always takes in strays."

Lucy thought, *apparently, I do too.* "Liz is the most honorable and generous person I know," she said aloud.

"Even if she is a notorious flirt."

"Yes, that too," Lucy agreed. "They didn't have an easy road to reconciliation."

"If I remember right, Maggie cheated on Liz with a man." Lucy smiled because Rebecca's engagement in the story meant she'd forgotten her own troubles for a moment.

"Well, it turned out that event wasn't exactly what it seemed, but that's another tale for another time."

"Lucy! You can't do that to me! What do you mean it wasn't exactly what it seemed?"

Lucy debated the best way to explain that intercourse had been impossible because it had been too long since Maggie had been with a man. "The affair wasn't consummated," she finally said.

"Well, to a lesbian having a dick inside you isn't really the same thing. Or it's everything, because it's a man you're cheating with, not another woman." Lucy eyed Rebecca. Her use of a crude expression wasn't like her. Lucy realized her friend had been guzzling her wine like water.

"That can go either way," Lucy agreed. "Either it means less because it's a man or it means everything."

When Rebecca batted away the statement with a wave of her hand, Lucy realized she was tipsy. She hadn't been eating much lately, so the alcohol had gone right to her head. "In Liz's case, it was a trigger because when they were dating in college, Maggie pretended to be normal by dating men. Maggie knew that sleeping with a man would really hurt Liz."

"So that's why it ended the marriage," concluded Rebecca pouring herself another glass of wine. The glasses were large but meant only to be filled a little at the bottom. Rebecca kept pouring. "But they didn't speak to one another for years. How did they work it out?"

"When Maggie got cancer again, she wanted Liz to manage her case like she did the first time. Liz tried to foist her off on her protégé, but Maggie wasn't having it. What a mess! But Liz came through for Maggie, because she's, you know, Liz. That's when they finally began speaking to one another. What complicated things was Maggie's relationship with Sam, Liz's best friend."

"Jealousy?"

Lucy compressed her lips and thought for a moment. "Yes, but not in the way you think. Liz was annoyed that Maggie was interfering in her friendship with Sam."

"But Sam's gone now."

"Yes, she is, and unlikely to come back. Even before they broke up, Maggie was afraid to be alone at Sam's house. That was one reason she'd moved back in with her daughter."

"Poor Maggie," said Rebecca with a sigh. "Always thinks she's found a home and ends up homeless. I hope that's not me. I don't have the money to buy a house on my own. I can't live with Mom. She'd drive me crazy. I love Jack, but it's clear he's the boss now."

"Well, don't worry. You can stay here as long as you want to."

"Of course, you'd say that, Lucy. You charge my sister a ridiculously low rent. You could get three times what she pays."

"They're saving up to buy a house, and I don't need the money. I'm glad the place is occupied. Empty beach houses get burglarized more often."

Rebecca's eyes started to close. Lucy took the glass out of her hand before she spilled the contents. The motion woke up Rebecca. "I'm sorry, Lucy. I haven't had much sleep."

"Why don't you go up and lie down on the bed and take a little nap? I can go over to your mother's and get your bags."

"Oh, my sister can bring them over. Let me send her a text." While she was doing that, Lucy corked the wine bottle, covered Rebecca's glass, and put a clip on the bag of chips. By the time she returned, Rebecca had passed out on the futon. Lucy covered her with one of the colorful afghans Liz's grandmother had crocheted.

She left her key to the apartment on the table and turned the button to lock the door behind her. As she descended into the garage, Lucy realized she hadn't gotten around to explaining that she was now part of a threesome. At least, she'd set the scene.

Chapter 13

Deborah Goldberg looked over the rim as she sipped a glass of Liz's best Chardonnay. She inspected the trio sitting on the living room sofa. Liz could feel the blonde's subtle judgments of each of the three women before her. Her dark eyes glittered as she inspected Liz. They widened a bit when they settled on Maggie, but they lingered on Lucy for a long time. Finally, Deborah smiled all the way into her hidden tucks from her last facelift. "I must say," she pronounced in carefully paced words, "you make a most attractive throuple."

"Glad you aren't disappointed, Deb," Liz said, "but I expected more surprise."

Deborah's merriment at the statement was perfectly controlled and ladylike, but her eyes were full of laughter. "Nothing you do surprises me, Liz, but I will admit that marrying a priest wasn't on my bingo card. The opera singer part I totally get. You and Erika were always running down to the Met to hear your favorite divas. And now you have one of your very own! Well done, Dr. Stolz."

Liz resisted the impulse to puff up with pride over her little family. Then Maggie jumped up, "Let me get the snacks. I'm sure you're hungry after the long train ride from New York."

"Actually, it was restful, and I got to see parts of New England I'd miss if I were driving. Caught up on some reading too. I reviewed all the news posts and articles in which your friend, Brenda, is mentioned."

"You didn't need to do that," Liz said.

"Of course, I didn't, but it's been a long time since I had a case with national attention. Keeps the blood pumping to my brain. Reminds me that I'm not dead yet." Deborah had five years on Liz, who heard an echo of her own comments on aging. She wondered if all older women needed reassurance that they were not just breathing, but still relevant.

Liz caught Deborah admiring Lucy with furtive glances. Lucy dismissed perfect looks as an accident of genetics, inherited from her mother, who'd been a model as well as a singer, but she was beautiful and deserved to be ogled. Liz was proud to watch Deborah notice her wife's virtues.

"Lucy, I hear you have a full schedule. All the major summer festivals and national opera companies, a revival of *Faust* at La Scala, Desdemona at Covent Garden, but no Met." Deborah clucked her tongue sympathetically. "Gelb is a fool. He'll take down that house yet."

"To be fair," Lucy began, "Covid crippled many arts institutions. They had to spend down their endowments to stay afloat. The Webhanet Playhouse has been going strong since the 1930s. If not for donors like Maggie and Liz and frankly, me, it would be out of business. It absolutely deserved to be rescued, but really, there's only so much individuals can do."

"Agreed, but private money may be their only salvation. They're not getting any money from the current administration. Now that he's taken over the Kennedy Center, I fear that's the end of it. He's such a petty, little man with no class. Like Hitler, he takes over institutions to prove he can push them around."

Liz settled back to listen to Lucy and Deb discuss the crisis of arts institutions since Covid. Despite a doctorate in theology and a popular book on sex, Lucy often doubted her intellectual abilities. Liz especially enjoyed watching her hold her own against Deborah's sharp mind.

"Lucy, I don't know how you do it," Deborah said. "You run a church and a busy summer chapel. You keep up a very active singing career, and you manage to keep my friend here in line." Deborah peered at Liz.

"Oh, Liz keeps herself in line," said Lucy, laughing. "I may be her better angel, but she's such a straight arrow, sometimes I have to remind her to relax. Besides, Maggie does all the heavy lifting. I just expect Liz to be her best self, and she always rises to the occasion."

Deborah laughed heartily, her natural just-a-girl-from-Queens guffaw. She liked Lucy and felt comfortable with her. *Good*, thought Liz. Then Deborah turned her dark eyes on Liz. "She has you all figured out. You needed a sharp woman like Lucy to make you behave yourself. If her life depended on it, Jenny couldn't stop you from working yourself to death and bedding every woman in the metropolitan area, never mind at those medical conventions."

Liz blushed. Few people could make her feel embarrassed about her sexual exploits, but Deborah knew every one of her pressure points. That quality was exactly what made her such a good publicist and spokesperson. She was incredibly observant and sucked up details like a sponge, carefully storing them away for future use.

Maggie returned with the tray of hors d'oeuvres. Deborah leaned over to inspect the wide variety of tasty treats, apparently overwhelmed by the selection. "These all look too good to eat. What do you recommend, Maggie?"

"Try the pâté crostini. I got the recipe for the chicken liver pâté from a Jewish friend, Ruth Morgenstern."

"You have Jews here?" said Deb, looking directly at Liz as if she needed confirmation of something she couldn't possibly believe. "Who knew?"

Liz laughed. "Oh, we have a few. The Morgensterns have a house on the marsh. The younger daughter, Melissa, is my attorney. The other daughter is a rabbi. She's been a friend of Lucy's since seminary. One of Lucy's partners in her psychotherapy practice is Gloria Parrish. She's non-practicing now but grew up Jewish."

"Parrish doesn't sound like a Jewish name," said Deborah with a thoughtful look. "It must have been anglicized at some point. Probably some unpronounceable East European name. We German Jews had it easy."

"If you stay a while, and I hope you will," Liz continued, "I'd be happy to introduce you to some of our friends. You'll enjoy Olivia Enright, who retreated to Hobbs after her hedge fund became a big scandal."

"Olivia Enright lives here?" Deborah widened her eyes.

"She does, and she has the biggest house on Gull Island."

"Of course, she does. I'd love to meet her and find out what really happened. She's lucky she escaped prison time. Martha Stewart was the high-profile fish they caught. They always prosecute the women while the men swim away unharmed."

"That's exactly what Olivia says," said Liz.

Deborah got up to get a plate and help herself to more canapes. "Maggie, your hors d'oeuvres are as delicious as they are beautiful. You outdid yourself." Deborah engaged the eyes of each of her hostesses. "Thank you all for making me feel so welcome."

***

After dinner, Liz and Deborah sat on the enclosed porch. Although it was June, the nights were still cool, so Liz had the propane stove cranking. Liz had offered Deborah her best cognac, while she sipped her favorite single-malt Irish whiskey.

"That pro-immigrant group has been protesting outside the police station since the news broke about the chief signing the 287g agreement," said Liz. "They're the source of the controversy, not the media."

"Everyone hates ICE now, thanks to the orange man and Stephen Miller's vile tactics. Obviously, we need to enforce immigration laws, but not this way. Obama deported more violent undocumented immigrants, but he did it legally and without the need for body armor and intimidation. I think half of those ICE agents are Proud Boys and Oath Keepers looking for a legal way to beat up brown people."

"I wouldn't be surprised if some of them are the January sixth insurrectionists he pardoned."

"Some say they are," Deborah agreed and took a sip of cognac. She held it up to the firelight. "This is good stuff, Liz."

"I don't share it with everyone, only people who can appreciate it. I know you have good taste."

"One learns fast when one comes from nothing."

"Oh, come on, Deb. Your father owned a drug store chain."

"Three stores. Not a chain like they have now. Those national chains put him out of business before he was ready to retire. My mother worked as a bookkeeper to help put me through Barnard."

"Forgot we have that Columbia connection. Lucy too, she got her social work degree there, and Union Theological has some connection to the university, I think."

Deborah raised her glass. "Here's to over-educated women who work twice as hard as men to get halfway to where they are."

"Oh, I don't know," said Liz, sitting back in her chair. "Some of us succeeded."

"Yes, but look at your friend, Olivia, and Martha Stewart. They were made to pay for their mistakes. Or poor Lucy, who was made to pay for being raped by a man who pretended to be her friend. Powerful men get away with everything."

"Not disputing that fact, Deb. We all worked our asses off to get where we were. Sometimes I miss the pace of a high-profile job, but I don't mind leaving it behind."

"Sounds like you're still working your ass off from what Maggie tells me."

Liz shook her head. "She never knew me when I was chief of surgery. She was busy playing a bored suburban housewife with her perfect engineer husband, who cheated on her the first chance he got. Who knows? Maybe he was cheating on her the whole time they were married. They couldn't get pregnant, and Maggie went through years of fertility treatments." Liz stared into her whiskey reflectively. "All the hormones they pumped into her probably contributed to her breast cancer risk."

"Poor woman," Deborah said in a genuinely sympathetic voice. "How lucky she found you at the right time."

"I told you how I discovered the breast cancer."

"Yes, you did. You were on a camping trip in Acadia National Park, if I recall."

"It was the first time we'd made love in forty years." Liz sat back in her seat, remembering that night. "It was wonderful until I felt the lump. It was all I could do not to react, but I'd been trained to stay calm, so I did."

"You were probably so horny, you just wanted to get the job done."

Liz grinned. "I sure did. I spent months trying to get her into bed."

"Oh, you're shameful!" Deborah shook her head. "So gleeful about your conquests. Worse than a man sometimes."

Liz touched her chin to her chest. "I beg your pardon!"

"But you are, with all your butch swagger, your surgeon's arrogance. I'm surprised you're not a stone butch and refuse to be touched."

"Deb, I'm butch, not crazy." Liz leaned toward Deborah and spoke behind her hand. "Don't tell, but Lucy absolutely *owns* me in bed."

Deborah cackled. "Why am I not surprised? It's always the tiny, feminine ones who can bring a big, strong butch to her knees. Well, good, Liz. I'm glad you met your match. But what about Maggie? How does she take being second fiddle? She once was the wife of the town doctor. Not the same as being married to the chief of surgery at Yale, but a prominent social position even so."

"That's a damn good question," said Liz, gazing into the fire. "Maggie's spent her entire life using sex to get ahead in life. Her mother drummed into her the goal of marrying up, so that's what Maggie did. She married the high school football captain who got a scholarship to engineering school. When they couldn't have a baby, Maggie convinced him to adopt two orphans from Romania. I must say Barry was a good father to those girls, who had lots of problems."

"Is he still around?"

Liz shook her head sadly. "No, he died of prostate cancer last year. Sophia, the older daughter, is an oncologist. She was so depressed because she couldn't do anything for her father, but the cancer was stage four when they discovered it."

"That's sad."

"It was. He was only a year older than Maggie. Seventy-three is young these days."

"Sounds like you forgave him. Last I heard, you wanted to castrate him in his sleep."

Liz laughed. "Yes, I used to have some colorful revenge fantasies. Relieves the need to execute on them. Plus, karma is a bitch. He's dead, and I have his wife...again."

"Yes, tell me about that, Liz. Why did you take her back after she cheated on you with a man?"

"Turns out it was more complicated than that. And in fairness, I was drooling over Lucy like the monster in *Alien*. I behaved awfully."

Deborah gave her a long critical look. "I'm not sure I like this Liz Stolz who confesses her sins and takes responsibility. Part of what I've always loved about you is your unrepentant bravado. You used to take what you wanted and never looked back."

"I still take what I want," said Liz defiantly. "And as you can see, I get it."

"Point taken." Deborah seemed surprised by the aggression of Liz's reply and sat back. "But you seem to have become more sensitive."

"We all grow up eventually. Maybe by the time I die, I'll get there."

"Hear, hear," said Deborah, extending her glass. They tapped in agreement.

Liz frowned. "You're running low there, Deb. A refill?"

"I thought you'd never ask."

*****

"Oh, my God!" Maggie exclaimed, unfolding the paper copy of the *New York Times*. After the expletive, she gave Lucy a sheepish look. "Brenda made the front page," Maggie quickly explained.

"What!" said Deborah, suddenly awake after sleepily hunching over her first cup of coffee. "Let me see."

Maggie handed her the paper. Deborah scanned it rapidly and turned to the continuance of the article on page twelve.

"I found it in the app," said Liz. "I'm sending you the link. Deb, kindly return Maggie's paper. She hates reading online." Deborah returned the section of the *New York Times* to Maggie and tapped open her phone. "Interesting that it's indexed under travel, but it made the front page."

"That's because they used the impact of the controversy on tourism as the hook," Deb explained. At the speed she read, she'd already finished the article. "Many of the comments are people swearing never to visit Hobbs again."

"That's not good," said Lucy, who'd been sipping her coffee to wake up. It had been an active night. The reminder that Liz was a stud had been an inspiration, and Lucy's toys had gotten a vigorous workout. "Hobbs is just getting back on its feet after the pandemic. This town lives and dies by its tourist season. It can't take another economic shock."

There was an extended silence while the others caught up to Liz, who was halfway down the comments. Almost every one of them was negative about the town and its police chief. "What is *wrong* with people?" Liz said in disgust. "Why is Hobbs a terrible place because the police chief signed up for some government-sponsored training?"

"It's gotten out of control," Deborah said calmly. "What I can't figure out is how this got on the front page from the travel section. I know there has been some national news coverage but being on the front page of the *New York Times* means someone got the managing editor's attention."

"Oh, I bet I know how that happened," said Maggie, carefully folding and stacking the newspaper. "Greg bragged that he knew a retired journalist who was advising him on strategy for the communications team. He used to write a column in the Portland paper."

"I know who you're talking about. He had a regular opinion column after he left hard news reporting. He made quite a name for himself for even-handed coverage of Maine politics." Liz snapped her fingers near her ear, trying to recall the writer's name.

"Yes, that's the one," Maggie said. "Greg liked to throw his name around like the man was his best friend. I doubt it. Greg is so full of himself. Maybe he talked to the guy once or twice, but in Greg's mind that made them bosom buddies." Liz smiled at the expression from their youth that no one ever used anymore.

"The man's name is Russell Bliss," Deborah said, scrolling through her phone. "Yes, he had a high profile, even out of state. He won a couple of journalism awards. Not exactly a Pulitzer winner, but I could see him knowing people in high places at The *New York Times*."

"The communication team was really focused on getting news attention for their ICE protests in front of the police station," said Maggie. "It became their one and only issue. Their obsession was annoying other teams and the officers. We saw what happened."

"What happened?" asked Deborah. "This is getting exciting!"

Liz listened to Maggie summarize how a riot broke out when Brenda went to answer the group's questions about the ICE agreement and how three of the four officers had resigned. Deb turned to Liz. "You never told me your little town was so exciting!"

Liz shrugged. "When you look under the hood, all little towns are full of conflict and passion. Remember our parents watching *Peyton Place* when we were young? But the shooting at Hobbs elementary was much more exciting." Liz leaned on her hand. "Honestly, I could do with less excitement."

Deborah barely waited until Liz finished speaking before ordering her to call Brenda. "Tell her not to react, not even with close associates. From now on, she needs to keep her mouth *shut*." Deborah passed her open hand in front of her face. "NO reactions. Once a story hits The *New York Times*, it never dies. Quick! Call her."

Liz picked up her phone to call Brenda, but it rang in her hands. The town manager's name and photo flashed on her screen. "Olivia is calling me. Guess what this is about?" Liz swiped open the call. "Olivia, I'll call you right back. My publicist friend is here and she's advising me to call Brenda right *now*."

"Liz, you're talking to *me* now," Olivia ordered angrily. "Did you see the article in the *Times*?"

"I sure did. That's why I'm calling Brenda. I'll call you back as soon as I get off with her. Okay?" Liz didn't wait for her to answer. She tapped closed the call and scrolled for Brenda's number.

Fortunately, she picked up on the first ring. "What? Don't you think I'm busy now?"

"Yes, but my publicist friend advises you to be calm and not to react. Make no statements to anyone. Put on your game face and pretend everything is fine."

Brenda grunted in exasperation. "You actually think that's possible?"

"Yes, it is. Just do it. Now, I know it's hard, but you're tough, Brenda. *Tough.* Remember that. I have to call Olivia back."

"Oh, Jesus!" exclaimed Brenda. "She's going to have me fired."

"No, she's not," said Liz, trying to sound confident, although it was a real possibility. "Now, take my advice. Shut yourself in your office and calm down. I'll call you in a few minutes after I deal with Olivia."

But Liz didn't instantly call Olivia. She sat at the kitchen island and took some deep breaths.

"Did you teach her that?" Deborah asked, turning to Lucy.

"She didn't," Liz said. "It's my fifteen seconds of Zen. I used it in surgery when I had my fingers clamping the patient's artery, and I needed to figure out what to do next."

Deborah continued to focus on Lucy. "Rev. Bartlett, what do you think about all this?" she asked in a casual voice.

"I feel bad for everyone involved, especially Brenda and her family. It's a mess of her own making, but I can see why she's afraid to back down. She didn't do anything wrong. Under another administration, without ICE acting like a backwoods militia, no one would have thought twice about her agreement with DHS."

"Exactly right," said Deborah. "Context is everything."

Liz had forgotten that maxim, which came right under "perception is reality" in Deborah's list of how to manage a bad situation. "Excuse me. I'm going to my office to talk to Olivia. It's going to be a loud conversation full of bad words, and I don't want to offend my wife."

"Liz, I've heard your filthy mouth before," Lucy said blithely. "Don't leave because of me."

Liz stayed, but when she called Olivia back, it went directly into her voice mail. She hoped that Brenda's worst fear wasn't being realized. She *really* needed that job.

Chapter 14

When Olivia finally called back, Liz retreated to her office as she'd planned. Lucy had heard her swear up a storm, so she didn't care about her language. She suspected Liz wanted privacy so she could give Olivia a piece of her mind.

"You don't think that woman will fire the chief, do you?" Deborah asked.

"Probably not," said Maggie. "Olivia has too much invested in Brenda. She refused to accept her letter of resignation when she ended up with Long Covid that affected her heart. She got her that spot on the Fox News show. But Olivia gets super anxious about anything that affects tourism. What matters to Olivia is the bottom line."

Lucy sighed and locked her phone screen. "I think I'll get dressed and go into the office for a while."

"You look dressed to me," said Deborah, looking Lucy up and down.

"Usually, she works at home on Wednesdays to write her sermon," Maggie explained. "She means she's going to put on her collar."

"Ooo! You mean I get to see you in your costume?"

"As a singer, I wear a lot of costumes, Deborah," Lucy said with a sigh. "This outfit is more like my uniform."

She left them in animated conversation and reluctantly went upstairs to put on a clerical shirt. She imagined how differently the day could have gone. She could have leisurely browsed her library of gospel commentaries for inspiration. At eleven, she would likely have taken a break with Maggie to catch up on the internal and external gossip. Then they might have had an extended yoga session. After lunch, she could have done her singing practice, which she'd skipped this morning because they had company. She hated giving up her work-at-home day, but she couldn't hide in her beautiful office overlooking the ocean while the whole town was on fire.

Mindful that Deborah was a chic dresser, Lucy leafed through her more colorful outfits, finally choosing the embroidered jacket Maggie had found for her in the thrift store. The rich colors were exotic but classy. New, the jacket would have been outrageously expensive. Maggie was an experienced thrift store shopper and always found the best deals.

While Lucy was putting on her makeup, she decided she would stop at Cherie's before heading to the office. No doubt Brenda had already called her with her worries about her job. Cherie was a gifted therapist, but when it comes to your own family, all your professional skills fall apart.

Lucy applied a deep red lipstick because she expected the day would require her to display some power as well as compassion. She pressed her lips together and gently blotted the excess, then stepped back to look at her image in the full-length mirror. With a change of wardrobe and a full coat of makeup she'd transformed from relaxed Lucy with fuzzy slippers to the Rev. Dr. Lucille Bartlett. She decided that Deborah wouldn't be disappointed seeing her in this "costume."

Lucy slipped the tube of lipstick into her pocket and texted Cherie. *Mind if I stop by in a little while?*

The text had barely been delivered when the response arrived. *Please do.* Lucy stared at the words, trying to discern their possible meaning. Like emails, text messages were tone-deaf. She doubted Cherie was simply being polite. More likely it was a plea for compassion and emotional support. After her wife had been shamed on the front page of the *New York Times*, Cherie would likely need both.

Lucy's return to the kitchen was met by a wolfish whistle. Liz's blasts of approval had a different tone, and Maggie made disapproving eyes at such behavior. Of course, it was Deborah. She got up from her stool at the island to get a better view. "Wow, Lucy, and I thought you were hot in your jeans. You are one *sexy* priest!"

"Thank you, Deb. Last year Maggie decided I needed a make-over of my clerical outfit, so she took me to the thrift shops."

Deborah turned to Maggie. "If that's what you can find up here, take me, take me!"

"This is a good time of year to shop," Maggie explained. "The rich people are changing over their seasonal clothes and cleaning out their closets."

Liz came into the kitchen like a storm, scowling as she filled a coffee pod and forcefully poked at the button of the coffee maker. She looked up to see the three expectant faces.

"Well?" Maggie finally asked, "what happened?"

"Thank God, Olivia has too much sense to fire Brenda. Never mind that she needs a vote of the select board to confirm it, and she hates asking them for anything. Apparently, the dressing down left Brenda in tears. How Olivia knew this without being there, I can't say. Maybe she was bragging. Olivia enjoys being an overbearing monster."

"But at least she didn't fire her on the spot," said Maggie, who had the good sense to ask for clarification. "Did she threaten to fire her?"

"No, but she demanded that she clean up this mess stat. A front-page story in the *New York Times* could have an economic impact on the town. Demographic trends are already against us. Retreating to the Maine shoreline is a Boomer's idea of an idyllic vacation. Younger people have other ideas."

"So what do we do now?" Maggie asked.

All eyes turned to Deborah, who began issuing assignments. "You, Liz, go to the police station and reassure your friend. Make sure she keeps her mouth shut. You, Lucy, comfort your flock as necessary. Maggie and I will stay here and draft a press release in response to this character assassination in the form of a travel article. We'll also write positive letters to the editor of the *Times*, using all our names to get as many posts into the comments while they're open. And I will write an article for *The Atlantic* that will be guaranteed to engender sympathy for Brenda. Hopefully, it will also expose the irrationality and hypocrisy of the *Times* story."

"But I thought the *Times* article was pretty even-handed," said Liz, stirring cream into her coffee.

Deborah rolled her eyes. "Liz, that's not the point. This is war, and we are going to fight!" She looked at each of them in turn. "Battle stations!"

Like obedient troops, they scattered.

***

Cherie's eyes were bloodshot when she opened the door for Lucy. She swung it wider and stepped back so she could pass. But as soon as it was closed, she threw herself into Lucy's arms. "Thank you for thinking of me!" she declared mournfully into Lucy's ear.

When Lucy was ready to let go, Cherie wasn't, so Lucy settled against her body and waited. Finally, the fierce grip on her lessened, and Cherie stepped back. She quickly wiped her tears with the back of her hands. "I don't want the kids to see I'm crying," she explained in a whisper.

Lucy didn't try to hide her surprise. "I thought school was open today."

"It is, but I kept them home. I don't want them listening to what other kids heard their parents saying about their mother."

In fact, most people in Hobbs never read the *New York Times*. Cherie probably needed her children home for her own comfort, not to shield them from thoughtless comments or bullying.

"Where are the children?" Lucy asked.

"Upstairs in their rooms reading. Aunt Simone is coming over in a little while to give them a lesson."

"Convenient to have a retired educator in the family," said Lucy.

"That it is. Come inside," said Cherie, taking Lucy's hand. "I'll make you some coffee." Lucy raised her thermal mug. "Keep it for later," said Cherie. "I'll make you some fresh."

Cherie settled Lucy at the kitchen table while she bustled about making a fresh pot of coffee and cutting Lucy an overly generous piece of coffee cake. Between Maggie and Cherie, Lucy was going to need a few extra laps in her beach walks.

"Liz is going over to see Brenda," Lucy said.

"I'm glad Liz is being there for Brenda. She's a real friend. I know she doesn't approve of the ICE agreement, but it doesn't matter."

"I don't think any of us approve of ICE or the contract, although rational people can see why Brenda thought it was a good idea," Lucy said. "But we can separate our opinions about the politics from our love for our friends."

"That's what makes you and Liz different. You see the big picture."

"I try," said Lucy modestly, "but I don't always succeed. Liz, who's studied the rise of the Third Reich, says the ICE aggression is deliberate intimidation."

"She's right. Those ICE agents are dressed for battle. One of my clients, a veteran, said he never used all that body armor and heavy weaponry when he was in Iraq! He has nothing but contempt for ICE. He says they're playing soldier, but they're too cowardly to sign up."

"But you understand why people are angry with Brenda for associating with ICE."

"Completely," said Cherie, sitting down with a cup of coffee. "And I've encouraged her to cancel that damn agreement, but she is the most stubborn woman I have *ever* met."

Lucy smiled. "But you love her, and her stubbornness is part of her appeal. I know because I'm married to someone like her. When she thinks she's right, she doesn't back down. She *doubles* down, and people don't always like it. Look how the gun club treated her when she testified for the enhanced yellow flag law."

"It's this cancel culture! It's as bad on the left as it is on the right."

"Maggie knows Pat and Maura through the adult education program at the high school. Since this started, they won't even speak to her. Never mind Greg."

Cherie shook her head. "This has ripped Hobbs apart. How could this happen?"

While Lucy thought about how to answer this question, she took a bite of coffee cake. Like everything Cherie baked, it was delicious. Lucy knew she didn't need the extra calories, but she ate it with pleasure. When she wiped her hands on the cloth napkin Cherie had provided, she wondered how this busy woman had the time to launder them with two jobs and two active kids.

"The chaos caused by this administration scares people," Lucy finally said. "Things look and feel out of control. Nothing is as it seems. He's sending troops into large cities in blue states, supposedly to reduce crime at a time when crime rates are down. The masked ICE agents are dressed for battle, which is clearly intended to intimidate all of us. When people are afraid they often turn on each other instead of the real enemy."

Cherie had been listening thoughtfully. "I realize all this, Lucy, but knowing it doesn't make it any easier for me or the kids."

Lucy covered Cherie's hand with hers. "No, it doesn't, and your pain is real. It's agonizing to watch someone you love being hurt. Never mind worrying about Brenda losing her job."

Cherie drew a ragged breath. "Thank God Olivia didn't ask for her resignation. She screamed at Brenda for ten minutes straight, but she never threatened to fire her."

"Olivia has always supported Brenda, even when she wanted to resign. Olivia will never admit she was wrong."

"What is it with these people who can't admit they were wrong?" asked Cherie, throwing up her hands.

Lucy raised her shoulders nearly to her ears. "Liz says it's a guy thing. Even if you realize you made a mistake you don't change course, or you look like you're weak. We can see it's counterproductive, but they don't. Being challenged just makes them dig in."

Out of the corner of her eye, Lucy saw a small person standing in the doorway. When she turned and smiled, Megan bounded into the room and crawled into her lap. She wiggled her small rear to establish a firm seat and settled back into Lucy's arms.

"When Megan has her Mother Lucy, no one else matters," said Cherie smiling at her daughter.

"That's because she knows she'll always get hugs from me." Lucy kissed Megan's silky blond hair, remembering the night Brenda had brought them to Liz to check them medically, after she'd rescued them from their parents' house. The moment Megan saw Lucy, she'd decided she was the safest person in the room, and it seemed they were bonded forever.

"Isn't this your day to stay home and write your sermon?" Cherie asked with a frown.

"It is, but I thought it would be a good idea to go into the office... and visit you."

Cherie's eyes filled. "Thank you," she said. "Thank you."

❊❊❊

Lucy was deeply involved in researching her sermon when she heard a soft knock on the door. She looked up to see her curate grinning. Her perfect teeth were shockingly white against her velvety black skin. Reshma was a true natural beauty, yet she wore it effortlessly.

"Good morning, Mother Lucy. I come bearing gifts!"

"Let me guess. Special delivery from Tiffany's shop?"

"Exactly. She figured your day could use a little sweetening," said Reshma, opening the box to display the beautifully decorated chocolate-covered strawberries.

"My favorite," said Lucy, helping herself to one dipped in white chocolate with dark chocolate drizzle. At least fruit counted as a relatively healthy treat. "You need to help me eat these," Lucy said, covering her mouth as she spoke with her mouth full.

Reshma sat down and reached into the white bakery box. "When we read the article in the *Times* this morning, we knew things would be busy for you."

"I've been putting out fires for most of the morning," Lucy replied, "but I finally found a few minutes to work."

"And I interrupted you."

"I'm always glad to see you, Reshma."

"Not only when I bring treats?"

Lucy pouted until Reshma said, "Okay, I believe you. I'm glad you don't mind me barging in on your sermon prep. Before I came, I brought some pastries to the police chief. She was behind closed doors and not to be disturbed. I hope her admin delivers them as I asked."

"I'm sure she will," Lucy assured her. "That's kind of Tiffany to think of Chief Harrison. I thought you were members of that group, Activate Hobbs."

"We were, but they were so nasty about the police chief. They refused to listen to me when I tried to explain that she was only trying to do what she thought was right. One of them told me to shut up. I happened to be wearing my collar, so I was surprised."

Lucy sighed. "Unfortunately, the collar means nothing anymore. Liberal clergy get lumped in with ministers of right-wing Evangelical churches. We're all equally bad in their eyes."

"But the Christian left fought along with civil rights leaders. Nuns and priests marched in Selma. I read about it in my history books."

"Your friends are too young to remember those days. And they don't teach history anymore."

"Maura and Pat are older than Liz. They remember, but they've lost their minds. They attend every select board meeting and insist on speaking even when the 287g isn't on the agenda. They say disruption is the only way to be heard, and they're expressing their First Amendment rights. When I took classes for my citizenship test, we spent a lot of time on the Constitution, especially The Bill of Rights. Many Americans have no idea what they're talking about. Tiffany and I quit that group. We're going to work with Melissa on organizing the next protest."

"That's brave. I thought you were afraid of being picked up in an ICE dragnet."

"I am afraid. But that's the definition of courage, isn't it? Doing the right thing, even when you're frightened? I may be the wrong color, but I am a naturalized US citizen, and I will exercise my rights to free speech and freedom of assembly, so help me God!" Reshma's statements were so fervent they made Lucy shiver and nearly brought tears to her eyes.

"Thank you for standing up for your beliefs."

"I never saw Tiffany so disgusted. She never met a liberal cause she didn't like." Tiffany's parents had raised her to be a political activist, but they also lived their beliefs. Her father, Brad Taylor, ran a charity dedicated to supporting artists in countries under oppressive regimes. "These people are out of control," Reshma continued. "They broke the Hobbs Democrats, and they won't rest until they destroy the police chief. That's just wrong!"

"Yes, it is. Sometimes, disruption is necessary, but usually only as a last resort," said Lucy, easily falling back into her role as Reshma's mentor. "Destroying someone else's good name to advance a cause is never right."

"When I went to deliver Tiffany's treats, the admin said that Dr. Liz was coming to see the chief. She's a good friend."

"Yes, she is," said Lucy, pleased to hear how much Reshma admired Liz.

Reshma glanced at Lucy's computer screen. "I'll let you go. I know you only came in today because there's so much going on." Reshma glanced at her phone. "And it's time for me to get on to my pastoral visits. Then I have a meeting with Mother Susan and Bobbie about their wedding."

"Thanks for offering to officiate. It was a little awkward for me because of our prior relationship."

Reshma raised a brow. "No worries. It is an honor to officiate at Mother Susan's wedding. If not for her, I wouldn't be a priest. You will come to the service, won't you?"

In fact, there was no way that Lucy could respectfully stay away, but Reshma's earnest anxiety made her smile. "Of course, I will. Susan has asked me to sing, and I will. Actually, I am looking forward to a big wedding. We need some joy amid all this fear and anger, don't you think?"

"I most certainly do," declared Reshma and rose. "Do you mind if I give one of those strawberries to Jodi?"

"Please. I can't eat them all."

Reshma grinned. "Oh I bet you can."

❋❋❋

Lucy returned home with a complete sermon and a hunger for real food after gorging on the box of chocolate-covered strawberries. At least she'd achieved her fiber target for the day. She opened the garage door to good smells wafting down the hall. Maggie and Liz must be cooking up a storm.

"Are we having company?" Lucy asked, taking off her collar at the door. Liz was always inviting people, so Lucy never knew who'd be there when she came home.

"Maggie invited Brenda and Cherie," Liz explained, "but they decided they need some privacy at home," Liz explained. "Maggie had already shopped for a crowd, so we invited Olivia and Amy instead."

"I thought it was a brilliant idea," said Deborah. "I'm dying to meet Olivia Enright. Plus, I get to watch Liz talk her friend out of making an ass of herself."

"It will be more relaxed because Olivia and Amy already know about us," Maggie said, turning away from the pots on the stove to give Lucy a quick kiss. "Honey, you look beat."

"I am," Lucy admitted.

"You're not the only one. When Deborah swings into action, she's not fooling around!"

Lucy gave Deborah a curious look. "Maggie helped me draft and write letters to the editor, send out press releases, and she proofread my article for *The Atlantic*. It will run in the next issue."

"Wow! You two have been busy." Lucy slipped into Liz's open arms, enjoying both her strength and softness.

"I love how you mesh with one another," observed Deborah. "It's like you were always meant to be together."

"Maybe we were," said Liz and kissed the top of Lucy's head.

"Karma," said Deborah, "It works both ways."

Lucy went upstairs to take off her clerical blouse. She'd noticed that Maggie looked as elegant as always. Even Liz had left on her perfectly pressed button-down shirt and dress slacks in honor of their guests. Olivia and Amy would be dressed from work, so Lucy decided to put on a silky maroon blouse that picked up a color in her jacket. She arrived downstairs just as Olivia and Amy were coming through the front door.

"An impromptu party. I love it!" Olivia declared. "Any excuse to savor one of Maggie's delicious meals." Of course, Olivia was taking up all the space in the room with her emphatic presence. Only Liz could achieve that when she put on her ex-surgeon persona, but she was clearly trying for a laid-back presence tonight. Knowing her, it was a deliberate attempt to lower the temperature after an overheated day.

There were hugs and kisses at the door, except Liz only shook Amy's hand because they were colleagues. The reserved Asian woman looked a bit overwhelmed at her partner's bluster and exchanged a look of commiseration with Lucy.

"I'm so glad I have an opportunity to meet you," said Deborah, insinuating herself into the knot at the door. "I'm Deborah Goldberg, Liz's former publicist."

"Oh, my God!" exclaimed Olivia. "I've heard so much about you. I've always wanted to meet you."

"Well, here I am. And I've always wanted to meet you, Ms. Enright. I've studied your case. You *never* should have resigned from the Enright Fund."

"Really?" said Olivia, intrigued. "Tell me more."

Liz chuckled, watching Deborah lead Olivia into the living room where Maggie had set out a charcuterie board worthy of a photo shoot. Liz brought Amy into the kitchen ostensibly to help with the drinks, but really to get an inside line on Olivia's mood.

"Well," said Maggie, taking Lucy's arm. "Shall we join the clash of the titans?"

"Oh, I think we're going to enjoy a front row seat at some very interesting social theater, don't you?"

Maggie smiled. "Lucy, I like your thinking."

They were, in fact, an audience to a fascinating analysis of how Olivia could have avoided giving up her controlling interest in the Enright Fund.

"You have an amazing grasp of the legal issues, Deborah," Olivia, who'd been conspicuously quiet for most of the evening, said.

"I studied law before I became a journalist and then a publicist," Deborah modestly explained.

"Then tell us how to get out of this mess we're in with our police chief."

Deborah smiled at Maggie and Lucy. "We're working on it."

By dessert, Lucy was tired from trying to keep up with all the moving parts in the conversation. Deborah had sold her plan to Olivia, who swore to stay out of police controversy and let an expert handle it. Over some excellent cabernet, they pledged to be lifelong friends. Liz was smiling, so she obviously thought this was a good outcome.

For a much-needed break from all the strategizing, Amy turned to Lucy. "I hear you have a full singing schedule this summer."

"I do. And my agent just landed me the soprano lead in a Covent Garden production of Charpentier's *Louise*. It's not often performed. I only sang it a few times as part of my *Fach* duty years ago in Stuttgart, so I'm practically relearning it."

"I'm not familiar with that opera," Amy admitted without an ounce of shame. One of the things Lucy most admired about Liz's partner was her effortless grace.

"Lucy sings the role superbly," said Liz. "I say we repair to the media room. I'm sure Deborah would love to hear you sing."

Lucy was startled that Liz hadn't asked before volunteering her to sing. "But I never had a chance to practice today."

Liz shrugged. "Go warm up. That will give us time to clear the table."

Lucy tried to stare her wife out of the idea, but Liz turned to collect dishes.

"Please, Lucy," said Maggie. "After you sing, we can sing some duets together to show off what a good voice teacher you are." Maggie turned to their guests and shyly admitted, "Lucy's been giving me lessons in classical singing."

Now, Maggie was betraying her. Lucy felt trapped and yet touched by their confidence in her. "All right," she finally said. "I'll meet you in the media room in twenty minutes... No sooner!"

"Promise." Liz rose and began clearing the table.

Lucy used the grand piano to cue the notes to her scales. Whenever she went through this quick warmup she thought of her mother, her first singing teacher, who'd taught her so many tricks she still used today. One was how to ready herself to sing publicly with hardly any preparation.

By the time the others arrived, Lucy was feeling like she was in good-enough voice to sing a few arias. While their guests settled into the home theater seats in the oversized room, Liz ran around behind the scenes, turning on the sound system and adjusting the lighting. Within a short time, the media room was transformed into a venue for a cozy, private concert.

"I'm ready if you are," Liz called after jumping down from the little stage. She took the seat next to Maggie.

"I'm going to sing the most famous aria from *Louise*, which you may recognize because it's a popular soprano concert solo." Lucy connected her phone to the sound system to stream the accompaniment to *"Depuis le jour."* She enjoyed watching the faces of her listeners as she sang the eloquent aria.

Liz was listening with a look of otherworldly devotion. She sat back in her chair, her legs were spread wide. Because Liz often sat that way, taking up space like a man, Lucy knew it wasn't meant to be an obscene gesture. When she sang, Liz responded erotically. Some of their most sublime nights together were after Lucy's performances. As she reached the crescendo, Lucy smiled directly at Liz. There was no need to imagine what the night would bring, because they were already making love.

Chapter 15

Brenda slammed the door of her SUV and leaned on the roof. She needed to get all her anger out before she went into the house and the kids saw her like this. Even worse than the fury was the blow to her confidence. She hadn't felt so unsure of herself since her first day in the homicide division when a shot-up body made her puke in front of half a dozen seasoned cops. After her boss had pulled her aside later, he told her to either learn to deal with such awful sights or find another line of work. With her extended cop family breathing down her neck, Brenda had learned to control her nausea...until now. She didn't know whether to beat the roof of the car, cry, or throw up.

The light went on by the front door. Cherie stepped out onto the little porch. "Come inside, honey bear. It's safe in here."

The simple statement finally brought tears to Brenda's eyes. Their home was a sanctuary, not only because she could hide from the criticism, but because her beautiful wife was there to welcome her home. For years after Marcia died, Brenda had longed for the refuge of another woman's arms. Thank God Cherie could put aside her fear of cops and guns and give her a chance.

Brenda clicked the key tag until the vehicle honked. She knew she was preoccupied, so she'd started doing things twice. Distraction was not a good thing in a cop.

Cherie enfolded her in her arms. The feel of her wife's soft breasts against her were like a soothing balm. "Sorry, I'm so late," Brenda murmured into Cherie's sweet-smelling hair. More than anything, the familiar scent reminded her that she was *home*. "Are the kids already in bed?"

"They were exhausted and couldn't stay up any longer. Aunt Simone was here all day. Her lessons are fun but intense. Those kids probably learned more in a day than in a whole week in school."

Brenda smiled for the first time that day. "Good for Aunt Simone. Their minds need a good workout now and then."

Cherie took Brenda's hand. "Come in. I'll give you your dinner, or did you eat some fast-food crap your staff brought you?"

"I didn't have time to eat. Didn't even notice. No appetite today."

"Well, then I hope you like my dinner. You need to eat, Brenda." Cherie pulled on her shirt sleeve. "You're losing too much weight over this bullshit."

Brenda followed her wife into the kitchen. "You're going to have a glass of milk with your dinner. All those beers aren't helping you sleep. They make you think you're relaxing, but when the alcohol wears off you're hanging off the ceiling." Brenda chuckled. Cherie had a way with words, and her Louisiana drawl made her statements even more colorful, but her description was accurate. Brenda could count on her hand the nights of uninterrupted sleep she'd had in the last month, and they were the result of exhaustion.

After locking up her service pistol in the hall closet, Brenda came into the kitchen. She was pleased to see that Cherie had made one of her favorite dinners. Before she'd tasted Cherie's meatloaf, with a little hot sauce added for zing, Brenda always thought her mother made it best. Cherie spooned a fluffy mound of mashed potatoes on her plate and covered it with gravy. Once she'd poured a large glass of milk from the gallon jug, Brenda's nostalgic visit to her childhood was complete. She released a long sigh. "God, it's good to be home."

"That's why I refused Maggie's kind invitation to dinner. For one thing, I couldn't guarantee you'd get out of work on time, but the real reason was I knew you'd want to be in your own house with your own people."

"Liz and Lucy are our people too," said Brenda after a long drink of the ice-cold milk.

"They have a house guest, so we couldn't really be ourselves. She's an old friend of Liz's, who helped her during the malpractice suit that actress bought against her. I didn't know Liz then, but even I was following that story."

"Yup, me too. It was hard to miss. It was all over the tabloids, even in *People* magazine." Brenda gulped down some more milk. "I hope Liz didn't bring her up here because of me," she said with a frown and felt prickly at the idea. "I told her I don't need help from a slick New York publicist."

"According to Lucy, Liz called her because they hadn't been in touch for a while and just wanted her opinion. You know how Liz is. She invites everyone to come up to Maine. Apparently, this woman accepted, so here she is."

"Well, I'm *not* interested," Brenda said, aggressively digging into her meatloaf.

"Sweetie Pie, your friend means well. Don't be angry. She gave you good advice on pausing the agreement."

"And now that damn law passed, but our governor won't sign it. I thought she was on our side! If she'd sign it, I'd have to cancel the agreement."

"Do you know why she won't sign it?" Cherie asked, replenishing the small mountain of mashed potatoes that Brenda had demolished.

"Sean follows legislation more closely than I do. There are situations when the Feds can force us to cooperate. He thinks she won't sign because she thinks it won't survive a court challenge."

"That seems like a weasel solution."

"It really is because if she doesn't veto the bill, it will eventually become a law. Meanwhile, we're in limbo."

"No, you're not. You can just cancel the agreement based on the law passing the legislature."

Brenda gave her wife a hard look. "You think I've put you, our family, the department, the whole town of Hobbs through all this just to drop it?"

Cherie shrugged. "Why not?"

"Because it doesn't work that way."

Cherie crossed her arms on her chest. "Well, then Chief Harrison, tell me how it works."

Brenda gave her a pleading look. "Please, honey, don't you get on my case. You have no idea how bad my day was. I can't take having you against me too."

Cherie rubbed Brenda's arm soothingly. "I know, honey bear. Eat your dinner in peace. I won't say another word about this. I promise."

***

Brenda would have been on time for her breakfast date with Liz if not for the reporters and protesters camped outside all the entrances of the police station. Fire Chief Paul Duvaney and Brenda watched the crowd from the window of his office.

"They really have me trapped," said Brenda. "I'll be late for my breakfast date with Dr. Stolz."

Paul scratched idly at the mutton chop sideburns he wore in honor of Wolverine, his pop culture hero. "Not if I drive you to the diner."

They went down to the fire garage and got into the Chief's red SUV. "You could make all this stop, Brenda," Paul said casually as they slipped past the press unnoticed. "I know why you're holding out, but at some point, it gets stupid."

She felt his blue eyes on her when he turned to see her reaction. "I know, Paul. But I'm not dropping it until the governor signs that bill. Otherwise, I'm backing down under pressure from the likes of them." Watching the protesters grow smaller in the rearview mirror, she thumbed over her shoulder.

"They're nuts, but they're not wrong," said Paul. "Those ICE agents are acting like assholes."

"Yes, they are. They're out of control, but that doesn't mean the training was a bad idea. And there was a good reason for it. We don't want ICE in our town."

"That's not why you did it, though," Paul said, turning to her.

"No, honestly, I hadn't thought that far ahead. We just have two holding cells. Sean was thinking if we had to arrest a large number of people, we'd have no place to put them."

"I get that part, Brenda, but this is making you look bad. Time to give it up."

"Thanks for your advice, Paul. I will take it under consideration."

"I hope you do. My guys are sick of driving around those protestors to get out of the station."

When Paul swung into the diner parking lot, the flashing lights made the customers inside come to the windows. Nothing like a dramatic entrance to draw a crowd.

There was another counter waitress on duty, so the first thing Brenda asked Liz was what happened to Paula. "You know I can't tell you, Brenda. Professional confidence."

"Well, then give me a hint."

"She's on her feet too much and needs a break."

"Her plantar fasciitis is bothering her," Brenda guessed.

Liz just shrugged and put her phone away. "How the hell are you?"

"Been better, but I finally got a full night's sleep with that pill Cherie gave me."

"Oh, good. She asked me to prescribe it for you. Glad it's working."

Lois arrived with Brenda's coffee. "I put in your orders because Paula's not here today."

"If you talk to her, tell her that we miss her and hope she gets well soon," Brenda replied.

Lois looked pleased at the show of concern. "I certainly will." She turned and scowled at a woman at the next table staring at them. "They never stop, do they?"

"Nope, haters gonna hate," said Liz. She turned to the woman with a big smile that showed threatening bared teeth. When the woman literally clutched her pearls, Liz laughed hilariously.

"Better stop that, Liz, or they'll hate you too."

"Fuck them. I don't care. I'm the only game in town. People are begging to get into our practice. I'll be glad when Teresa qualifies as an NP."

"If they don't deport her," replied Brenda glumly.

"She's here legally. She has her green card, her work permits, every piece of paper she can get."

"You think that matters to them?" asked Brenda, staring into her coffee. "The only thing they see is her brown skin and her foreign accent."

"She lived in a British area. She speaks better English than we do."

"But she sounds funny to them, so that makes her dangerous."

Liz leaned down to look at Brenda's face. "Is that regret I'm hearing, Chief Harrison?"

"When I signed up for that agreement, I never imagined it would get this bad. Those ICE agents are animals."

"Yes, they are." Liz leaned back so Lois could serve her breakfast. "My friend, Deborah, wrote a nice piece defending you in *The Atlantic*."

"I don't read that paper."

"It's a magazine," Liz corrected casually. "I'll send you the link. She makes your critics look like the bad guys, but I worry it might cause a Streisand effect."

Brenda smashed her egg yolks with her fork. "What the hell is that? You mean like Barbra Streisand?"

"She sued a photographer, which only increased the number of people who wanted to look at the photo he took. Sometimes, just talking about something draws more attention to it."

"That's why I'm not talking to anyone. I learned my lesson. The more I try to explain, the more people twist my words to make me look bad."

"The press certainly has sensationalized the whole thing."

"Liz, you know I try to stay out of politics. I didn't even want to go to your election watch party last year, but Cherie talked me into it."

"We only invited the friends we know are on our side. You had nothing to worry about."

Brenda gave Liz a hard look, wondering if she understood. "Policing can't be partisan. No one should ever know my party affiliation or who I vote for."

"Except now the people planting signs showing the black flag with a blue stripe think you're on their side."

"Tell me about it. The other day, a guy flying a Trump flag out of his truck gave me the thumbs up when he passed. I'm not supposed to take a side. As police chief in this town, I'm on *everybody's* side."

Liz studied her with a little frown. "Take it easy, Brenda. You don't have to convince me."

"I feel like I need to convince myself! I'm really starting to hate those protesters. And now people are harassing my family."

Liz looked up sharply. "You mean the kids?"

"The kids in Keith's class are old enough to understand what their parents are saying about me. Those with liberal parents won't play with him. The kids with parents who support the administration now want to be his best friend. How inside out can this get?"

"Very," said Liz.

"How can people think like this?" Brenda asked with disgust. "Isn't there anything such as truth anymore?"

"Not in the way that we understand it. According to Deborah, 'perception IS reality.' Those who control the narrative 'make' the truth."

"That is shameful!" declared Brenda.

"To us, maybe, but look how much money is made spinning lies."

"Thanks for cheering me up, Stolz."

"If it makes you feel any better. I hate what those people are doing to you too."

Brenda frowned as she considered what Liz's friend had said about the situation. "Your friend sounds smart."

"Deborah? She's one of the smartest people I know. You should talk to her."

"Maybe. Let me think about it," said Brenda, mopping up the last of her eggs with her toast.

***

Brenda texted Duvaney to pick her up from the diner. This time he sent a fire truck with lights and sirens. Liz and Brenda laughed, watching the diner patrons glue themselves to the windows. "Well, my ride is here," Brenda said, tossing a twenty on the table.

Liz smacked it back into her hand. "Get going. I've got this."

Brenda enjoyed riding shotgun in the town's premier pumper. Maybe she'd chosen the wrong branch of safety service. The fire department had the flashier vehicles.

The vibration of her phone in her pocket interrupted Brenda's joy ride. Olivia had texted: *Let's talk this morning. Come to the town hall as soon as you can.*

I'm in hiding, Brenda texted back. She smiled to herself, wondering how Olivia would respond.

After a short delay came the answer. *Never mind. I'll come to you.*

That was a first. Olivia always summoned her reports to her domain. She never came to theirs. Brenda felt generous, so she texted back: *Thanks. Really appreciate it.*

After Brenda put away her phone she realized that Olivia could have changed her mind and decided to fire her. After a brief fit of paranoia, Brenda consoled herself with the knowledge that Olivia's management of the town's business had always been deliberate and carefully orchestrated. Besides, she'd know soon enough.

Punctual as always, Olivia was standing outside Brenda's door at the appointed hour. She didn't wait for Cynthia to announce her. She just strode right in and sat down. "Good morning, Chief Harrison," she said in a brisk, formal tone.

"Thanks, Cynthia," Brenda said to acknowledge the staring admin. Cynthia walked away shaking her head.

"What can I do for you, Olivia?" asked Brenda, clasping her hands on her desk.

Olivia sighed dramatically. "Brenda, I must apologize for speaking to you so harshly yesterday."

Brenda managed to restrain herself from doing an exaggerated double take. *Olivia was apologizing!* She started to say she accepted the apology, but Olivia raised a hand to silence her.

"No, there's no excuse for what I said, but you must agree that front page coverage of the ICE issue in the *New York Times* is *not* good."

"Olivia, I don't usually read the *Times*. If I read the New York papers, I usually read the *Daily News* or sometimes *The Post*."

"Ugh! They're rags, especially *The Post*. Fox News in print form."

"But they have good local coverage. I like to keep up on the old neighborhood. The *Times* is trying to be our national newspaper."

"Which it is since that so-called savior of *The Washington Post* bent the knee. 'Democracy dies in Darkness', my ass! With the help of the orange man's cronies, it's 'lights out' everywhere!" Brenda hid a smile. When Olivia was on a roll, she could be quite entertaining. "I'm glad Liz has advised you to keep a low profile."

"It's kind of hard. I can't even get out the door without jumping into a fire truck."

Olivia finally smiled. "I heard about that. Very clever, and it made quite an impression at the diner. The tourists loved it!"

"Can't miss my standing breakfast date with Liz. I also don't want people to think I'm hiding, even though I am."

Olivia affected an exaggerated expression of sympathy. "This must be so hard on your family."

"It is. My wife had to take leave from her job because she's so upset, and my son is being bullied at school. Meanwhile, the kids from Police Lives Matter families think he's great."

"It's crazy," said Olivia, shaking her head. "Wrong is right. Down is up. Lies are true. Truth is false. I dread to think what's coming next."

"But you see what's happening," said Brenda. "The craziness is dividing us and making us hate one another, even people who used to be on the same side."

"I used to think that those ex-nuns were the soul of rationality and civic duty. They always volunteered at the polls. They wrote intelligent letters to the editor of the local paper. Now, they're harpies at every select board meeting, demanding to be heard and making shrill accusations!"

"I know," said Brenda with a sigh. "I don't know what came over them."

"You know that LD1971 passed the legislature," said Olivia.

"My administrative captain keeps me informed, but why won't the governor sign it?"

Olivia frowned and looked thoughtful. "I have no idea. She was defiant when the president picked on her at the last governor's meeting. She said, 'See you in court.' And she won. She obviously loathes him. It makes no sense that she won't sign it."

"It would take me off the hook," Brenda said.

"I know, but you paused the agreement, pending the outcome of the legislation. Unfortunately, it hasn't made any difference."

"Obviously, not. The old hippies are still outside my office every single day."

"Because they have nothing else to do." Olivia shook her head. "I hope the furor dies down soon. With the season starting, the town doesn't need the bad publicity. We need immigrants in Hobbs to bus tables and cook in our restaurants. We need them to clean the motel rooms after the tourists leave."

"Ironically, we are the ones who will protect them if ICE threatens them illegally."

"Would you really?"

"If we can. I know other departments have hired green card holders. Guards in our jails are often immigrants. Sometimes, they get snatched in plain sight and then taken to a location in a red state that's out of our reach."

Olivia huffed out a sigh. "Dear God! It's out of our control, isn't it?"

"I'm afraid it is."

"Reasonable people support enforcement of immigration laws, but that's not what this is."

"No, it's intimidation," said Brenda. "It's dehumanizing people who are coming here for a better life, just like my Irish ancestors did years ago."

"Like mine, who came from Poland."

"Really? Poland?" This time, Brenda did a double take. "I thought you were a WASP through and through."

Olivia winked, shocking Brenda. "Don't tell."

"Scout's honor," said Brenda, forming her fingers in the oath position.

"I'm glad we talked, Brenda. I think we understand each other. If you don't mind some advice, I think you should talk to Liz's friend. She's very savvy about how to deal with this kind of thing."

"I thought you told me to lay low."

"I did, and you should, but you should meet Deborah Goldberg. She's one of us."

"You mean a New Yorker? I think I knew that."

Olivia wiggled her eyebrows significantly, and finally, Brenda got it. "Oh, she goes to our church." Being of a certain age, Olivia would know she didn't mean the Episcopal Church Lucy ran.

"Melissa Morgenstern is holding an organizing meeting for the next protest in Liz's media room next week. You could come for informational purposes, out of concern for public safety...if you know what I mean."

Brenda grinned. "And by the way, I could meet Liz's publicist friend."

"You're a quick study, Brenda. One of the many reasons I like you."

Chapter 16

Lucy looked at each of the women sitting in her office. Rebecca had made some effort with her appearance. She wore makeup to disguise her pallor. Despite living on the beach, she hardly ever went outside. She'd washed and brushed what she called her "Jewish hair," unruly tight curls that turned into a bushy mass in humid weather. Her wife, Judith, had cut her hair short since Lucy had last seen her. She stared at her feet, like a child waiting outside the principal's office to hear her punishment. Guilt hung over both women like a shroud.

"We're meeting in my office because we all decided it's neutral territory," Lucy finally said, "but I'm not here as a therapist or a priest. I'm here as your *friend*. You will do all the talking. I'm merely the facilitator. Can you both agree to that?"

Two heads nodded.

"Thanks for driving down here, Judith," Lucy said. "I know it's a trip for you."

"You're welcome," Judith murmured, then stared belligerently at her wife.

Lucy sighed. This was going to be one of those "pulling-teeth" sessions. *No, don't think like that,* Lucy told herself. *It's not a session. Remember what you just told them.* "Now, I'd like you each to tell us what you hope to get out of this meeting."

Rebecca raised her hand. She was the good girl and always the smartest person in the room. Lucy could bet that when the teacher was looking for the answer to a hard question, Rebecca's hand had been the first to go up. "I'd just like to have a conversation with Judith in a civil tone," said Rebecca, sneering in Judith's direction. "For once, I'd like to discuss it without screaming."

"If you'd stop telling me how much I hurt you, maybe I wouldn't scream," said Judith. "I didn't do it to hurt you. It wasn't about *you.*"

"No, it was selfish. It was all about *you*. You wanted to fuck your old school friend, so you did."

Judith recoiled from the accusation. "It was more than just a fuck. You cannot understand." Although Judith had been in the US for over twenty-five years, since she was a foreign student at Columbia Teacher's College, she still had a faint Israeli accent.

"What don't I understand? I was home keeping our family going, taking care of *our* children while you were on an extended vacation with your parents."

"I was only there for a week before the bombs began to fall. What a great *vacation*! It was terrifying. Even my parents, who have been through many wars, were frightened. You have never been in a war. You have no idea what is!"

Rebecca huffed, but Lucy could see a flicker of sympathy in her dark eyes. "Did you go looking for this school friend or did she find you?"

"She was visiting her parents. My parents were always friends with Rachel's." Judith pronounced her friend's name with the emphasis on the second syllable and a guttural "ch" sound. She also called Rebecca by her Hebrew name, Rivka, which often puzzled listeners, including Lucy at first. "Rachel was the first girl I loved, and the first is always special, even if it ended sadly. My parents didn't realize they were breaking up a romance when they sent me to the English school for two years. But I didn't dare tell them I was in love with a girl. I missed Rachel so much and wrote her passionate letters every day. I cried into my pillow every night."

"Sounds like you never really got over her," said Rebecca frowning.

"Oh, I did. When I met you. I fell completely and absolutely in love with you."

Rebecca looked skeptical. Lucy stared at her until her expression relaxed. "Is that the truth, or was I just the rebound?"

"No, it's completely true. I almost forgot about Rachel until she came with her parents to dinner at our house a few weeks into the war."

"Is that why you kept delaying your return to the states? Be honest!"

Judith shook her head. "Not at first. I was really worried about my parents being in a war zone. I was expecting to be called up along with other reservists to fight."

"But then you saw that war is really hell, and you chickened out," said Rebecca.

Judith glared at her. "I am not a coward! I would defend my country to the death from the pigs that raped those women and cut those people to pieces. I would gladly die if it meant killing them." She was practically spitting with fury. Her dark eyes glowed with molten rage.

"I know you're not a coward, Judith," Rebecca said quietly. "You're a brave woman to even think of signing up with the IDF. I couldn't do it. Or maybe I should say, I wouldn't do it. Both sides are to blame for this war." Rebecca frowned when Judith responded with a huff.

"You have no idea what you're talking about. You weren't there."

"Ladies, let's not diverge into a political debate," said Lucy. "We're here to talk about your relationship."

"If we still have a relationship," Rebecca remarked bitterly. "Judith, you said you were drunk the night you first slept with Rachel. Do you think that excuses what you did?"

Judith swallowed audibly. "No, of course not, but it does explain why I made such a bad decision. You have to understand. We were under bombardment for hours. The lights were knocked out in our district. Rachel and I were huddling in my childhood bedroom. We were drinking wine to numb the fear. Then...it happened."

While Judith was speaking, Rebecca's face had grown stony. Her sharply defined brows dipped to the base of her nose. "Just like that?"

"No," stammered Judith. "It was like our school days, when we used to steal wine from my father's cabinet and tell secrets in the dark. The association, the fear, and missing you so much..."

"You fucked your friend because you missed me? Oh, come on, Judith, that won't fly. Try again."

"I was very drunk at the time it happened. I don't remember much."

Rebecca turned to Lucy. "What am I supposed to say?" she asked.

"I don't know," said Lucy. "What do you want to say?"

"You broke my heart, Judith. Even worse, you broke my trust. I don't know if I can ever believe a word you say again."

"I'm not a liar, Rebecca. I have always told you the truth. That's why I told you what happened with Rachel."

"To get it off your chest? Was the guilt too much for you?"

"No, because I couldn't keep lying to you. No more lies. From now on, only the truth between us."

"Okay. Then, answer this. Are you still in contact with Rachel?"

"We still text from time to time, but I think she regrets what we did as much as I do. She was just beginning a new relationship when this happened. That's over now because she told the truth to her boyfriend."

"The texting has to stop," Rebecca sad flatly. "Absolutely no more contact. I need your promise on this, Judith."

Judith stared at Rebecca for a long time before she said, "If that's what you need to trust me again, but Rachel is my oldest friend."

"It doesn't matter. If you want to save our marriage, that's my number one condition."

Judith hung her head and sighed. "I agree."

"I have to trust you on this, Judith, but I may ask to look at your computer or phone to see if you're keeping your word."

"What! You know you can trust me!" was Judith's fiery response.

"No, I don't. I will check on you, when you're least expecting it."

"Like an unannounced drug test?"

"Something like that. Once you prove you're keeping your word, maybe I can learn to trust you again. Meanwhile, our marriage is on probation. Do you understand?"

Judith nodded sadly. "But please come home. The girls miss you so much. I miss you!"

"Not today. Maybe not for a while. I need to think about what we've said here today. I need some time to heal."

Lucy could see how disappointed Judith was, but she said, "I understand. Would you like to talk more? Would you like to know how the girls are?"

"Not right now," said Rebecca firmly. "They text me all the time. I know how they are."

"I will bring them on Friday night, as we agreed."

"Good," said Rebecca. "I can't wait to see them."

Judith looked at Lucy. "Thank you for arranging this."

"You're welcome. I am willing to meet with you once more, but after that, I'll refer you to someone who does couple's counseling. You have a lot of things to work out, but I'm friends with both of you, so I can't be objective."

"I understand," said Judith and rose. She started to head toward her wife, but she shook her head.

"Not yet," said Rebecca. "I'm hurting too much, but I love you... and if you really and truly love me, I'm willing to try again."

Judith sighed and headed toward the door. Before she left, she turned and said, "Thanks, Lucy."

"You're welcome," Lucy called after her.

After the door shut, Rebecca covered her face with her hands. "That was the hardest thing I ever did," she mumbled.

Lucy got up and rubbed her friend's shoulder. "I know, but it was a good start. You had an honest conversation, and you set some boundaries."

Rebecca sat up straight. "I know. We were so adult I could

hardly stand it. I really wanted to scream and pull her hair. I wanted to punch her so hard…"

"But you didn't. I'm proud of you."

Rebecca leaned back and sighed deeply. "Do you really think we have a chance?"

"I do. You have a lot going for you. You've been together for twenty years. You share children. You've built a comfortable, secure life together. You have a family who loves and supports you."

"I have you."

"Yes," said Lucy, sitting down beside her. "You have me."

"You said Liz had finally forgiven Maggie for cheating on her. Did you do therapy with them too?"

Lucy could feel her heart beat faster. They were getting uncomfortably close to the truth. Lucy assumed her professional mask. "It felt like that at first. After Maggie moved in next door, I often felt like I was playing referee. I'd call out each of them when they were being unfair to the other or landed a low blow. Their wounds go way back. Liz's fear and terror of Maggie leaving her for a man. Maggie's guilt over abandoning someone she loved. In a way, they were replaying their childhood trauma."

"But they weren't children back then."

"They were about the same age as your daughters. Maggie was only nineteen when she abandoned Liz in college. Liz was seventeen. In those days, there weren't the resources for LGBT youth we have now. Liz was afraid if she went for counseling it would be a black mark against her when she applied to medical school. Then her parents disowned her, and she was even more alone."

"Wow, she's strong!"

"But don't think all that rejection didn't leave a mark."

"Lucy, doesn't it bother you that Liz has her ex living right next door?"

"It was a little uncomfortable at first. But remember that Maggie and I were close friends before the breakup. We kind of just eased back into our old patterns. Maggie was around more often. We had group dinners. Then we started eating together all the time, watching movies."

"But it doesn't bother you?"

Lucy sighed and looked Rebecca directly in the eye. "No, because we have taken Maggie into our marriage."

Rebecca flinched away. "You're kidding."

"No, I'm not," said Lucy, steadily holding Rebecca's gaze.

"And the three of you have sex together?" asked Rebecca, looking increasingly anxious.

Lucy nodded.

"Oh, Lucy, this is so unfair! Here, you're pretending to help me with my fucked-up marriage, and now you're inflicting your shit on me."

"No, I'm not. I'm not asking for your help. I'm fine. I'm just telling you the truth, which is something I've wanted to share since we got back in touch. I love both Liz and Maggie. It's messy at times, but it works."

"But how can it work?" Rebecca demanded. "I'm so jealous of that bitch, Rachel, I could scratch her eyes out."

Lucy thought for a moment. "We talk a lot. We negotiate things that could become a problem before it does. We complement one another, so we share chores. Maggie loves to cook. I hate it. Liz takes care of the guy stuff: the maintenance, the cars."

"And what do you do? Look beautiful?"

Lucy laughed. "Sometimes, that's what it seems like. But I'm the interpreter. My specialty is being the Liz whisperer. In some ways, I'm the glue that holds us together. When Maggie initiated the event that started this, she seduced me, not Liz."

"Because she already had Liz. I don't know, Lucy. This is crazy. If your bishop finds out, you could lose your job!"

"I know. That's why we choose who to tell very carefully."

"You know this really goes against everything I believe."

"Does it?" challenged Lucy. "Rebecca, you're the Old Testament expert. All those "Biblical" marriages? Those prophets with multiple wives, bedding their slave woman at God's command?"

"So is that what it's like? Liz has a harem, and you and Maggie are the sister wives, like the TV show?"

Lucy laughed. "No, it's not like that at all. We're just a different kind of family. Maggie needs us for security. That's all she's ever wanted. She really needs Liz. She's the first person Maggie goes to when she's sick or frightened. Liz is the only safe person Maggie has ever known. That's why she kept coming back."

"And what do you get from Maggie?" asked Rebecca, her dark eyes enormous with curiosity. "I'm sorry if I'm asking too many questions."

"No, and I'm happy to answer them." Lucy sat back and thought for a moment. "What do I get? I get the sister I desperately wanted and never had. I hated being an only child. My mother was so determined to make me an opera star, I was always practicing. I never had time to make friends. Having Maggie around is wonderful. We do girl things together. We shop, get massages and pedicures. Liz would die before she'd do those things with me."

"But you have sex with Maggie."

"I do, but Maggie has a lower sex drive since her breast cancer. The treatment lowered her libido. Sometimes, I wonder how important sex is to her. Maybe she only uses it to get love and affection."

"Many women do," said Rebecca.

"But what about Liz, your legal wife?"

Lucy smiled slyly. "Oh yes, we have sex. Maggie complains we're like horny teenagers."

"Shut up. I hate you," said Rebecca, then grinned.

Lucy didn't mirror her smile. "Liz and I have a lot of sex, but not because we're horny. I can't explain it exactly. It's like we can't touch one another enough. Like our skin is an impediment, and our bones and organs are a barrier to touching one another. The sex is great, but what we really want is to merge and become one." Lucy noticed Rebecca's eyes widening. "Too much information? You're not disgusted, are you?"

Rebecca glanced away. "No, I think it's beautiful. I'm so jealous. Even before Judith went to Israel, our sex life was pathetic."

"I'm sorry, but you know that happens to a lot of couples."

Rebecca nodded sadly.

"You know, Rebecca, there's a lesson to be learned here. To heal a relationship after a betrayal requires raw honesty. The roles and familiar patterns are suddenly broken, and you have no choice but to look, really *look* at yourself and your partner. It opens possibilities for growth. If you're lucky, the disruption frees you from the old baggage and deepens the relationship. That's what happened with Maggie and Liz. Maybe it can happen for you too."

Rebecca drew a long breath. "Well, first we need to learn how to have conversations without screaming at each other."

"Yes, you do. And with good counseling and support from your family and friends, you could."

"I hope so," said Rebecca, but she didn't sound optimistic.

"Did you call Gloria Parrish?"

Rebecca nodded. "I have an appointment next week.".

"Good," Lucy said in an encouraging tone. "That's a step in the right direction."

✳✳✳

After Rebecca left, Lucy sat in her office for a long time, thinking about the conversation with Rebecca. Everything about the throuple arrangement was so new. They were still struggling to navigate the pitfalls and articulate the ground rules. Lucy could fall back on time-tested couple counseling wisdom to advise Judith and Rebecca, but there were no marriage manuals or sex guides for polyamory.

Lucy was enormously relieved that Rebecca hadn't recoiled from the revelation. Yes, she was skeptical, but she listened. It was so freeing to finally tell her "rabbi" the truth about this basic fact of her life. Lucy expected there would be plenty of questions. She herself had questions.

She glanced at her watch and decided to have a cup of coffee before she left for home. Heading down the hall, she saw Tom come out of the library with a book under his arm. He approached with an ominous look. "How did it go?" he asked, flexing his bushy brows. She'd shared her concerns before she'd met with Rebecca and Judith.

"Everyone left alive, which is always a good sign."

"Do you think there's hope for a reconciliation?"

"Time will tell."

"Indeed. As you saw with Liz, healing can take a long time, and the parties are never the same again."

"I like to think of their relationship as *Kintsugi*, where broken pottery is fused together with gold. Broken things can be even more beautiful."

"Correct as always," said Tom. He glanced toward the kitchen. "Are you getting a coffee? Do you mind if I join you?"

"No, if you can spare the time away from writing your sermon."

"Yes, and I'm bored with all the bread metaphors this week. The bread this, the bread that. I was looking for a new angle."

"Don't look at me," said Lucy with a grin. "Exegesis is your thing."

"Oh, come on, Lucy," said Tom, falling into step beside her. "You're every bit the Bible scholar I am, even if you're obsessed with sex." He grinned to let her know he was teasing.

"Just because I wrote my doctoral thesis on it, doesn't mean I'm obsessed." Then she remembered what she'd confessed to Rebecca about her intimate life with Liz. Maybe she was too interested in sex. "You know, Tom. I'm glad you're here," she said, preparing a coffee pod. "I have questions."

"Don't look at me, Lucy. At this point, I have more questions than answers myself. Please don't tell me you're not still agonizing over being discovered."

"Not as much," said Lucy, positioning her cup under the coffee spout. "I told Rebecca."

"That's good. It's hard to keep important things from such a close friend. Sooner or later, it comes out and the other person feels hurt that you didn't trust them."

"That's one reason, but really, there wasn't any point to being friends if I couldn't be honest with her. Before we argued about Gaza, I told her everything."

Tom released a long sigh. "It's sad that your comment about Gaza could disrupt such a deep friendship, but there's a lot of that going around, isn't there?"

"Oh, poor Brenda. She's being tortured over this stupid ICE agreement."

Tom pursed his lips. "She could say I made a mistake and cancel it."

"Oh puleeze!" said Lucy, rolling her eyes. "Don't get me started on that subject."

"Admitting you're wrong is very hard for some people," said Tom, switching positions with Lucy so he could make his coffee.

"That's never been one of my problems," Lucy said. "Someone shows me evidence that I'm wrong, and I adjust. But even I used to find it harder to rearrange my thinking. This whole throuple thing has made me reconsider so many things I thought I knew. 'Settled law' as they say in the Supreme Court, and then they overturn half-century precedents."

"I certainly didn't agree with that decision. But it's good to have your assumptions tested and change your mind. It means you're still growing."

"I just wish I didn't have to do it this fast."

Tom leaned closer. "But you are doing it beautifully."

"Part of me still feels like I'm breaking my marriage and ordination vows, but I wonder if I'm the same person who said them."

Tom looked thoughtful. "Yes, and no." Tom sat down at the

table with his coffee. "We shed our skin like snakes many times during our lives. It's not only our appearance that changes. Other parts of us are altered too, yet something essential stays the same. It's a mystery. But the good news for you, Lucy, is you're still changing because you're open to new thoughts and experiences."

"What if I lose my way?"

"You won't," said Tom, smiling. "I have every confidence in you."

Chapter 17

Cherie carried the last covered dish to the car. When she looked over what she'd already brought out, she realized she'd gone overboard. Maggie had accepted her offer to help with the food for the meeting, but it hadn't been necessary to cater the whole event.

It was impossible not to cook too much. Isabelle Bois had taught her daughter that it was always better to have too much food than not enough. That's why, when storage containers were on sale at the discount store, Cherie stocked up, so people could take food home with them. Some of their friends, especially those who lived alone, were grateful for a homemade meal instead of prepared food from the supermarket.

That's what Cherie told herself as she searched for a place to put the bowl. She ended up setting it down on the driveway so she could rearrange the space. Brenda came out of the house with a case of beer. She instantly put it down to help her wife. Cherie stood back to let her wife work her magic. No one could pack a trunk like Brenda Harrison.

"Is that the last of it?" Brenda asked, looking hopeful.

For space, they'd dropped the backseat, so they'd sent the kids ahead with Aunt Simone. She'd volunteered to watch the children while the adults gathered to organize the next protest. When Cherie had asked Simone if she would regret missing the meeting, her aunt had said, "Honey girl, I don't need no pep rally to whip me into a frenzy! I am there, and I have been there since before you were even born." Simone Ballou had been one of the few early feminists in her conservative Southern community. When she felt passionately about something, the refined woman slid into the black speech of Louisiana for emphasis. "I am loaded for bear as these Mainers say. I have all my signs ready, and I will be standing there alongside the rest of you!" Her righteous fervor gave Cherie goosebumps.

When they arrived at the long driveway leading up to Liz's house, cars were parked along it all the way down to the street. "Looks like Melissa has a good turnout for her meeting," Brenda said, hunched over the steering wheel, "but where the hell are we going to park?"

Cherie whipped out her phone and texted Liz. An answer shot back instantly. *Park in front of my garage bay. I'll open the doors for you to bring in the food.*

"Looks like your friend reserved a space for you," Cherie said after reading the instructions aloud. "She looks after you."

"Of course, she does," said Brenda.

Liz was waiting in the open bay. She took the beer from Brenda. "Thanks. This is a thirsty crowd." Liz always had plenty of alcohol on hand, but her graciousness wasn't lost on Brenda, who handed over the beer with a big smile.

Aunt Simone had gathered the kids in the backyard to keep them out of the flow of traffic through the house. In the kitchen, Maggie was issuing orders like a field commander. She instantly made room on the countertop for the dishes Cherie had brought. "Before you go back to the car, Cherie, can you bring this veggie tray out to the deck?" Maggie asked. "That will make some room. Meanwhile, I'll rearrange here to make space for the other things you brought."

Cherie went out to the deck, which was swarming with people. She waved to Bobbie and other co-workers from Hobbs Family Practice because she couldn't get through the throng. Lucy came out with a bowl of hummus and set it down beside the tray of raw vegetables. As soon as her hands were empty, she turned and embraced Cherie warmly. "Thanks for helping Maggie with the food," she whispered in her ear. "You never know how many people will show up at these meetings."

"Cherie!" a male voice boomed across the crowd. She turned and saw Tom and his husband hemmed in by people. He waved to her with both hands and a big smile.

The festive atmosphere made it seem like any other summer party at Liz's house. From the smiling faces and laughter, no one would ever guess they were gathered for a political meeting. Cherie sighed. Their last protest in April had drawn nearly a thousand people. The favorable long-range weather forecast, and the arrival of the summer visitors meant that this event could be even bigger. It also meant the other side would step up their trolling of the protesters. Trucks flying flags displaying right-wing messages drove up and down the protest route. A confrontation was becoming inevitable.

When Brenda called Cherie from the doorway, she told herself this was no time to dwell on her anxiety. There was more food to bring into the house.

***

Cherie had admired Melissa's gifts as an orator since the young trust lawyer out of Boston had stepped up to plead their adoption case pro bono. Young was a relative term. Melissa Morgenstern was in her forties, a dozen years Cherie's junior. She was taller than her sister, the rabbi, fair-haired and blue eyed. Both women were attractive, but Melissa clearly had the edge where looks were concerned. Cherie chided herself for judging other women by their looks, but it was so ingrained in everyone to value women for their beauty.

Melissa's girlfriend, Courtney Barnes, was also an attractive woman with blond hair and warm, brown eyes the color of fine brandy. She'd come along to support her partner, but as the elementary school principal shouldn't be perceived by the townspeople as partisan. Instead, Courtney would contribute behind the scenes by minding the kids in the church nursery during the protest.

After Melissa discussed the childcare arrangements, she went on to the safety plan. "Once again, Dr. Stolz will be our lead marshal as well as our chief medical officer. Bobbie Lantry will be her backup on the medical side. Cherie Harrison will be in charge of the first aid tent. Marshals will wear reflective green vests, which we will provide. Medical officers will wear white vests with a green first aid cross on the back."

"But Melissa," Liz called from the rear of the media room, clearly feeling good after a few beers. "I only have one body. How can I wear two vests?"

Everyone laughed.

"We'll put a green cross on the back of the green vest."

"But won't the colors clash?" asked Maggie to more laughter.

"Don't worry. We'll figure it out," said Melissa. "Maybe we can get an orange vest for Dr. Stolz."

There were hoots of approval from the crowd. They were clearly in a partying mood.

"I'd advise against wearing orange," said Lucy, raising her hand. "I know construction workers wear that color because it's visible, but it's also provocative. We want to keep people calm, not rile them up." Cherie nodded in agreement. Although she'd been a therapist longer than Lucy, she would never have considered the impact of the colors.

"Now, I want everyone to remember that all our protests are non-violent," Melissa said. "As the host, I sign an agreement that says we will not tolerate *any* weapons." Melissa peered at Liz, sitting in the back. "That means you, Liz Stolz." Liz responded with a double thumbs up to indicate she understood.

Melissa's eyes focused on Brenda. "Chief Harrison, do you have anything to add regarding safety?"

Sitting beside Cherie, Brenda shifted uncomfortably. Finally, she got up and turned around to face the audience. "First, I want to commend your group for your organization. At the previous event, the only incident requiring our assistance was a lady who stepped off the curb and twisted her ankle."

Cherie had assisted the elderly woman who'd fallen. She'd been transported to Southern Med for what had turned out to be a sprain.

"Last time, we had officers stationed at several locations," Brenda continued, "but we ordered them to only intervene if there was violence or a medical emergency. This time, we won't be around as much. With all the publicity about the Hobbs PD, our presence might not be a benefit, so we'll only come out if you call us. I have every confidence in your ability to run another incident-free event. And I know you'll all listen to Dr. Stolz because you're afraid of her."

The crowd roared, and Brenda sat down grinning at Liz in the back. Liz shot her friend a filthy look, then smiled to let her know she was kidding.

The discussion turned to the sign-making party in the library ahead of the protest. Cherie volunteered to make cookies. The rest of the meeting proceeded as efficiently as Cherie expected of Melissa. They adjourned ahead of schedule.

The participants hung around to catch up with their friends and neighbors. For many, the involvement in politics was an excuse to get away from the busyness of daily life and focus on the community. Cherie overheard a gray-haired woman say behind her: "I never expected to spend my golden years fighting fascism, but it certainly gives me something to do!"

Aunt Simone brought the children down to reunite them with their parents. She volunteered to drive Megan and Keith home and tuck them into bed. "That will give you time to collect your dishes," Simone whispered into Cherie's ear. "And I get out of cleanup! Yipee!" She flashed a brilliant smile at her niece. "See you later, alligator."

"In a while, crocodile," replied Cherie, ready to head to the kitchen to help organize the cleanup. As she turned, she was cornered by Bobbie Lantry.

"Now, you won't forget the rehearsal dinner is a week from Saturday."

Cherie had been touched when Bobbie had invited her to be in the wedding party. Bobbie had insisted on going all out with a big church wedding with white dresses. Cherie found it surprising that shy Susan had agreed to it, but she knew that Bobbie could be persistent.

"I will absolutely be there," Cherie assured her.

"Good, but just in case, I'll send an email to remind you. I'm getting so excited!" she declared like a kid and fast clapped.

Out of the corner of her eye, Cherie saw Liz's friend, Deborah Goldberg, approach Brenda, who was separating deposit cans and bottles from the other trash. Whatever Ms. Goldberg said, it made Brenda sit down beside her in the front row of home theater seats. Olivia's plan was working!

While Bobbie went on about the horrors of planning a big wedding, Cherie kept an eye on her wife speaking to Liz's friend. She was pleased to see that Brenda was listening intently to what Ms. Goldberg was saying. Maybe someone could finally talk some sense into her and get them out of this awful mess.

Susan approached her fiancée and gently tugged on her arm. "Bobbie, I hate to pull you away from your colleague, but I have school tomorrow," the taller woman said emphatically. The holy card saint had disappeared, replaced by the stern ex-nun.

Bobbie turned to Cherie apologetically. "Sorry, but I have to go. You know how it is."

Cherie chuckled and glanced at Brenda. "I most certainly do."

"Susan, can't we stay a few more minutes to help Liz clean up?" Susan's eyes became steely.

"I guess not," Bobbie turned to Cherie, looking for sympathy.

"Don't worry," said Cherie. "I've got it covered." She gestured toward Brenda, who was deep into a tête-à-tête with Deborah Goldberg. "I think we may be here for a while."

Cherie took one of the large black trash bags from the big roll on one of the home theater seats. She went around the room, searching for used cups and other refuse. Brenda's conversation with Deborah seemed to be reaching a crescendo, so Cherie decided to give them some privacy. Maybe Brenda would admit something to Deborah that she wouldn't say in front of her wife.

They'd eaten dinner on the deck. Cherie went out to see what its state was after their outdoor feast. Most of the food had found its way into the kitchen, but in the far corner, Cherie found a tray of raw veggies and a half-empty container of hummus. She peeked into the media room as she passed the door and saw that her wife was still deep in conversation. She left them and headed to the kitchen.

"It was a great success," Cherie heard Liz's voice say. "Cherie's food was just as amazing."

"Thank God, she brought so much," said Maggie. "Otherwise, we never would have had enough."

"But you outdid yourself," Liz murmured.

Cherie considered pitching the tray of vegetables and the hummus into the trash bag she was carrying, then realized her hosts might have other plans for the leftovers and decided to bring them into the kitchen.

Her eyes widened in disbelief at what they saw. Liz's mouth was locked on Maggie's. Their cheeks pulsed from a deep tongue kiss. Liz's hands clamped to Maggie's backside were sensually kneading her buttocks.

The tray fell from Cherie's hands. Left-over hummus spattered across the floor tiles. Slices of pepper and baby carrots escaped under the stools at the island. Cherie instantly fell to her knees, trying to pick up the scattered vegetables.

Lucy came into the kitchen and saw what had happened, snatched some napkins from the counter and got down beside Cherie to help.

"I didn't see anything. I swear. I didn't see anything!" Cherie declared, furiously wiping up the spattered hummus with a paper towel, which was effectively pointless.

"What did you think you saw?" asked Lucy. She glanced at Maggie and Liz who looked like two guilty children.

Lucy turned to Cherie. When their eyes met, Cherie saw a moment of panic followed by pleading.

She knows all about it! Cherie realized and scrambled to her feet. *She knows because she's in on it!* "Sorry, but I gotta go!" She dashed out of the kitchen and hurried down the hall to the media room, where Brenda and Deborah Goldberg were still deep in conversation. She yanked on Brenda's arm. "We need to leave."

Brenda looked at her curiously. "What's the matter? Something happen to one of the kids?"

"No, but we need to go. *Now!*"

Brenda heard her urgency and got to her feet. "Sorry, Ms. Goldberg, but I need to go."

"Call me Deborah," said the publicist, rising. "Don't worry. We can talk more tomorrow."

Cherie gripped Brenda's arm and practically dragged her to the front door. Brenda resisted, trying to slow her down. "Honey, what's wrong?"

"I'll tell you later, but we have to get out of here."

"Okay, okay. We're going, but what's the matter?"

"I can't explain now. I have to get out of here. *Now!*" In her frenzy, Cherie couldn't figure out how to unlock the front door, so Brenda leaned over and flipped the lever of the deadbolt. She opened the door and Cherie flew out, pounding down the porch stairs. Brenda unlocked the car doors just as Cherie reached for the handle.

"Okay, Cherie. What's going on?" asked Brenda, getting into the driver's seat. "You're shaking. What happened?"

"I saw something I can't unsee."

"What?" asked Brenda, sounding frustrated but curious.

"Liz was kissing Maggie like they were still married. She practically had her tongue down her throat."

Brenda glanced toward the house sharply. "Are you sure?"

"I know what I saw. Then Lucy came in. When she looked at me, I realized she knew all about it because she's in on it."

"No!" said Brenda in complete disbelief. "Not Lucy!"

"It's none of our business," Cherie said but couldn't convince herself that it was true, so she said it again. "None of our business!" She shook her head to clear the images that wouldn't go away.

Chapter 18

Liz was huddled in the kitchen with Maggie and Lucy when Deborah arrived. "What's going on?" she asked. "I almost had the chief convinced to follow my direction when her wife flew in and demanded they leave." Deborah studied each of their faces. Liz imagined what she saw—Maggie hanging her head in guilt, Lucy so distraught her face was ghostly pale, and she herself, grimacing with anger over being so *stupid*.

The light of understanding dawned on Deborah's face. "Uh oh, your secret's out."

"Damn right it is. Cherie came into the kitchen and caught me and Maggie tongue kissing," said Liz. "If only I'd been kissing Lucy, everything would have been fine."

"It was stupid," Maggie agreed.

"It's my fault. *I* kissed *you*." Liz turned to Lucy. "I'm so sorry, honey."

"Nice of you to apologize, Liz, but it's too late now," said Deborah, briskly cutting off Lucy before she had an opportunity to respond. "Yes, that was stupid, but what are you going to do about it?"

Liz pulled out her phone. "I'm going to talk to Brenda."

"I wouldn't do that if I were you," Deborah said, hand on Liz's arm to stop her. "Let them sit with their shock. But don't be surprised if they're angry because you didn't tell them sooner."

"I wanted to tell them," said Liz. "But Lucy is so paranoid about her job."

"Liz!" said Deborah with a sharp look. "Lucy is right to be worried about her job. If you could keep your tongue in your mouth in public, you wouldn't be feeling bad now."

"I'm not in public. I'm in my own home, in my own kitchen!"

"But you had people roaming the house," Deborah countered.

"You were in the media room. I thought you had them occupied."

"I did, but after I cornered Brenda to give her my sales pitch, Cherie got antsy. I guess she decided we needed privacy to talk, so she tried to make herself useful."

"Well, now what do we do?" asked Liz. "You're the expert on cleaning up messes."

Deborah drew a long breath. "Leave them alone until at least tomorrow. Then, if you care about the friendship, try to talk to them. Don't apologize for your relationship but do express regret for not telling them sooner. That will be their real issue. You didn't trust them enough to tell them."

"Both Liz and I work with Cherie," Lucy said.

"That complicates the problem," Deborah agreed.

"In a small town like Hobbs, it's hard not to mix business and pleasure," Liz explained.

"Like the saying goes, 'candy is dandy, but incest is best,'" Deborah quipped with a sad smile.

Maggie whose Irish-Catholic heritage enabled her to do guilt better than any of them had been mostly silent. "I've caused enough damage. I think I'll go back to my place." She hugged Lucy and murmured. "I'm so sorry."

Lucy clung to her. Liz realized she'd already forgiven Maggie, and as usual, she'd get the blame when things went wrong. Lucy stared at her. Her green eyes held no reproach, but a hint of despair. "I think I'll go up to bed too," she finally said.

After she left, Deborah nodded in the direction Lucy had departed, indicating Liz should follow her. "If you value your marriage, you need to make amends. And don't defend yourself. Just listen for a change!"

Liz found Lucy in the bathroom, taking off her makeup. She stood in the doorway until Lucy's eyes met hers in the mirror. "You can come in," said Lucy. "I'm almost done." She was already in her nightgown, an old one she wore to be comfortable. She flung the makeup pad into the trash and picked up her toothbrush.

"I'm sorry," said Liz. "Really sorry." Lucy only nodded because her mouth was full of foam, but after she spat into the basin she didn't say anything. "I don't know what I was thinking," Liz continued. "Everything went so well. People had a good time at the party. The meeting went well and ended on time. I was feeling good, and there was Maggie, looking so damn beautiful..."

"Tom predicted that it would be something simple, and it was."

"I swear I meant no harm."

"I know you didn't do it to hurt me."

"I'm glad you understand," Liz murmured.

"I understand, Liz, but it doesn't mean everything is okay. That was a real lapse of judgment. It could have real implications for all of us."

"I know," said Liz, hanging her head.

"Don't give me your naughty boy look, Liz. This is serious!"

Liz raised her eyes to meet Lucy's. As always they were loving, but she meant business. "I will clean it up. I promise."

Lucy turned around and leaned against the counter. "If you can. Sometimes, we do things, and they take on a life of their own. Look what happened to Brenda. When she signed that ICE agreement, she never imagined it would make her the most hated person in Hobbs."

"I'm sure she didn't," Liz murmured.

Lucy nodded. "I'm not worried about Cherie. She's a mature, integrated woman and an excellent psychotherapist. She keeps professional confidences scrupulously. She will see reason. It's Brenda I'm worried about."

"Brenda would never spread gossip about us, Lucy. She thinks you walk on water."

Lucy managed a little chuckle. "Haven't mastered that trick yet. I'm working on it." She stepped forward and looked up into Liz's face. "You and Brenda have been friends for a long time. She'll be crushed that you didn't tell her, and she had to find out by accident."

"I know."

"And Liz, you'll be so busy defending yourself, you'll forget to listen."

"No, I won't."

Lucy nodded and headed out of the bathroom. Liz scrambled out of her jeans and T-shirt and underwear. She put on the old shirt and cotton shorts she slept in during the summer and hurried to brush her teeth.

In the dark, she approached the bed. She found Lucy turned on her side, facing the edge of the bed. Liz slipped in beside her. As usual before lying down to sleep, Lucy had wound her red hair into a loose braid. Liz gently moved it aside, so she could kiss the soft nape of her neck. Lucy loved to have her neck kissed, but tonight, there was no response. Liz reached around and cupped Lucy's breast. She closed her eyes, enjoying the delicious weight and softness, then gently pinched her nipple.

"Liz," said Lucy in a sad tone. "I don't feel like making love tonight. Sex isn't going to fix this."

Liz withdrew her hand and lay on her back to consider this development. Lucy almost never refused her overtures. "Okay. I'll leave you alone. Do you want me to sleep in another room?"

"No, you can sleep here. Just let me be for a while. I need to think."

"Okay." Liz clasped her hands behind her neck and stared at the ceiling. She was wide awake, but her thoughts and emotions were a jumble. Usually, Lucy helped her sort them out, but she was dealing with her own feelings and not available to listen.

Liz tried to put herself in Lucy's place, imagining a scandal that could deprive her of not only her job, but her priesthood. It was like the malpractice suit, but not really because the case had no merit. Her medical career was never in peril. The bishop could pull Lucy's priest's license, which would crush her.

After lying there for ten minutes, Liz said, "I think I'll go downstairs for a while."

"Okay," Lucy said in a skeptical tone, turning her head slightly. "Don't drink too much. That will only make everything worse."

"I know," said Liz, getting out of bed.

"I love you, Liz."

"I love you too," replied Liz with a sigh.

When Liz went into the kitchen to pour herself a glass of whiskey, she saw a glow from the enclosed porch. The propane stove was blazing. Deborah was a low-maintenance guest, who didn't require being waited on or entertained. She quickly read the household routines, memorized where things belonged, and made herself at home wherever she was. After Liz got her drink, she joined her.

"I thought you might be back," Deborah said as Liz slid open the door.

"Lucy needs some alone time."

"And you need to talk."

"How did you know?" asked Liz as she sat down.

"Like most people, you figure things out by talking about them."

"Gee, sorry I'm so typical."

Deborah laughed. "You can't be exceptional at everything, Dr. Stolz. Sometimes, it's good to be normal."

They sat in silence for a few moments, gazing into the flames. "How do I get myself out of this mess?" Liz finally asked.

"Clearly, your friends love you, so they'll be inclined to forgive you. Neglecting to loop them in on your secret will be a harder sell. They both look up to you and see you as larger than life. Did you hear what Brenda said about everyone being afraid of you? She was really saying she's in awe of you, even a little afraid. She looks up to the brilliant and successful Dr. Stolz."

"Me? Brenda looks up to me?" asked Liz, surprised.

"Of course, she does. Don't tell me you haven't noticed. Your worst crime here is falling off your pedestal. There's nothing more despised than a fallen idol."

Liz frowned as she considered what Deborah had said. "I never asked for admiration."

Deborah laughed softly. "Liz, you don't have to. You are an amazing person. No matter what you try your hand at, you do it better than anyone else. It's not even that you are that competitive, except with yourself. You must always prove that you're the best, not to others but to yourself." Liz nodded as Deborah spoke, absorbing the comments and seeing their validity. "I bet you shoot better than Brenda Harrison."

Liz turned to her. "How did you know?"

"Because I know you. You immerse yourself in anything that interests you. Learning a new skill? You'll practice every day until you do it perfectly. By the way, you could be a little less critical of Lucy when she rehearses or, at least, learn to say what you think more gently."

Liz began to wish she hadn't allowed Deborah to listen to Lucy's morning singing practice. "I don't do it to be mean. Lucy is a world-class classical singer. She has important engagements coming up."

"I know, Liz, but she's your wife, and you're not her vocal coach."

Liz downed her whiskey in a gulp. "I should be paying you for all this good advice."

Deborah sighed. "For you, it's free. You're a quick study, Liz. All I have to do is tell you something's not working, and you fix it. You make my job too easy to charge you. No challenge in it."

"What about Brenda?"

"Now, she's a problem," said Deborah, looking into the flames. "Like you, she pays careful attention, but she has that stubborn look in her eyes like you had when I first met you. She hears but doesn't *listen*."

"So, she won't let you help her, even for free?"

"No, she says she'll wait to see if the governor signs that bill."

"And nothing you said could persuade her?"

Deborah's exaggerated head shake was her only response.

"You want another cognac? I'm thinking of going into the kitchen for a refill."

"No, thanks, Liz," said Deborah leaning on the arms of the chair to help her get up. "I've had enough alcohol. I'm going to bed, and you probably should too. Your wife needs you close, even if she doesn't say it out loud."

Liz looked up into Deborah's handsome face reflected in the firelight. "How is it that a smart, good-looking woman like you never found a mate?"

"That's a good question. I always thought it was because I was too busy and traveling too much. Then I thought I was too picky. Now, I realize I haven't met anyone who gets me, if you know what I mean."

Liz thought of Lucy and knew exactly what Deborah meant. "I do know."

Deborah sighed deeply. "I'm too old now to date and too set in my ways."

"Don't give up," said Liz. "You never know."

"Says Dr. Stud." Deborah grinned as Liz feigned offense.

"I'll never forgive Olivia for sharing that with you."

Deborah patted Liz's shoulder. "Sure you will."

After Deborah left, Liz shut off the stove. Although the evening had grown cool, there was no need to waste propane. She sat in the dark for a few minutes, listening to the quiet, before going upstairs.

She crept quietly into the bedroom. Lucy's still form was still turned away from the place where Liz slept. The mattress had been advertised as not conducting motion, ensuring a restful sleep for a companion, but as soon as Liz slipped into bed, Lucy sighed. "I'm glad you're back," she murmured, rolling over. She tentatively sniffed Liz's lips. "Good, you don't smell too much like whiskey."

"I only had one."

Lucy pressed her lips softly against Liz's mouth. "I need you."

"I'm here."

Lucy lifted her nightgown and placed Liz's hand between her legs. "Touch me," she whispered.

***

After scraping the foredeck by hand in the hot afternoon sun, Liz was sweating fiercely. For over an hour, she'd been visualizing the cold beer in the galley refrigerator. She could see the droplets of condensation on the outside of the can, fogging the label. She'd wondered when she first saw it on the on-tap board at Dockside how it got its funny name: *Lunch*. Was it meant for midday meals only? Then she read up on the brewery and learned that the Maine Beer Company donated part of its profits to protecting marine mammals and named its IPAs after whales. The whale that had inspired this moniker had a big chunk out of its fin. The lame sense of humor of the marine biologists tracking it had resulted in its unlikely name. Liz reflected on how easily she'd mistaken the intention without knowing the whole story.

By now, she wanted that beer so badly she could taste it. Her physician brain told her that water would be a healthier choice, especially after all the alcohol she'd consumed at last night's party. But that beer was just sitting in the fridge waiting for her. Finally, she threw the scraper aside, wiped her brow with the back of her hand, and went below. She was rummaging in the refrigerator, when something made her stop and listen. Without the racket of cans banging around, she clearly heard her name.

"Stolz! Are you in there?"

Liz popped her head out of the front hatch. She saw Brenda clinging to the ladder. "Hey!" Liz called. "Why don't you come aboard?"

"I'm waiting to be invited," said Brenda.

Liz climbed out of the hatch and walked over to Brenda. "You know you're always welcome. You don't need an invitation."

"Maybe I do," said Brenda.

"Why?"

"I'm not sure I really know you."

"Oh, come on, Brenda. Don't be an asshole. I'm the same Liz you've known since I came to Hobbs."

"Are you?" said Brenda, shading her eyes against the sun.

Liz threw her head back in disgust. "Okay. I'm sorry. All right?" She reached down her hand. Brenda stared at it for a long moment before she took it. She let Liz tug hard before she relented and climbed up the ladder.

"Being difficult, are you?" Liz asked when Brenda finally stepped onto the deck. "Want a beer? I was down in the galley getting one when you showed up."

"I'm not here for social reasons."

Liz stood up to her full height. Being slightly shorter, Brenda had to look up to her. "Fine. You can tell me why you're here while *I* have a beer."

Brenda squinted at the hot sun. "In that case, maybe I'll have one too."

"Red ale or the IPA I was going to drink?" asked Liz, throwing plastic pads on the coaming so they could sit down.

"I'll take a red if you have one." Liz always kept a few cans of red ale on hand in case Brenda showed up. She also had a stock of Brenda's favorite salty snacks. Liz went below again and returned with the beer and peanuts. Maggie wasn't there, so she hadn't bothered with plastic beer cups. She plopped down beside Brenda "I would have brought out some sling chairs, but since you're not here for social reasons," she said, deadpanning, "I assumed we wouldn't be sitting long."

"Thanks for the beer," Brenda murmured.

"You're welcome."

While they drank their beer, they silently watched the seagulls dive for clams. Finally, Brenda turned to Liz and said, "I need you to tell me the truth."

Liz moved down on the bench so she could see Brenda's face. "I don't know exactly how to explain it because there are a lot of moving parts, and they keep changing."

"Start by telling me what's going on. Are you involved with both Lucy and Maggie?"

"Yes." The direct, single-word answer visibly upset Brenda. Frowning, she turned away.

"When did it start?"

"Remember when we went up to Moosehead after the election? That weekend."

"I can understand doing something stupid while you were away. It was a bad time, and you probably drank too much. But since then, you all decided it was more than a fling?" asked Brenda, narrowing her eyes.

"I never stopped loving Maggie, and I love Lucy, so yes, we decided to continue."

"Who else knows about it?"

"Not many people. Lucy's daughter, Emily. Maggie's daughter, Sophia, figured it out. So did Tom Simmons. Olivia and my lawyers know. Maggie wanted some security. She didn't even have a lease because that little apartment over the garage isn't legal. So, I took it a step further and we created the LLM Corporation to hold our assets. Melissa, Olivia, and Harriet helped me draw up the papers. I assume their girlfriends know too."

Brenda stared into the harbor. The gulls were getting nasty with one another. A fight had broken out, raising a terrible racket. When the noise finally settled down, Brenda turned to Liz. "Why didn't you just tell me?"

"Brenda, you had so much going on that I thought…"

"Don't give me that, Liz!" Brenda said, cutting her off. "It started in November. The reporters didn't start hounding me until March. You had all that time to tell me." It was hard to argue with the timeline.

"The truth is, Brenda," said Liz quietly. "We weren't sure what we were doing. There's no road map for a relationship with three people, so we had a lot to negotiate. We're still figuring out how this works."

"I understand, Liz, but I'm your friend. We used to be the Three

Amigas when Sam was around. We were the first people she told when she was breaking up with Olivia. We used to share *everything*."

Liz inhaled a deep breath. She needed to come clean with Brenda.

"It's not that I didn't want to tell you. Lucy is afraid to tell people because if our secret gets out, she'll lose her job."

Brenda frowned as she considered Liz's words. "You didn't tell me because you didn't trust me."

"I do trust you, Brenda. But you know how these things are, the more people who know, the more likely everyone will know. Lucy's denomination is open-minded about a lot of things, but this may be a bridge too far."

Brenda peered into Liz's eyes. "You know I only go to church to please her, and now, because of the kids. Cherie is a true believer. This is blowing her mind."

"I bet it is," said Liz, nodding. "I know Cherie is religious and looks up to Lucy."

"She suspected something was going on with the three of you."

"But it's one thing to suspect something, and another knowing it."

"Exactly! Last night I was really mad, especially because Cherie was so upset. She kept me awake for hours talking about it. She's still not all right with it. She's hurt and angry because Lucy isn't the person she thought she was."

"Lucy is a good priest. She tries to live according to her principles. This whole thing took her by surprise too. She's really struggling to square this circle."

"Meanwhile, you're thinking, what the hell? If having one woman in bed is good, two might be even better!" Brenda elbowed Liz with a rakish smile. "Right?"

"I admit it's not always easy to keep them happy," Liz said, playing along. "And they gang up on me."

"Figures."

"So, you understand why I didn't tell you?"

"Your reason kind of makes sense, but please, Liz, never do that again. Apart from Cherie, you are my best friend. I trust you with my life, and you can trust me. If you tell me something in confidence, I will never tell anyone. I swear."

Liz looked directly into Brenda's earnest blue eyes and saw how much withholding the facts had hurt her. "Brenda, I would have said something sooner, but we decided we all need to agree on who we tell. There were times when I really wanted to tell you. It's kind of weird having to tell people. It's like coming out all over again. Now, instead of coming out as gay, I'm coming out as married to two women."

"Is that how you see it?" asked Brenda, curious.

"Well, yes. We're equal partners, but that doesn't mean things are all that different. I'm still legally married to Lucy and will continue to be. See, to me, marriage is nothing more than a legal contract."

"God help me if I ever said such a thing to Cherie. She loves all that romantic stuff. Flowers, candlelit dinners, date nights."

"Lucy and Maggie are the same. They like it if I bring them gifts or take them out for a nice dinner. Good thing no one pays attention because older women are always going out together. People probably assume we're a bunch of lonely widows hanging out together because there's no one else. Hah! If they only knew! If we were younger, I'm not sure we could get away with it."

"Maybe not," said Brenda.

"I will admit there are awkward situations. When Lucy and I appear as a couple, Maggie is the third wheel. People invite us, but not her. When we're on the singing circuit, Lucy introduces Maggie as her publicist. Like when we used to say our lovers were 'roommates.'"

"People never believed it, even then." Brenda finished her beer and shook the can to see if she'd gotten the last drop.

"Want another?"

"Sure. There's nowhere I need to be right now."

The crisis was over. Liz could finally take a deep breath. She went below and brought up two beers and the bag with the lobster rolls she'd picked up for her lunch. "Want one? I was hungry when I ordered, so I bought two," Liz said, offering one of the red plaid, cardboard boxes to Brenda.

"Are you sure, Liz? I know how you love your lobster rolls."

Liz gazed longingly at the sandwich in Brenda's hand. Then she looked up into Brenda's face, friendly now since the air had been cleared. "Yeah, I'm sure."

***

While Liz waved on the cars into the parking lot, she saw the truck flying right-wing flags pass again. The driver was trolling the crowd, and the look in his eyes, when they caught hers, was pure hatred.

She shook off her anxiety to focus on the traffic, backed up because of the speed bumps in the school driveway. People waved as they passed. She nodded but maintained her game face while using the hand signals Brenda had taught her to direct traffic. She was wearing the green vest with a cross identifying her dual role as head marshal and medical officer. So far, Cherie had dealt with the sole medical incident, a bee sting.

The groups sponsoring the protest had set up tables along the route, offering free bottled water and cards from the ACLU, outlining the constitutional rights of protesters.

When Liz had walked the crowd in her role as the head marshal, she saw many of her staff members: Teresa, their immigrant nurse, and her daughter, Grace, along with the Somalian medical assistant, who'd recently joined the practice. Reshma had encouraged them to participate. She'd also volunteered to be a marshal. Under her green vest, she proudly displayed her collar and a rainbow stole. Liz had never been a fan of mixing religion and politics, but she remembered the nuns and priests marching alongside civil rights leaders. Martin Luther King had been a minister. Maybe it was time for the Christian Left to rise again.

Melissa approached to ask whether the parking lot had reached capacity. "When it does, only let the elderly and handicapped people through."

"Most people here fit that description." Liz gestured to the stream of people coming from the parking lot. Some pushed walkers. Others hobbled to the protest line using canes. "The old hippies are out in droves. Do we have any idea how many people are here?"

"Someone did a count and says it's close to twelve hundred."

"Wow! I'm surprised so many came out in this heat."

Melissa patted Liz's arm. "Thanks for taking this spot. It's a bottle neck, between the entrance to the school and the crosswalk. Everyone is clustering here."

Liz nodded toward a woman pushing a man in a wheelchair. "When you can barely walk, you stick close to where you park."

"I'm heading to the other end," Melissa said, looking Liz in the eye. Being one of the taller women in their group, she could. "You okay by yourself here?"

"Fine," said Liz. "I've got this."

After Melissa left, Liz noticed a man and woman suddenly stop on their way to the street. They were both elderly. He was swaying precariously. Liz grabbed a sling chair and a water bottle and ran to where they stood. "You okay?" she asked the man, opening the chair. Breathing heavily, he plopped into it. Liz opened the water bottle. "Here, take a few sips." Her fingers went to his pulse, which was rapid.

"It's so hot," the man said, wheezing. He took off his hat, embroidered with the name of the navy ship he'd served on in Vietnam, and wiped his brow. The sweat was running off him.

"Sit here for a while. Drink the water slowly," Liz advised. "If you still feel dizzy, make sure you sit in the shade. There's some over there." Liz pointed in the direction of the trees.

"Thank you," said the woman with a beatifically grateful expression.

Liz had no time to respond because she heard shouting from the entrance to the school. She jogged back to her post and saw the truck with the right-wing flags stopped in the crosswalk. A male protester was shouting, "You fucker! You almost hit me!" He brought his fist down on the hood of the truck. "Fuck you!," he screamed. "You could have killed me!"

Liz ran into the crosswalk and dragged the protester away by the arm. "Get back!' she ordered the crowd that had gathered in the street. "Get back on the sidewalk!"

"He's got a gun!" a woman's voice shouted.

Liz turned around. The driver was pointing a pistol at the protester who'd slammed his truck. She was standing between them. Liz raised her hands and engaged the eyes of the man holding the gun. "Put it down," she said calmly. He didn't move. "Now!" Liz ordered. For a long moment, they stared at one another. Finally, he lowered the gun. "Now, get back in your truck and get out of here!" Liz pointed in the direction the truck had been heading.

She went back to where the protester was still shouting. "Why did you let him get away? He almost hit me!"

"I saw it," said a woman. "He was in the crosswalk and the guy didn't stop. It looked like he was trying to hit him."

"I'm calling the police!" the protester declared.

There goes our perfect record with the town, thought Liz. She glanced at the man, sitting in her chair, still recovering from the heat, and realized she was breathing as heavily as he was. Her mind flashed the image of an assault weapon pointed in her direction. She suddenly smelled marijuana smoke and saw Peter Langdon's bloodshot eyes. Her breaths came faster. She began to feel light headed.

"Dr. Liz, are you all right?" a woman beside her asked.

Liz took her own pulse. It was rapid, but not thready. It wasn't shock. She did a quick scan of her body. She was breathing too fast. She tried to slow it down, but she couldn't. Two police cars wailed down the street and pulled into the school driveway. Brenda got out of the first cruiser and ran in her direction.

"The guy had a gun," a man next to Liz was explaining to Brenda. "Dr. Stolz broke up the fight. The man with the gun drove away."

Liz heard Brenda giving orders to pursue the driver of the truck. Then she felt a strong hand take her arm. "Liz, you're coming with me." Brenda turned to an officer and said in a quiet voice, "Find Rev. Bartlett and get her down here. Now!" The hand on her arm tugged her in the direction of the squad car. The back door opened. "Get in," Brenda ordered and put her hand on Liz's head like she was under arrest.

"I'm okay," Liz protested.

"Get in and sit down." Brenda's voice was firm, but her eyes were kind. "Come on, Liz. Listen to me for a change."

Liz got into the back of the police car. Brenda got in next to her and closed the door. Liz's breaths came faster. She couldn't stop them. Brenda reached into the pocket behind the driver's seat and took out a barf bag. She snapped it open. "Here, Liz. Breathe into this. You're having a panic attack." Liz was insulted that Brenda was telling her something she already knew. She tried to push the bag away. "Stolz, don't argue with me!" Brenda ordered and moved the bag into position around Liz's nose and mouth. "Breathe into the bag. Deep breaths," Brenda encouraged gently. "That's it."

After a few breaths, Liz began to feel better. Brenda put her arm around her. Her grip on her shoulder was tight but reassuring. "You're going to be all right, Liz. You're going to be just fine."

The door swung open and Lucy peered in. "Not again!"

"Yup," said Brenda. "Again." She moved over, encouraging Liz to move in the same direction, so Lucy could get into the car.

Brenda never, not even for a second, released her grip on Liz's shoulder.

Chapter 19

Cherie was hanging up her robe when she saw Lucy pass by the choir room door. The priest was still fully vested from the morning service. As usual, she'd stayed afterward to receive handshakes and hugs from members of the congregation.

"Lucy!" Cherie called. The priest turned and smiled in a way that made Cherie feel like the most important person in the world. "Do you have a minute to talk?"

"For you, Cherie," said Lucy, approaching, "I always have a minute." Her red hair was unbound and streamed over the emerald-colored chasuble. She looked as elegant in brocade vestments as she did in one of her concert gowns. The deep red color she'd painted her fingernails, a new feature since last fall, provided contrast. Lucy had confessed she'd shied away from nail color so not to draw attention to her hands during the Eucharist. In Cherie's opinion, the colored fingernails added drama to the solemn ritual and reminded everyone that, in the Episcopal Church, priests could be male or female.

Lucy reached for Cherie's hand. "If you like, we can talk while I change." Cherie didn't instantly take the offered hand. Reading the rejection, Lucy let her hand drop at her side. *No!* thought Cherie, *don't withdraw. I don't understand, but it's okay!*

"Come," said Lucy with a nod in the direction of the robing room, "we can talk for a few minutes before coffee hour."

Cherie fell into step beside her. The scuffs of their high heels on the floor slates echoed against the stone walls. "Let me apologize on behalf of my partners," Lucy said, jumping right into the vexed topic. That was her way, always get to the point directly, but gently. "Liz and Maggie drank too much before, during, and after the meeting. That's no excuse for their behavior." Lucy stopped and turned to Cherie. "I'm sorry you had to find out that way."

Nearly miscalculating for the difference in their heights, Cherie flung her arms around Lucy's neck. "Thank you for apologizing, but you didn't need to."

Lucy gently untangled herself from Cherie's arms, so she could see her face. "Oh, yes I do. It was a shock to you. I should have prepared you by telling you the truth long ago. There were many times when I was tempted." When Lucy reached for Cherie's hand, this time, she gave it. "Come into the vestry. We can speak privately there." They went into the large room, where long closets full of albs, surplices, and brightly colored stoles and chasubles lined the walls. Although the acolytes had changed long before and wouldn't interrupt them, Lucy closed and locked the door behind them.

"You look good in green," Cherie observed, for want of something to say.

"Thank you. Maggie says it's my best color," said Lucy before pulling the chasuble over her head.

"Maggie must think I hate her," Cherie confessed. "I feel terrible for avoiding her this morning. I didn't know what to say."

"I'm sure she doesn't either." Lucy took off her priest's stole and kissed the cross on it before hanging it up. She untied and took off the white alb, then shook out her hair, trying to impose some order on her unruly red mane. Humid weather made Cherie's hair frizzy too. Unconsciously, she smoothed it.

"Lucy, it's none of my business what you do in the privacy of your home," Cherie said to the top of her head.

Lucy stood straight, a little flushed from bending over. "Sure it is. You and Brenda are our friends. My relationship with Liz and Maggie is an essential fact of our lives. We should have been honest with you. Do you know why we weren't?"

"Of course. If word gets out, you could lose your job."

"Exactly. And the more people know, the more likely it will happen." Lucy found an elastic band in her bag and tied back her hair. She instantly looked more civilized. She glanced at her watch. "We could go to my office for a few minutes to talk more, or we can talk tomorrow when we'll have more time."

"Let's talk now. I'll text Brenda and tell her I'll be a little late for coffee hour."

While Cherie was texting, Lucy refreshed her lipstick. She slipped on a colorful cardigan. Lately, she'd been giving Reshma real competition when it came to vivid clothing.

"Did Maggie pick that sweater for you?" asked Cherie.

"As a matter of fact, she did," said Lucy, glancing at the sleeve. "She has an eye for clothes that work together. Probably from her theater training. Costume design is one of the things they teach in the Yale drama program."

"She has a real flair," Cherie agreed.

"Before the divorce, she was my thrift store buddy." Lucy looked suddenly sad. "I missed her so much when she decided she didn't want to see me anymore. She was my best friend." She brightened. "But she's back in my life now, and I'm grateful." Lucy took Cherie's arm. "Come on, let's go to my office before someone decides to look for us."

After they sat down on the comfortable, well-worn furniture in Lucy's office, Cherie suddenly didn't know what to say. Across from her sat the woman who had all the answers, or at least, that's what Cherie used to think. Lucy wasn't only her priest. She was her role model as a therapist. Cherie could easily become impatient with her clients or angry when they couldn't see something right before their eyes. Lucy always seemed to have infinite patience. She never seemed discouraged, even when she had every right to be.

"Brenda told me about her conversation with Liz on the boat," Cherie volunteered, trying to be helpful.

Lucy's green eyes were bright with amusement. "You're telling me that I don't have to start from the beginning. Well, that's a relief." She wiped imaginary sweat from her brow and beamed one of her solar flare smiles.

For a long moment, Cherie basked in its warmth. Then she remembered that time was short, and they should get on with the conversation. "I know the basic story and the timeline. I know it happened when you went away after the election."

"*It*," repeated Lucy, grinning wickedly. "Like *it* was an accident or a disease we suddenly got. It wasn't like that at all, not a lapse of judgment during a lost weekend in the woods. It's true none of us expected it. The stress and being away from home probably inclined us to take risks we wouldn't ordinarily take. But when it happened, it seemed organic, the next step in the evolution of our relationship."

"Tell me more," said Cherie. Lucy smiled at the therapist's trick.

"After becoming our neighbor, Maggie spent more time with us. It had once been her house, after all. She's a trained chef and that little efficiency kitchen in her apartment is no place to cook a gourmet meal. We began eating together. Living alone, Maggie wanted company. We invited her to watch movies with us, then the evening news. As we invited her more deeply into our private spaces, we were becoming a family without even realizing it. We had the foundations before sex was involved. Liz and Maggie have loved one another for over half a century. Maggie was my best friend. When we made love it felt entirely natural."

"But Mother Lucy..." Cherie started to say.

"Uh, uh. Cherie, I thought we'd lost the 'Mother' title some time ago. We're partners now in our practice. Colleagues and friends. Just Lucy to you, if you don't mind."

"I can leave off the title, but, Lucy, I look up to you!"

Lucy shook her head sadly. "Heaven save me from my pedestal. My fans think I'm a diva. My congregation thinks I'm God's messenger."

"Well, aren't you?"

Lucy's auburn brows flexed. "I am ordained to preach the Gospel, so technically, yes. The truth is, I'm just another human being struggling to keep the faith in difficult times. Just like you."

"That's what is so hard for me. I can't think what you're doing is anything but adultery."

Lucy nodded sadly. "I understand. That's what the commandment says, right? But it's not that simple. Do you want the church perspective, the theological perspective, or my perspective?"

"If you have time, all three."

"I have time," said Lucy. "Do you?"

"The kids love playing with the other kids at coffee hour, so I have a few more minutes."

Lucy settled back in her seat. "The church perspective is that marriage is between two consenting adults. It used to be only between those of the opposite sex. Until a few years ago, I couldn't be married in the church, and neither could you. In England, gays or lesbians still can't be married in the church. That's church law, which as you see, can differ, based on geography. If that's the case, the restrictions can't be God's immutable law. Rules about marriage are cultural. They can be changed."

"So, it's all relative?"

"Not completely, but things can change. The Anglican Communion is broad and ranges from modern, liberal society to the developing world. In some of those places, Victorian morality still rules. The Anglican churches of the Global South want to break away over the ordination of women and LGBT. They think same-sex marriage is an abomination, whereas in the Episcopal Church, we bless it."

"So, it depends," Cherie said to indicate she understood.

Lucy drew breath to continue the lesson. "We know both from the Old Testament and historical records that polygamy was common in ancient times. A man might have a primary wife to bear his legitimate heir and other lesser wives, even slaves, as concubines. Even the primary wife was considered his property. Any other man who had sex with his wife devalued his property. A woman who had sex with another man defiled herself, reducing her value."

"Obviously, that's not what we think now."

"No," said Lucy, gazing out the window. "The church has overlaid two thousand years of tradition, cultural influences, and theology on the Old Testament commandments. We have marriage as a metaphor for Christ's mystical marriage with the Church, which is always thought of as 'she.' We have natural law theory, justifying marriage only for reproduction. During the Middle Ages, things started to get really technical. The consummation needed witnesses."

Cherie made a face. "Ew!"

"Right? And sex is only intercourse, meaning penetration with a penis. Remember when Bill Clinton declared, 'I did not have sex with that woman'? That's what he meant."

"So lesbians don't have sex?"

"Technically, no."

"It all sounds very patriarchal to me."

Lucy laughed softly. "You should have heard my first wife, Erika, on this subject. To her, marriage was merely a tool of the patriarchy and to be avoided at all costs. At least, I didn't have to twist Liz's arm. She believes in marriage as a legal institution."

"But you can't legally marry Maggie."

"No, the law, like the church, holds that marriage is between two people, but Liz, being Liz, made sure Maggie is secure legally and financially within our arrangement. She and Olivia came up with the clever idea of creating a corporation, as if our relationship is a business!"

"That sounds like Liz. Always practical."

"Don't you know it?"

"Okay, Lucy. I've heard the official views. What's *yours*?"

Lucy thought for a moment. "Let's say, it's evolving. When I wrote my book, I was firmly in the marriage-is-exclusive-to-two-people camp. Liz kept challenging this position when I was prepping for my dissertation defense. As a philosopher, she was trained to look at all sides of an issue. She knew the job of the examiners was to pick apart my thesis. She came up with convincing arguments for polyamory, so that I could 'bullet proof' my defense."

Cherie rolled her eyes. "Don't you hate it when they use those gun metaphors? Every time Brenda means 'go ahead,' and says 'shoot,' I literally jump."

"I'm trying to wean Liz off them," said Lucy, shaking her head. "Not with very much success, so far. Those two and their guns."

Cherie remembered their time was short, and she was impatient to have her questions answered. "When you said your thinking is evolving, where is it now?"

Lucy took a long moment to reflect. "We impose rules on sex so people don't get hurt. If no one gets hurt, why is having two partners wrong? As Tom put it, something done out of love that hurts no one is not sinful."

"Obviously, Tom knows about this. That's good. He's very wise as well as smart."

"He is, but I don't want you to think this is a 'don't do what I do, do what I say' situation. Don't think the priests say this might be okay, so it's okay to throw out everything we believe."

Cherie shook her head. "You and Tom are theologians, and I'm sure you talk about things on a different level than I could even begin to understand. But I know both of you. You're not hypocrites."

"Thank you for saying so," Lucy said. "We try to be as honest and authentic as we can be. Sometimes, it's hard to get past the conventions, the church rules, and patriarchal theology. In moments of insecurity, my mind wants to revert to the familiar model we were all brought up to believe in. When I first became involved with a woman, it was hard to wrap my brain around that too. Once I did, I knew that's what I'd been looking for all along."

"It was the same for me," Cherie admitted, "but after my first female partner, it was a long time before finding my Brenda."

"But you found her," said Lucy with a smile.

"And I can't imagine sharing her with *anyone!*"

"That's fine, and a heck of a lot easier. Society has come such a long way in seeing same-sex relationships as normal. Being a threesome doesn't have precedents, except polygamy. But that's not what we have. We're trying to invent something new, but even coming up with ground rules is challenging. Sometimes, even I wonder if it can work."

The little pucker between Lucy's brows testified to her ongoing struggle. Her raw honesty touched Cherie.

"I don't think I could ever do what you're doing. I believe in the sanctity of marriage to one person, both as a matter of faith and conviction. Brenda is *mine* and mine alone. That's the hardest part for me to understand. I've seen how you and Liz look at one another. Your passion is so hot I often worry if I stand too close I'll be scorched." Cherie grinned and shook her hands to mime being burned. "Your love for that woman is so deep and strong, I can't imagine you sharing her with anyone, not even your best friend."

Lucy looked at Cherie for a long time before she said, "My love for Liz is so big, which is why I can share her, if that makes any sense."

Cherie shifted uncomfortably. "Sort of, but I still don't get it."

"That's all right, Cherie, you don't have to understand or even accept it. Just try not to judge us."

"Oh, Lucy, I'm trying. I'm really, *really* trying."

Lucy smiled one of those brilliant smiles that could melt a glacier. "I know you are, Cherie. I appreciate you asking questions and trying to understand. Thank you."

A sharp knock at the door startled them. "Cherie, are you in there?"

Cherie whispered loudly, "I knew it was only a matter of time."

"Yes, Brenda, she's here," Lucy called out. "You may come in."

The door opened and Brenda tentatively entered. "So, this is where you've been hiding."

"We're not hiding," Cherie protested indignantly. "Lucy and I had some things to discuss."

Brenda looked from her wife to Lucy and back again. "That's fine, but I need to talk to Lucy too." Lucy gestured to the place beside Cherie on the love seat.

"Where are the kids?" Cherie asked.

"Teresa and Reshma are entertaining them," said Brenda, sitting down. "Keith likes Grace."

"Oh, really?" Cherie said in a suggestive tone.

"Not in that way." Brenda waved dismissively. "They both like model rockets. They're building them in science class."

Lucy smiled at Brenda. "Cherie and I have been talking about the religious and social aspects of my relationship with Liz and Maggie. Would you like to join in?"

"I'll take a rain check. I have lots of questions, but I need to talk to you about something else."

"Sure," said Lucy and settled back in her seat. "Go ahead."

"I've decided to end the 287g agreement with Homeland Security, effective tomorrow."

"That sounds like a wise move," said Lucy, "but I thought you wanted to wait and see if the governor will sign the new law."

Brenda scowled. "I can't wait around for her to decide. My friend could have been killed yesterday. My pride and how people perceive me aren't worth someone getting hurt in my town. I just called Liz's friend to ask her to draft a statement. She'll be with me tomorrow at the news conference when I will announce it. I already asked Liz to come, and she said she would. Lucy, I hope you'll be there too."

"Of course, Brenda," Lucy said without hesitation. "Tell me the time and place, and I'll be there."

"Good. That's all I wanted to say," said Brenda, getting up. "Maybe, one more thing." A little smile played on Brenda's lips. "Please encourage your wife to stop standing in front of guns. I know she likes to play hero, but she doesn't have to do it every time. My officers like to have something to do."

"Well, honey," said Cherie, getting up, "maybe you should put an officer at that intersection, so your friend doesn't have to do the police's job."

"Next time we have a protest, that's exactly what I'll do. Deterrence is better than waiting until there's violence." Brenda leaned down and hugged Lucy. "Thank you for all you do."

Lucy returned the hug. "Right back at you. And I'll be there tomorrow. I promise."

***

"Want to ride with me to the station?" Cherie had an ulterior motive in asking Lucy to accompany her to the news conference. Mostly the offer came from simple generosity, but she was also trying to prove their relationship hadn't changed. They were still friends and colleagues.

Lucy closed her laptop and smiled. Because of the news conference, she was wearing a formal black skirted suit and an impeccably pressed linen clerical collar. Her big hair had been smoothed into submission, and her makeup was flawless. Lucy always knew how to make a good impression. "Thanks for the invitation, Cherie, but I'm not coming back right away. Liz is taking me out for lunch afterward. She's also invited her friend, Deborah, and our partner, Gloria Parrish." Lucy's little smile and arched brow told the rest of the story.

"Ah, I get it. A little matchmaking." Cherie laughed. "Her idea or yours?"

"What do you think? She came to bed after one of her long talks on the porch, feeling sorry for Deborah and wondering why she never found a partner."

"So, you scanned the inventory of available women of the right age and came up with Gloria."

"She checks all the boxes," Lucy said, counting with her fingers. "They're about the same age, well-educated and wicked smart, interested in the arts, and of similar ethnicity. Deborah grew up in Philadelphia, not New York, but they share that city-dweller street smarts people up here can only imagine."

Cherie pursed her lips and nodded as she considered the similarities between the two women. "Sounds like the makings of compatibility."

"Trouble is, Deborah is just as stubborn as Liz, so we didn't tell her that Gloria is joining us for lunch. Deborah is so sharp, she'd instantly know we were trying to set her up."

"So, you're just going to blind side her?"

"Sometimes, even priests have to resort to dirty tricks."

"Mother Lucy!" Cherie said, this time using her title as a tease. "I'm shocked."

"My motto is, keep everyone guessing." Lucy winked and took her purse out of her laptop bag. "We should go. It's important to Brenda that we be there. We don't want to be late."

When they were leaving the church parking lot, a car stopped to let Lucy out because she was wearing her collar. Cherie was right on her tail to make the turn with her.

At the police station, the department admin opened the door for them. "The meeting room is down the hall to the left," Cynthia explained. "It's packed."

"Bigger response than last time?" Lucy asked, hopefully.

"Ms. Goldberg sent all the invitations. I'm so grateful. This thing is beyond me. I hardly have time to do my real job, like reviewing the permit requests for the chief and dealing with Augusta." Cynthia leaned forward to speak confidentially. "I just wish the governor would sign that gosh darn bill!" She eyed Lucy's collar when she used the watered-down expletives, but she'd made her point. "I need to stay here to check credentials. You two should go in and find a seat," she urged.

The meeting room was jammed with people. Lights were set up in front. A man with a shoulder-held TV camera was filming the crowd. Liz, dressed in one of her power suits, was in the front, speaking to Deborah. Sean, Brenda's administrative captain, was trying to appear calm, but looked nauseous. The senior officers of the Hobbs PD were lined up on one side of the room.

At the podium, Brenda had her head down, reviewing her statement. She noticed Cherie and Lucy come in and motioned to them to join her the front. She gave Cherie a discreet kiss on the cheek, while reaching out her other hand to Lucy. "Thanks for coming, ladies. We're about to get started. I'd like you to stand up here with me." Sean pointed to a spot next to him.

Brenda tapped the microphone to get people's attention. "Would everyone please find a seat? We're about to begin." The TV camera lights switched on, nearly blinding everyone in the front of the room. Lucy reached for Cherie's hand and gave it a little squeeze.

"Thank you all for coming today," Brenda began. "You all received the statement in advance, so I'm not going to repeat the information in it. I'm here to answer your questions. Please raise your hands, and I'll call on you."

A dozen hands shot up. Brenda pointed to a woman in the front row. "Chief, in your statement, you said that you believe the extreme polarization politicized your agreement, and you are terminating it to avoid violence. Can you elaborate?"

"Yes, I can. As soon as people began protesting our 287g, other people were posting signs in front of the station with the black flag and a blue stripe. Of course, I agree that police lives matter, but that sign has become a symbol of right-wing anger. The driver of the truck in Saturday's incident was flying that black flag with the blue stripe along with a flag from the last presidential campaign. Let me be clear. You are not supporting me or the Hobbs PD by threatening protesters with a gun."

Brenda picked another reporter, this time from the back. "Chief Harrison, you already paused the agreement, pending LD1971 being signed into law by the governor. Why wasn't that enough for your detractors?"

"I don't know the answer to that question. You'll have to ask them. Next question, please."

A very young woman raised her hand, and Brenda called on her. "You mentioned that the driver of the truck had been detained for questioning. Can you update us on the investigation?"

"It's department policy not to comment on on-going investigations unless it is a matter of public safety. We are still receiving voluntary statements from the public on the incident. We will update you as soon as we have more information. Another question?"

An older man that Cherie recognized from the evening news rose in the back. "Chief, you said the threat of violence ultimately convinced you to cancel the agreement. Did you feel that anyone was ever in serious danger?"

Brenda paused to consider for a moment. "Whenever someone draws a gun, especially in a large crowd, there is the possibility of people being harmed. Fortunately, Dr. Stolz has tactical training and is experienced in facing gunmen. She also knows how to de-escalate a volatile situation. She was able to defuse the tense moment before anyone got hurt."

"Why did she wave the driver on instead of waiting for the police?"

Brenda turned to Liz. "Dr. Stolz, would you like to answer that question?" She stepped aside so that Liz could approach the podium.

"As a civilian marshal at a protest, I had no authority to detain someone. The parked truck stopped traffic, causing it to back up on Route One, so as soon as the light changed, I encouraged the driver to leave."

Every hand shot up. Liz turned to Brenda, who nodded. Liz pointed to a woman who wore an NPR hat. "Did you witness the incident that caused the argument?"

"No, I was assisting a man in respiratory distress. I heard the shouting and a loud thump, which I interpreted as the sound of soft tissue striking a vehicle. I left my patient in the care of his wife and proceeded to the intersection, where I saw the driver of the truck and the protester arguing. I pulled the protester back to the sidewalk, where he belonged."

Every hand was raised. Liz called on a man in the front. "Did you see the gun?"

"Not at first. When the driver of the truck opened the door, it blocked the view of his body. I only knew about the gun when someone shouted that he had one. I turned around and saw the gun pointed at the protester." Liz called on someone in the back.

"Dr. Stolz, a few years ago you were involved in the shooting at Hobbs Elementary." Cherie saw all the color drain from Liz's face. "Did that experience help you deal with this situation?" Liz stared at the podium for a long moment and took some deep breaths. Cherie braced herself to move quickly, but then Liz looked up.

"They were two completely different situations. In the school situation, I was directly threatened by the shooter. In this one, I just happened to be between the gunman and his target. My only objective was to defuse the situation and remove the danger as quickly as possible."

Liz pointed to another reporter. "Was the protester injured and was there any damage to the truck?"

"I did not observe any injury. As for the condition of the truck, I'll let Chief Harrison answer that question." Liz switched places with Brenda.

"There was no observable damage to the truck, although the driver alleges that the protester slammed his hand down on the hood. Eyewitnesses corroborate that. The protester was examined by paramedics at the scene but showed no signs of injury. And that is all I will say about the details of the incident until we review the statements and interview witnesses. Thank you. Now, one more question."

Although he was considerably grayer than the photo that used to appear next to his column, Russell Bliss was instantly recognizable.

"Chief Harrison, do you have a plan to rehabilitate the image of the Hobbs Police Department and the town after all the negative publicity?"

"First of all, I did not cause the negative publicity. In the beginning, I tried to be transparent with the press and provide factual answers to their questions. If they chose to spin what I said and make the town look bad, that is not because of what I did or the town. The media twisted what I said for their own purposes. However, I understand that Deborah Goldberg has offered her services pro bono to the town to, as you say, 'rehabilitate' our image. That's Ms. Goldberg standing next to Dr. Stolz." Deborah nodded to acknowledge Brenda's comment. "If we had more time, I'd ask Ms. Goldberg to take questions. But now, the Hobbs Police Department needs to get back to work of protecting this town. Thank you all for coming. This news conference is concluded."

As the senior officers of the Hobbs PD filed out of the room, the reporters were still raising their hands and calling Brenda's name, but resolutely, she made her exit.

Chapter 20

Cherie watched Brenda button up the elegant suit she had worn for their wedding. It had been a hand-me-down from Liz, who had rescued Cherie from marrying a woman wearing a police uniform. The designer suit might be a few years out of style, but in Hobbs, who even would notice? The exceptions might be Liz's partners and her New York guest. Olivia was also a fashion plate, so she might look askance, but otherwise, no one else would care.

Cherie was relieved that Liz had put her foot down and refused to wear the matching gowns the bridal pair had chosen for the wedding party. When they'd shown up at the bridal shop for a fitting, Liz had completely lost it. She held up the sample, a flouncy, pastel chiffon number, and declared to the red-faced attendant at the bridal shop, "Nope! I will not look like an escapee from a 1970s cotillion!" After Liz's meltdown, all the female attendants were allowed to choose their own formal wear.

Cherie was glad for an excuse to splurge on a new gown. Lucy would be singing in Boston in a few weeks and had given the Harrisons tickets.

Cherie didn't mind another occasion to dress up, but Brenda might need some convincing.

"I was scared shitless at our wedding. I hardly remember a thing, so I'm looking forward to this one," Brenda said, inspecting herself in the mirror. "For the first time since that stupid ICE agreement, I feel like I can relax and enjoy myself."

"At least, now you can admit it was stupid."

"Signing up for it wasn't stupid," Brenda said earnestly. "There was nothing wrong with the training or our motives. The problem is who's running the government and the assholes he's appointed to run these agencies. One is crazier than the next."

"I can't argue that point, Brenda, but it did look bad."

Brenda hung her head. "Yes, it did."

"Why did it take Deborah explaining it before you realized it?" Cherie asked, raising Brenda's face with her fingertips under her chin. Brenda's blue eyes looked sad.

"I don't know. She had a way of explaining it that made me see why it made people think I was one of them. I'd never be one of them. They're cruel. I thought I was just doing my job and preparing my people to deal with a problem. I didn't realize how much it would hurt you and the kids."

Cherie put her arms around her. "Oh, Brenda. You did what you thought was right. I'm just sorry it took a guy pointing a gun at your friend to wake you up. I love you with my whole heart and soul. I forgive you. And now, you know I'll always stand by you."

Brenda wiggled her blond brows suggestively. "Maybe they'll play that song at the reception. I love slow dancing with you and getting to feel up your curves in front of all those people." Brenda pressed closer, demonstrating.

"Brenda Harrison, don't get me started! We need to get to this wedding. We can celebrate afterwards." Cherie gave her a soulful tongue kiss. "There. That will have to hold you for a while. We need to leave soon. Now, I need to fix my lipstick and so do you. Come with me, honey bear. Let mama take care of you."

***

Ablaze with stargazer lilies, the church looked spectacular. Reshma was wearing the ornate white vestments that Bobbie had donated to thank St. Margaret's clergy for their attentive care at the end of Joyce's life. The young priest looked uncomfortable in the stiff brocade, but she wore it beautifully, looking like an icon in an Eastern-Rite Basilica. Her almost black skin contrasted sharply with the brilliant white.

Cherie only peeked in because she was in the wedding party and was supposed to stay hidden until the ceremony began. She kissed Brenda at the door and sent her down the aisle to sit beside Olivia

Enright and Dr. Hsu. The kids were at home with Aunt Simone because this was an adults-only wedding. Susan had decided she couldn't invite the Harrison kids and Teresa's daughter, Grace, but not her students, which would be her entire class and their parents. Bobbie had been willing to pay the extra expense, but Susan worried some of the parents would balk at their children attending a same-sex wedding. Apparently, this conversation went back and forth until they'd arrived at the no-child policy. Since returning to work, Cherie had become a captive audience to Bobbies's complaints about the wedding planning. Her tales had more twists and plot reversals than a daytime soap opera.

On her way to the rectory conference room where the bridal party was gathering, Cherie heard a powerful soprano voice singing scales—Lucy warming up in her office. Another soprano was singing accompanied by a guitar in Tom's office. Maggie would be the cantor and sing "The Wedding Song" with the lyrics adjusted to feature two women.

Cherie found the others in the conference room. Liz, in spike heels, towered over the women. Her eyes were glued to her phone. Cherie presumed she was reviewing the scripture passages she was to read during the ceremony. She was wearing a maroon pants suit with shimmering highlights that instantly drew the eye, but in a way that wouldn't detract from the brides. The others also wore outfits reflecting their personalities. Teresa's brightly patterned gown and headdress matched. Courtney's understated formal dress was simply elegant. The other attendants on Susan's side included the school secretary, who'd also been a hostage during the school shooting, and Sally, Susan's AA sponsor. Everyone looked perfect. As Liz had said, serendipity was an excellent wedding planner.

Liz noticed Cherie come in and approached. She leaned down to whisper, "May I say, Mrs. Harrison, that you look absolutely gorgeous?"

"I promise I won't report you, Dr. Stolz. We're at a wedding, not the office."

Liz grinned wickedly. "This old dinosaur is still learning the rules."

"You're not an old dinosaur, and you're doing just fine. I never could understand why complimenting another woman is offensive." Cherie looked Liz up and down. "You're looking pretty gorgeous yourself, although those high heels make you *very* tall."

"Why I hardly ever wear them. Plus, they make me too sexy. Women can't resist me." Liz winked rakishly.

"I heard your wife practicing when I came in. Actually, both of them. This will be quite the spectacle."

Liz bent low to say, "Joyce wanted Bobbie to have her money. Throwing a big party for the town is not the worst way to spend it."

Maggie came into the conference room. Because she had directed many theater productions, she'd volunteered to choreograph the ceremony. She reviewed what they had practiced during the previous night's rehearsal.

Lucy had joined them just in time to hear her speech. Cherie's jaw dropped a little. If Liz's outfit had drawn the eye, Lucy's deep-green, black-satin gown with amazing folds to emphasize the sheen demanded everyone's attention. Her red hair was styled in a dramatic upsweep, and her elegant rhinestone jewelry looked real. Across the room, Liz gave her a smoldering look. The raw desire in it was a little shocking.

Lucy signaled to Liz with a bent finger. Her wife instantly came to her side. Lucy took a brass tube and a small mirror out of her purse and handed them to Liz. After she applied the darker lipstick, there was no doubt it looked better. Lucy caught Maggie's eye. She smiled and gave the improvement a thumbs up. Watching their wordless communication was fascinating.

Lucy left to take her position in the front of the church, where she'd be singing the processional music. Maggie herded everyone into the narthex of the church to await the brides. The sense of anticipation was palpable.

Finally, the limousine carrying Bobbie and Susan arrived. They were wearing different wedding gowns, both white. Bobbie's dress was cleverly designed to drape beautifully on her short, stocky frame. Befitting an ex-nun, who was now a priest, Susan's gown was modest and somehow ethereal. Neither bride wore a veil. Instead, they wore wreaths of red and white rosebuds.

Maggie opened the back door slightly and signaled to Lucy. The brass ensemble from the Boston Symphony began the accompaniment to Bach's "*Bist du bei mir*." Lucy's connections always ensured the best accompaniment.

In a departure from the usual order of the service, Reshma greeted each bride with a kiss on the cheek and opened the ceremony. Liz read from the *Song of Songs*, seemingly relishing the erotic metaphors, but followed with Corinthians 1:13 in a more respectful tone. Tom Simmons read John's Gospel on love. As Reshma rose to deliver the homily, Cherie wondered what the young priest would say.

Reshma nodded to the brides, but she didn't ascend to the pulpit. Instead, she stood in the main aisle.

"Susan and Bobbie waited a long time to marry, even though they were both free. It wasn't uncertainty that kept them apart, but judgment, our judgment about their relationship." Reshma paused for effect and glanced around the church. A few people visibly squirmed.

Cherie adjusted her long dress under her to be comfortable and sat back. This was going to be interesting.

"When Susan first met Bobbie, she was caring for Joyce, her longtime partner, who was suffering from dementia. Bobbie and Joyce never married, even when the Supreme Court voted to make it the law of the land. Joyce didn't believe in same-sex marriage, but she planned for their financial security as if she did. Joyce left enough money for her long-term care. Bobbie could have put her in a facility, but she took care of her, ensuring she lived her best life.

I was with them when Joyce left this world. Bobbie was there until her last breath."

All eyes turned to Bobbie. People were nodding in approval.

"Susan, an ordained priest, had come to Hobbs seeking a new start. She'd struggled with alcoholism. Chief Harrison quietly helped her deal with the consequences. Dr. Stolz pulled strings to get her into rehab. Sally, her sponsor, stood by her when she faltered. Despite Susan's history, members of this community, like her principal, Courtney Barnes, and her rector, Lucy Bartlett, were willing to give her a chance.

"Bobbie too. She became friends with Susan working for common causes. She fell in love, but Susan was afraid to return her love because of us. She feared our judgment." Reshma looked at members of the congregation, acknowledging rather than accusing them. "I heard the whispers. People said how terrible it was for Bobbie and Susan to be in love because Joyce was still alive.

"Meanwhile, Bobbie was showing the purest love for Joyce that any human being can give another. You see, romantic love is selfish. It expects to be returned. Joyce's brain was dying and she couldn't reciprocate. Yet Bobbie was there for her at the worst time of life, expecting nothing. That is the kind of fidelity a marriage requires.

"Exclusivity is nice, but being there when things are hard is more important than anything else. That's why the old marriage vows say, 'in sickness and in health, for richer or poorer...'

"Today, Bobbie and Susan will say those old vows and mean them in a way that comes from their lived truth. Bobbie never gave up on Susan. She held space for her after she was a hostage in the shooting at Hobbs Elementary. She helped Susan heal from the worst trauma imaginable, almost losing her life. You see, friends, fidelity means being there no matter what happens. *Being there.*"

Cherie noticed Tom and Lucy exchanging a satisfied look. She wondered if they'd coached Reshma while she was writing this sermon. Maybe she wasn't giving the young priest enough credit.

Since she'd first arrived in Hobbs as a transitional deacon, Reshma had come a long way. Susan, who'd mentored her, beamed with unabashed pride. A single tear ran down her cheek.

"So, what are we to take away from what these two women have lived?" Reshma continued. "For one thing, don't judge another's relationship. You don't know what hell someone else is living, so don't judge their joy. The other is, romantic love is just one form of love. Our readings today remind us there are many ways to love. As the LGBT meme says, 'Love is Love.'

"So, as we bless the marriage of Bobbie and Susan, learn from their stubborn persistence in loving one another and their service to others. Learn from their lives, what fidelity really means...and love. Today, I encourage you not only to feel love, but to live it, every day of your lives, and to give it away, passionately, joyfully, and extravagantly. Amen."

Gazing fondly at Reshma, Liz reached for Maggie's hand and smiled across the nave at Lucy. Pure joy glowed in their faces. Cherie wondered if Reshma knew about their relationship. Then she realized the young priest didn't need privileged knowledge to have arrived at her simple but profound message. She only needed eyes.

Also by Elena Graf

HOBBS SERIES

HIGH OCTOBER

Liz Stolz and Maggie Fitzgerald were college roommates until Maggie confessed their affair to her parents. When Maggie breaks her leg in a summer stock stage accident, she lands in Dr. Stolz's office. Is forty years too long to wait for the one you love?

THE MORE THE MERRIER

Maggie and Liz's plans of sitting by the fire, drinking mulled wine, and watching old Christmas movies get scuttled by surprise visits from friends and family.

THIS IS MY BODY

Professor Erika Bultmann, a confirmed agnostic, is fascinated by Mother Lucy, the new rector of the Episcopal Church, especially when she discovers Lucille Bartlett was a rising opera star before mysteriously disappearing from the stage.

LOVE IN THE TIME OF CORONA

Police Chief Brenda Harrison shows an interest in Liz's biracial PA, but first Cherie needs to get past her loathing for all law enforcement since a state trooper shot and killed her sister.

THIRSTY THURSDAYS

Liz Stolz initiates Thirsty Thursdays, a weekly cocktail party on her deck, so her friends can socialize safely during the pandemic. Pretentious, overbearing Olivia Enright pursues Liz's friend, architect Sam McKinnon, and tries to push her way into the tight-knit group.

THE DARK WINTER

Erika hires Sam to build a soundproof practice room for Lucy. Fortunately, the early Christmas gift is ready before tragedy strikes.

As the women of Hobbs pull together to help a beloved friend deal with her loss, the dark winter brings tension and realignment in their small community.

SUMMER PEOPLE

Melissa Morgenstern, a high-profile lawyer from Boston, is spending the summer with her widowed mother. She's doing some trust work for Liz who introduces her to the attractive Courtney Barnes, Hobbs Elementary's new assistant principal. The arrival of Susan, Lucy's ex, complicates her deepening relationship with Liz.

STRANDS

Cherie hears her biological clock ticking and would like to start a family. When a shocking tragedy creates an opportunity for her and Brenda to become parents, their friends need to step up to make it happen.

THE RECTOR'S WEDDING

The sudden opportunity for Lucy to return to her singing career throws everything in her life into doubt—her vocation as a priest, her settled life in Hobbs, even her upcoming marriage to the woman she loves.

THE VANISHING BRIDGE

Rev. Susan Gedney tries to rebuild trust after her humiliating exit from Hobbs. Bobbie Lantry always needs to rush away to take care of a mysterious elderly woman. They need to share their secrets, but do they dare?

EXTENDED CAPACITY

A school shooting was a nightmare that only happened in other towns until it came to Hobbs. Liz finds herself in the middle when the shooter's identity is revealed. The town is shocked to learn how the shooter got into the school.

RIP TIDE

A small town in Maine has begun to recover from a school shooting when another mass shooting and divisive politics threaten to divide friends and end relationships. Town doctor Liz Stolz and Episcopal rector Lucy Bartlett, used to bringing people together, find their own alliances threatened.?

THREE'S COMPANY

What if the love of your life is not one person but two? A warm-hearted look at how love never really dies and how forgiveness opens new possibilities.

PASSING RITES SERIES

THE IMPERATIVE OF DESIRE

A coming-of-age story that takes a brilliant aristocratic woman from La Belle Époque, through a world war, a revolution that outlawed the German nobility, the roaring twenties, and finally, to the decadent demimonde of Weimar Berlin.

OCCASIONS OF SIN

For seven centuries, the German convent of Obberoth has been hiding the nuns' secrets—forbidden passions, scandalous manuscripts locked away, a ruined medical career, and perhaps even a murder.

LIES OF OMISSION

In 1938, the Nazis are imposing their doctrine of "racial hygiene" on hospitals and universities. Margarethe von Stahle has always avoided politics, but now she must decide whether to remain on the sidelines or act on her convictions.

ACTS OF CONTRITION

After the fall of Berlin, Margarethe is brutally assaulted by occupying Russian soldiers. Her former protégée, Sarah Weber, returns to Berlin with the American Army and tries to heal her mentor's physical and psychological wounds.

About the Author

In addition to the Hobbs series of contemporary novels set in a small town in Maine, Elena Graf has published four historical novels set in twentieth-century Europe. Two of the titles in the Passing Rites series have won Golden Crown Literary Society and Rainbow awards for best historical fiction. She pursued a Ph.D. in philosophy but ended up in the "accidental profession" of publishing, where she worked for almost four decades. She lives in coastal Maine.

Find out about events and new books at her website, www.elenagraf.com. You can write to Elena at elena@elenagraf.com, and find her on Facebook and BlueSky.

SILVIANO SANTIAGO

O ENTRE-LUGAR DO DISCURSO LATINO-AMERICANO

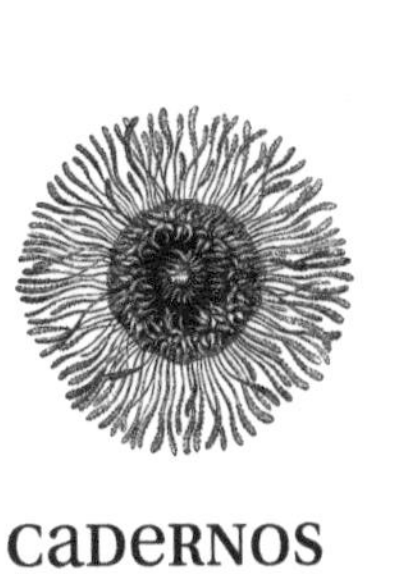

CADERNOS ULTRAMARES

ORGANIZAÇÃO E PROJETO GRÁFICO

Marcos Lacerda, Ana Paula Simonaci e Sergio Cohn

CONSELHO EDITORIAL

André Botelho

Bernardo Esteves

Boaventura de Souza Santos

Evelyn Goyannes Dill Orrico

Fréderic Vanderberghe

José Luis Garcia

Maria João Cantinho

Renato Rezende

Teresa Arijón

Vagner Amaro

ISBN 9786586962413

azougue press |
coordenação geral Sergio Cohn
coordenação editorial
Sergio Cohn — Darien Lamen — Cristián Jiménez Plaza
Brasil | CNPJ 12.272.339/0001-26
Portugal | Oca Editorial NF 515805394
USA | E. Id. 803650511
Chile | Tucán Ediciones RUT 77.369.106-1

A proposta dos Cadernos Ultramares é transpor fronteiras. Não apenas geográficas, com a edição de um amplo panorama do pensamento brasileiro para o público português, mas também entre as áreas do saber, criando uma coleção transdisciplinar, acessível não apenas para leitores especializado, pesquisadores e acadêmicos, como para interessados em geral.

Para isto, os Cadernos Ultramares privilegiam a leveza do ensaio, a "brigada ligeira", utilizando-se de um gênero marcado pela abertura e experimentação, uma forma privilegiada para a proposição e a apresentação de interpretações da cultura e da sociedade. Nos últimos anos, o gênero ensaio tem sido revalorizado como um importante meio de diálogo entre a pesquisa acadêmica e a sociedade.

O Brasil possui uma produção riquíssima de pensamento em diversas áreas, que vão da física à antropologia, da matemática às artes. Os Cadernos Ultramares, ao trazerem importantes textos de alguns dos nossos mais renomados pensadores, sejam clássicos ou contemporâneos, busca possibilitar ao leitor um olhar amplo e qualificado sobre essa produção.

Interessa-nos a constituição de um diálogo entre áreas, de uma conversa aberta que escape das armadilhas do pensamento especializado e do produtivismo acadêmico. Interessa, antes de tudo, a valorização do encontro do leitor com o sabor do texto, do prazer da leitura e da troca livre de pensamento.

apresentação

POR MARCOS LACERDA

No texto de introdução à 2º edição do livro *Nas malhas da letra* (1989), Silviano Santiago (1936) faz uma boa reflexão a respeito do sentido da sua obra crítica em especial, apontando uma gradação histórica, política e conceitual entre o seu segundo livro de ensaios críticos: *Uma literatura nos trópicos* (1978), o livro imediatamente posterior, *Vale quanto pesa* (1982) e este, *Nas malhas da letra*. No primeiro, havia ainda uma certa euforia advinda da acumulação crítica, política e social da geração de intelectuais associados às discussões a respeito da relação entre teorias sociais potentes, como a teoria da dependência, e criação artísticas originais: a euforia da criação acompanhava o ímpeto da crítica, cuja principal feição era também criadora. No segundo, mantendo o espírito de rigor e invenção acesos, o ambiente já começa a se modificar, com a consolidação da lógica de economia de mercado, capitaneada pela ditadura civil-militar, e da figura do consumidor – inclusive da literatura – no centro dos interesses, o que significa também a consolidação dos critérios da cultura de massas como padrão de avaliação nivelador. Ao mesmo tempo, um certo desencanto crítico com a questão econômica e social que atravessa a crítica da esquerda feita através de bens culturais, como os livros, por exemplo, e a recepção em geral restrita apenas aos circuitos pequeno-burgueses.

No terceiro, por fim, o tom mais maduro atesta a consolidação de sua forma de pensamento crítico e o lugar da sua análise em relação, por exemplo, com o grupo de críticos paulistas que se constituiu em torno da figura de Antonio Candido e, em especial, de Roberto Schwarz, em ensaios como, entre outros, "Poder e Alegria: a literatura brasileira pós-64" (de que falaremos mais adiante) e "Além da história social", em que apresenta algumas das limitações, segundo a sua análise, da perspectiva "realista" e histórico-social na crítica literária (associada ao grupo dos críticos paulistas), procurando mostrar situações nas quais a crítica da arte e da literatura, em especial, com a poesia, podem pensar a autonomia imanente e interna da arte, sem a colocar necessariamente na condição de revelação – complexa e tensa – de processos sociais e históricos específicos.

Sem desconsiderar a vasta obra do autor, também poeta, contista e romancista, neste último caso, tendo ganhado um dos principais prêmios de crítica do Brasil: o prêmio jabuti de 2017, pelo romance *Machado* (2017) sobre Machado de Assis, o nosso maior escritor, além de ter organizado uma das mais importantes seleções do pensamento social brasileiro, com um texto introdutório dos mais importantes já escritos para quem quer compreender a vida intelectual brasileira (*Intérpretes do Brasil*, 2000), parte expressiva do seu pensamento crítico pode ser situado entre estes três livros mencionados. Para a coleção ultramares foram selecionados dois ensaios: "O entre-lugar do discurso latino-americano", publicado no livro *A literatura nos trópicos* (1978) e "Poder e alegria: a literatura brasileira pós-64", publicado, por sua vez, no livro *Nas malhas das letras* (1989).

No primeiro, Santiago apresenta uma perspectiva original do lugar do discurso latino-americano em relação à literatura e ao pensamento em geral, em sua situação ambivalente especialmente em relação ao discurso europeu, em grande medida, o discurso do "colonizador" mas, ao mesmo tempo, uma espécie de discurso "fundador" de uma tradição de conhecimento, arte e cultura inevitáveis. "O entre-lugar do discurso latino-americano" pode ser considerado um texto inaugural, no sentido de ser o texto que traz para o âmbito das discussões que ficam entre a análise estilística e a reflexão histórico-sociológica, a filosofia pós-estrutural, em especial, Derrida e Foucault, além da perspectiva propriamente antropológica. No segundo, uma forma de abordagem da literatura e da arte brasileira que emergem associadas aos movimentos subversivos e libertários e às lutas pelos direitos civis de minorias, em grande parte, não de todo associados ao ideal nacional-desenvolvimentista das movimentações da esquerda cultural pré-64 que foi desalojada do poder (ou de qualquer ambição realista ao poder) com o golpe militar de 64. "Poder e alegria" sugere uma perspectiva a respeito da cultura brasileira que a coloca numa situação diferencial em relação ao período imediatamente anterior: um distanciamento dos temas associados ao projeto nacional-popular, como a anunciar uma primeira dimensão mais propriamente "pós-moderna" no discurso literário e artístico brasileiro, com o advento das temáticas associadas ao maio de 68, ao movimento ecológico e, no caso do Brasil, a movimentos artísticos como o tropicalismo, não à toa mencionado pelo ensaísta como exemplo da linguagem subversiva, corrosiva e, ainda assim, descolado do ideário pré-64, na voz de um dos seus principais criadores.

Os dois textos, assim, tem muito em comum, com o primeiro trazendo para os estudos mais importantes da crítica literária e do pensamento social brasileiro a perspectiva filosófica de Derrida e Foucault, como contraponto, em certa medida, às perspectivas do marxismo ocidental, de Lukács, Adorno e, por extensão, a chamada Escola de Frankfurt, que tanta influência teve no desenvolvimento do pensamento crítico, de cunho formal e histórico-social a um só tempo. Não deixa de ser interessante notar que o próprio Foucault disse em conhecida entrevista que, se tivesse conhecido os teóricos da "Escola de Frankfurt" antes, isso o teria poupado tempo de reflexão, mostrando que os caminhos do pensamento e da crítica são bem mais ambivalentes e complexos do que podemos imaginar. Já o segundo ensaio, é uma espécie de afirmação crítica da literatura brasileira do imediato pós-64 feita através de um desvinculo dos quadros de referências principais da cultura brasileira mais interessante do pré-64, não mais tendo como o seu objeto principal o tema da exploração do homem pelo homem, da desigualdade social profunda, dos impasses da modernização conservadora, do capitalismo, do imperialismo e da possibilidade de sua superação estética e social. A cultura brasileira mais inventiva do pós-64 atuaria numa dimensão mais comportamental, numa atenção maior às formas complexas de realização dos micro-poderes e aos modos de subje-tivação, rebeldia e reação baseados em comunidades alternativas transnacionais.

O ENTRE-LUGAR DO DISCURSO LATINO-AMERICANO

Para Eugenio e Sally

O jabuti que só possuía uma casca branca e mole deixou-se morder pela onça que o atacava. Morder tão fundo que a onça ficou pregada no jabuti e acabou por morrer. Do crânio da onça o jabuti fez seu escudo.
ANTONIO CALLADO, *Quarup*

Antes de mais nada, tarefas negativas. É preciso se libertar de todo um jogo de noções que estão ligadas ao postulado de continuidade. [...] Como a noção de influência, que dá um suporte — antes mágico que substancial — aos fatos de transmissão e de comunicação.
Michel Foucault, *Arqueologia do saber*

Montaigne abre o Cap. XXXI dos Ensaios, capítulo em que nos fala dos canibais do Novo Mundo, com uma referência precisa à História grega. Esta mesma referência servirá também para nos inscrever no contexto das discussões sobre o lugar que ocupa hoje o discurso literário latino-americano no confronto com o europeu. Escreve Montaigne:

> Quando o rei Pirro entrou na Itália, logo depois de ter examinado a formação do exército que os Romanos lhe mandavam ao encontro, disse: "Não sei que bárbaros são estes (pois os greos assim denominavam todas as nações estrangeiras), mas a disposição deste exército que vejo não é, de modo algum, bárbara."

À citação histórica em Montaigne, metafórica sem dúvida na medida em que anuncia a organização interna do capítulo sobre os antropófagos da América do Sul, ou mais precisamente do Brasil — a metáfora em Montaigne guarda em essência a marca do conflito eterno entre o civilizado e o bárbaro, entre o colonialista e o colonizado, entre Grécia e Roma, entre Roma e suas províncias, entre a Europa e o Novo Mundo etc. Por outro lado, as palavras do rei Pirro, ditadas por certa sabedoria pragmática, não chegam a esconder a surpresa e o deslumbramento diante de uma descoberta extraordinária: os bárbaros não se comportam como tais — conclui ele.

Na hora do combate, instante decisivo e revelador, no momento em que as duas forças contrárias e inimigas devem se perfilar uma diante da outra, arrancadas brutalmente de sua condição de desequilíbrio econômico, corporificadas sob a forma de presente e guerra, o rei Pirro descobre que os gregos subestimavam a arte militar dos estrangeiros, dos bárbaros, dos romanos. O desequilíbrio instaurado pelos soldados gregos, anterior ao conflito armado e entre os superiores causa de orgulho e presunção, é antes de mais nada propiciado pela defasagem econômica que governa as relações entre as duas nações. No momento exato em que se abandona o domínio restrito do colonialismo econômico, compreendemos que muitas vezes é necessário inverter os valores que definem os grupos em oposição e, talvez, questionar o próprio conceito de superioridade.

Segundo a citação extraída dos *Ensaios*, ali onde se esperava uma *disposição do exército* delineada segundo os preconceitos sobre os romanos espalhados entre os gregos, encontra-se uma armada bem organizada e que nada fica a dever às dos povos civilizados. Libertamo-nos de um arrancão do campo da quantidade e do colonialismo, visto que a admiração do rei Pirro revela um compromisso inabalável com o julgamento de qualidade que ela inaugura. Apesar das diferenças econômicas e sociais, os dois exércitos se apresentam em equilíbrio no campo de batalha. Mesmo que não se apresentassem em equilíbrio, nunca é demais lembrar as circunstâncias inusitadas que cercam a morte do monarca grego a que se refere Montaigne. O acidente inesperado e fatal guarda, por sua atualidade, um aviso seguro para as poderosas nações militares de hoje: Pirro, rei de Éfeso, "foi assassinado na tomada de Argos por uma velha senhora que lhe atirou uma telha na cabeça do alto de um telhado" — como nos informa deliciosamente o *Petit Larousse*.

Vamos falar do espaço em que se articula hoje a admiração do rei Pirro e de um provável processo de inversão de valores.

I

Mas antes é preciso estabelecer certo número de distinções, de modo que se possa ao mesmo tempo limitar e precisar o nosso tópico. Analisemos, primeiro, por razões de ordem didática, as relações entre duas civilizações que são completamente estranhas uma a outra e cujos primeiros encontros se situam no nível da ignorância mútua. Desde o século passado, os etnólogos[1], no desejo de desmistificar o discurso beneplácito dos historiadores, concordam em assinalar que a vitória do branco no Novo Mundo se deve menos a razões de caráter cultural do que ao uso arbitrário da violência e à imposição brutal de uma ideologia, como atestaria a recorrência das palavras "escravo" e "animal" nos escritos dos portugueses e espanhóis. Essas expressões, aplicadas aos não-ocidentais, configuram muito mais um ponto de vista dominador do que propriamente uma tradução do desejo de conhecer.

Nesse sentido, Claude Lévi-Strauss nos fala de uma enquete de ordem psicossociológica empreendida pelos monges da Ordem de São Jerônimo. À pergunta se os índios eram capazes "de viver por eles próprios, como camponeses de Castilha", a resposta negativa se impunha de imediato:

1 Jacques Derrida, salientando a contribuição da etnologia de abalo da metafísica ocidental, comenta: "... a Etnologia só teve condições para nascer como ciência no momento em que se operou um descentramento: no momento em que a cultura européia [...] foi deslocada, expulsa do seu lugar, deixando então de ser considerada como a cultura de referência." E acrescenta: "Este momento não é apenas um momento do discurso filosófico [...]; é também um momento político, econômico, técnico etc." *A escritura e a diferença*. São Paulo, Perspectiva, 1972, p. 234.

Na verdade, talvez seus netinhos possam; além do mais, os indígenas estão de tal modo entregues ao vício que ainda se pode duvidar da sua capacidade; como prova, evitam os espanhóis, recusam-se a trabalhar sem remuneração, mas levam a perversidade até o ponto de presentearem os próprios bens; não admitem repudiar os companheiros que tiveram as orelhas decepadas pelos espanhóis. [...] Seria melhor para os índios que se transformassem em homens escravos do que continuassem a ser animais livres...?[2]

Em visível contraste, os índios de Porto Rico, seguindo ainda as informações prestadas por Lévi-Strauss nos *Tristes trópicos*, se dedicam à captura de brancos com o intuito de os matar por imersão. Em seguida, durante semanas ficam de guarda em torno dos afogados para saber se eles se submetem ou não às leis de putrefação. Lévi-Strauss conclui não sem certa ironia:

[...] os brancos invocavam as ciências sociais, ao passo que os índios mostravam mais con-

2 *Tristes Tropiques*. Paris, Plon, 1955, p. 82.

fiança nas ciências naturais; enquanto os brancos proclamavam que os índios eram animais, estes limitavam-se a supor que os primeiros fossem deuses. Ignorância por ignorância, a última atitude era, certamente, mais digna de homens (p. 83).

A violência é sempre cometida pelos índios por razões de ordem religiosa. Diante dos brancos, que se dizem portadores da palavra de Deus, cada um profeta a sua própria custa, a reação do indígena é a de saber até que ponto as palavras dos europeus traduziam a verdade transparente. Pergunto-me agora se as experiências dos índios de Porto Rico não se justificariam pelo zelo religioso dos missionários. Estes, em sucessivos sermões, pregavam a imortalidade do verdadeiro Deus, da ressurreição de Cristo — os índios, em seguida, tornavam-se sequiosos de contemplar o milagre bíblico, de provar o mistério religioso em todo seu esplendor de enigma. A prova do poder de Deus deveria se produzir menos pela *assimilação* passiva da palavra cristã do que pela visão de um acontecimento verdadeiramente milagroso.

Nesse sentido, encontramos informações preciosas e extraordinárias na carta escrita ao rei de Portugal por Pero Vaz de Caminha. Segundo o testemunho do escrivão-mor, os índios brasileiros estariam *natu-ralmente* inclinados à conversão religiosa[3], visto que, de longe, *imitavam* os gestos dos cristãos durante o santo sacrifício da missa. A imitação — imitação totalmente epidérmica, reflexo do objeto na superfície do espelho, ritual privado de palavras —, eis o argumento mais convincente que o navegador pôde enviar a seu rei em favor da inocência dos indígenas. Diante dessas figuras vermelhas que macaqueiam os brancos, caberia perguntar se eles não procuravam chegar ao êxtase espiritual pela duplicação dos gestos. Não acreditariam também que poderiam encontrar o deus dos cristãos ao final dos "exercícios espirituais", assim como os índios de Porto Rico teriam se ajoelhado diante do espanhol afogado que tivesse escapado à putrefação?

Entre os povos indígenas da América Latina a palavra europeia, pronunciada e depressa apagada, perdia-se em sua imaterialidade de voz, e nunca se petrificava em signo escrito, nunca conseguia instituir em *escritura* o nome da divindade cristã. Os índios só queriam aceitar como moeda de comunicação a *representação* dos acontecimentos narrados oralmente,

---

3 Consultar nosso artigo "A palavra de Deus", na revista *Barroco*, nº 3, 1970.

enquanto os conquistadores e missionários insistiam nos benefícios de uma conversão milagrosa, feita pela assimilação passiva da doutrina transmitida oralmente. Instituir o nome de Deus equivale a impor o código linguístico no qual seu nome circula em evidente transparência.

Colocar junto não só a representação religiosa como a língua europeia: tal foi o trabalho a que se dedicaram os jesuítas e os conquistadores a partir da segunda metade do século XVI no Brasil. As representações teatrais, feitas no interior das tabas indígenas, comportam a *mise-en-scêne* de um episódio do *Flos Sanctorum* e um diálogo escrito metade em português e a outra metade em tupi-guarani, ou, de maneira mais precisa, o texto cm português e sua tradução em tupi-guarani. Aliás, são numerosas as testemunhas que insistem em assinalar o *realismo* dessas representações teatrais. Um padre jesuíta, Cardim, nos diz que, diante do quadro vivo do martírio de São Sebastião, patrono da cidade do Rio de Janeiro, os espectadores não podiam esconder a emoção e as lágrimas. A doutrina religiosa e a língua europeia contaminam o pensamento selvagem, apresentam no palco o corpo humano perfurado por flechas, corpo em tudo semelhante a outros corpos que, pela causa religiosa, encontravam morte paralela. Pouco a pouco, as representações teatrais propõem uma substituição definitiva e inexorável: de agora em diante, na terra descoberta, o código linguístico e o código religioso se encontram intimamente ligados, graças à intransigência, à astúcia e à força dos brancos. Pela mesma moeda, os índios perdem sua língua e seu sistema do sagrado e recebem em troca o substituto europeu.

Evitar o bilinguismo significa evitar o pluralismo religioso e significa também impor o poder colonialista. Na álgebra do conquistador, a unidade é a única medida que conta. Um só Deus, um só Rei, uma só Língua: o verdadeiro Deus, o verdadeiro Rei, a verdadeira Língua. Como dizia recentemente Jacques Derrida: "O signo e o nome da divindade têm o mesmo tempo e o mesmo lugar de nascimento."[4] Uma pequena correção se impõe na última parte da frase, o suplemento de um prefixo que visa a atualizar a afirmativa "...o mesmo tempo e o mesmo lugar de renascimento".

Esse renascimento colonialista — produto reprimido de uma outra Renascença, a que se realizava concomitantemente na Europa — à medida que avança apropria o espaço sócio-cultural do Novo Mundo e

4 *De la Grammatologia.* Paris, Minuit, 1967, p. 25. (Tradução brasileira: *Gramatologia*, São Paulo, Perspectiva, 1973.)

o inscreve, pela conversão, no contexto da civilização ocidental, atribuindo-lhe ainda o estatuto familiar e social do primogênito. A América transforma-se em *cópia*, simulacro que se quer mais e mais semelhante ao original, quando sua originalidade não se encontraria na cópia do modelo original, mas em sua *origem*, apagada completamente pelos conquistadores. Pelo extermínio constante dos traços originais, pelo esquecimento da origem, o fenômeno de duplicação se estabelece como a única regra válida de civilização. É assim que vemos nascer por todos os lados essas cidades de nome europeu cuja única originalidade é o fato de trazerem antes do nome de origem o adjetivo "novo" ou "nova": New England, Nueva España, Nova Friburgo, Nouvelle France etc. À medida que o tempo passa esse adjetivo pode guardar — e muitas vezes guarda — um significado diferente daquele que lhe empresta o dicionário: o *novo* significa bizarramente fora de moda, como nesta bela frase de Lévi-Strauss: "Les tropiques sont moins exotiques que démodés" (p. 96).

O neocolonialismo, a nova máscara que aterroriza os países do Terceiro Mundo em pleno século XX, é o estabelecimento gradual num outro país de valores rejeitados pela metrópole, é a exportação de objetos fora de moda na sociedade neocolonialista, transformada hoje no centro da sociedade de consumo. Hoje, quando a palavra de ordem é dada pelos tecnocratas, o desequilíbrio é científico, pré-fabricado; a inferioridade é controlada pelas mãos que manipulam a generosidade e o poder, o poder e o preconceito. Consultemos de novo Montaigne:

> Eles são selvagens, assim como chamamos selvagens os frutos que a natureza, por si só e pelo seu progresso habitual, produziu; quando, na verdade, são os que alteramos por meio de nosso artifício e desviamos da ordem natural é que realmente deveríamos chamar selvagens. Nos primeiros são vivas e vigorosas as verdadeiras, mais úteis e naturais virtudes e propriedades, as quais abastardamos nestes outros na medida em que apenas os acomodamos ao deleite do nosso gosto corrompido.

O renascimento colonialista engendra por sua vez uma nova sociedade, a dos *mestiços*, cuja principal característica é o fato de que a noção de *unidade* sofre reviravolta, é contaminada em favor de uma mistura sutil e complexa entre o elemento europeu e o elemento autóctone — uma espécie de infiltração progressiva efetuada pelo pensamento selvagem, ou seja, abertura do único caminho possível que poderia levar à descolonização. Caminho percorrido ao inverso do percorrido pelos colonos. Estes, no desejo de exterminar a raça indígena, recolhiam nos hospitais as roupas infeccionadas das vítimas de varíola para dependurá-las com outros presentes nos atalhos frequentados pelas tribos. No novo e infatigável movimento de oposição — de mancha racial, de sabotagem dos valores culturais e sociais impostos pelos conquistadores —, uma transformação maior se opera na superfície, mas que afeta definitivamente a correção dos dois sistemas principais que contribuíram para a propagação da cultura ocidental entre nós: o código linguístico e o código religioso. Esses códigos perdem seu estatuto de pureza e pouco a pouco se deixam enriquecer por novas aquisições, por miúdas metamorfoses, por estranhas corrupções, que transformam a integridade do Livro Santo e do Dicionário e da Gramática europeus. O elemento híbrido reina.

A maior contribuição da América Latina para a cultura ocidental vem da destruição sistemática dos conceitos de *unidade* e de *pureza*[5]: estes dois conceitos

Em artigo de significativo título "Sol da meia-noite", publicado em 1945, Oswald de Andrade detectava por detrás da Alemanha nazista os valores de unidade e pureza, e em seu estilo típico comentava com rara felicidade: "A Alemanha racista, purista e recordista precisa ser educada pelo nosso mulato, pelo chinês, pelo índio mais perdem o contorno exato de seu significado, perdem seu peso esmagador, seu sinal de superioridade cultural, à medida que o trabalho de contaminação dos latino-americanos se afirma, se mostra mais e mais eficaz. A América Latina institui seu lugar no mapa da civilização ocidental graças ao movimento de desvio da norma, ativo e destruidor, que transfigura os elementos feitos e imutáveis que os europeus exportavam para o Novo Mundo. Em virtude do fato de que a América Latina não pode mais fechar suas portas à invasão estrangeira, não pode tampouco reencontrar sua condição de "paraíso", de isolamento e de inocência, constata-se com cinismo que, sem essa contribuição, seu produto seria mera cópia — silêncio —, uma cópia muitas vezes fora de moda, por causa desse retrocesso imperceptível no tempo, de que fala Lévi-Strauss. Sua geografia deve ser uma geografia de assimilação e de agressividade, de aprendizagem e de reação, de falsa obediência. A passividade reduziria seu papel efetivo ao desaparecimento por analogia. Guardando seu lugar na segunda fila, é no entanto preciso que assinale sua diferença, marque sua pre-

atrasado do Peru ou do México, pelo africano do Sudão. É preciso ser misturada de uma vez para sempre. Precisa ser desfeita no melting pot do futuro. Precisa mulatizar-se." Ponta de lança. Rio de Janeiro, Civilização Brasileira, 1972, p. 62.

sença, uma presença muitas vezes de vanguarda. O silêncio seria a resposta desejada pelo imperialismo cultural, ou ainda o eco sonoro que apenas serve para apertar mais os laços do poder conquistador.

Falar, escrever, significa: falar contra, escrever contra.

II

Se os etnólogos são os verdadeiros responsáveis pela desmistificação do discurso da História, se contribuem de maneira decisiva para a recuperação cultural dos povos colonizados, dissipando o véu do imperialismo cultural — qual seria pois o papel do intelectual hoje em face das relações entre duas nações que participam de uma mesma cultura, a ocidental, mas na situação em que uma mantém o poder econômico sobre a outra? Se os etnólogos ressuscitaram por seus escritos a riqueza e a beleza do objeto artístico da cultura desmantelada pelo colonizador — como o crítico deve apresentar hoje o complexo sistema de obras explicado até o presente por um método tradicional e reacionário cuja única originalidade é o estudo das fontes e das influências? Qual seria a atitude do artista de um país em evidente inferioridade econômica com relação à cultura ocidental, à cultura da metrópole, e finalmente à cultura de seu próprio país? Poder-se-ia surpreender a originalidade de uma obra de arte se se institui como única medida as dívidas contraídas pelo artista junto ao modelo que teve necessidade de importar da metrópole? Ou seria mais interessante assinalar os elementos da obra que marcam sua diferença?

Essas perguntas não poderão ter uma resposta fácil ou agradável, pelo fato mesmo de que é preciso de uma vez por todas declarar a falência de um método que se enraizou profundamente no sistema universitário: as pesquisas que conduzem ao estudo das fontes ou das influências. Porque certos professores universitários falam em nome da objetividade, do conhecimento enciclopédico e da verdade científica, seu discurso crítico ocupa um lugar capital entre outros discursos universitários. Mas é preciso que agora o coloquemos em seu verdadeiro lugar. Tal tipo de discurso crítico apenas assinala a indigência de uma arte já pobre por causa das condições econômicas em que pode sobreviver, apenas sublinha a falta de imaginação de artistas que são obrigados, por falta de uma tradição autóctone, a se apropriar de modelos colocados em circulação pela metrópole. Tal discurso crítico ridiculariza a busca dom-quixotesca dos artistas latino-americanos, quando acentuam por ricochete a beleza, o poder e a glória das obras criadas no meio da sociedade colonialista ou neocolonialista. Tal discurso reduz a criação dos artistas latino-americanos à condição de obra parasita, uma obra que se nutre de uma outra sem nunca lhe acrescentar algo de próprio; uma obra cuja vida é limitada e precária, aprisionada que se encontra pelo brilho e pelo prestígio da fonte, do chefe de escola.

A *fonte* torna-se a estrela intangível e pura que, sem se deixar contaminar, contamina, brilha para os artistas dos países da América Latina, quando estes dependem de sua luz para o seu trabalho de expressão. Ela ilumina os movimentos das mãos, mas ao mesmo tempo torna os artistas súditos de seu magnetismo superior. O discurso crítico que fala das influências estabelece a estrela como único valor que conta. Encontrar a escada e contrair a dívida que pode minimizar a distância insuportável entre ele, mortal, e a imortal estrela: tal seria o papel do artista latino-americano, sua função na sociedade ocidental. É-lhe preciso, além do mais, dominar esse movimento ascendente de que fala o crítico e que poderia inscrever seu projeto no horizonte da cultura ocidental. O lugar do projeto parasita fica ainda e sempre sujeito ao campo magnético aberto pela estrela principal e cujo movimento de expansão esmigalha a originalidade do outro projeto e lhe empresta *a priori* um significado paralelo e inferior. O campo magnético organiza o espaço da literatura graças a essa força única de atração que o crítico escolhe e impõe aos artistas — este grupo de corpúsculos anônimos que se nutre da generosidade do chefe de escola e da memória enciclopédica do crítico.

Seja dito entre parênteses que o discurso crítico que acabamos de delinear em suas generalidades, não apresenta em essência diferença alguma do discurso neocolonialista: os dois falam de economias deficitárias. Aproveitemos o parêntese e acrescentemos uma observação. Seria necessário algum dia escrever um estudo psicanalítico sobre o prazer que pode transparecer no rosto de certos professores universitários quando descobrem uma influência, como se a *verdade* de um texto só pudesse ser assinalada pela dívida e pela imitação. Curiosa verdade essa que prega o amor da genealogia. Curiosa profissão essa cujo olhar se volta para o passado, em detrimento do presente, cujo crédito se recolhe pela descoberta de uma dívida contraída, de uma ideia roubada, de uma imagem ou palavra pedidas de empréstimo. A voz profética e canibal de Paul Valéry nos chama:

> Nada mais original, nada mais intrínseco a
> si que se alimentar dos outros. É preciso, po-

rém, digeri-los. O leão é feito de carneiro as-
similado.

Fechemos o parêntese.

Declarar a falência de tal método implica a necessidade de substituí-lo por um outro em que os elementos esquecidos, negligenciados e abandonados
pela crítica policial serão isolados, postos em relevo,
em benefício de um novo discurso crítico, o qual por
sua vez esquecerá e negligenciará a caça às fontes e
às influências e estabelecerá como único valor crítico a diferença. O escritor latino-americano — visto
que é necessário finalmente limitar nosso assunto de
discussão — lança sobre a literatura o mesmo olhar
malévolo e audacioso que encontramos em Roland
Barthes em sua recente leitura-escritura de *Sarrasine*,
este conto de Balzac incinerado por outras gerações.
Em *S/Z*, Barthes nos propõe como ponto de partida a
divisão dos textos literários em textos *legíveis* e textos
escrevíveis, levando em consideração o fato de que a
avaliação que se faz de um texto hoje esteja intimamente ligada a uma "prática e esta prática é a da escritura". O texto legível é o que pode ser lido, mas não
escrito, não reescrito, é o texto clássico por excelência,
o que convida o leitor a permanecer no interior de seu
fechamento. Os outros textos, os escrevíveis, apresen-

tam ao contrário um modelo produtor (e não representacional) que excita o leitor a abandonar sua posição tranquila de consumidor e a se aventurar como produtor de textos:

> remeter cada texto, não a sua individualidade,
> mas a seu jogo

— nos diz Barthes. Portanto, a leitura em lugar de tranquilizar o leitor, de garantir seu lugar de cliente pagante na sociedade burguesa, o desperta, transforma-o, radicaliza-o e serve finalmente para acelerar o processo de expressão da própria experiência. Em outros termos, ela o convida à práxis. Citemos de novo Barthes:

> que textos eu aceitaria escrever (reescrever),
> desejar, afirmar como uma força neste mun-
> do que é o meu?

Esta interrogação, reflexo de uma assimilação inquieta e insubordinada, antropófaga, é semelhante à que fazem há muito tempo os escritores de uma cultura dominada por uma outra: suas leituras se explicam pela busca de um texto escrevível, texto que pode incitá-los ao trabalho, servir-lhes de modelo na organização de sua própria escritura. Tais escritores utilizam sistematicamente a digressão, essa forma mal integrada do discurso do saber, como assinala Barthes. A segunda obra é pois estabelecida a partir de um compromisso feroz com o *déjà-dit*, o já-dito, para empregar uma expressão recentemente cunhada por Michel Foucault na análise de *Bouvard et Pécuchet*, de Gustave Flaubert. Precisemos: com o já-escrito.

O segundo texto se organiza a partir de uma meditação silenciosa e traiçoeira sobre o primeiro texto, e o leitor, transformado em autor, tenta surpreender o modelo original em suas limitações, suas fraquezas, em suas lacunas, desarticula-o e o rearticula de acordo com suas intenções, segundo sua própria direção ideológica, sua visão do tema apresentado de início pelo original. O escritor trabalha *sobre* outro texto e quase nunca exagera o papel que a realidade que o cerca pode representar em sua obra. Nesse sentido, as críticas que muitas vezes são dirigidas à alienação do escritor latino-americano, por exemplo, são inúteis e mesmo ridículas. Se ele só fala de sua própria experiência de vida, seu texto passa despercebido entre seus contemporâneos. É preciso que aprenda primeiro a falar a língua da metrópole para melhor combatê-la em seguida. Nosso trabalho crítico se definirá antes de tudo pela análise do uso que o escritor fez de um texto ou de uma técnica literária que pertence ao domínio público, do partido que ele tira, e nossa análise se completará pela descrição da técnica que o mesmo escritor cria em seu movimento de agressão contra o modelo original, fazendo ceder as fundações que o propunham como objeto único e de reprodução impossível. O imaginário, no espaço do neocolonialismo, não pode ser mais o da ignorância ou da ingenuidade, nutrido por uma manipulação simplista dos dados oferecidos pela experiência imediata do autor, mas se afirmaria mais e mais como uma escritura sobre outra escritura. A segunda obra, já que ela em geral comporta uma crítica da obra anterior, impõe-se com a violência desmistificadora das planchas anatômicas que deixam a nu a arquitetura do corpo humano. A propaganda torna-se eficaz porque o texto fala a linguagem de nosso tempo.

O escritor latino-americano brinca com os signos de um outro escritor, de uma outra obra. As palavras do outro têm a particularidade de se apresentarem como objetos que fascinam seus olhos, seus dedos, e a escritura do segundo texto é em parte a história de uma experiência sensual com o signo estrangeiro. Sartre descreveu admiravelmente essa sensação, a aventura da leitura, quando nos fala de suas experiências de menino na biblioteca familiar:

As densas lembranças e a doce insensatez das crianças camponesas em vão as procuraria em mim. Nunca esburaquei a terra nem procurei ninhos, não colecionei plantas nem joguei pedras nos passarinhos. No entanto, os livros foram meus passarinhos e meus ninhos, meus animais de estimação, meu estábulo e meu campo...

Como o signo se apresenta muitas vezes numa língua estrangeira, o trabalho do escritor em lugar de ser comparado ao de uma tradução literal, propõe-se antes como uma espécie de tradução global, de pastiche, de paródia, de digressão. O signo estrangeiro se reflete no espelho do dicionário e na imaginação criadora do escritor latino-americano e se dissemina sobre a página branca com a graça e o dengue do movimento da mão que traça linhas e curvas. Durante o processo de tradução, o imaginário do escritor está sempre no palco, como neste belo exemplo pedido de empréstimo a Julio Cortázar.

O personagem principal de *62 Modelo para armar*, de nacionalidade argentina, vê desenhada no espelho do restaurante parisiense em que entrou para jantar esta frase mágica: "Je voudrais un château saignant." Mas em lugar de reproduzir a frase na língua original, ele a traduz imediatamente para o espanhol: "Quisiera un castillo sangriento." Escrito no espelho e apropriado pelo campo visual do personagem latino-americano, château sai do contexto gastronômico e se inscreve no contexto feudal, colonialista, a casa onde mora o senhor, *el castillo*. E o adjetivo, *saignant*, que significava apenas a preferência ou o gosto do cliente pelo bife malpassado, na pena do escritor argentino, *sangriento*, torna-se a marca evidente de um ataque, de uma rebelião, o desejo de ver o *château*, o castillo sacrificado, de derrubá-lo, a fogo e sangue. A tradução do significante avança um novo significado — e, além disso, o signo linguístico nuclear (*château*) abriga o nome daquele que melhor compreendeu o Novo Mundo no século XIX: René de Chateaubriand. Não é por coincidência que o personagem de Cortázar, antes de entrar no restaurante, tinha comprado o livro de um outro viajante infatigável, Michel Butor, livro em que este fala do autor de *René* e de *Atala*. E a frase do freguês, pronunciada em toda sua inocência gastronômica, "je voudrais un château saignant", é percebida na superfície do espelho, do dicionário, por uma imaginação posta em trabalho pela leitura de Butor, pela situação do sul-americano em Paris, "quisiera un castillo sangriento".

É difícil precisar se é a frase ouvida ao acaso que atrai a atenção do sul-americano, ou se ele a vê porque acaba de levantar os olhos do livro de Butor. Em todo caso, uma coisa é certa: as leituras do escritor latino-americano não são nunca inocentes. Não poderiam nunca sê-lo.

Do livro ao espelho, do espelho ao pedido do freguês glutão, de château à sua tradução, de Chateaubriand ao escritor sul-americano, do original à agressão — nessas transformações[6], realizadas, na ausência final de movimento, no desejo tornado coágulo, escritura —, ali se abre o espaço crítico por onde é preciso começar hoje a ler os textos românticos do Novo Mundo. Nesse espaço, se o significante é o mesmo, o significado circula uma outra mensagem, uma mensagem invertida. Isolemos, por comodidade, a palavra índio. Em Chateaubriand e muitos outros românticos europeus, este significante torna-se a origem de todo um tema literário que nos fala da evasão, da viagem, desejo de fugir dos contornos estreitos da pátria eu-

Seguimos de perto os ensinamentos de Derrida com relação ao problema da tradução dentro dos pressupostos gramatológicos: "Nos limites em que ela é possível ou pelo menos PARECE possível, a tradução pratica a diferença entre significado e significante. Mas se essa diferença nunca é pura, a tradução não o é menos, e será preciso substituir a noção de tradução pela noção de TRANSFORMAÇÃO, transformação regulada de uma língua por outra, de um texto por outro." Positions. Paris, 1972, p. 31.

ropeia. Rimbaud, por exemplo, abre seu longo poema "Bateau Ivre" por uma alusão aos "peles-vermelhas barulhentos", que anuncia em seu frescor infantil o grito de rebelião que se escutará ao final do poema: "Je regrette l'Europe aux anciens parapets." Aquele mesmo significante, porém, quando aparece no texto romântico americano, torna-se símbolo político, símbolo do nacionalismo que finalmente eleva sua voz livre (aparentemente livre, como infelizmente é muitas vezes o caso), depois das lutas da independência. E se entre os europeus aquele significante exprime um desejo de expansão, entre os americanos, sua tradução marca a vontade de estabelecer os limites da nova pátria, uma forma de contração.

Paremos por um instante e analisemos de perto um conto de Jorge Luis Borges, cujo título é já revelador das nossas intenções: "Pierre Menard, autor del *Quijote*." Pierre Menard, romancista e poeta simbolista, mas também leitor infatigável, devorador de livros, será a metáfora ideal para bem precisar a situação e o papel do escritor latino-americano, vivendo entre a assimilação do modelo original, isto é, entre o amor e o respeito pelo já-escrito, e a necessidade de produzir um novo texto que afronte o primeiro e muitas vezes o negue. Os projetos literários de Pierre Menard foram de início classificados com zelo por Mme. Bachelier: são os escritos publicados durante sua vida e lidos com prazer por seus admiradores. Mas Mme. Bachelier deixa de incluir na bibliografia de Menard, nos diz o narrador do conto, o mais absurdo e o mais ambicioso de seus projetos, reescrever o *Dom Quixote*: "Não queria compor um outro *Quixote* — o que é fácil —, mas o *Quixote*." A omissão perpetrada por Mme. Bachelier vem do fato de que não consegue *ver* a obra *invisível* de Pierre Menard — nos declara o narrador do conto —, aquela que é "subterrânea, a interminavelmente heróica, a sem-igual". Os poucos capítulos que Menard escreve são invisíveis porque o modelo e a cópia são idênticos; não há diferença alguma de vocabulário, de sintaxe, de estrutura entre as duas versões, a de Cervantes e a outra, a cópia de Menard. A obra invisível é o paradoxo do segundo texto que desaparece completamente, dando lugar à sua significação mais exterior, a situação cultural, social e política em que se situa o segundo autor.

O segundo texto pode no entanto ser *visível*, e é assim que o narrador do conto pôde incluir o poema "Le Cimetière Marin", de Paul Valéry, na bibliografia de Menard, porque na transcrição do poema os decassílabos de Valéry se transformam em alexandrinos. A agressão contra o modelo, a transgressão ao modelo proposto pelo poema de Valéry situa-se nessas duas sílabas acrescentadas ao decassílabo, pequeno suplemento sonoro e diferencial que reorganiza o espaço visual e silencioso da estrofe e do poema de Valéry, modificando também o ritmo interno de cada verso. A originalidade, pois, da obra *visível* de Pierre Menard reside no pequeno suplemento de violência que instala na página branca sua presença e assinala a ruptura entre o modelo e sua cópia, e finalmente situa o poeta em face da literatura, da obra que lhe serve de inspiração. "Le lion est fait de mouton assimilé."

Segundo Pierre Menard, se Cervantes para construir seu texto não tinha "rejeitado a colaboração do acaso", o escritor argentino tinha "contraído o misterioso dever de reconstituir literalmente sua obra espontânea". Há em Menard, como entre os escritores latino-americanos, a recusa do "espontâneo" e a aceitação da escritura como um dever lúcido e consciente, e talvez já seja tempo de sugerir como imagem reveladora do trabalho subterrâneo e interminavelmente heróico o título mesmo da primeira parte da coletânea de contos de Borges: "O jardim das veredas que se bifurcam." A literatura, o jardim; o trabalho do escritor — a escolha consciente diante de cada bifurcação e não uma aceitação tranquila do acaso da invenção. O conhecimento é concebido como uma forma de produção. A assimilação do livro pela leitura implica já a organização de uma práxis da escritura.

O projeto de Pierre Menard recusa portanto a liberdade total na criação, poder que é tradicionalmente delegado ao artista, elemento que estabelece a identidade e a diferença na cultura neocolonialista ocidental. A liberdade, em Menard, é controlada pelo modelo original, assim como a liberdade dos cidadãos dos países colonizados é vigiada de perto pelas forças da metrópole. A presença de Menard — diferença, escritura, originalidade — instala-se na transgressão ao modelo, no movimento imperceptível e sutil de conversão, de perversão, de reviravolta.

A originalidade do projeto de Pierre Menard, sua parte visível e escrita, é consequência do fato de ele recusar aceitar a concepção tradicional da invenção artística, porque ele próprio nega a liberdade total do artista. Semelhante a Robert Desnos, ele proclama como lugar de trabalho as "formas prisões" (*formes prisons*). O artista latino-americano aceita a prisão como forma de comportamento, a transgressão como forma de expressão. Daí, sem dúvida, o absurdo, o tormento, a beleza e o vigor de seu projeto visível. O invisível torna-se *silêncio* em seu texto, a presença do modelo, enquanto o visível é a mensagem, é ausência no modelo. Citemos uma última vez Pierre Menard:

O escritor latino-americano é o devorador de livros de que os contos de Borges nos falam com insis-
tência. Lê o tempo todo e publica de vez em quando.
O conhecimento não chega nunca a enferrujar os de-
licados e secretos mecanismos da criação; pelo contrário, estimulam seu projeto criador, pois é o princí-
pio organizador da produção do texto. Nesse sentido,
a técnica de leitura e de produção dos escritores latino-americanos parece com a de Marx, de que nos falou recentemente Louis Althusser. Nossa leitura é tão
culpada quanto a de Althusser, porque estamos lendo
os escritores latino-americanos "observando as regras
de uma leitura cuja impressionante lição nos é dada
na própria leitura que fazem" dos escritores europeus.
Citemos de novo Althusser:

de exato e para criticar o que de falso disse-
ram...

A literatura latino-americana de hoje nos propõe um texto e, ao mesmo tempo, abre o campo teórico onde é preciso se inspirar durante a elaboração do discurso crítico de que ela será o objeto. O campo teórico contradiz os princípios de certa crítica univer-sitária que só se interessa pela parte *invisível* do tex-to, pelas dívidas contraídas pelo escritor, ao mesmo tempo que ele rejeita o discurso de uma crítica pseu-domarxista que prega uma prática primária do texto, observando que sua eficácia seria consequência de uma leitura fácil. Estes teóricos esquecem que a eficá-cia de uma crítica não pode ser medida pela preguiça que ela inspira; pelo contrário, ela deve descondicio-nar o leitor, tornar impossível sua vida no interior da sociedade burguesa e de consumo. A leitura fácil dá razão às forças neocolonialistas que insistem no fato de que o país se encontra na situação de colônia pela preguiça de seus habitantes. O escritor latino-ame-ricano nos ensina que é preciso liberar a imagem de uma América Latina sorridente e feliz, o carnaval e a *fiesta*, colônia de férias para turismo cultural.

Entre o sacrifício e o jogo, entre a prisão e a trans-gressão, entre a submissão ao código e a agressão, entre à obediência e a rebelião, entre a assimilação e a expressão — ali, nesse lugar aparentemente vazio, seu templo e seu lugar de clandestinidade, ali, se realiza o ritual antropófago da literatura latino-americana.

março de 1971

PODER e aLEGRIA

A Celso Cunha

Nós temos que dar ao Brasil o que ele não tem e que por isso até agora não viveu, nós temos que dar uma alma ao Brasil e para isso todo sacrifício é grandioso, é sublime. E nos dá felicidade. [...] Toda a minha obra é transitória e caduca, eu sei. E eu quero que seja transitória. [...] Mas que importa a eternidade entre os homens da Terra e a celebridade? Mando-as à merda. Eu não amo o Brasil espiritualmente mais do que a França ou a Cochinchina. Mas é no Brasil que me acontece viver e agora só no Brasil eu penso e por ele tudo sacrifiquei.
Mario de Andrade (1924)

Tentemos, primeiro, uma distinção básica que servirá para caracterizar tematicamente a literatura brasileira pós-64. Deixa esta de apresentar como tema principal e dominante a exploração do homem pelo homem. Esse tema foi em geral dramatizado pelo processo de conscientização político-partidária de personagens pertencentes ao campesinato e ao operariado, acompanhado de crítica velada (simpática) ou aberta (radical) à oligarquia rural e ao empresariado urbano. O jogo entre as duas forças sociais opostas escamoteava por vezes as camadas médias e urbanas da sociedade e era composto de forma a antecipar dramaticamente uma evolução otimista e sem tropeços do capitalismo para o comunismo no Brasil. Otimismo e utopia se aliavam para mostrar a vitória definitiva das forças de esquerda.

E pelo abandono gradativo desse tema (e seus subtemas) que a literatura pós-64 se diferencia da literatura engajada que lhe foi anterior e encontra a sua originalidade temática. Esse abandono não significa que a igualdade econômica e social tenha sido atingida nesta parte do mundo, que a utopia tenha virado realidade cotidiana entre nós. Pelo contrario. Nos anos 60, através de expedientes de incalculada violência, a desigualdade foi acentuada de tal modo pela América Latina que seria ingénuo acreditar que o modelo ficcional proposto pelos modernistas para a superação política da exploração do homem pelo homem ainda fosse valido depois de 64.

De maneira tímida e depois obsessiva, a literatura brasileira, a partir da queda do regime Goulart e do golpe militar de 1964, passou a refletir sobre o modo como funciona o poder em países cujos governantes optam pelo capitalismo selvagem como norma para o progresso da nação e o bem-estar dos cidadãos.

Refletindo sobre a maneira como funciona e atua o poder, a literatura brasileira pós-64 abriu campo para uma crítica radical e fulminante de toda e qualquer forma de autoritarismo, principalmente aquela que, na América Latina, tem sido pregada pelas forças militares quando ocupam o poder, em teses que se camuflam pelas leis de segurança nacional.

De maneira paralela ao deslize temático mencionado, opera-se uma guinada importante no processo evolutivo linear do modernismo, concretizado por um gesto de ruptura que, por sua vez, determina o aparecimento de um novo período da nossa historia literária, chamado de pós-modernista, passível de ser estudado dentro do ideário mais amplo do que se convencionou chamar de pós-moderno.

Estilisticamente, a literatura brasileira pós-64 pode, por um lado, retomar uma lição do passado, ajustando-se — após a obra genial de Guimaraes Rosa e o esforço universalista dos vários concretismos — a princípios estéticos fundamentados pelo realismo dos anos 1930. Pode também, por outro lado, aproximar-se da literatura hispano-americana que lhe é contemporânea, abrindo mão do naturalismo na representação, em virtude de problemas graves de censura artística. Neste segundo caso, adentra-se o texto literário por uma escrita metafórica ou fantástica, até então praticamente inédita entre nós. Valendo-se, pois, de uma escrita realista ainda comprometida com os anos 1930 ou de uma outra comum aos latino-americanos, a literatura pós-64 guarda sempre a obsessão temática a que nos referimos.

Na crítica ao autoritarismo e ao poder militar, a literatura brasileira pós-64 também se distancia ideologicamente dos anos 1930: os escritores das mais diversas posturas politicas se irmanavam então, contraditoriamente, numa opção radical pela demolição do liberalismo clássico, rechaçando a escolha de governantes através do sufrágio universal e defendendo a tomada de poder por um líder carismático a que se entregaria o caminho do país. O projeto totalitário de Getúlio Vargas foi um entre vários, e se foi ele o vencedor foi porque soube congregar de forma habilidosa as diversas forças conservadoras em jogo no Brasil e no estrangeiro. À partir de 1964, gradativamente, as diversas facções esquerdistas foram se aglutinando para formar uma frente ampla que acabou por rejeitar qualquer forma de ditadura, até mesmo a do proletariado, ficando no palco do autoritarismo apenas os velhos *compagnons de route* que se recusaram a pensar o próprio passado tenentista, como é o caso de Luís Carlos Prestes.

A autocrítica no plano ideológico efetuada após 1964 por si só comenta a mudança temática significativa a que estamos nos referindo no plano artístico. Ambas são formas de uma mudança geral que vai afetar o todo das forcas que compõem o cenário político do país, deixando primeiro que o desejo de democracia explodisse para que em seguida o conceito pecasse — e ainda peque — pela sua imprecisão semântica. O conceito de democracia frequenta hoje discursos que vão da direita ofendida por uma manifestaçao de povo na rua à esquerda que volta a tomar assento no Parlamento nacional. Essa indiscriminação, essa imprecisão política do conceito é grave, mas simboliza uma vez mais a inércia da história social brasileira, ou seja, simboliza as ambiguidades, covardias, estratégias retóricas, espertezas etc., de períodos que se convencionou chamar de transição e que fundamentalmente acabam por não o ser.

O surgimento do Partido dos Trabalhadores na década de 1970, sua aliança com os movimentos sociais das minorias e sua possível absorção de facções que defendem a ecologia, não é apenas signo de mais uma dissidência interna no chamado Partidão, como tantas outras no passado. É antes a necessidade de um novo programa de participação política para o campesinato e os trabalhadores urbanos, afinado com os novos tempos negros dos desmandos do poder por estas terras. Não se trata de lutar apenas contra o poder burguês sob a sua forma de centralização burocrática, legislativa e jurídica; a luta é e deve ser mais ampla, pois o poder toma as mais inusitadas formas no cotidiano do cidadão, sub-repticiamente gerando — a partir da negação da *diferença* — forças repressoras que visam à uniformidade (racial, sexual, comportamental, intelectual etc.).

O deslize das questões dos e sobre os oprimidos para o questionamento amplo do opressor (do lugar de onde ele fala, da ordens e dita leis; do modo como, mesmo revolucionário, pode ser conservador etc.) não é uma simples reviravolta retórica a gosto de políticos com ranço tático militar. O deslize esta no centro das rebeliões de jovens que se multiplicaram nas décadas de 1960 e 1970 e nas suas explosões libertárias, inspiradas como sabemos no *Free speech movement*, inicialmente localizado na Universidade de Berkeley, e nos acontecimentos de maio de 68 em Paris. Os jovens do Primeiro Mundo, irmanados por uma educação universitária que conseguira desprestigiar a alta burguesia como única merecedora de escolaridade completa, quiseram impor ao todo da sociedade os seus valores autênticos como justos e pregaram uma compreensão ética (e não pragmática, como é de praxe nos partidos políticos tradicionais) das relações humanas na ordem sócio-econômica e política do capitalismo. Para tal, elegeram como inimigo fundamental as várias forças repressoras que mantém o *status quo*, em nível tanto macro como microestrutural.

Como consequência, gerou-se uma surpreendente reviravolta na politica estudantil latino-americana: passa para fundo de cena a atitude típica dos anos 1950 na União Brasileira de Estudantes, expressa pelo *slogan* "Yankee, go home", e ficam no proscénio os jovens libertários americanos c europeus, a se exprimirem pela voz de Joan Baez ou Bob Dylan, de Jim Morrison ou Jimi Hendrix, de John Lennon ou Mick Jagger. De Chico Buarque ou Caetano Veloso.

No âmbito dos países do Primeiro Mundo, a preocupação maior dos estudantes era com as microestruturas de repressão do poder (daí o surgimento nos anos 1970 de um neo-individualismo liberado que explodiu, primeiro, em anarquia e, depois, em narcisismo alimentando a sociedade de consumo). Mas, ao repensarem a atuação dos países líderes ocidentais no plano mundial, esses mesmos estudantes descobriram tanto os perigos da corrida armamentista, responsável por um proximo apocalipse nuclear como no filme *Zabriskie Point*, quanto as grandes vítimas da historia atual, os países do Terceiro Mundo. A rebelião estudantil alicerça a busca do "novo homem", não nos partidos políticos de esquerda inspirados pela Revolução Russa, mas em Che Guevara e Cuba. Ao mesmo tempo atua de maneira radical contra as intervenções militares feitas pelas grandes potências a favor do colonialismo europeu (nos países africanos) ou do colonialismo americano (nos países asiáticos). Atua ainda contra as intervenções econômicas feitas pelas multinacionais a favor do neocolonialismo americano (nos países da América Latina). Os movimentos contra a guerra do Vietnã, dos sit in nas reitorias ou nas vias publicas à queima de cartões de reservistas nos *campi*, resumem tudo.

A guerrilha rural do Terceiro Mundo passa a modelo para a guerrilha urbana do Primeiro, e poucos meses depois a diferença desaparece, pois o importante passa a ser a teoria dos focos, os 1001 Vietnas de que fala Guevara. Eis o traço de união que irmanava a liberação do povo vietnamita aos *black panthers* americanos, que justificava o expansionismo de Cuba pela América Latina e a luta armada contra a ditadura militar no Brasil, que ligava o jovem *soixante-huitard* de Paris aos estudantes mexicanos que tomavam de assalto Tlatelolco. A revolta era ocidental.

Ficou por vir o pior da história. A reorganização da direita pelos países do Terceiro Mundo, impondo aqui e ali regimes opressores e totalitários de âmbito nacional (embora articulados pelo governo americano), de uma violência organizada e burocratizada inédita desde os movimentos de independência frente ao colonialismo europeu no século XVIII, mas que palidamente relembrava o extermínio dos índios e as torturas da escravidão.

Uma errata vai sendo pouco a pouco apensa ao livro da década de 1960 pelos acontecimentos vitoriosos na década de 1970: onde estava movimento libertário, dever-se-ia ler regime repressor; onde estava imaginação no poder, dever-se-ia ler censura policial; onde estava liberação do homem, dever-se-ia ler tortura militar; e assim por diante. Como a errata era imprudente e desanimadora para os meios de comunicação de massa, impunha-se escondê-la atrás de uma fachada. A fachada é nossa conhecida, e a propria atualidade dos anos 80 encarregou- se de desmistificá-la: tratava-se de enquadrar a economia dos diversos países da América Latina aos padrões do capitalismo tecnológico, através do domínio autoritário de uma tecnocracia burocratizada. Esta seria responsável, na sua racionalização do progresso e pela competência indiscutível dos técnicos. pela modernização das diferentes nações do hemisfério sul, optando-se para isso por uma entrada maciça do capital estrangeiro. Por detrás da fachada milagrosa, além do autoritarismo e da repressão, vê-se hoje a realidade do endividamento extemo típico do capitalismo selvagem dominante nos nossos países.

Nesse contexto mais amplo é que se pode entender melhor a reação revolucionária da inteligência brasileira ao golpe militar de 64 e ao seu recrudescimento a partir de 1968.

As "maos dadas" de que nos falou Carlos Drummond de Andrade na década de 1930 ficaram soltas no ar. O companheirismo revolucionário e esperançoso de que todos nos falaram utópica e chaplinescamente nas décadas de 1930 e 1940 perdeu a sua razão de ser como luta primeira, em virtude de uma desagregação das forças de esquerda operada por uma violência insuspeitada. A violência pode ser visível nas ruas, com a militarização progressiva do Estado, com o grupo dirigente outorgando a si o direito de reprimir o cidadão em nome da segurança nacional; pode ser visível de forma quase invisível na carteira de identidade e nos crachás que se requisitavam para se entrar num edifício público ou num escritório; e pode ser visivel de forma invisível na ficha a ser preenchida pelos moradores de um edifício para, caso necessário, posterior controle policial. A violência pode passar praticamente invisível como um todo se se atenta para os meios de comunicação de massa, em especial a televisão, direcionados pelo Estado para o controle subliminar da sociedade. Tanto a violência visível quanto a invisível restringiram ao mínimo o universo de pensamento e o campo de ação dos cidadãos inconformados (e, entre estes, o do artista).

Retomemos. A descoberta assustada e indignada da violência do poder é a principal característica temática da literatura brasileira pós-64. São tematizadas as várias origens do poder, na sociedade ocidental e na época colonial brasileira, no tenentismo de 1930 e no Estado Novo, também nos nossos dias com o aparato policial convenientemente resguardado da imprensa pela censura; reflete-se sobre suas formas globais e centralizadas, como também sobre seus esfarelamentos em infinitas partículas moleculares pelo cotidiano. A abrangência do poder repressor e vingativo pode ser total ou localizada, conseguindo eficazmente neutralizar os assaltos que lhe são feitos pela razão crítica e pelas grandes questões do século. Dessa forma, o escritor brasileiro pós-64 coloca em segundo plano nos seus textos a dramatização dos grandes temas universais e utópicos da modernidade, da mesma forma como guarda distância dos temas nacionais clássicos, e ainda discute sem piedade os temas oriundos de 1922 que falavam da indispensável modernização industrial do país.

A opção dramática é, de maneira geral, pelos temas que, no particular e no cotidiano, na cor da pele, no corpo e na sua sexualidade, representariam uma alavanca que pudesse balançar a sólida e indestrutível planificação do Estado militarizado e o aprisionamento de uma população pelas fronteiras "naturais" do país.

Esboçado o quadro, deve-se acreditar que haja *atraso* na proposta da nova literatura com relação, por exemplo, à proposta dos anos 1930? Pode-se dizer que a proposta da literatura brasileira pós-64 seja alienada ou alienante? Não houve "atraso" artístico nem alienação política no melhor da produção literária pós-64; houve, sim, a compreensão profunda de que a tão reclamada modernização e industrialização do Brasil (que, teoricamente, não tenhamos medo em dizer, era o cerne do projeto modernista e estava nos programas políticos tanto da direita quanto da esquerda nos anos 1930) estava sendo feita, mas a custa de tiros de metralhadora e golpes de cassetete, espancamentos e mortes, numa escalada de violência militar e policial sem precedentes na historia deste país, já fora dos padrões universais de justiça por efeito de uma colonização europeia que se valeu de meios de transformação hoje reconhecidamente discutíveis.

Colocar corretamente a questão do poder (e isso foi o que o melhor da produção literária fez) já é investir contra os muros que se ergueram impedindo que o cidadão raciocinasse e atuasse, constituísse o seu espaço de ação e levantasse a sua voz de afirmações. É orientar, pois, o país para uma necessária democratização, ainda que esta tenha chegado só sob forma institucional. É também investir contra o silêncio a que o já oprimido economicamente ficou reduzido, perdendo os direitos trabalhistas e de reivindicação de classe. É dar voz, portanto, a todos e a qualquer para que possam manifestar desejo e vontade políticos no plano nacional, comunitário e profissional, para que mais tarde possam ser constituídos governos e organizações sindicais dignos do nome.

Pode-se dizer que houve atraso na problematização das questões modernas e universais, mas não se pode dizer que houve atraso nas questões que a literatura colocou. Para ficar no fundamental: houve, sim, atraso na própria historia social do país, nas tentativas que houve no passado por tornar a sociedade mais justa e igualitária. Uma coisa ficou patente: nos vinte anos que seguem a 1964 os donos do poder resolveram por as mangas de fora de vez, assumindo como *rosto* algo — o poder conservador — que sempre foi dado como transparente pelos trópicos.

Sabia-se que o poder existia lá fora, mas como falar dele aqui dentro se dele se participava sem participar, se dele não se tinham o rosto e as mãos?

A partir de 1964, a literatura mostrou que os donos do poder no Brasil tem olhos e ouvidos reais, boca e nariz como qualquer um, mãos injustas e, sobretudo, inteligência para se manter indefinidamente assentados na direção do país. Agora, ou do poder conservador não se participa ou inocente não se é. Acabam de vez as infindáveis imagens pias dos pôncios pilatos nacionais, fossem eles senhores de engenho, cafeicultores ou capitães de indústria. Acabam pouco a pouco, num processo altamente positivo de rarefação, as *caricaturas* grotescas, fáceis e animalescas, dos donos do poder reacionário (e, portanto, como caricaturas que eram, escamoteavam o conhecimento). Refiro-me as famosas caricaturas de macacos ou outros quadrupedes abundantes em períodos populistas.

Para descrever o poder reacionário como algo de concreto, dotado de corpo e também de espírito, teve o artista brasileiro (e o intelectual contestador de maneira geral) de se distanciar dele. Por isso, a postura politica na literatura pós-64 é a do total descompromisso para com todo e qualquer esforço desenvolvimentista para o país, para com todo programa de integração ou de planificação de ordem nacional. É certamente por essa razão que a boa literatura pós-64 *não carrega mais o antigo otimismo social que edificava,* encontrado em toda a literatura política que lhe é anterior. Por essa razão também é que o texto literário deixa de se expressar pelos tons grandiloquentes e pelos exercícios de alta retórica. A boa literatura pós-64 prefere se insinuar como rachaduras em concreto, com voz baixa e divertida, em tom menor e coloquial.

Passa a ser do conhecimento de todos o que antes era o grande segredo do bruxo Machado de Assis: num pais de tradição bacharelesca e jesuítica, sabe-se finalmente o que otimismo e retórica recobrem. Já se sabe qual é a retórica do otimismo e qual é o otimismo da retórica. Antes tarde do que nunca.

Perdendo o otimismo social edificante e construtivo, a literatura pós-64 não pode também ser aproximada, por movimentos de semelhança, da sua precedente imediata — a produção dos chamados anos democráticos, que vão de 1945 a 1964. Seja na construção de Brasília a partir do nada, sonho de todo arquiteto e metáfora ideal para o artista de vanguarda,

seja no transplante maciço de uma indústria automo-
bilística estrangeira para o pais, seja nas palavras de
um teórico da poesia concreta que pedia aos pares
para construírem "poemas à altura dos objetos racio-
nalmente planejados e produzidos" — em tudo isso
perpassava um otimismo construtor de tipo interna-
cionalista que dizia que o bem e o bom estavam na *capitalização*. Na capitalização das forças humanas e na
capitalização dos recursos econômicos estrangeiros e
nacionais, ai também estava a "capitalização" de um
saber brasileiro que trabalharia em favor de um Estado nacional forte e pujante, atrevido e esperançoso,
que se langaria a uma inédita explosão internacional.

O velho Brasil estava então sendo rejuvenescido
pelo soro da industrialização e do capital estrangeiro.
A descoberta do subdesenvolvimento pela geração de
1930, que retirou o pais do paraíso ufanista, era a garantia histórica para uma politica de país-em-desen-
volvimento a partir dos anos 1950. O alicerçamento
de um pensamento de esquerda nos anos 1930 foi a
garantia para a criação do ISEB (Instituto Superior de
Estudos Brasileiros). A Sudene foi o romance do Nor-
deste no plano das realizações admissíveis pela oligarquia rural progressista. E assim por diante.

Nos dezenove anos que precedem 1964 a ética política brasileira foi a do *fazer*, mas a do fazer cegamen-

te, já que os ideólogos nacionais do nacional acreditavam que princípios éticos advindos da reflexão sobre o agir só poderiam vir depois do já-feito. Apenas dois exemplos meio soltos para aclarar a ética do construtivismo otimista brasileiro que estamos tentando apreender. É sintomática a ausência da figura do *operário* nos textos da época — você só poderá falar dele depois de ele existir, ora ele ainda não existe por aqui e é por isso que ele "inexiste" no nosso universo de discussão. Talvez seja essa a razão pela qual poucas conquistas fez o sindicalismo durante aqueles dezenove anos, e tenha ele conhecido em contrapartida — grande vitalidade a partir de meados da década de 1970. É ainda sintomática a ausência de qualquer reflexão sobre o *público* nos textos sobre a literatura escritos na época. Os produtores e teóricos da literatura só deverão se preocupar com o público depois que o país se alfabetizar integralmente; até lá, faça-se a nossa literatura no vácuo do mercado cultural. Assim como não se discute o objeto de uma revolução social, assim também não se discute a eficácia do texto artístico. Ou, quando se a discute nos anos que precedem imediatamente 1964 —, é para considerar o publico como uma massa amorfa, passível de fácil manipulação.

Em ambos os casos citados como exemplo, elide-se a questão da dominação, do poder no plano interno, agigantando-se em contrapartida uma ideologia que, para esconder a própria cegueira, beira a xenofobia e se expressa — como vimos — pelo "Yankee, go home". As lutas contra o imperialismo americano, ainda que justas, camuflavam as insondáveis questões sociais internas e, consequentemente, não deixavam que se visse a problemática do poder nacional. Pairava este como aura — dourada mas transparente a circundar as poucas cabeças privilegiadas, dando origem a rodízios previsíveis na chefia dos interesses (econômicos, políticos, sociais, artísticos etc.) nacionais.

Apesar de os anos que precedem 1964 se proporem como democráticos, é preciso caracterizá-los melhor, talvez e simplesmente como menos centralizadores. O carisma do chefe foi a forma como os meios de comunicação de massa transmitiam e impunham a voz e a imagem do mestre supremo e dos mestres estaduais e municipais, sem que se tocasse na aura deles, pois das verbas deles se alimentavam. Era com o carisma que programavam a curiosidade publica e o jogo eleitoreiro nos vários espaços do poder. Eis ai os indícios que permitem compreender o surgimento de uma TV nos moldes realizados por Assis Chateaubriand, uma rede ao mesmo tempo descentralizada e todo-poderosa. (A Rede Globo inverte astuciosamente o programa de Chateaubriand adaptando-se a 64: para suplantar o império da rival se centraliza desativando as várias estações com sede nas capitais dos estados; em outras palavras, passa a "comprar tempo" das estações regionais, impedindo o trabalho de produção que antes ali existia.) Eis ai um possível retrato da enorme importância de revistas de ampla circulação nacional cuja base e fundamento era a fotografia (do homem e dos seus feitos), como *O Cruzeiro* e *Manchete*. O carisma é, pois, a forma pela qual o politico (e mesmo o artista enquanto intelectual) falava e continuava a falar como "consciência nacional", sem que na sua voz transparecesse o mandonismo centralizador ou a ânsia secreta de poder. O mandonismo não era falado às claras porque os chefes o contrabalançavam com a atitude descentralizadora, que se exprimia em última instância por uma retórica otimista no melhor estilo populista. A transferência definitiva da capital da República para Brasília e a inflexibilidade dos programas de integração nacional propostos pelo golpe de 64 dão um fim trágico a esse benéfico esfarelamento politico-ideológico do nacional. O fazer de Juscelino é substituído pelo fazer de Andreazza.

A geração que dominou os anos que precederam 1964 foi a dos administradores do lugar político possível em favor do nome próprio. O nome próprio no lugar apropriado. A perda do lugar na administração das coisas públicas e nacionais não foi certamente tão desastrosa quanto se pensa e teoriza, quanto nos querem fazer crer os ex-isebianos. Pelo contrario: a perda do lugar apropriado proporcionou que todos, pela primeira vez e indiscriminadamente, enxergassem a aura que cercava e cerca o poder. Puderam enxergar a cara da aura. A cara do carisma. A cara da retorica populista. O espelho não-narcisista não sendo o forte dos intelectuais brasileiros (que me perdoe Mário de Andrade), a aura do poder reacionário só chegou a ser vislumbrada quando foi adornar a cabeça do outro, ou seja, do usurpador. E muitos dos antigos, já fora do poder, continuam procurando cegamente o lugar apropriado perdido, o nome próprio perdido, como se lugar e nome pudessem ser os mesmos nos anos 1980. Restou-lhes o cultivo em estufa do nome próprio em lugar inapropriado.

Se falta à literatura pós-64, como dissemos acima, o otimismo social que edifica, não se pense que o melhor da produção literária dos últimos anos tenha caído, rastejado, vivido e se alimentado de sombrio pessimismo, interiorizando uma pura negatividade diante dos desmandos políticos da ditadura. Assim como a questão do poder deslocou o tema da exploração (sem abandoná-lo, é evidente, como horizonte) para a reflexão sobre quem e o que está por detrás dela, impossibilitando ou dificultando a almejada igualdade social, assim também se retirou da cena a oposição maniqueísta entre otimismo e pessimismo, tão do nosso agrado e do agrado da nossa imprensa desde a publicação do *Retrato do Brasil* por Paulo Prado, em 1927. Abandona-se a oposição maniqueísta, não para que se diga que somos todos otimistas & pessimistas, dependendo da ocasião — caso em que não haveria deslocamento semântico, apenas o surgimento de certa *tolerância* cúmplice do agrado dos oportunistas de primeira e última hora. Catando palavras no cotidiano (ou: catando feijão, como diria Joao Cabral de Melo Neto), digamos que na cena pós-64 nem o sorriso nem a fossa, nem o sambinha bossa-nova nem o samba-canção de Dolores Duran. Na cena, a boca de Caetano Veloso, na Tropicália: Alegria! Alegria!

A sensibilidade para o que existe de impreciso nas oposições maniqueístas já está em Mário de Andrade desde a década de 1920 e ficou em silêncio até os anos 1960. Enquanto instrumental descritivo para se chegar ao saber, as oposições maniqueístas tem de ser trabalhadas por um exercício na linguagem que o próprio Mário chama de "desassociação de palavras". Aconselha ele, por exemplo, a desassociação da palavra *felicidade* da sua correspondente *prazer*, abrindo a brecha para que se desconstrua o sentido clássico do conceito e se chegue a uma associação mais exata para explicar o que na realidade experimentava. Acabou por escrever em prosa e verso e inúmeras vezes, como a atestar a sua legitimidade e perenidade: "A própria dor é uma felicidade." A felicidade, tal como articulada por Mário em associação à inesperada dor, parece-me próxima da lição dionisíaca e nietzschiana do que se deve entender pelo grito de alegria na cultura brasileira pós-64, grito dado no momento mesmo em que o corpo do artista era dilacerado pela repressão e a censura.

No caso de Mario de Andrade, a desconstrução do conceito clássico de felicidade tinha, pelo menos, função dupla. Primeiro: distanciar a sua atuação intelectual do bom-mocismo de Graça Aranha, que pregava uma alegria superficial, prenuncio do otimismo-vencedor tão ao gosto dos futuros fascismos. Segundo: precaver os jovens companheiros contra os estragos que o anatolismo havia feito com os moços brasileiros no início do século. Ao jovem Carlos Drummond, vítima provinciana de mestre Anatole France, aconselha Mario: Anatole "escangalhou os pobres moços, fazendo deles uns gastos, uns frouxos, sem atitudes, sem coragem. duvidando se vale a pena qualquer coisa, duvidando da felicidade, duvidando do amor [...]. Isso é que esse filho-da-puta fez".

No caso de 1964, a desconstrução do conceito de alegria visou, como vimos, a retirar a produção artística da pura negatividade, como ainda a liberá-la do espírito de ressentimento. A resposta mais evidente da esquerda tradicional ao autoritarismo repressor e à perda do lugar na administração pública teria sido o ressentimento. Este teria conduzido o intelectual a se afirmar de novo por um não sistemático, contraditoriamente. A alegria foi o que permitiu que se alicerçasse a possibilidade de o artista afirmar — sempre em oposição às forcas do terror, do dilaceramento e da dor — pelo sim, ainda que, para isso, precisasse chegar ao "dérèglement de tous les sens", ou abrir "as portas da percepção". Alijado do poder, o artista compreendia o papel corruptor de um mando privado de reflexão ética. Condenado à inexistência política, o artista não perdia a bossa e a raça. Destituído de um lugar na administração pública, o intelectual constituía um lugar envolvente de onde podia demolir, sem comprometer-se, a construção precária (dada como invencível) do golpe de 64.

A alegria desabrochou tanto no deboche quanto na gargalhada, tanto na paródia e no circo quanto no corpo humano que buscava a plenitude de prazer e gozo na própria dor.

A alegre afirmação do indivíduo numa sociedade, no entanto, autoritária e repressora talvez tenha

sido a ideia principal na boa literatura pós-64. Aliada
à análise e à crítica radical do poder, essa ideia soli-
dificou a necessidade de uma sociedade democrática
na América Latina e o descompromisso para com as
forças militares no exercício do governo; retirou ainda o pensamento e a ação de oposição dos meandros
tortuosos seja do ressentimento, seja do totalitarismo.

Otimistas e tristes ficaram as figuras do poder,
contraditoriamente. Sacrificados e alegres ficaram
os opositores do regime, afirmativamente. A ditadura militar foi-se esfarelando nesse jogo de forças, ao
mesmo tempo que a sociedade brasileira se preparava
como nunca para aceitar um governo legitimamente
democratico. Que não seja decepcionada!

[1988]

Da Formação ao entre-lugar

**ENTREVISTA PARA SERGIO COHN E
MARCELO REIS DE MELLO, 2016**

Silviano, a poesia surge muito cedo na sua vida?

Para falar a verdade, eu só consigo falar do aparecimento da poesia na minha vida de maneira biográfica. Porque há um detalhe da minha vida que as pessoas desconhecem: eu comecei a trabalhar muito cedo, com 12 anos de idade. Meu pai era cirurgião dentista e resolveu montar comércio. E ao montar comércio, ele precisava de funcionário. Então o filho virou funcionário. Eu fui de início menino de entrega, depois balconista, e depois fiz a contabilidade da firma. Eu trabalhei nove anos nessa firma. Dos 12 aos 21 anos. Então acontece o seguinte: eu sempre tive muito pouco tempo disponível para fazer o que eu gostava. Porque além do trabalho, eu estudava. Fazia o ginásio, que ocupava toda manhã. E adorava ir ao cinema. Ia ao cinema todo dia, ao sair do trabalho, o que ocupava a noite. Então havia quase uma necessidade imperiosa de começar a literatura pela poesia, porque era curto. Eu podia ler um poema, podia ler dois poemas, não precisava ler um livro inteiro. Então tanto a prosa quanto o ensaísmo chegam muito tarde na minha vida. Porque ambos requerem muito tempo. Você tem que passar horas e horas lendo um livro.

Eu só comecei a ler prosa, para falar a verdade, muito tardiamente, quando eu entrei para a universidade. Eu li antes um ou outro livro, mas de uma maneira estudiosa, ou analítica, só quando eu entrei na universidade. Eu só entro na universidade em 1956. Mas já estava interessado em cinema e poesia desde 1952. Tanto que meu maior interesse por livro vai ser pelos poetas franceses, porque eu estava fazendo também Aliança Francesa. A poesia francesa me interessou antes mesmo da brasileira. Era parte do meu estudo na Aliança Francesa.

Qual era o acesso a essa poesia francesa na época?

A Aliança Francesa de Belo Horizonte tinha uma biblioteca maravilhosa. E foi ali que eu comecei a ler desde cedo Valéry, depois passei para Mallarmé. Adorei Baudelaire, que realmente foi um autor importante para mim naquela época. E assim por diante. Eu fui lendo esses livros e só depois cheguei na poesia brasileira. Carlos Drummond e sobretudo João Cabral. Depois os concretos... É um caminho muito nítido, que está claro no primeiro livro onde reuni alguns dos meus poemas, que foi o *4 Poetas*. Os meus poemas na época eram uma mistura de poesia renascentista francesa, como os três poemas, que gosto muito, chamados "Cauchemar Oublié". Três sonetos que são paródias ou imitação do tema clássico do "déclose rose", de se aproveitar o dia de hoje porque amanhã você será velho e não poderá mais. Esses poemas, assim como o "Três árvores", que também está no livro, fizeram um certo sucesso e me lançaram primeiro como poeta do que como prosador. Naquela época eu morria de vergonha de ser poeta e escrevia com pseudônimo, Antônio Nogueira. Os dois nomes que o Fernando Pessoa não utilizava. Como pode-se ver, eu também estava lendo muito o Fernando Pessoa. Na época, em 1957, eu mandei para o Mário Faustino alguns poemas, e ele publicou na página "Poesia Experiência", que editava no *Suplemento Dominical do Jornal do Brasil*. E teve boa repercussão. Isso me fez poeta em Belo Horizonte.

E o livro *4 Poetas* foi publicado nessa época, também?

Não, ele só seria publicado alguns anos depois, em 1960. E nele tem claramente essas influências: de um lado o poeta Ronsard e seus poemas sobre o tema da rosa, que dura pouco tempo e depois se despetala, assim como a beleza feminina. E depois Mallarmé e Valéry, que influenciou um dos poemas que mais gosto do livro, que é o "Fala de Narciso". Um poema tipicamente valeryano. Então esse é o meu começo. E daí, é claro, não é difícil me aproximar dos irmãos Campos, porque de certa maneira Ronsard, Valéry e Mallarmé fazem parte do paideuma concreto.

O livro foi publicado na época em que eu entrei na Faculdade de Filosofia e fiz parte do Diretório Acadêmico, que o editou, reunindo quatro jovens estudantes de Letras: Affonso Romano de Sant'Anna, Teresinha Alves Pereira, Domingos Muchon e eu. Nós já pertencíamos mais ou menos ao mesmo grupo. Nessa época, inclusive, eu fiz o primeiro número de uma revista chamada *Mosaico*, onde eu publico um longo ensaio sobre Carlos Drummond de Andrade. Agora, anterior, eu participei da revista *Complemento*, que existiu entre 1955 e 1957, e onde eu publiquei alguns poemas.

E como era o ambiente da revista *Complemento*?

Era um ambiente fantástico, porque nós todos nos encontrávamos no cineclube. O cineclube era um lugar de reunião. Aos sábados se exibia um filme, normalmente um filme de altíssimo nível, porque nós tínhamos contato com a Cinemateca Brasileira de São Paulo e ela nos mandava um clássico do cinema toda semana. Então pudemos ver "O encouraçado Potekim", "O gabinete do dr. Caligari", toda uma série de grandes filmes clássicos, muitos deles do cinema mudo. E nos reuníamos lá para conversar depois. Era um grupo extraordinário, muito heterogêneo, porque faziam parte dele pessoas que gostavam do cinema, mas que muitas vezes trabalhavam em outras áreas, como no teatro, que é o caso do Carlos Kroeber e João Marschner. Havia o Frederico Morais, que era crítico dc arte, e a esposa dele, Wilma Martins. Eu conheci o Ivan Ângelo e o Ezequiel Neves lá, também. E, o que era mais fascinante, era o pessoal da dança que frequentava o cineclube, o Klaus e a Angel Vianna. Então esse grupo se reunia todos os sábados, e era uma coisa muito ampla, muito rica.

E foram nesses encontros que surgiu o pequeno grupo de jovens que fez a revista *Complemento*. E surgiu, de maneira muito mais ampla, a *Revista de Cinema*, que a Azougue editou uma antologia. A *Revista de Cinema* foram 25, 26 números. E se você for ver, todas essas pessoas participavam da *Revista de Cinema*. Todos esses tópicos estão contemplados pela revista. Foi um momento muito extraordinário, que eu tive a sorte de participar. Mas devo dizer que eu participei muito mais ativamente como crítico de cinema do que como poeta ou prosador. A prosa só vai ganhar força na minha vida quando eu resolvi me especializar em literatura francesa. E foi nesse momento que a poesia vai perdendo lugar, porque a minha tese de doutorado será sobre romance.

Esse ambiente era plural só em linguagens artísticas, ou também na questão ideológica? Alguns dos nomes citados vão se envolver de maneira mais ou menos direta com questões políticas nos anos seguintes. Isso já estava claro?

Olha, a questão ideológica é um pouco tardia. Ela começa a surgir de maneira mais forte depois. A nossa geração era estética e comportamental. O que era muito importante no grupo era o questionamento do comportamento provinciano. E esse questionamento se dava exatamente através do cinema, em particular o cinema europeu, e também através da música. Porque é o momento em que começa a surgir o rock'n'roll. Eu diria que antes de mais nada o que tínhamos era o comportamento estético. O que é muito parecido com o que acontece com o Movimento Concreto, que só vai dar o salto da onça em 1961, em Assis. A preocupação ideológica é um pouco tardia. E aí acontece uma grande lacuna na minha vida, porque eu deixo a cidade de Belo Horizonte em 1960. Eu venho primeiro com bolsa de estudos para o Rio de Janeiro e depois vou para a França fazer o doutorado. Então esse período de ideologização é exatamente o período em que eu saio.

Nos anos 1960, há um processo rápido de ideologização da cultura e isso vai aparecer tanto na poesia, quanto na prosa e na participação política. E as pessoas começam a fazer jornalismo. As pessoas que estão mais implicadas politicamente, não serão tanto nas artes, mas na atividade jornalística. O melhor exemplo seria uma pessoa que não foi contemporânea minha, mas que começa a ganhar muito destaque logo depois que eu saio de Belo Horizonte, que é o Fernando Gabeira. É quem mais ganha destaque desse grupo, embora não fizesse parte da formação inicial.

Só havia uma expressão ideológica muito precisa antes de 1960 no Partido Comunista. E aí existe a figura do Fritz Teixeira de Salles, entre os mais velhos, e entre os mais novos o Argemiro Ferreira. São pessoas que já tinham uma visão muito política de cinema. No fundo, a grande questão nos anos 1950 é o cinema. E aí esse debate vai aparecer numa discussão sobre o realismo. Existe a versão do realismo italiano, que vai ser defendida por aqueles que estão comprometidos com uma visão política de esquerda tradicional, e existe o realismo norte-americano, que é de muito bom nível também e vai ser defendido por um grupo com ideias mais liberais. E, finalmente, havia um terceiro grupo, que seria um grupo que tinha uma visão mais esteticizante de arte, que se interessava muito por um cinema dito poético. Naquela época a grande figura desse cinema poético era o Jean Cocteau.

O processo de ideologização vai se dar nos anos 1960. E no meu caso, na minha biografia, vai ser um negócio totalmente estapafúrdio, porque eu vou me politizar nos Estados Unidos. Eu fui para a França, passei lá os anos de 1961 e 1962, mas em setembro de 1962 já vou trabalhar nos Estados Unidos como professor. E fico lá até 1974. E nesse momento está acontecendo lá a revolução jovem. E eu vou mais e mais me politizar pela política das minorias, nos movimentos estudantis. Foi um processo de politização gradativo, e que vai ser curioso porque eu vou ter um problema sério com Haroldo de Campos em 1967, quando eu faço a resenha do livro dele *A arte no horizonte do provável.* Eu faço uma resenha muito crítica, porque eu estou muito engajado naquela época. E o Haroldo me manda uma carta violentíssima me chamando de Zdanov, dizendo que eu tinha virado um crítico zdanovista, se referindo a um realismo socialista. Então eu já estava muito metido nas grandes questões políticas. Mas devo dizer que tinha muito pouco a ver com o que estava acontecendo no Brasil na época. Estava respondendo muito mais às questões que eu estava vivenciando por lá.

O seu primeiro de poesia solo, *Salto*, saiu em 1970, e traz um diálogo muito próximo com as experiências da poesia concreta. Como começou essa relação?

O diálogo com os concretos foi muito bom. Eu sou extremamente agradecido a todos eles, em particular ao Augusto de Campos. Porque eles tinham um trabalho de comentário extraordinário. Você mandava para ler e eles comentavam, corrigiam, dialogavam. Não era uma relação distante, era muito próximo. E, além do mais, havia um intermediário no meu relacionamento com eles, que era o poeta mineiro Afonso Ávila. E isso ajudava, porque o Afonso era uma pessoa muito querida deles. Ele pertencia, junto com o Rui Mourão e o Fábio Lucas, a um grupo muito ligado aos concretos. Eu cheguei a publicar na revista *Invenção*. Fiz uma série de quatro poemas, com uma veia irônica, quase grosseira, e que chamei de "Alguns floreios". Eram poemas que eu gozava de Drummond, Bandeira e João Cabral. E "Alguns floreios" porque eram ao mesmo tempo flores e também estocadas. Os concretos gostaram muito e publicaram os poemas na revista. Havia uma relação muito boa.

E, por outro lado, como eu estava fora, primeiro na França e depois nos Estados Unidos, eu pude sempre mandar livros para eles. Porque era muito difícil conseguir livros naquela época. Por exemplo, eu lembro que mandei Khlebnikov para eles. E, quando eu estava no Canadá, mandei o Marshall McLuhan. Existia uma relação muito fraterna e recíproca. Até que surge esse problema, que eu me torno um pouco exagerado nas questões políticas, de forma até juvenil. O que na prosa vai se concretizar no *Em liberdade*. Mas esse era o ambiente em que eu vivia. Essa coisa meio esquizofrênica, de tentar uma atividade, não política, ativista, mas engajada nos meus escritos, na minha maneira de pensar, de conceber arte e literatura, e ao mesmo tempo um enorme prazer em brincar com a linguagem. Uma relação quase lúdica com a linguagem.

A própria poesia concreta estava vivendo alterações nesse período, com uma abertura a novas experiências de linguagem, como vai acontecer com o _Galáxias_, do Haroldo de Campos. Você, estando nos EUA, conseguia se informar do que estava sendo produzido aqui?

Sim, eu era muito bem informado. Essas pessoas todas eram muito amigas minhas, então eu recebia o material. Nós somos até hoje bastante amigos. É claro que com o passar da vida nos afastamos um pouco, por questões práticas. Além do mais, em 1969, quando eu vou para a Universidade de Buffalo, eu conheço o Hélio Oiticica. E fazer amizade com o Hélio não foi difícil, porque eu estava a par das coisas no Brasil, em particular do concretismo e do neoconcretismo, e estava estudando o pós-estruturalismo, que era algo que o interessava. Ele queria saber o que era o pós-estruturalismo, e em particular, e ele chega a mencionar isso em textos, como o que ele publicou na revista _Pólen_, ele estava interessado nas novas leituras de Nietzsche, que eu fui apresentando para ele. Eu mostrei para ele meu livro _Salto_, e ele vai aproveitar aquele ideograma chinês que eu faço, "man hat tan", "o homem se esconde do sol", e citar na revista _Navilouca_, que foi feita em 1972.

Tem um ponto importante, que vai marcar muito minha biografia. Eu diria que a minha sorte grande foi o fato de eu não ter ido para os EUA diretamente do Brasil. Foi ter ido para lá através da França e trazendo uma formação francesa relativamente sólida. Isso me levou a ter uma vida muito diferente do que a normal de um latino-americano numa universidade norte-americana. A ponto de em 1969 eu poder me transferir definitivamente para o Departamento de Francês. O que é um caso inédito. Não há latino-americano que foi lecionar francês. Naquele época, especialmente. Você tinha que ser *native speaker*. E isso me permitiu participar de mundos muitos diferentes e muito divididos. Eu pude me dar o luxo, em determinado momento, de não concentrar a atenão na América Latina. É o momento em que eu ajudo a fundar, em 1970, o Porto Rico Study Center, em Buffalo. Eu me aproximo dos porto-riquenhos, fico muito amigo deles, e começo a trabalhar com eles, ao invés de lidar com o pessoal da América do Sul, como normalmente acontece. Eu consegui inclusive que o Abdias do Nascimento fosse contratado para trabalhar lá. Naquele momento, eu consegui realizar muita coisa em Buffalo. O Hélio Oiticica vai falar lá, o "Arena conta Zumbi" se apresenta com elenco completo. O Glauber Rocha apresentou quatro filmes por lá. Eu pude fazer muito mais pelo Brasil estando no Departamento de Francês do que se estivesse em Português, onde eu estaria sozinho e sem nenhum tostão.

Curioso que, mesmo falando que não estava concentrando sua atenção na América Latina, você fez textos que se tornam paradigmáticos nos estudos latino-americanos, como "O entre-lugar no discurso latino-americano".

O que aconteceu é que naquela época eu tinha uma alta produtividade de ensaios sobre literatura brasileira. Escrevi textos sobre Machado de Assim, sobre *Iracema*, um dos primeiros estudos sobre a homossexualidade em Raul Pompéia. Mas, embora estivesse fazendo minha carreira em estudos sobre literatura brasileira, a minha tese era em francês. Havia essa dualidade, que foi muito importante. A tese foi defendida em 1968, e logo depois eu fui para o Departamento de Francês, onde a concorrência era muito pesada, quase insuportável. Para se ter uma ideia, o René Girard era meu colega e amigo em Buffalo. Eram nomes de primeiríssima qualidade. Se eu quisesse escrever alguma coisa sobre literatura francesa, provavelmente não conseguiria me sobressair. Então apareceu uma figura muito importante para mim, que foi o Eugenio Donato, um introdutor do estruturalismo nos Estados Unidos. O Eugenio fez junto com Richard Macksey o primeiro grande evento sobre estruturalismo nos Estados Unidos. Ele ficou muito meu amigo e me aconselhou a explorar essa área, onde ele acreditava que eu conseguiria mais espaço. Foi um conselho importante. E o Eugenio me convidou para fazer uma conferência em Montreal, onde ele estava como professor visitante. Éramos três conferencistas: eu, o Michel Foucault e o René Girard. Com os outros conferencistas sendo desse peso, eu achei melhor tratar sobre um tema diverso ao deles, e decidi aproveitar a curiosidade que havia naquela época em relação à América Latina. Foi então que escrevi "O entre-lugar no discurso latino-americano". O Eugenio não gostou do título, achou que ninguém iria entender. E então o texto foi apresentado com outro título, sugerido por Eugenio, falando sobre antropofagia. Mas eu sempre preferi o título original e o mantive quando publiquei o texto no Brasil, em 1973. De qualquer forma, eu devo muito ao Eugenio. Ele foi uma daquelas pessoas de muita sensibilidade, de muita inteligência, que dão uma dica que transforma a sua vida.

cadernos ultramares